Lynda Chater grew up in Ashford, Middlesex, and was educated at Twickenham Girl's School. She trained as a landscape architect in Leeds and has practised in West London for a number of years. Now living in Guildford with her husband and cat, she is currently working on her second novel for Pocket.

THAT DEVIL CALLED LOVE

LYNDA CHATER

LONDON · SYDNEY · NEW YORK · TOKYO · SINGAPORE · TORONTO

First published in Great Britain by Pocket Books, 1999
An imprint of Simon & Schuster UK Ltd
A Viacom Company

Simon & Schuster UK Ltd
Africa House
64–78 Kingsway
London
WC2B 6AH

SIMON & SCHUSTER AUSTRALIA
SYDNEY

A CIP catalogue record for this book is available
from the British Library.

1 3 5 7 9 10 8 6 4 2

ISBN 0–671–01802 7

Typeset in Melior by Palimpsest Book Production Limited,
Polmont, Stirlingshire
Printed and bound in Great Britain by
Caledonian International Book Manufacturing, Glasgow

With thanks to Luigi Bonomi for all his help,
encouragement and good advice.

CHAPTER 1

I met the Devil for the first time on the day I was sacked from the library. Mephisto, I should call him, now that we're on first-name terms. Maybe he's not the actual Devil himself, but he assures me that he's not far down in the hierarchy. Do I believe him? Does the Devil speak the truth? I don't know, but I'm going to find out very soon.

It was a wet Friday afternoon in December and I was taking my turn at the front desk. The computer had just thrown one of its sulking fits – pretending it had never seen a bar code before – and the queue of borrowers was getting restless, jostling for space with damp shoppers who had come in to shelter from the rain.

A group of expensively dressed women pushed their way through the crowd, flapping their umbrellas and glancing around with expressions of mild surprise, as if they had never seen a library before. Maybe they hadn't – in their mental maps of Guildford, it would probably be a blank space somewhere between Laura Ashley and Jaeger. One of those annoying dead spots on the shopping circuit.

They gathered near the desk, checking progress on their gruelling schedules of Christmas shopping and comparing purchases. Designer labels fluttered discreetly into view: *Gucci. Armani. Chanel. Lapinique – for the woman who wants a little more.*

I watched them with envy. I badly wanted a little more, but no one was going to buy me a bottle of *Lapinique* this Christmas. Andrew would give me a book as usual, and I would try not to show my disappointment that he was going away. If only I'd plucked up the courage earlier to invite him for Christmas lunch. It might have been just the thing that was needed to jog our relationship out of its long-standing platonic inertia.

What good would a bottle of *Lapinique* do for me? It would take a whole lot more than a pretty smell to make an attractive proposition of this fifty-year-old frump.

'The stuff probably smells of cat's piss, anyway,' I muttered, taking a vicious swipe at a particularly stubborn bar code.

'Sorry?' A well-groomed woman handed me her next book with a look of surprise.

'Nothing.' I glanced at the cover. *A Marriage Made in Heaven.* Beneath the elaborate gold lettering of the title, an impossibly handsome man with smouldering eyes embraced a dopey-looking blonde on a tropical beach.

I stared at the woman, curious. Did people really enjoy reading this crap?

'It's the sequel to *A Dream Romance,*' she explained, reading my expression as a sign of interest in the book. 'They were about to get married at the end, when she was kidnapped by bandits, and Brett – that's him on the cover – swore he'd search to the ends of the earth until he found her.'

'Looks like they met up again,' I said, indicating the picture.

'I know,' she gushed. 'I'm dying to find out how it happens.' She touched the cover lightly with a gloved fingertip and gave me a coy smile. 'Don't you think he's gorgeous?'

I grinned. 'Not bad – if you like a man with a palm tree growing out of his left ear.'

'I never noticed that,' she exclaimed, examining the illustration closely. 'Perhaps I ought to write in and tell them they've made a mistake.' She tucked Brett into her shopping basket and patted him fondly. 'You can win prizes sometimes by doing that.'

Silly cow. I turned to the next person in the queue, a mild-looking man with a huge stack of books. My smile froze when I saw his selection: *Written in Blood: An Anthology of True-Life Crime Stories; Body Count: A Survivor's Gruesome Tale; I Married an Axe Murderer; Ten More Great Serial Killers of Our Time.*

Why doesn't anyone read *real* books any more? Books by real writers, with proper stories? If you wanted to find the classics in a library today, you would have to wade your way through shelves filled with sex and shopping sagas, murder mysteries and historical romance, together with whole sections devoted to the likes of Mills and Boon.

Everyone enjoys an easy read from time to time – even I would occasionally put my feet up with a Jilly

Cooper or take a bath with the latest Jackie Collins – but this library doesn't even have a complete set of Dickens. As for Jane Austen, we were caught on the hop by the television success of *Pride and Prejudice* – our single dog-eared copy had disappeared in a bungled inter-branch loan.

The computer bleeped to tell me that my current borrower was hoarding an overdue copy of *Anatomy for Beginners*. I began to explain the rules, but I was interrupted by a tap on the shoulder. The library manager.

'Harriet, would you come into my office for a moment? I'd like to have a few words.'

I left Dr Crippen to have his wrists slapped by an enthusiastic junior, and followed the manager to his dingy office upstairs.

'We're facing another huge cut in funding,' he said, closing the door behind me. 'There has to be a certain amount of . . . er, rationalisation. We've decided to streamline the content of some of the less popular subject areas, and give the space over to an expanded "Living and Learning" section, with an emphasis on audio-visual material. We have to adapt to today's needs – change our image. Clear out some of those dusty old books and make the library more accessible to young people.'

'Why not do away with the books altogether?' I muttered. 'Play pop music over the PA system and get a licence to sell drinks. You could stay open all night, and they'd pay good money to come in. You'd soon solve your funding problem.'

He gave me an embarrassed stare.

'Annette Baker is very keen to run this new department . . .'

'That's good,' I interrupted. 'I can't really see myself advising fifteen-year-old yobs about the best handbook on do-it-yourself euthanasia. I'd much rather . . .' My voice tailed away as the real purpose of the interview began to dawn on me.

Taking the cue, he gave it to me straight, without frills – anxious to get the unpleasant task out of the way, so he could go home for the weekend with a clear conscience.

'I'm so sorry . . .' he concluded vaguely, reaching with a comforting gesture to pat my arm. Flinching, I turned and bolted clumsily from the room, my cheeks wet with tears. Everyone seemed to be staring at me. Hiding my face, I pushed my way through a cluster of people on the landing and ran upstairs, not pausing for breath until I reached the sanctuary of the upper gallery.

'Philistines,' I gasped, gripping the balcony rail. My reading glasses swung wildly on their chain, clattering against the metal rail as I fought back a fresh wave of angry tears. One or two people glanced up at me. A middle-aged woman in a state of disarray – a figure of fun.

Taking a deep breath, I wiped my eyes and surveyed the kingdom which was no longer my own. My loyal subjects were ranked obediently on the shelves, unaware that their queen had been deposed – unaware of the purges they would suffer under the new regime. My beloved books – my friends. I had passed many lonely nights in their company, escaping with them to a world where values hold their meaning, where virtue has its reward, and where the plain heroine always triumphs over the frivolous beauties, winning the man who appreciates her true worth.

If only it could happen in the real world, I thought. But it was too late now. What hidden qualities could atone for the crime of ageing? I had been consigned to the scrap heap along with my 'dusty old books' – cleared out of the way to make room for glossy new paperbacks which trumpeted the shallow cult of youth. I leaned forward dizzily and watched the figures moving amongst the shelves below. If the balcony had been higher, it would have been easy – just a little push, and my wasted life would all be over.

Then I saw her. She was coming out of the archive room with an armful of newspapers, clad in the usual aggressive little suit with padded shoulders. Her hips swung insolently as she strutted across the room, moving with the easy self-assurance of those who never have to make an effort.

Ms Annette Baker. The bright young hope of the Surrey Library Service. A list of qualifications as long as your arm, drop-dead good looks, and – worst of all – popular with the rest of the staff. Rumour had it that she was sleeping with the manager, which was probably her only conception of what 'Living and Learning' was about. I could teach the jumped-up little tart a thing or two.

She deposited the newspapers on a desk and returned towards the archive room. Her route would take her directly below the edge of the balcony. I picked the first volume from a pile of oversized encyclopaedias on a table beside me and weighed it experimentally in my hand. A to D. It was heavy, but maybe I should combine it with E to H to be on the safe side. I'd show them a good use for these 'dusty old books' no one wanted. I imagined the screams as she hit the floor, felled by the very material she sought to corrupt.

Then I put it back on the table. They would know straight away that it was me. And I suddenly wanted to carry on living. I wasn't going to do any more work that afternoon, though. I made my way back down the stairs, stopping briefly at the supply cupboard to collect a large pot of binding glue. In the staffroom, I emptied its entire contents into Annette Baker's smart leather handbag, then picked up my coat and went home.

Closing the door of my flat behind me, I entered the loneliness of my private life: a gas bill and two circulars on the door mat; a bag of rubbish in the hallway, which I had forgotten to put out for the dustmen; no messages on the answering machine, which stared at me in silent reproach for my failure to provide it with regular employment. My table was in its usual state, resembling a scene-of-crime exhibit from an explosion in a bookshop. Dropping the gas bill out of sight in a narrow slot between Thackeray and Trollope, I hunted around for the coffee cup with the least fungal growth.

The coffee-making was accomplished on autopilot,

my eyes half closed to avoid the disturbing sights: the dirty plates in the sink, the frayed cord I hadn't repaired on the electric kettle and, worst of all, the unused fondue set – an unwanted gift I couldn't bring myself to throw away – a symbol of the society I at once loathed and longed to be part of.

A large measure of whisky went into the coffee, and I perched stiffly on the window seat, unable to relax because the room was so bloody cold. But I had surmounted the first hurdle – I had established my presence in the flat. Some days I just sat at the table in my coat and scarf, feeling like a burglar in my own home – an intruder surveying the sad evidence of a solitary and fruitless existence. It wasn't until I forced myself to pick a book from the table and start reading that I came back to life.

But this evening I couldn't even look at a book. I gazed numbly out of the window at the twinkling lights of Guildford – the view which was supposed to justify the exorbitant rent I paid. I hadn't waited to hear the details of the redundancy payment. How long would I be able to last out here?

It wasn't just the money – I had loved my job. And the job which would still be mine if Ms Annette Baker hadn't come along. The job which would have seen me through to retirement if the manager wasn't running the library with his dick instead of his brain.

Sex. That was the problem. The powerful secret weapon in the battle of the haves and the have-nots, the winners and losers in life. What chance did I have – a plain old woman of fifty with aching limbs and varicose veins? Not only was I permanently disqualified from taking part in the game, but I was also forced to watch from the sidelines, constantly reminded of what I was missing. Everywhere I looked – in books, films, television, advertising hoardings on the street, even the junk mail which came through my door – there was no escaping the message. *Everyone is doing it.* Everyone but me, so it seemed. So I was a failure – a sad, inadequate human being.

What could I do about it? Women of fifty aren't supposed to feel physical desire, it's undignified, a guilty secret, an embarrassing problem to be ignored and brushed out of sight under the carpet. What did the postman think was in the small parcel I received last week? A box of chocolates from a guilty relative? A new hair dryer? Did he guess, as he rattled it thoughtfully and handed it over with a conspiratorial smile, that it contained the latest multi-speed King Dong vibrator with super-added texture and realistic finish?

No one admits to masturbation – least of all a woman of my age. But why should I be ashamed? It's better than nothing, and also better, as far as I can remember, than the vague fumblings of my youth. I did once experience sex, long ago, when I was desperate to find out what it was like – desperate enough to give it a go in the back of Barry Thompson's van one night after a sixth-form party. It was a brief and unrewarding encounter which left me wondering what all the fuss was about. After spending the best part of a month waiting anxiously for my next period to arrive, I vowed that I would never do it again until I was married.

Fat chance of that, as it turned out.

I blame it on my looks or, rather, the lack of them. It's poor consolation, even now, to be told that looks aren't everything. As a fat, unattractive teenager, I had no time for a statement which was so obviously untrue – especially when I found out that Barry Thompson had only deflowered me to win a bet. Instead of turning my attention to other things, such as raising my career sights or developing the self-confidence which might have made a difference to my life, I shut myself away with my books and waited for a transformation to occur. Ugliness like mine couldn't last forever, I told myself. One day, I was convinced, I would wake up and find that I had blossomed into an attractive young woman. Then my real life would begin.

My school friends drifted away – first to experiment with free love and flower power, then later to marriage and child-rearing. I took a menial job in the local library – intended to tide me over until my knight turned up on his white charger. Eventually, at some point in my late twenties, I did wake up – and I discovered that I had thrown away my youth waiting for something that was never going to happen. The impediment was no longer my appearance, but my age. All the decent men – the ones who might have been able to look beneath the surface and appreciate the person inside – had been snapped up by other women.

Panic-stricken, I began to hunt for a man in earnest. Progressively lowering my expectations, my knight was downgraded first to a squire, then to a mere peasant, and finally, to anyone who would have me. But I had left it too late. The only single men remaining were either failures, like myself, unwilling to team up with someone who would reflect their own deficiencies, or else they had concentrated on career and money-making and were now successful enough to hold out with confidence for the perfect woman.

Why had no one warned me? The years ticked by with increasing loss of hope as the time left on my biological clock ebbed away and I was forced to come to terms with the painful realisation that I had missed out. I would never marry and have children, a home life, security and companionship in my old age.

I used to fear the menopause – the hot flushes, the drying up of my body, nature's cruel confirmation of my status as defunct breeding stock. Now I was becoming impatient to get it all over and done with. I was tired of facing the monthly reminder of never having fulfilled my physical purpose.

What had I achieved instead? Nothing. And now I'd lost my job.

The whisky began to hit the spot. I felt an urge to get drunk – drunker than I had ever been before. I had good enough reason, didn't I? Wasn't it the traditional solace of the unemployed?

I was abandoning the pretence of the coffee and heading towards the kitchen to find a proper glass when the telephone rang. The answering machine quivered eagerly on the starting blocks and I didn't have the heart to disappoint it. I listened from the doorway, whisky bottle in hand, as it chuntered into life and delivered its message.

'Harriet, are you there? I phoned the library and they said you'd gone home sick. Are you all right?'

Sally. My best and, at present, my only female friend. There have been others, but they always seemed to drift away, dispirited, no doubt, by my failure to return their calls. How can I explain that it's fear of rejection which stops me from keeping in touch? That I'm protecting myself by ending the acquaintance before they do?

Sally's impervious to these subtleties – she's too busy organising other people's lives to waste time worrying about rejection. This will be a routine check-up call to make sure that I haven't topped myself or done anything foolish in the few days since she last saw me.

'Harriet?' Her voice is the cluck of a stern mother hen rounding up her brood. She knows I'm here and she's not going to let me get away with pretending otherwise. She's probably ready for one of these long sessions where she grills me about my lifestyle and drinking habits before suggesting sound, sensible remedies. Why don't I get out more and meet new people? What about joining a social club?

A *social club*? She really has to be kidding. Sometimes I almost enjoy my solitude, just to spite her.

'Harriet, are you there? I was ringing to make sure you hadn't forgotten my party tonight.'

I had. But I had also told her that I wasn't going. She knows I hate parties, with their cosy couples and spoilt, arrogant youngsters. Single, middle-aged women are about as popular as rattlesnakes in a lucky dip. Sally's got Duncan – the ideal husband. She doesn't know what it's like to be alone and past your sell-by date.

Then again, it struck me that a party might just suit my mood tonight. I could get drunk more disgracefully in company than on my own. Andrew might even be there.

'Sally?' I picked up the phone.

'Harriet, what's wrong?'

'Nothing,' I snapped defensively. How can she always tell – damn her? 'Nothing much, anyway. I just got made redundant, that's all. Early retirement, they call it.'

'Oh, Harriet . . .' I could picture her face twisting into that expression of agonised sympathy she does so well. 'What are you going to do?'

I knew I wouldn't have to wait long before she told me. I laid the receiver on the table and fetched a glass from the kitchen. When I came back she was yammering away about job advertisements and training courses. I poured a large whisky and began to count the lines of the wood grain in the end of the bookshelf. She gave me fifteen minutes of good, solid advice, every word of which I ignored except for her final injunction to indulge myself in a stiff drink and then get round to her place for another one.

CHAPTER 2

The mix of guests at the party was much as I had predicted: Sally's fashionable friends from the design studio and Duncan's colleagues from the university, each with their 'partners' – how I hate that word, that smug apology for the superior status of coupledom. There was also a sprinkling of Duncan's students – his token display of keeping in touch with the younger generation. Andrew wasn't there, but Sally informed me with a wink that he had been invited. I handed her my coat, blushing. Did she know? Had she finally guessed how I felt about him?

Andrew was the only exception to the Law of Ineligibility of Single Men that I knew of – the law which states that, if they're single, there has to be something wrong with them. He was a few years older than me, taught English at the university, and had no visible deformities which couldn't be cured by a bottle of Head and Shoulders. We met several years ago, fighting over a boxed set of George Eliot at a jumble sale for one of Sally's good causes. Inexplicably, he chose to befriend me. It was a strictly platonic relationship – no other variety had ever been hinted at – but it was the main thing that kept me going and held me back from the brink of despair. Secretly, along with most of the women over thirty-five on the university campus, I fancied him badly.

Escaping from Sally's questioning smile, I went into the living room. The couples took centre stage, earnestly discussing mortgages, school fees and gardening. Small groups of students lurked in the corners, purposefully consuming Sally's food and drink, and jealously guarding the cans of lager they had brought with them for when the wine ran out. Mindful of this eventuality, I visited the kitchen and, waiting until I was alone, slipped a couple of bottles into the narrow space between the Welsh dresser and the Aga. No one would think of looking there.

When I returned to the party, I noticed him for the first time. A young man leaning against the wall by the doorway, clad in a long black coat. He had unkempt curly black hair and was unshaven, but it was his eyes which drew me. Mocking eyes – eyes which saw and judged. The eyes of an outsider. For a moment I was transfixed in his cold stare. Then somebody pushed past behind me and his expression changed, his face relaxing into a smile. I instinctively looked round to see whom it was meant for.

'So you've noticed me at last?' he asked in an imperious tone. 'I think it's time I introduced myself.'

I turned back, realising with a start that he was addressing me. 'Sorry?'

'The name's Mephisto, servant to Lucifer, arch-regent and commander of all spirits.'

Sally's told me how Duncan's students get carried away with these dungeon and dragon games, but I wasn't in the mood for this sort of rubbish right now.

'And I'm Jesus Christ,' I replied. 'I'd love to stop and talk to you but I want to get some of the Last Supper before your friends over there polish it off. Excuse me.' I turned towards the buffet table.

'Do you realise who I am, Harriet?'

How did he know my name? I stared at him. He looked just like any other student, but there was something odd about him, something I couldn't define.

'I thought you'd have noticed that I was different from the others.'

Was he some kind of loony? One of Sally's lame ducks – just like myself?

'I come from the Devil himself to offer you what you most desire.'

I laughed. 'You won't impress anyone around here with an opening like that. No one believes in the Devil any more.'

'Don't they? Why are they all so scared of him, then?' He gave me a cool stare. 'Why has the world spent so much effort building up its defences – civilisation, I think you guys call it – if not through fear of the Devil? Art, society, religion – it's all a kind of insurance against Hell. Against chaos. It's God they really don't believe in, because deep down they know they invented him themselves.'

I paused. He was just a student talking nonsense –

probably on drugs – but he had a point. I felt an urge to engage with him on his own terms. Take up the challenge – show him I was a worthy adversary.

'So, if you're really the Devil, what are you doing here?' I asked. 'I'd have thought you'd have your hands full in the third world right now. Why are you hanging out in a middle-class drinks party in Guildford?' Keep it light, I thought. Lull him into a false sense of security, give him enough rope . . .

'Oh yes, we're busy out there all right. But those guys don't really need much convincing of the Devil's existence – I'd only be preaching to the converted. There's much more fun to be had in a cosy little town like Guildford. We like to knock a few holes in all that nicely structured order and let some draughts in.'

A blast of music drowned the hubbub of voices around us, indicating that one of the students had discovered the controls on the stereo. Sally rushed past with a look of alarm and the volume rapidly subsided to a level which was quieter, but still clearly audible. I found my foot tapping to the beat and felt an uncharacteristic surge of confidence. I was beginning to enjoy myself for a change.

'So why the parlour games?' I asked with a smile. 'If you're out to destroy us, why not just whip out the heavy artillery and blow us all away?'

'Ah, there are limits to my powers, I'm afraid. We have to play by the rules. And though it might look like a great idea to wind the universe backwards and have a seafood barbecue on the day that first little fish crawled out of the primeval sludge, it wouldn't leave us with much to do afterwards. We devils would get a bit lonely all on our own. Forever damned with Lucifer and no one else to play with.'

We both laughed. Surely he would drop the pretence now and let the joke come to an end? I glanced down. My glass was empty. Alcohol was a poor substitute for happiness, but it was the only comfort I was likely to get tonight. I looked round for a refill, but there were no bottles in sight. I felt a sense of panic. There was something about the young man's manner which I found strangely compelling. I might never get a chance to continue this conversation if I broke it off now. But I desperately needed another drink.

'Getting drunk won't help you, Harriet. You need a whole lot more than that to make you happy.'

I stared at him suspiciously. Had I spoken aloud without realising it? 'What do you mean?' I asked.

'You tell me,' he said with a smile. 'If you could have anything you wanted, what would you choose?'

I sighed. It was just another parlour game. 'Anything at all?'

'Anything at all. No limits.'

'Well, there are a few little things I wouldn't mind having right now. A job, for example. Some money to live on. Maybe a few years knocked off my age – let's say twenty-five to make it a round figure. You Devils do a nice line in rejuvenation, don't you? Faustian pacts and all that?'

I paused and glanced at the doorway. Andrew had just arrived, accompanied by a young woman – probably one of his English students. She was tall, slim and elegantly dressed, in contrast with his habitually scruffy attire. As she crossed the room ahead of him, her hips swayed gently in time with the music and her short dress revealed a pair of shapely stockinged legs. Andrew caught up with her by the fireplace and she turned to him, smiling. A mane of chestnut-brown hair framed an attractive face with sparkling eyes. I felt a surge of envy.

'While we're at it,' I added, turning back to Mephisto, 'I could use a few improvements in the looks department. It's pretty tough being born with a face like the back of a bus.'

Was I hoping he would contradict me? Tell me that beauty is more than skin deep? If only more people thought so. But he wasn't even listening – he was gazing at Andrew's companion.

'*Was this the face that launch'd a thousand ships/And burnt the topless towers of Ilium?*' he murmured.

Marlowe's *Doctor Faustus.* Was that where he'd got the idea for all this Devil nonsense?

I took a deep breath. I was a fool to have thought this attractive young man was actually enjoying my company. All it had taken was a half-way decent looking woman to come into the room, and he'd lost interest in our conversation straight away.

'If you want to go and chat up Helen of Troy over there, don't mind me,' I said. 'I was just off to get myself another drink.'

I lifted my empty glass by way of explanation, then started as a warm splash of dark red wine ran across my hand. The glass was full. I sipped at it nervously to avoid further spillages and a pungent, earthy flavour flooded my taste buds. Much better than Sally's usual plonk. My mind raced to work out how he had performed the manoeuvre without my noticing. Plenty of room for a wine bottle under that big coat – an easy enough trick.

The music increased in volume again, intruding on my thoughts. A love song. A young couple on the other side of the room began to dance, their arms wrapped around each other. I felt a wave of self-pity, an urge to let myself go – to drop the pretence of conversation and allow the party atmosphere to carry me away to a drunken oblivion. Mephisto continued to stare at the girl.

'He's not screwing her, you know,' he said eventually, nodding at Andrew.

'How the hell would you know that?' Curiosity dragged my attention back to what he was saying.

'Trust me, and I'll show you. You've not believed a word I've said so far, have you?'

'Most certainly not.' This game was getting out of hand.

'Look around you,' he said. 'All these people – they look as if they've got it together, don't they? Playing by the rules, keeping up the right attitudes, never saying what they really think. They've paid their insurance money to keep the Devil away – set up their defences and dug their moats around them. It all looks pretty cool on the surface, but what do you think's going on underneath?'

'God only knows,' I muttered.

'Not God, Harriet – you're backing the wrong guy there. Let me tell you something. You're not the only sinner in this room. These people might think they're safe in their cosy little bastions of civilisation, but what they don't realise is that they've locked the gates and thrown away the key with the Devil still inside. They're all rotten to the core.'

'What makes me a sinner?' I asked indignantly. 'I haven't done anything wrong.'

'Don't fool around with me, Harriet – the Devil can see everything you do. Have you forgotten the little show you put on in the library this afternoon? It was that murderous impulse of yours which dragged me up from Hell to visit you here – I don't waste my time on venial sins.'

'I . . . I didn't . . .' My head began to spin. How could he know? I took another large mouthful of wine and stared at my glass dizzily. It still seemed to be full to the brim. 'I didn't actually do it, did I?'

'I know. I stopped you. It would have messed up my plans. But it was a great performance – you could have scooped an Oscar for your rendition of wrath, not to mention pride and envy. That's three of the seven deadly sins covered already.'

I opened my mouth, then closed it again, not trusting myself to speak.

'What about the rest?' he continued, glancing round the room. 'I think we'll find that they're all here.' He caught my eye and nodded towards a smartly dressed woman standing on the edge of the central group, one of Sally's friends.

'I hear gluttony in action over there. Listen.'

I gasped and clutched his arm for support as the music faded around me and a voice began to speak inside my head. What was this? Telepathy?

Will anybody notice if I take another chicken drumstick? There's only three left and I know I've had four already but I don't think anyone was counting. I recognised the woman's voice – I had overheard her telling Sally about her latest diet plan when I first arrived.

'Don't worry,' said Mephisto. 'It's just a trick I know. It can't hurt you.'

If I scoop it into a napkin, I could take it to the bathroom and eat it there – then I could get to chew all those lovely gristly bits on the ends without anyone noticing. If I pretended to be taking the plate into another room to offer them round, then maybe I could get away with all three!

The woman began to edge towards the table. I stared at Mephisto with awe. Some trick.

'Now for sloth,' he whispered, indicating a student slumped in an apparently comatose state on the sofa. The voice in my head changed to a lazy masculine drawl.

Why the fuck did I tell Sandra I'd see her after the party? There's no way I'm walking all the way up that hill to her digs at this time of night. She's bound to have a go at me if I phone her, though. Maybe it's best just to pretend I forgot – play it cool. I'm a free man, aren't I? God, I'm busting for a pee. But it's so comfortable here. I really can't be bothered. Where did I put that lager?

Duncan crossed in front of the sofa to change the

tape on the stereo and the voice faded away. The music blasted out again, louder this time, and he turned with a smile to a man standing beside him.

'George, how goes it? Ready for some disco action?' Duncan pumped his arms back and forth in imitation of an aggressive dance movement and the two men laughed.

'Avarice coming up, I think,' murmured Mephisto.

Don't look so smug, George. You might have a new Citroën parked outside, but I'm in line for a promotion, and if Sally's new client comes up with the goods I'll be getting that BMW before long. If only the school fees weren't crippling me, I'd go to the top of the range – show you who really packs the muscle on the road. When Sally's mother dies, we'll be able to pay off the mortgage . . . the old bat can't last out that much longer . . .

'How on earth did you do that?' I asked Mephisto, unable to suppress a grin. Duncan was well known for his socialist ideals. 'Is it some kind of hypnotism?'

'Keep quiet,' he replied, pressing a finger to his lip. 'I haven't finished yet. I've saved the best one for the end.' He took my elbow and swivelled me round so that I was looking at Andrew and his companion, deep in conversation by the fireplace.

I wonder what she thinks of me? I gave an involuntary shiver. It was a shock to hear Andrew's familiar voice at such close range. *I suppose it was only coincidence that we arrived here at the same time. She's standing so close to me, though – I can feel the warmth of her skin.*

'Lechery.' Mephisto gave a dark chuckle.

I can see her nipples through her dress. What would happen if I touched her? Oh God, I must stop thinking these things – she'd probably hit me if I even tried to kiss her goodnight. Concentrate. I mustn't make a fool of myself. She's asking about her grades for last term – that's the only reason she's talking to me. But imagine . . . imagine cupping those breasts in my hands, resting my cheek against the silky softness . . .

I blinked back a tear of jealous resentment. Andrew was never likely to think about me in that way. Why were men all the same – unable to see beyond the superficial pleasures of the flesh?

Mephisto touched my arm. 'You'd give a lot to be in her shoes, wouldn't you?'

I swung to face him angrily, unnerved by the suggestion that he also knew *my* every thought. 'I wouldn't want to be like *her*! If I was young and beautiful, I'd have better things to do than flirt with men old enough to be my father. I'd live a decent life – try to find some happiness in this bloody miserable world!'

He just stood there with a supercilious smile. I took a deep gulp of wine and watched in disbelief as the dark red liquid swirled and rose again to the rim of the glass. He must have drugged me – that was it. I stared at him wildly.

'If you're the Devil, with all these powers, why don't you give me what I want?' I could feel the hysteria in my voice, but I couldn't control it. 'What do you want in return? My soul? Well, you're welcome to it! Nobody else bloody well wants it, do they?'

'Harriet? What's wrong?'

Someone grabbed my shoulders and twisted me round. Sally. Staring into my face with a worried look.

'Leave me alone!' I pulled away from her and turned back to Mephisto. But he was gone.

'Harriet? Come and sit down.' Sally put her arm round me and led me towards the sofa. 'I know you've been under a terrible strain. Don't worry – it's all right now.'

People were staring at me. I sat down dizzily. 'That man . . .'

'What man?' Sally looked around with a puzzled expression. 'Has Andrew been teasing you again?'

I began to describe Mephisto, noticing as I did so that Sally was fingering her necklace – some glittery piece of junk she had recently picked up in a street market. An elaborate chain decked out with a cluster of metallic charms. I looked at it closely. The charms were shaped like pentangles.

Sally's voice floated distantly into my ears. 'Really, Harriet, I think you must have imagined it. There's been no one like that here tonight.'

CHAPTER 3

My neck hurt. Someone had exchanged my pillow for a sandbag and glued it to the bed. Why wouldn't it move? I struggled to turn over and came up against a soft vertical surface, which I gradually identified as the back of a sofa. Where was I?

I sat up, wincing as a sharp pain stabbed into my right shoulder, and opened my eyes. Sally's living room. Cold morning light filtered through the cracks in the curtains to reveal a grey and unfriendly version of the place which had held so much warmth the night before. Empty wineglasses glinted on the coffee table. A stale aroma prickled at my nostrils and a dull ache began to invade the numbness in my head. I shivered, clutching at the duvet which must have covered me in the night, and a thin film of cold sweat enveloped my body. I felt a rush of nausea.

'Are you awake, Harriet? I've brought you some coffee.'

Oh Christ, not Sally. Please God, I thought, burrowing under the duvet, let me close my eyes and wake up in my own bed. I'll behave myself from now on – cut down on the drinking, stop thinking bad things about people, do my job better . . .

But I didn't have a job any more. And God didn't exist. I sat up, my mind numb with self-pity, and took the steaming mug of coffee from her with trembling hands.

'How are you feeling?' she asked. 'We thought it would be better not to wake you up – you were sleeping so soundly.'

'Have you seen the car keys, darling?' Duncan breezed into the room, fastening the collar of his shirt. He stopped abruptly when he saw me. 'Oops, sorry Harriet. Clean forgot you were here.' He gave a broad grin. 'Feeling any better?'

I stared at him, remembering confused fragments of the previous evening. I had been given the power to read people's thoughts. Duncan wanted a BMW. Andrew wanted to screw that girl. I wanted . . . I wanted to be young again. I shook my head. It was a dream, just a bad dream.

Escaping to the bathroom, I gazed at myself in the mirror. A plump, rounded face with red creases on one side from the arm of the sofa. Crinkled skin around unfocused, slightly bloodshot eyes. Cheeks with broken veins. A sagging chin. Brown wispy hair cut in a short, no-nonsense style. An ugly old woman. No use to anyone.

I felt dirty. The bathtub gleamed with false promise, flanked by rows of brightly coloured bottles and baskets of sweetly scented soaps. I longed to immerse myself in hot, fragrant water, but to do it here would be overstepping the bounds of hospitality. What was the point? I had slept in my clothes and had nothing clean to put on – I didn't even have a toothbrush. I imagined Sally bathing, drifting in a sea of bubbles. Emerging fresh and clean and beautiful, wrapped in a soft towel which would fall silently to the floor as Duncan took her in his arms.

I would have to make do with a wash. Splashing water on my face, I shivered as it trickled down my arms and wet the sleeves of my blouse. The towel smelled of aftershave. I inspected it thoughtfully, picking off a dark curly hair. Had it made contact with Duncan's body that very morning? I dried my face slowly, imagining its brisk journey around his damp masculine parts. Private parts, accessible only to Sally. What was it like to be married? What was it like to know another person's body as intimately as your own?

Guiltily, I picked a pale blue container from the shelf above the bath. *Lapinique. Total Skin Control. Moisturises, Nourishes, Revitalises.*

Was this Sally's secret? I plunged my fingers into the pot and spread a thick layer of the cream over my face. It took a long time to rub in and I eventually had to wipe off the excess with Duncan's towel. I peered hopefully into the mirror, gently prodding the delicate skin under my eyes with the tip of my finger. The dry crinkly feeling had gone – but was it *revitalised*? I couldn't tell.

A rattle at the door startled me. I snatched a toothbrush at random from the rack over the sink and quickly brushed my teeth, drying it afterwards on the now damp and greasy towel. Scouring the shelves in vain for a comb, I restored some semblance of order to my hair with the help of a long-handled scrubbing brush that I found on a hook behind the door. I flushed the toilet for no particular reason, took a deep breath, and emerged into the hallway.

Voices drifted from the kitchen as I made my way downstairs.

'It makes a lot more sense to trade it in before the warranty runs out.'

'But what's the point of having a warranty if you don't use it up?'

'Oh God, I'm not going to explain all that again. Besides, those trips to your mother's are pushing the mileage up. I won't get such a good deal if we wait until the spring.'

'But Duncan, I like the car we've got. I can't see why you want to spend all that money on a BMW.'

I coughed loudly, preparing to enter the kitchen, but the door opened before I reached it and Duncan bustled into the hallway, jangling car keys.

'Did you see Jenny upstairs? She's late for her riding lesson.' He flashed me an indulgent smile, then disappeared through a doorway into the garage without waiting for an answer.

So he really did want a BMW, after all. I went into the kitchen, where Sally was stacking glasses into the dishwasher.

'Would you like some breakfast, Harriet?'

I wanted to leave, but I found myself agreeing to toast and coffee. I sat at the scrubbed wooden table that matched the Welsh dresser and watched her busy movements around the kitchen.

Sally was in her mid-forties, but looked a lot younger. This morning, she was smartly dressed in a dark-green suit, her shoulder-length blonde hair neatly brushed and styled. Her face was glowing with that finished look only attainable through the expert use of cosmetics.

'I'm meeting a client at eleven,' she said, consulting her watch. 'But I can't leave until Duncan gets back from the riding school, so there's no need for you to rush.'

She fed slices of bread into a large chrome toaster. 'I don't usually work on a Saturday, you know, but Duncan thinks I should push this client for more private jobs. He says I could make more money if I left the practice and set up my own consultancy. I'm not so sure, but you have to check out the possibilities, don't you? Otherwise you'd just stick in the same boring job all the time.'

She fell abruptly silent, presumably remembering what had just happened to *my* boring job. Sally's job wasn't in the least boring. Sally was an interior designer – a creator, a builder of dreams. She conjured up the backdrops to the lives of the idle rich, invented the settings in which they played out their fantasies. An Arabian Nights nursery for the spoilt child of a local industrialist, a Gothic dining room for an American banker, a Roman theme for an exclusive health club, complete with mosaics and statuary.

A mug of coffee and a plate of hot, buttered toast appeared under my nose. 'Tuck in,' said Sally, flopping into the opposite seat and inspecting me with curiosity. 'You look like you need it.'

I crunched miserably at the toast. Sally had everything: good looks, a rewarding and well-paid job, a husband, children, a secure home. I often wondered why she bothered to be friends with me. Did she need an example of failure to spur her on – the way dieters tape pictures of fat women on the fridge door? A warning: one false step and you too could be like this.

A glint of something shiny caught my eye at the side of the Welsh dresser and I queasily remembered the bottles of wine I had hidden there the night before.

'Sally?' I asked tentatively. 'What happened? Last night, I mean. Did I behave badly?'

She laughed. 'Goodness, no – I've never seen you enjoy yourself so much! It must have been just what you needed, letting your hair down and all that.'

I didn't remember this. I gave her a look of surprise. 'What did I do?'

'Well, let's see.' Sally frowned. 'You were acting a bit strangely at one point, going on about some student who you thought had drugged you. You were asking everyone if they'd seen him putting things in your drink.' She smiled. 'Then Duncan cranked the music up a bit and asked you to dance. You're a dark horse, Harriet. I didn't know you could move like that.'

I shuddered. What must Andrew have thought?

'Then you danced with Andrew . . .'

'I didn't!'

'Oh yes you did – all the way through that Dire Straits album. I didn't think he had it in him either – maybe you two had been drinking the same stuff.' She leaned forward confidentially. 'I don't suppose you're going to tell me that you've forgotten your date with him today?'

'Date?'

'Well, afternoon tea or something. It amounts to the same thing. After you'd hogged the dancing space for the best part of the evening, you were having this big debate with him about good and evil. Some intellectual stuff I'm not going to pretend to understand. He said it was all there in Marlowe's *Faust*, and he'd show you if you went round to see him this afternoon. Promised you toasted crumpets.'

'You don't happen to recall what time he said?' I asked foolishly, wishing I could remember what had happened. It was all a blank. What on earth had I said to Andrew?

'Four o'clock,' replied Sally with a grin. 'I think he's getting fond of you, Harriet.'

What did she know? Hadn't she noticed the way he was carrying on with that student? But her words were already working a strange magic, filling me with wild hopes that I might somehow be mistaken – that he might care for me after all. I looked at my watch. Eleven o'clock. Only five hours to wait.

I escaped just as Duncan returned with the car, bumping into him on the path and spilling his armful of glossy BMW brochures all over the flower bed. As soon as I got home, I had a long bath and washed my hair, determined to purge all unpleasant traces of the previous night from my mind and body. The afternoon passed slowly. I tried to read a book, but I couldn't concentrate. My mind kept wandering to the events of the previous night, searching for a clue about what had happened. Why had I allowed myself to get so drunk? What were Andrew's motives for inviting me round?

At five minutes to four I was standing nervously at the door of Andrew's flat, feeling like a teenager on a first date.

He let me in with a smile. 'Feeling better today?'

I followed him into the living room and took my usual seat in the armchair by the fireside. Would he fall at my feet, declaring his secret and undying love?

'I think we all had a bit too much to drink last night,' he said, stroking his beard thoughtfully. 'It was hard work this morning – getting started on these essays.' He waved his hand vaguely towards a heap of papers on his desk. 'I've got to have them all marked by Tuesday. Monday's crammed with meetings, and I've got a student coming for an extra tutorial tomorrow. I'll have to crack down to it this evening if I'm going to have any chance at all of getting them done.' He wandered through the open door of the kitchen. 'Can't have the system collapsing because of Duncan's wild parties, eh?'

'You're a busy man, Andrew,' I said, my hopes of the visit being extended into a romantic evening crushed. Sally had been exaggerating again.

'All work and no play,' he murmured, reappearing with a paper bag in his hand. He pulled out a cellophane package. 'Fancy a crumpet?'

I know you do, I thought, biting my tongue. I hadn't

forgotten the way he was eyeing up that student of his the night before. No prizes for guessing who needed the 'extra tutorial' which seemed to require the whole of Sunday to be kept free. A toasting fork was thrust into my hand, and I waited patiently while he struggled with the plastic wrapping, finally spilling the crumpets all over the hearthrug.

'Just like student days, eh?' he said, bending down and spiking one on the fork which hung limply from my hand. He guided it towards the crackling fire. Why couldn't he just stick them under the grill like anyone else, I wondered? But then, I reminded myself, Andrew wasn't like anyone else – that was why I loved him.

Andrew cared about traditional values. He shared my taste for Victorian novels and believed in happy endings – in fiction, at least, if not in reality. He also held to his principles, refusing to cut corners in his teaching while budgets were being slashed and standards were dropping all around him. Some thought he was eccentric or old-fashioned, but to me, he was a man of integrity. Well, most of the time, anyway.

'I'll just put the kettle on,' he said, returning to the kitchen. I watched him surreptitiously through the doorway, trying to reconcile my romantic picture of him with the domestic reality. Did all knights give up their white chargers with advancing years, exchanging them for carpet slippers and tea-making? He wore baggy brown corduroys and a rumpled, sporty kind of jacket with fraying cuffs and patched sleeves. A black polo neck jumper gave him an arty touch, contrasting nicely with the silvery hairs which flecked his light brown beard, and also providing an accidental showcase for the flakes of dandruff which fell in profusion each time he pushed his fingers through his hair. His hair was long – almost shoulder length – with no definable style. I loved it that way, grieving secretly each time he had it trimmed.

The kettle did its duty and he finally joined me by the fire, fussing with a tray of elaborate tea-making equipment – teapot, knitted cosy, delicate little cups and saucers, strainer, sugar bowl and tongs, milk jug, coasters, spoons. I speared the third crumpet and held it to the flames, enjoying the familiarity of the ritual. As he poured the tea, I gazed at his profile, fascinated by the endless permutations of his face when viewed from different angles. His prow-like nose shone in the firelight and the dry, papery surface of his cheek sprang into relief – each line a hieroglyph pregnant with hidden meaning.

He raised an eyebrow. 'You're looking rather thoughtful, Harriet. Is everything all right?'

I hesitated. Had Sally told him what had happened?

She hadn't. His face took on an expression of shocked concern as I gave him the brief details of my unexpected redundancy. Mumbling phrases of sympathy, he leaned forward and touched my hand.

'If there's anything I can do . . .'

Put your arms round me, you idiot! screamed a voice in my head. I willed him to move closer.

The third crumpet burst into flames. Startled, I dropped the toasting fork, which bounced on the hearth and sent burning fragments flying in all directions.

'Bugger!' muttered Andrew, leaping to stamp out several small fires on the carpet. 'I knew I should have got an extra packet.' He turned and grinned. 'You'll have to fight me for the last one now.'

The opportunity for romance had clearly been missed. But how could he make jokes at a time like this? Didn't he realise that my whole world had fallen apart?

Crouching by the hearth, he reloaded the fork and lifted it towards the flames, obviously unwilling to risk my incinerating the rest of his tea. 'You know, Harriet,' he said slowly, 'these things can sometimes be a blessing in disguise.'

Sniffing back a tear of self-pity, I stared at the still-smouldering burns in the worn patch of carpet in front of the fire. What on earth was he on about now?

'Are you telling me,' I suggested with a weak smile, 'that I've given you the excuse you needed to buy a new carpet?'

'Why would I need a new carpet?' He gave me a bewildered look. 'I was talking about early retirement. It could be the start of a new way of life for you – give you the time to develop your interests and so on. To tell the truth, I rather envy you.'

Envy me? That was the last thing I wanted right now. I wanted sympathy – bucketloads of sympathy. I wanted to spend hours complaining about the injustice of my redundancy, about the declining standards at the library, and to hear Andrew agree with me that Ms Annette Baker and her kind were a menace to civilisation – undermining the literacy of future generations.

'I'd jump at the chance myself,' he continued, 'but

I've got a good few years to go before I can take up that option. Too many long-term commitments in my job.' He twirled the toasting fork. 'Besides, the department's in such a mess at the moment, it would fall apart if I wasn't there. Someone's got to hold things together, eh?'

Why did men always think they were so indispensable? He had forgotten about my woes and was talking about himself now. He would be on to his writing soon.

'How's the book coming along?' I asked, pre-empting him. I wasn't going to give him a chance to accuse me of self-pity.

'Ah, well, that's exactly the problem, isn't it?' he said, depositing a fourth crumpet on the plate with a clunk and reaching for the butter. The last one was obviously being saved for after I had gone. 'Not enough time.'

Andrew's book. He had been working on it for at least five years. Something to do with myths and legends, as far as I could tell from his guarded remarks on the subject. I had never laid eyes on a single word he had written, and I sometimes wondered if the whole thing was a myth itself, a handy excuse for social unavailability when it suited him.

'That's why you've got to see the positive side of your situation, Harriet,' he continued. 'You could . . . mmmf . . .' He bit greedily into a dripping crumpet, flapping his hand to indicate that I should take one too. 'You could write something yourself – I'm sure you've got the ability. You should take a course or something – creative writing – we do them up at the university.

Now you've got the time – it's the ideal moment to begin.'

He didn't understand. He didn't understand me at all. Had it never occurred to him that I already had plenty of time? More time than I wanted? All those lonely evenings and weekends that stretched with interminable dreariness between the distantly spaced and brightly coloured landmarks of my meetings with him? Had he ever realised that my voracious appetite for reading was fed not just by a passion for literature, but by a need to escape the bleak reality of my life?

'You were telling me some fascinating things last night, Harriet. About the Faust legend. Have you been studying it?'

'Not really,' I replied, grateful for the change of subject. 'I saw the Marlowe play once, but I don't remember much. Do you know anything about it?'

'Let's see . . .' He went to the bookshelf and selected a handful of volumes. 'I've got Marlowe and Goethe here, plus a couple of commentaries – you might like to borrow them.'

I flicked through the books at random while Andrew scoffed the remaining three crumpets and drank four cups of tea. A line of Marlowe's leapt from the page: *Arch-regent and commander of all spirits.* Hadn't I heard that somewhere recently?

'A lot of writers have tried to get to grips with the Faust legend,' said Andrew, taking the Marlowe from my hand. He produced reading glasses from an inner pocket and put them on, turning the pages thoughtfully. 'It's a simple morality tale really – Faust makes a pact with the Devil, and gets twenty-four extra years of life in return for his soul. He fritters away the time with worldly pleasures, finds that none of them are worthwhile, and by the end he's wishing he could repent – but it's too late. Mephistophilis turns up on the stroke of midnight and whisks him off to Hell.'

He held up the book, angling it towards the light, and began to read:

The stars move still, time runs, the clock will strike,
The Devil will come, and Faustus must be damn'd.

His glasses sparkled with reflections of the firelight, adding a layer of mystery to his features. The greedy schoolboy had become an elusive intellectual – his image more vital, more attractive, more inaccessible.

'Goethe, on the other hand,' he continued, 'was a child of the Enlightenment. He saw redemption as man's natural destiny – believed in salvation through constant striving towards a higher good.' He took a vigorous bite at his last piece of crumpet and a stream of molten butter squirted from the side of his mouth, trickling in a greasy rivulet down his chin and soaking into his beard. Resisting an impulse to reach out and wipe it away with my handkerchief, I opened the second book, browsing through the pages as he spoke. Again, certain phrases triggered memories of the previous night.

'In Goethe's interpretation of the myth, Faust escapes damnation – he's snatched up to heaven at the last moment. And Goethe introduced a new theme: *Das ewig Weibliche.*'

'Das what?'

'The Eternal Feminine.' Andrew's face took on a dreamy look and he gave a little laugh. 'Saved by the love of a good woman.'

I felt a sharp pang of jealousy. Who was he thinking of? He reached for the book, but I pulled it back towards me, pretending to read. Look at me, Andrew, I told him silently. I'm a good woman. I wouldn't chew you up and spit you out like that young student would. I'd look after you. I'd save you. And I wouldn't even mind you having butter all over your chin.

'Of course, in later interpretations,' he went on, 'a whole new set of problems arise.'

But I had stopped listening. I was staring at the page in front of me.

You find my pentagram embarrassing?

My memory suddenly jolted back to life and I remembered everything that had happened the previous night. The pentangles on Sally's necklace. The student who called himself Mephisto. His outrageous promises and conjuring tricks. How nobody knew who he was or remembered seeing him there. I remembered how abruptly he had disappeared when Sally arrived.

I tapped Andrew's arm and pointed at the page. 'What does this bit about the pentagram mean?'

He repositioned his glasses and peered at the book. 'Oh, it's just a little joke of Goethe's. Mephistopheles can't leave the room because of Faust's amulet over the door. The five-sided figure is a traditional sorcerer's talisman – it's used to protect them against demons.'

Was it possible? I asked myself. Was it ever so

remotely possible that it had all been true? That I had really met the Devil last night? But if he was the Devil, why would he want to talk to me? Surely he had bigger fish to fry?

'Andrew,' I asked. 'Why is Faust always a man?'

He looked surprised, then gave a broad grin. 'I suppose the feminists haven't got round to him yet.' He chuckled. 'I expect they will soon enough, though. A female Faust would certainly give the Devil a run for his money.'

'Maybe women wouldn't be so easily tempted by worldly pleasures,' I said, bristling. 'Maybe they have a little more self-respect than to go throwing themselves at every new experience which comes along.' I gulped and fell silent, aware that I was unexpectedly on the verge of tears. What a hypocrite I was. If anyone offered me a new experience of any kind, I wouldn't be sitting around worrying about self-respect, I'd be tearing their arms off in my eagerness to get at it.

'I'll have to be going now,' I said, standing up. 'I've got a few things to get done this evening. And I'm going out later.' Pointless lies, but I wasn't going to hang around until he started dropping hints about his essays to be marked. Self-respect. Why did it always involve doing the exact opposite to what you wanted?

'Oh, already?' He glanced at his watch and looked disappointed. 'I was going to suggest a visit to the pub.'

'But I thought . . .' I gazed at him in frustration. Damn, I'd blown it! Why couldn't I have waited a few moments longer before I opened my big mouth?

He stood up and patted me lightly on the shoulder. 'You're quite right, of course, Harriet. I really ought to finish those essays tonight. Where would I be without you to keep me on the straight and narrow?'

'I . . . er . . . might be able to rearrange . . .'

'Nonsense, Harriet,' he said, smiling. 'I wouldn't dream of messing up your plans. I was being completely selfish – I should have thought to mention it much earlier.'

'Another time, then?' I asked in a studiously casual voice. 'Later in the week, maybe?'

'Oh yes, of course.' He frowned. 'I'm tied up most evenings, though – what with all the boring end-of-term parties at the university. Have to put in an appearance at these things to keep inter-departmental relationships sweet.'

He laughed, so I laughed with him, although I couldn't see anything funny in what he had said.

'I'll give you a call,' he promised, showing me to the door.

'Harriet?' he asked as I reached the top of the stairs. I turned back eagerly.

'Yes?'

'I'm sorry about your job. But you mustn't let it get you down – these things often turn out for the best in the long run.' He reached for the doorhandle to show that the meeting was over. 'Have a good Christmas if I don't see you before then.'

I walked quickly home through the dark streets, taking a masochistic pleasure in the slap of the icy wind on my face and pretending it was the sole cause of the stinging tears that streamed from my eyes. It was fairly obvious that I wasn't going to hear from Andrew until after Christmas. What was I going to do with myself until then? How would I cope with the loneliness once I had finished my job? The future loomed as a dark chasm, its entrance fringed with twinkling Christmas lights.

CHAPTER 4

As I let myself into the flat, I was mentally unscrewing the lid of the whisky bottle. Not stopping to remove my coat or turn on the light, I headed straight into the living room to the windowsill where I had left it. It wasn't there. Surely I hadn't finished it all the night before?

I paused and sniffed the air. Smoke. What in hell's name . . .

A voice cut through the stillness. 'Your drink's over here, Harriet.'

My heart gave a thump of fear and I opened my mouth and screamed. I was half-way to the door when the light flicked on of its own accord and I swung round to see a man reclining on my sofa. It was the student from the party. Mephisto. He had a glass of my whisky in one hand and a cigarette in the other.

'You take it straight, don't you?' he asked, indicating a second glass on the table. 'I've poured you a double measure.'

I stared at him in disbelief. 'How did you get in?' I croaked.

'What kept you so long at Andrew's? Were you hoping he'd give you a Christmas kiss?'

'Get out of my flat!' My voice rose to a hysterical squeal. 'Get out before I call the police!'

He blew a smoke ring towards the ceiling. 'I expected something more original than that from you, Harriet. Now, why don't we just skip the tantrums and enjoy another drink together. The bottle will last longer if you share it with me, remember?'

I tried to think of a cutting reply, but I needed the whisky more than ever now. I gulped down the generous measure he had poured me and helped myself to another, savouring the warm glow which spread through my body and soothed the lingering remains of that morning's hangover.

'I think it's about time you explained yourself,' I said, giving him what I hoped was a challenging look. 'And you can take those muddy boots off my sofa.'

He looked at his boots with surprise, as if seeing them for the first time. 'Your sofa? Oh, I see.' He shrugged and swung his feet lazily to the floor. The boots were black leather, worn cowboy-style outside tight denim jeans. He pushed the sleeves of his jumper back to the elbows, revealing a dense covering of dark hair on his forearms.

'Well?' I said.

'*Sometimes indiscretions/Are our most valuable possessions.*'

Oh God, he was showing off with quotations again. Was it Marlowe or Goethe this time? 'Look,' I said, trying to sound authoritative – trying to speak with the wisdom of my years. 'I think you're getting a bit mixed up between fiction and reality here. This is all very amusing, but why don't you just return to real life for a moment and tell me what you're doing here?'

'I'm not the one with a problem, Harriet. It's you who can't tell the difference. What do I have to do to make you believe me?'

'To believe that you're the Devil?' I said with a laugh. 'Something pretty bloody convincing! You don't really think I'm going to be taken in by any more of your party games, do you?'

He gave me a long stare, and I felt an odd tingling in my stomach which had nothing to do with the whisky. My poor deluded body was sending out little chemical signals of desire. He moved closer, transfixing me with his gaze, then his hand snaked forward and brushed against my leg.

'You find me attractive, don't you?'

'No!' I jumped to my feet and backed away from him, trembling. How could I even think of such a thing? A woman of my age? It was disgusting.

But it was true. I felt a strange thrill – a combination of desire and repulsion. Standing with my back to the window, I tried to view him objectively. An unkempt young man with swarthy good looks, and a hint of the gipsy – the adventurer – about him. A face which refused to fit into the crowd, the face of a rebel. Cruel lips, suggestive of pleasures withheld, and therefore the more to be desired by those who fell under his influence. An air of cynicism, of cold-heartedness, a man who would never feel emotion or regret. A dangerous man, a man not to be trusted.

'I want you Harriet,' he said.

'What do you mean, want?' My mind was spinning with confusion. 'I'm old enough to be your . . .'

'Oh dear, no,' he interrupted, laughing. 'I wasn't talking about that kind of desire. That can wait for another day.'

'But you said . . .' I felt a hot flush of embarrassment. How could I have been so stupid as to think he was attracted to an ugly old woman like me?

'It's not your body I want, Harriet.' His eyes twinkled at me mockingly. 'It's your soul. And I want you to give it to me willingly. That's why I'm going to prove this to you once and for all. Come here.'

What was he going to do? I gave a weak moan of protest, but I felt my will letting go. He had me in his power. I didn't care what happened to me any more. No one else did, so why should I? I walked across the room and stood before him.

'Sit down,' he said. 'There's something I want to show you.'

Sunday 14th December

I can't believe this is happening to me. I'm writing it down here to prove to myself that I'm not going mad. Maybe I'll look back at it in a few days, or even a few years, and laugh at my own stupidity – the delusions of a desperate old woman. Maybe, but at the moment, I'm certain that it's real. This is it. The turning point I've been waiting for all my life.

I woke up this morning to the sound of church

bells ringing. They shatter my peace every Sunday, but today I was aware of their purpose for the first time. God calling the lost souls to seek redemption. What chance could there ever be for a soul as lost as mine?

Last night I had been prepared to sin, but to sin in other people's eyes, not my own. Mephisto might be young enough to be my son, but why shouldn't I have taken pleasure when it was offered to me? It would have been the first time in nearly thirty years. I was convinced until the very end that he was playing a game with me, using his subversive talk about the devil to camouflage a sexual preference for older women. If I'm truthful, I was excited by the idea. I would have done it, too – how often would such a chance come my way again?

But I was completely wrong about Mephisto. It wasn't a game at all. It wasn't my body he wanted. Last night I committed the greatest sin of all. I made a pact with the Devil and sold my soul.

How can I believe this? I don't believe in God, after all, so why should the Devil have any more credibility? How did Mephisto convince me?

As I might have expected, it was another trick. But it was a trick which I couldn't explain away as coincidence, because I know the odds against it. Everyone knows the odds. Fourteen million to one. Half an hour before the National Lottery draw took place last night, Mephisto predicted the winning numbers. He wrote them on the back of a Sainsbury's till receipt and placed them in my hand. Half an hour. I could have sprinted down to the late-night newsagent's, bought a ticket, and become an overnight millionairess. But I didn't, of course. I just laughed at him. Laughed all the way through the stupid television programme he made me watch, with all its razzmatazz of gipsy fortune-tellers and spinning balls. Then, when the numbers had finally been chosen, I realised the joke was over. I stopped laughing and began to listen to him very carefully. For he actually did possess magical powers. And he was offering me something money could never buy. Youth. Youth and beauty. A chance to recover all those wasted years.

The terms of the pact seemed straightforward enough at first. Twenty-five extra years of life, together with youth and beauty, in return for my soul. I asked him how he would claim it. When would it happen?

He told me that the twenty-five years were guaranteed – as long as I didn't start walking under buses or doing anything stupid. Beyond that, I would have to take my chances. He could come for me at any time he chose – a matter of pure whim. I would simply die and go to Hell, just like any other sinner.

Am I afraid of dying? It's going to happen one day, whether I make this bargain or not. Another twenty-five years would take me up to seventy-five years of being alive – that's not bad innings. What about Hell? Isn't that where I'd end up anyway, supposing it actually exists? I'm certainly not planning to rush off to that church down the road – the one with those bloody bells – to join in with their hypocrisy and pretence, as insurance against the off-chance that I'm backing the wrong side. That there really is a God sitting up there in a fairytale Heaven full of cherubs and angels floating around on clouds. What would I do in a place like that? Even Hell sounded better than an eternity trapped in Disneyland.

So I asked Mephisto how it was done. Would I be sent back in time to my youth? He explained that it couldn't work that way. Apparently time travel is a bit of a no-no in diabolical circles – you would get people interfering with things that have already happened, or turning up twice in the same place. He reminded me of the science-fiction story where the hero travels back in time and accidentally kills a butterfly. When he gets back to the present again, he finds that everything is different to how he remembered it – the entire course of history has been affected by this tiny event. How did Mephisto know I had read that story?

More to the point, I wouldn't gain much in the beauty stakes if I went back to the body of my younger self. I remember all too clearly my looks, or rather the lack of them, at the age of twenty-five. I'd be facing all the same handicaps all over again.

The way it would actually be done – and this is the scary bit – is that I would get someone else's body. One that wasn't needed any more. I asked what he meant by 'not needed', but I had already guessed the answer. I would get the body of someone who had died, conveniently, at the age of twenty-five. Who would it be? He couldn't tell me. He would have to see what the universe had to offer at the precise moment of transition. But what if he picked someone who was even uglier than I had been? Or someone horribly disfigured by an accident? I would have to trust him, he told me. He would make sure he got me a good deal.

But could I trust him? What if he was lying to me? What if I just ended up dead? I suppose there wouldn't be much point in going to all this trouble if he simply wanted to kill me. There wouldn't be any need for all this stuff about pacts, he could just do it – he's got the power. I didn't really have any choice but to trust him.

So I asked him if I had to sign my name in blood, like Doctor Faustus. He laughed at me then. Told me not to get mixed up between fiction and reality. That they didn't go in for all that paraphernalia any more – all I had to do was go to sleep, and, when I woke up again, it would all be done.

But what if I didn't agree to this pact? I started to get worried then. If there was nothing to sign, how could I stop him from going ahead with it anyway? He gave me a funny look then. Said that I wasn't going to want to stop him, was I? That I had already made up my mind.

He was right, of course. I had. What had I got to

lose? I was more worried that he would change his mind and tell me the offer was closed. So that was it. The pact was sealed.

I'm going to do it. There are still a lot of unanswered questions – things I don't understand. Things he wouldn't tell me. What happens to my old body, for example. People are going to wonder where I've gone. I don't have many friends, but there's the postman, the milkman and the old lady downstairs to worry about. There's also the landlord, who calls round from time to time to check that I haven't painted the living room purple or sub-let the broom cupboard to a family of illegal immigrants. If I wake up in my own bed with a new body, twenty-five years younger, how am I going to explain what I'm doing here? Pretend to be a friend or relative staying for a while? The landlord wouldn't like that. And what if no one believes me? What if they think that I've been murdered? They might accuse the new me of doing it, and the last thing I'm going to want is the police asking questions about who I am. I could end up in prison – that would be a nice twist to Mephisto's plot. There has to be a catch somewhere, doesn't there?

This is getting complicated – I need time to think things through. But I don't have time. It's afternoon already, and tonight, when I go to sleep, is when it will happen. I've only got as much time as I can force myself to stay awake. I need to think of a way to postpone discovery – pretend that I've gone on holiday, maybe. There are things I need to organise – paying the rent on the flat, and working out how, if I no longer exist, I can get my hands on my redundancy money from the library. I'll need to have some source of finance to begin with. Then I can leave Guildford and start a new life. I'll be well away from here before anyone finds out.

Other people – people like Sally or Andrew – would never have believed Mephisto. They'd have laughed it off as a joke and carried on with their smug little lives, never knowing what they'd missed. But I'm different. I believe in magic. When I was a child, I read all the story books and knew that one day my fairy godmother would arrive to wave her magic wand and make everything all right. I never thought I would have to wait this long, but it's happened at last. I've been offered a second chance at life – a chance to find happiness.

What am I going to do with my new life? With youth, beauty, and the knowledge which I have now, I should be able to get anything I want. I could have a brilliant new career and achieve fame and fortune – put the likes of Ms Annette Baker into the shadows. I could be really ruthless and make it right to the top – get my revenge on all the people who wrote me off as a useless old woman. That would give me great satisfaction, but there's something else I want – something I haven't told Mephisto. I want to find love. I want to know what it's like to be secure and have someone to care for you – to have a family life, children, someone to come home to at night. I want to hear the words that no one has ever spoken to me – my hand trembles to write them even now – I want to hear someone say 'I love you'.

I feel hot and dizzy. Beads of perspiration are breaking out all over my body. But the menopause can't get me now. It's too late. I'll soon be young and beautiful – able to have any man I choose. There's someone out there who's right for me, and I'm going to find him.

I must put my affairs in order. Pay the rent. Cancel the milk. Write letters to Sally and Andrew – tell them I'm going on a world cruise with my redundancy money. I'll probably never see them again, but it doesn't matter. I don't want any reminders of my old life – my unhappiness.

Then I'll go to bed and wait for Mephisto to come. I'm frightened. I feel as if I'm standing on the edge of a precipice and trying to summon the courage to jump.

But I will jump. I'm going to do it.

CHAPTER 5

I gradually became aware of a low bleeping noise, punctuated by distant metallic clinks and the sound of muffled voices. There was a nasty taste in my mouth and the smell of antiseptic in my nostrils. I explored with the tips of my fingers and found that I was lying on my back in a hard and unfamiliar bed. Where the hell was I?

I opened my eyes. A blurred shadow loomed towards me against a background of harsh white light. I flinched and tried to turn away, but I couldn't move. What had Mephisto done to me?

The shadow bobbed into focus. A woman's face. A face I didn't recognise.

'Cindy? Can you hear me, honey?'

Was she talking to me?

'She's waking up.' A loud whisper.

'Careful.' Another woman's voice. 'She's still very weak.'

'Cindy?' The first woman spoke again, leaning over me so that I could feel her breath on my cheek. 'You're gonna be all right, Cindy, honey. The doctor says you're doing just fine.'

Cindy? There must be some mistake. That was the name of a bloody *doll*, for Christ's sake. There was something wrong. Something horribly wrong. Where had these strange people come from?

'You just hang on in there, honey,' continued the woman in a nasal drawl. 'We'll have you out of here in no time.'

I tried to sit up, but the effort was too much and I sank back on the bed. 'Gently, now,' said the second voice. Unseen hands flew busily into action, cradling my head and plumping pillows until I was comfortably settled in a semi-upright position.

'There we go. That's better.'

My surroundings swam hazily into focus. A hospital room. Tubes coming out of my nose. Another tube taped to my wrist. Flickering green lines on a monitor at the bedside which pulsed in time with the low bleeping noise I had first heard.

'What happened?' I asked, my voice coming out in an unfamiliar squawk. 'Where am I?'

One of the women wore a nurse's uniform. 'You've had a bad accident,' she said calmly, placing a cool hand on my forehead and stroking away a wisp of hair. 'But you're through the worst of it already, and you're going to be just fine.'

'Just fine,' echoed the other woman, patting the back of my hand. 'Everything's going to be just fine.'

I stared at her. She was young – probably in her thirties – with a pretty face and pale blonde hair. Looking more closely, I could see lines of tiredness around her eyes and darker colouring at the roots of her hair. She patted my hand again, acting as if she knew me.

'Who's she?' I asked the nurse.

The woman looked up, her face stricken. 'What's wrong with her? How can it be that she doesn't know her own sister? Oh Jesus, don't tell me she's brain-damaged!'

Sister? I didn't have a sister. Who the hell was this imposter?

'It's Babs, your sister Babs,' said the woman earnestly, leaning right over me again. 'You recognise me, don't you, hon?'

'She's sure to have some memory loss after the nasty knock she's had,' said the nurse, fussing with something at the foot of the bed. 'But don't worry, she'll be as fine as apple pie in a few weeks. Once you get her home, and she's got familiar things around her, it'll all come flooding back.'

Home? Where was home, for Christ's sake? Then I realised what had been bothering me all along. As fine as *apple pie?* Why were they giving me all this American stuff? Stretching my neck sideways, I caught a glimpse of the view from the window. A palm tree swayed in a gentle breeze. It didn't look much like Guildford – or anywhere else I knew, for that matter.

'Where am I?' I demanded, as loudly as I could. My voice didn't sound like my own any more. Was it just the effect of the tubes in my nose, or had I mysteriously acquired a new accent?

'Why, honey,' said my so-called sister Babs. 'You're right here in LA, of course.

'LA?' I echoed. There didn't seem to be any 'of course' about it to me. 'You mean *Los Angeles?*'

'Where did you think you'd be? Acapulco?' Laughing nervously, she turned to the nurse. 'That's my ditzy sis for you – she's always been like that. Wouldn't know her ass from her elbow without a map.' She sighed. 'She never tired of talking about the place when she was a kid: The City of Angels and all that. She was coming here to be a movie star when she grew up.' She sniffed and dabbed her eyes with a tissue.

'Broke her mother's heart, she did – running off when she was only eighteen. Thought she was too good for Sioux Falls. Now look where it's got her.'

'But I'm not . . .' I tried to get her attention, but she carried on talking over me as if I wasn't there. Sioux Falls? Los Angeles? There had been nothing about this in the terms of the pact. And who the hell was this Cindy character? 'Thanks, Mephisto,' I muttered under my breath. 'You've really sold me down the river.'

'I don't know who's gonna look after her now,' Babs went on. 'I sure can't cope with it, with Dale and the kids to worry about. If only we'd taken out that extra insurance – I told Dale it was dumb not to – I mean, you never know when things might turn bad on you.'

'You sure as hell don't,' murmured the nurse.

'But I've done my duty. You can't deny that. I came straight out here as soon as the hospital called, even though I couldn't even get a fare beater on the plane ticket, let alone the fourteen-day discount at such short notice. It's just, I have to be back at work the day after next and I can't expect Dale's mom to have the kids for long. I have a family to look after, you know.'

'There, there,' said the nurse. 'Nobody's asking you to do anything right now.'

'Besides . . .' she let out a muffled sob. 'She never did anything for me. I was the one left at home to look after Mom . . .'

'Now, now, that's enough excitement for today,' said the nurse, ushering my would-be relative towards the door. 'She needs to rest.'

Rest was the last thing I needed. As soon as I was alone, I struggled to sit up properly without dislodging the tubes. What did I look like? I had expected to wake up alone in Guildford but, instead, I'd been transported half-way around the world and delivered into the hands of strangers. What about the rest of the bargain? Just how far had Mephisto betrayed me?

I looked at my hands and saw smooth skin, unmarked by signs of age. My fingernails – previously well-bitten and flecked with spots of white – were now long and elegant, filed carefully into shape and coated with pale-pink polish. My forearms were slender and lightly tanned. Summoning my courage, I lifted a hand to my face. My cheeks were taut and smooth. No sign of the double chin. My hair, tied loosely at the back of my neck with a ribbon, felt soft and silky. I pulled a strand forward for inspection. It was long, shiny, and very, very blonde.

The rest of my body was swathed in a frilly white nightdress. I plucked at the bedclothes in a feeble attempt to explore further, but the nurse returned before I could get anywhere.

'The doctor says these can come off now,' she said with a smile, removing the tubes from my nose and flicking switches on the banks of equipment at the side of the room. She tucked the rumpled sheets back into place, pinning me to the bed 'You just carry on resting like a good girl. You're doing real well.'

'May I have a mirror?' I asked. 'Please?'

'Why honey, whyever do you want one of those?' She paused. 'I don't know if the doctor will allow it,' she added doubtfully. 'I'll have to go and ask.'

I waited impatiently for her return. Why was there a problem with my having a mirror? Had Mephisto really done the dirty on me? I touched my face anxiously. Did I have disfiguring scars? Some hideous deformity?

The nurse reappeared with a white-coated doctor and conducted a long whispered conversation in the far corner of the room. Eventually, she approached the bed and held out a small rectangular mirror with a plastic handle. 'I have to warn you, there's a little bruising,' she said. 'Be prepared for what you see.'

I leaned forward eagerly to see my reflection, then let out a gasp of surprise.

'Don't be alarmed,' said the doctor, moving quickly to the bedside. 'The bruises are only superficial.' He grinned. 'We'll have that pretty face of yours back to normal in no time at all.'

I gave him a dazed look. My injuries were of a very minor nature – a slight swelling and discolouration on one cheek, and a small cut on my forehead – I had barely noticed them.

Mephisto hadn't let me down after all. I was young – younger than I had expected. Probably in my early twenties. I had a delicate, doll-like face which, as I pulled the ribbon from my hair, was framed by a mass of golden tresses. Big blue eyes gazed back from the mirror with trusting innocence. My lips were full and moist. I smiled at the mirror, revealing a perfect set of white teeth.

My eyes sparkled with pleasure. The doctor was wrong. My face wasn't just pretty. It was stunningly beautiful.

I spent the next few days trying to work out exactly who I was. If anyone suspected that I wasn't who I was meant to be, it would lead to all sorts of awkward questions. How would I explain myself?

The terms of Mephisto's pact had seemed straightforward at the time. I would get a new body, but it would be inhabited by my own mind and personality, which would be unaffected by the transition. I had been very careful about this point. If you replace the head of a hammer, and then you replace the handle, does the original hammer still exist? What use would a new life be if I wasn't myself any more?

Mephisto had kept this part of the bargain to the letter, but what I had somehow overlooked was the baggage which would come with someone else's body. I had foolishly assumed that I would have a fresh start – that I could take on any identity I chose. I hadn't anticipated being dropped into the middle of somebody else's life and having to take on all their ongoing relationships and responsibilities.

Now I would have to keep up the pretence of actually being this person called 'Cindy' – at least until I could get out of the hospital. I would have to find out as much as I could about her – enough to convince the doctors that I had recovered from my so-called memory loss. Otherwise they might send for the shrinks – as they so quaintly called their psychiatrists over here – and then there would be trouble.

My first source of information was Cindy's handbag, which I discovered in the bedside locker. Feeling like a character in a detective story, I searched it eagerly at the first opportunity. She could have opened a small chemist's shop with the contents – make-up, perfume, toiletries, face creams, several different kinds of hair-brush and even a small, battery-powered hair dryer.

A side pocket yielded Cindy's driving licence and purse. The purse contained bank and credit cards, keys, two five-dollar bills and some assorted change. The driving licence told me that my full name was Cindy Louise Mary Brown and that I was twenty-one years old. Twenty-one! So Mephisto couldn't even get his sums right – I had gained an extra four years through his treachery and incompetence.

There was also a small box of tampons and an unopened packet of three condoms. These last items brought a smile to my lips – proof of my admission to the ranks of the sexually active. Then it struck me that a girl with Cindy's looks would probably have a boyfriend. What if I found some beefcake waiting for me when I got out of here, expecting his rights? Could I convince him that I was Cindy? And what would it be like, having sex with a stranger? No, I thought. He'll just have to find himself back on the market sooner than he expected. If I have sex with anyone, it's going to be someone I choose for myself, and this time I'm planning to set my sights higher than the back of Barry Thompson's van.

At the bottom of the handbag were a dog-eared matchbook from Marty's Diner – wherever that was – and a laminated plastic calorie chart, which I threw in the wastepaper bin.

When I was able to get up and walk about, I spent a lot of time in the hospital bathroom getting to know my new body. I couldn't see that I needed to worry too much about calories – I was tall and slender, with legs that went on forever and a stomach so flat you could roll pastry on it. Turning sideways, I was able to admire a pert bottom without an ounce of superfluous fat – a marked contrast to the cellulite-dimpled cushions of sagging flesh which had embarrassed me in my previous life. My breasts were firm and perfectly symmetrical, with upturned nipples which became hard at the lightest caress of my fingers.

Adapting to my new body presented some curious problems. I wasn't used to being so tall and my balance was all different. When I walked, I tended to misjudge distances and bump into things. My voice, or – more specifically – my accent, took some getting used to. Each time I spoke, I winced at the uneducated nasal drawl which came from my mouth. I found myself struggling to pronounce familiar words – words which were not, presumably, part of Cindy's vocabulary. How could I expect anyone to take me seriously if I sounded like this? Was my personality to be trapped inside this beautiful new body, unable to communicate in my own language? Cindy, I decided, would need to brush up on her elocution.

My handwriting was another surprise. Presented with a form to fill in, I grappled unsuccessfully with the pen for several minutes before realising that Cindy was left-handed. When I transferred it to my other hand, the pen produced an unfamiliar childish script which was agonisingly slow. Impatiently, I tried to accelerate into my habitual scrawl, but my co-ordination disappeared and I was left with undecipherable scribbles. It was a disorientating experience. Where exactly were the boundaries between the mind and the body?

My new-found sister returned the next day, obviously pleased by my rapid recovery.

'I just thank my lucky stars you woke up from that coma,' she said with a melodramatic sigh. 'I didn't know *what* to think when they first told me – I had this picture of you hooked up to some machine costing hundreds of dollars a day. You know, totally dependent on your family for the rest of your life. And with me having Dale and the kids to look after . . .'

I privately thanked my lucky stars that I'd woken up too. How long would she have waited before she had me switched off?

'Tell me,' I mumbled. 'The accident. What happened?'

Babs launched into a tale rich with told-you-so's and should-have-known-better's, from which I gathered that I – or rather, Cindy – had been in a car crash. She had missed her turning on the Pasadena freeway and had hit another car while trying to back up the entry ramp. I was lucky to have escaped without visible damage, Babs told me sternly. Luckier than poor Cindy, I thought. She, presumably, had cashed in her chips at this point, providing the 'unwanted body' Mephisto was looking for. It must have been a quiet night for the Grim Reaper if he had needed to come all the way to Los Angeles in his search.

The other car, apparently, had been a Rolls-Royce.

'Trust my smartass sister not to run into any ordinary car,' continued Babs with a hysterical note in her voice. 'I just hope your insurance payments are up to date, that's all I can say. The guy driving it sounded like some real big shot – Harvey something, the nurse said he was called. Something to do with the perfume business. He was lucky to get out with just a nosebleed – you might have killed him! Then he'd have sued us all to kingdom come and where would we have been then?'

I wanted to ask her how he would have sued us if he was dead, but something told me it was best to keep quiet. At least I was getting some kind of background to my new life.

'I don't know how all this happened,' she went on, her voice becoming a whine. 'I don't know why you had to come to this terrible place. Three years you been here – and what do you have to show for it? What do you have that's worth anything more than what you could have done back in Sioux Falls?'

A gleam of hatred and resentment appeared in her eyes. 'Nothing,' she hissed. 'Nothing! They all said that you were the pretty one and that I was the plain Jane who would get nowhere, but I've got myself a respectable life. My Dale might not be a movie star but he's a good husband and a hard worker. I have a happy home and two great kids. But you – where were you when I was looking after Mom the last time she was sick?'

I remained silent, waiting for her to tell me.

'Out here waiting on tables in some two-bit diner, that's where!' she spat triumphantly. 'After all your airs and graces about being a model . . .'

Waiting on tables? 'Cheers, Mephisto,' I muttered under my breath. I had hoped for a slightly more glamorous start to my new career.

'And about that friend of yours . . .'

'What friend?' I interrupted. I had been wondering if Cindy had any.

'You'll find out soon enough – she's coming this afternoon.' Babs stood up. 'Which means that I'm out of here.' At the door she paused and threw me a contemptuous stare. 'Memory loss, sure! You can't fool me!'

Thanks for the support, Sis, I thought bitterly, as the door slammed shut. If this was a taste of family life in Sioux Falls, I wasn't surprised that Cindy had run away.

*   *   *

When I asked the nurse about the 'friend' my sister had mentioned, I learned that someone called Trish was coming to see me that afternoon. I waited impatiently for her arrival. Much of Cindy's life was still unknown to me and I desperately needed someone to help me fill in the gaps.

'Surprise!' A woman in her twenties burst through the door and clattered towards me on five-inch heels. She wore a short black leather skirt and jacket and her dyed red hair was piled high on the top of her head.

'Jeepers, Cin,' she gasped, flopping into a chair at my bedside. 'You scared the pants off me pulling a stunt like that! I thought you were a goner!' She peeled off her jacket to reveal a bright red T-shirt with *Too Hot To Handle* written across the front in shiny gold lettering. 'I thought I'd have to start looking for somebody else to share the apartment – and you know what a pain in the butt that would be, having to sift through all the geeks and weirdos that always turn up.'

I smiled weakly. I had rather been hoping that Cindy lived on her own. What was life going to be like sharing with Trish?

'Speaking of pains in the butt,' she added, glancing around and lowering her voice, 'I hope that poisonous sister of yours is out of the way. With due respect and all that, but you know what I think of her.' She shook her head, pushing loose strands of hair away from her face and inspecting me with curiosity. 'So, Cin, how d'ya feel? I never knew anyone who had a coma before.'

'Better than I did this morning,' I said, looking at her shyly. She wore bright-red lip gloss the same colour as her T-shirt, and her eyes were fringed with thick layers of shadow and mascara that made her look like a panda.

'I hear you've been trading paint with the high rollers,' she said with a grin. 'Did you know it was *Harley Brightman* in the car you hit?'

'Who?'

'The nurse told me – she says he escaped with just a nose . . .' She stopped and stared at me. 'Did I just hear you ask who Harley Brightman is?'

I nodded.

'Jeez, Cin, I thought they were kidding about you losing your memory!' Her eyes widened. 'It was him who brought you in here. Rode with you in the ambulance and everything, the nurse said. Probably saved your life.'

'Is he a friend of mine, then?'

'A *friend*? You should be so lucky. Harley Brightman is only the most eligible dreamboat bachelor in LA!' She let out a long sigh. 'Rolling in money too, since he inherited *Lapinique*. You know, the cosmetics company?'

I nodded again, this time with a smile. Even I had heard of *Lapinique*.

'Maybe you could sue him,' she said thoughtfully. 'After all, if you were backing up, he must have run into you from behind. You could probably say it was his fault.'

'Perhaps I should consider myself fortunate that *he* isn't suing *me*.'

'*Perhaps I should consider* . . .' She stared at me,

giggling. 'Hey Cind – what happened to your voice? You never talked all highfalutin' like that before.'

'I, er . . . I dunno,' I mumbled. I was going to have to be careful what I said around Trish. Her relationship with Cindy seemed just a little too close for my liking.

After a few hours spent with her, however, I had learned a lot more about Cindy's life than I was likely to find out elsewhere. I was relieved to learn that there were no other close relatives who might turn up unexpectedly. Her mother, as Babs had so painstakingly pointed out, had died shortly after Cindy left home, but Trish reckoned it had more to do with a bottle than with a broken heart. Her father had disappeared long ago.

Cindy had set off for the bright lights of Los Angeles, hoping to make it as a fashion model, but ended up waitressing in Marty's Diner, a sleazy-sounding establishment on an unfashionable stretch of Sunset Boulevard. Here she met up with Trish, who had ambitions to be an actress, and moved into the spare room of her apartment.

Cindy's only modelling engagement to date was as an extra in a baked bean commercial, while Trish had achieved the dizzy heights of a three-second exposure during a crowd scene in *Melrose Place*, together with a brief appearance on CNN News when she happened to be passing the scene of a bank robbery.

'You just can't give up, though, Cin,' she advised me repeatedly. 'You never know when your big break might come.'

When I questioned her about Cindy's relationships with men, she wasn't very helpful.

'How should I know?' she asked, shrugging. 'You never tell *me* anything. I always said you were too secretive for your own good.'

'Surely you would have noticed if I had a boyfriend?'

'Oh, come on Cin,' she said petulantly. 'How would you like it if you found out that I'd been spying on you? Keeping notes or something just in case you got hit on the head and lost your memory? You don't fool me with that little Miss Virgin act. I bet you're at it whenever you get the chance, just like the rest of us. Like that time you stayed out all night with Howard Weinburger.'

'Who's he?'

'Oh come on, Cin, don't pretend you don't remember Howard. I know you had this accident and everything, but honestly Cin, you went out with him for three whole weeks!'

Was that some kind of record? It certainly didn't look as if Cindy had any long-term commitments on the romantic front.

'You must have been giving him something he liked,' she added thoughtfully. ''Cause he sure was pissed off when you dumped him.'

Trish was a frequent visitor during my stay at the hospital, while Babs visited only one more time, on her way to the airport. She made it clear that she was not expecting to return to California again, and made no suggestion that I should stop by if I happened to be passing through Sioux Falls.

'Stuck-up bitch,' muttered Trish when I told her.

'You're better off without her, Cin, believe me. Even if she did cheat you out of that money your Mom left you.'

'What money?'

'Oh – er . . .' Trish looked vague. 'It was just something you said to me once. I don't think you had any proof.'

She began to study her fingernails. 'Speaking of which,' she continued, 'you do, um . . . remember that the rent's due at the end of this week, don't you?' She gave me an embarrassed look. 'Marty did say he'd hold the job open, and that you could do some extra shifts if you wanted.'

I hadn't thought much about money until then, but it suddenly loomed large on the agenda. How was I going to support myself? The next day, I wheeled myself down to the hospital foyer where the cash dispensers twinkled invitingly, and inserted the bank card from Cindy's purse into one of them. There were several numbers scribbled on a scrap of paper in the back pocket of her handbag and I keyed these into the machine, gaining access to Cindy's account on the third attempt.

I quickly wished I hadn't. Cindy's finances were in a sorry state, which was to say that she had hardly any cash in her account. I had already decided that I would rather rot in Hell than ask Babs for any handouts, so it looked as if I was going to have to get back to work at Marty's on the double.

Things could be worse, I told myself. I had a job – which was more than Harriet could say for herself –

and I had somewhere to live. Mephisto might have cheated me on some of my expectations, but I couldn't complain about the main part of the bargain. He had delivered youth and beauty to me in abundance. I might have been dislocated from my roots by several thousand miles, but it seemed that I had few ties and responsibilities, and I was free to do as I wished – within the limits of having to earn a living.

I wanted to get back to Guildford sometime – even if just to show Annette Baker what real good looks were about – but I would have to wait until I could save up the fare. Meanwhile, wasn't America supposed to be the land of opportunity? The place where people could reinvent themselves?

I had been given a second chance at life and I wasn't going to blow it this time.

CHAPTER 6

I left the hospital just before the Christmas holiday period began. Cindy's car had been completely written off in the accident, so Trish came to collect me in a battered red convertible which looked as if it had seen its fair share of collisions.

'Well, what are you waiting for?' she asked, gathering an armful of sweet wrappers, magazines and Coke cans from the front passenger seat and throwing them in the back. She donned a pair of sunglasses and started fiddling with the buttons on the car stereo. 'Come on, get in!'

A deafening blast of music filled my ears as we hurtled through the exit of the hospital car park.

'*Bo – orn to be wi – i – ild*!' sang Trish, accelerating. There was a scream of tyres as a pickup truck swerved to avoid us.

'Spin on it, tosser!' she yelled, sticking a finger in the air. The truck mounted the opposite pavement and crunched into a palm tree. As we drove by, a huge Alsatian dog leapt from the back of the truck and began to pursue us down the road, barking excitedly.

Gripping the edges of my seat with white knuckles, I fumbled for the seat belt. 'Er, Trish . . .' I mumbled. 'Would you mind, er . . .'

Trish stabbed at the stereo buttons, cutting off the music and replacing it with a radio talk show. 'Sorry, Cin,' she muttered ungraciously. 'I forgot that you're a Country and Western girl.'

When we reached the freeway, it was jammed with slow-moving traffic, and I was able to observe my surroundings clearly for the first time. It was certainly a change from Guildford – particularly the weather, which was mild and sunny only a few days before Christmas. I had never travelled outside Europe in my past life and, not having seen America with my own eyes, I had always secretly doubted whether it really existed at all.

Now, I still wasn't completely sure. I gazed around at road signs bearing the names of exotic sounding places like Santa Monica, Malibu and Beverly Hills, and wondered if I really was here or if it was all a dream. I felt completely disorientated. Most people have to sit on a plane for twelve hours or so to get to Los Angeles – and they usually know exactly where they're going. They've planned it, after all. It's a bit different to just wake up and find yourself over five thousand miles away from the place you went to sleep in the night before.

'Hey babe,' said a gruff voice beside me. Startled, I looked round to see a fat middle-aged man leering from the open window of a car that was cruising beside us at exactly the same speed. 'You wanna see my dick?' He guffawed with laughter and reached into his lap. 'I can get it out right here if you want.'

The two cars moved closer together and I glimpsed something pink out of the corner of my eye. 'Trish,' I yelped. 'Can we go faster?'

'Leave this one to me, Cin,' she muttered, leaning across to take a look. 'Hey jerk! Call *that* a dick?' She squealed with laughter. 'When are you going to hand out the free microscopes?'

'Why, you stinkin' bitch . . .' The man reached out of his window towards our car. Trish yanked at the wheel and swerved into another lane, prompting a cacophony of horn blowing. I shrank into my seat, hoping that I wasn't going to end up back in hospital before I even found out where I lived.

Then the traffic began to flow again and we moved forward, leaving the man with the penis of questionable proportions fuming impotently in a stalled lane.

It took us nearly an hour to reach Trish's Hollywood apartment. I had been excited by the glamorous sounding address but, as we left the freeway and drove through a series of run-down neighbourhoods, I saw that we were hardly going to be swapping cups of sugar with the stars. An old woman stood at an intersection on Sunset Boulevard carrying a sign which read 'Will Work for Food'. Was it something about her features that made me think of Harriet, or was it just her age and the dowdy clothes she wore? Towering above her was a huge billboard advertising *Lapinique* cosmetics. *For the woman who wants a little more . . .*

I felt a shiver of uneasiness. If I hadn't met Mephisto,

I might have ended up like that. Somehow, my financial problems, bad as they were, didn't have the same sense of desperate urgency about them as hers. Was it because I was young – with a future ahead of me – while for her, time was running out?

'Here we are, home sweet home,' said Trish gaily, pulling up outside a grim apartment block in a litter-strewn street.

We climbed several flights of stairs, picking our way through torn plastic bags of rubbish and unsavoury looking puddles. The smell was disgusting. On the top floor, Trish fiddled with a series of complicated locks and bolts before opening the door to admit me to my new home. Trying to look as if I knew my way around, I stepped into the narrow hallway and went straight through the first door I came to, which led to the broom cupboard.

'This way, dummy,' said Trish with an exasperated sigh, pulling me out and manoeuvring me through a second doorway. 'Honestly! You'd get lost falling out of a window if someone didn't tell you which way was down.'

We entered a small and dingy room crammed with furniture. Another doorway led through to a larger and much brighter room containing a huge double bed. Exhausted from the journey I made straight for the bed, dropped my bags on the floor and sat down.

'I'm worn out,' I sighed, stretching back on the soft, patterned quilt. 'I think I need to rest for a while.'

Trish stared at me with a look of disbelief. 'Hey,' she said eventually. 'Stop kidding around Cin – you know that this is *my* room.' She shook her head. 'Memory loss, sure!'

'But I only . . .'

'Yours is over here,' she said, opening another door. She gave me a sly smile. 'Just in case you forgot.'

I picked up my bags and dragged them through into a space that wasn't much larger than the broom cupboard. A narrow bed took up most of the floor area, leaving just enough room for a wardrobe and a chest of drawers. The only natural illumination came from a high window which could more accurately be described as a roof light.

A pink teddy bear sat against the pillow, the bed sheets tucked carefully around it. Was it my imagination, or did the bloody thing wink at me? 'Hi, bear,' I muttered, waiting for Trish to go away.

'Just in case you really *have* lost your memory,' she said in a warning voice 'I think I better remind you of a couple of things. My stuff is on the *left* side of the bathroom, and I wrote my name on the things in the fridge that are mine.' She leaned against the doorway, one hand on her hip. 'I told you about the rent, and an electricity bill came while you were in the hospital. You owe me thirty-six fifty. You also owe me the seventy-five bucks that I paid out to have what was left of your car towed away.' She paused and gave me a sympathetic look. 'Shame about your car, Cin – figures this would happen as soon as you'd finished paying it off. Still, if you need a lift anywhere, just let me know. That's what friends are for, eh, buddy?' She smiled. 'As long as you pay for the gas, of course.'

'Cheers Trish,' I murmured, closing the door behind her. Friendship didn't seem to come cheaply in this town. Was she going to send me a bill for her visits to the hospital? Charge me for the journey home?

But I was alone at last – properly alone for the first time since I woke up after the 'accident'. There had always been people around in the hospital, and the strain of constantly having to pretend to be someone else was wearing me out.

'Sorry, bear,' I yawned, removing it from the bed. 'My need is greater than yours.' Throwing the revolting pink creature on the floor, I crawled between the sheets and fell immediately into a deep sleep.

The next day was Christmas Eve and Trish departed to spend the holiday with her family in Bakersfield. 'See you in a couple of days, Cin,' she said breezily, fitting a large padlock to her bedroom door. As she was about to leave, she paused and gave me a searching look.

'Are you sure you'll be all right?' she asked. 'All on your lonesome over the holidays?' I nodded, hoping it wasn't obvious how keen I was to get rid of her.

'I should have invited you,' she murmured guiltily. 'I didn't really think . . .'

'I'll be fine,' I assured her.

'It's better this way anyhow,' she said in a relieved voice. 'My folks always make such a fuss if I take anyone home to meet them. I kind of figured it might be too much excitement for you after your accident and all that. You just rest up and get yourself fit enough to go back to work.'

'Bye then, Trish,' I said, uneasy at this reminder of what lay ahead.

'I'll pick up some groceries on the way back,' she promised. 'And you can use some of my *Lapinique* bubble bath if you want.'

As soon as she had gone, however, I began to feel differently. I realised that a little bit of homely fuss was exactly what I needed right now. I felt frightened and insecure – alone in a strange city with no transport and hardly any money. I didn't know a single person in Los Angeles and it was Christmas – the time of the year when everyone was at home with their families, secure in the knowledge that at least one or two people on this planet loved them.

I remembered the lonely Christmases I had spent in the past, when I was Harriet. At least I'd had Sally and Andrew to call on. Right now I was totally, mind-numbingly, terrifyingly alone. What had I gained by selling my soul to Mephisto?

I had to look in the mirror to remind myself. What would Sally or Andrew think if they could see me now? What would Andrew think of my beautiful new body? I sighed. They probably hadn't even noticed that I was gone. I felt a sudden pang of homesickness for Guildford – the place I had always affected to despise when I lived there. It was a whole continent away now, and it was going to be a long time before I could afford a trip there to find out if anyone had missed me.

Meanwhile, I had a whole new life to deal with right here. Exploring Cindy's tiny bedroom, I tried to find some further clues about the person whose body I was inhabiting. She seemed to have few possessions other than clothes, make-up and cheap jewellery, which told me very little about what Cindy was like. There was a well-thumbed Jackie Collins paperback on the floor under the bed. *Hollywood Wives*. Had Cindy shared my secret weakness? Had she spent time in the same fantasy world that I used to escape to in the steam of Harriet's bathroom back in Guildford?

For me it had been nothing more than entertainment – a diversion from the grinding monotony of the library. But Cindy lived right here in Hollywood, only a few miles from the homes of the rich and famous. Had she come all the way to Los Angeles in the hope of gaining access to their lifestyle? Looking around the room, with its peeling paint and shabby furnishings, I figured that she would have been better off staying in Sioux Falls.

Continuing my search, I hunted under the clothes in her drawers in the hope of finding a secret journal or notebook – anything that might give me an insight into her personality. But there was nothing. I began to reach the conclusion that Cindy had no personality – that what you saw on the surface was all you got.

Time passed slowly while Trish was away. On Christmas Day, I dressed in an old tracksuit and sneakers from Cindy's wardrobe and ventured out to buy some food. I had seen a grocery store from the apartment window which looked as if it was open.

As I left the building, a group of young women turned to stare at me.

'Hey, look at Pretty Woman over there,' shouted one

of them, pointing. As I drew closer, their garish clothes and make-up told me that they must be prostitutes.

'Looking for Mr Right, darlin'?' shouted another. 'I bet *you* don't swallow!'

Embarrassed, I tried to hurry past, but they began to jostle me.

'Stuck-up bitch,' snarled the first woman, pushing me off the pavement into the gutter. 'We'd better not catch you sucking dicks on our pitch, or you'll hear about it from me.'

I sprinted the rest of the way to the shop with insults ringing in my ears and spent the last of my money on some basic provisions: bread, eggs, milk and cheese.

'All on your lonesome, darlin'?' grunted a thickset man at the till, taking my money with a greasy paw. He snatched at my hand and held on to it, breathing heavily as he leaned over the counter towards me. 'Wanna come out with me tonight, baby? I'll give you a Christmas to remember.'

His breath smelt rich and pungent – like old sewage. 'No thanks,' I spluttered pulling my hand away and rushing out of the shop. A police siren began to wail nearby.

A man turned the corner of the street, glancing over his shoulder and running fast. As he came closer, a police car swung into view behind him, taking the corner with a squeal of tyres and hurtling up the street with siren and lights going full pelt. The prostitutes scattered and vanished from sight as it skidded to a halt beside him, disgorging four cops.

'Freeze!' shouted one of them, pointing his gun with

both hands, while the others surrounded the man and began to beat him up in a well practised manner.

Terrified, I crossed the street and ran back towards the apartment building. Inside the lobby, I stumbled over an unkempt youth who was slumped against the wall. I jumped back in alarm, but he didn't seem to notice me. He was too busy doing something horrible to himself with a needle, his whole body shaking in the dim light.

I didn't go out on my own again after that, and reduced the scope of my exploration of Los Angeles to channel-hopping on the TV. I learned that the average Angeleno viewer had an attention span slightly shorter than that of a bluebottle and a complete lack of interest in any concept that wasn't supported by a full range of tie-in merchandising. There seemed to be about three hundred channels of the stuff and I couldn't find a single thing worth watching. I yearned for a decent book to read.

Unable to face Jackie Collins, I settled for browsing through the piles of magazines in the living room. The articles seemed strange at first: *Winning Ways with Your Wardrobe. How To Get Your Man and Keep Him. Ring the Changes with Your New Look.* Then I realised that they were addressed at me – at the twenty-one-year-old single girl I had become. I would have to learn to stop thinking like an old woman.

After studying the magazines carefully, I went to Cindy's wardrobe and began to experiment. Her tastes weren't exactly conservative – the colours were vibrant and the styles left little to the imagination regarding her natural assets. It looked as if Cindy liked to have fun with her clothes.

I tried on a series of tops with plunging necklines and tiny short skirts that threatened to disappear around my waist when I sat down. There was a full-length mirror fixed to the back of the bedroom door and I spent much time parading up and down in the narrow gap between the bed and the wall, trying out different effects. At first I felt faintly foolish – like a child playing with the dressing-up box – but, as I grew accustomed to my new reflection in the mirror, I began to feel properly connected with my new body for the first time. I could feel myself moving differently in these clothes. No longer the self-conscious and clumsy Harriet, I approached the mirror with a sinuous walk and struck a seductive pose. A shiver of physical excitement ran through me. Breathing huskily, I touched my lips to the glass in imitation of a kiss. What kind of effect, I wondered, would this have on a man?

I was dreading the prospect of going out to work. Not only would I have to take on an unfamiliar job, but I would also have to pretend to be someone else. How would I deal with Cindy's friends? How long would it be before someone guessed I was an imposter?

By the time Trish returned from Bakersfield, however, I was bored, lonely and desperate to get out of the apartment. I also needed some money fast – I had eaten most of the food in the place and was reduced to a diet of dried waffle mix and ketchup sandwiches.

The following morning, we both got up early. I had

assumed we would walk to work as Trish had mentioned it was just a few blocks down Sunset, but it turned out to be a twenty-minute drive away. We pulled into a huge parking area fringed by a gas station, a Kmart and an Econo Lodge, and stopped outside a long, low building with a huge neon sign on the roof. *Marty's Diner*, read the sign. *Famous Breakfast Specials.*

'That's a buck fifty for gas,' muttered Trish, making a note in her pocket diary. 'Come on Cin, what are you waiting for? You don't want to be late for your first day back.'

We entered through a door at the side and plunged straight into a scene of pandemonium. Clouds of hissing steam issued from a bank of deep fryers and people bustled back and forth with plates of sizzling food. The air was thick with the smell of grease. A plump white-aproned man bellowed instructions from the grill, waving his spatula at a row of frying eggs as if he were conducting an orchestra.

'Hey Marty,' said Trish, touching his shoulder. 'Look who's here.'

He swung round. 'Hi, Cindy, honey,' he said with a broad grin. 'How's my favourite girl?' Deftly flicking two eggs on to a plate proffered by a waitress, he swooped forwards and squeezed me around the waist. A waft of stale body odour briefly masked the other kitchen smells and my stomach lurched queasily. Why did people keep wanting to touch me? 'Don't just stand there, girl,' he added, pinching my arm and giving me a lecherous wink. 'Get your apron on – we've got customers waiting.'

I followed Trish into a back room where we changed into sludge-coloured polyester uniforms with skirts that were too short, even by the standards of Cindy's wardrobe. Then we walked out into the public area of the diner. Someone thrust a jug of coffee into my hand and I stood helplessly by the end of the counter, frozen with panic as I wondered what on earth I was supposed to do next.

'Hey, miss, give me a refill,' grunted an elderly man, pointing at his coffee cup. That seemed easy enough, so I began to move slowly along the room, filling up cups as I went.

The place looked as if it belonged to the set for a fifties movie. Huge plate-glass windows ran down one side of the room, offering panoramic views of the car park and gas station outside. Fake leather banquettes formed seating areas around tables finished in wood-effect Formica, each with an elaborate chrome menu-holder shaped to look like an old-style juke box. These were chained to the tables, presumably to stop them being taken as souvenirs. A real juke box stood at the far end of the room, but I couldn't tell if it was playing or not over the hubbub of voices and clatter of plates. A long counter ran down the side of the room opposite the window, where a row of customers sat on chrome and plastic stools and jabbed each other with their elbows as they ate.

'Hey, waitress! Over here!'

I cautiously approached two men in grubby overalls who were beckoning me towards them.

'Two eggs over easy with hash browns and a French

toast special. Double syrup,' said one. 'Hold the whipped cream.'

'Scrambled eggs, bacon and a side order of blueberry pancakes,' said the other. 'Double whipped cream, hold the syrup.'

I stared around helplessly. I could see Trish taking orders further down the room, but no one had given me a notebook.

'Oh, and by the way,' said the first man in an innocent voice, 'I think someone dropped their wallet under that seat over there.'

'Maybe you should take a look,' suggested the other.

Confused, I stooped to look under the seat. There was nothing there. As I stood up I felt a hand tweak at my knickers and the two men dissolved into helpless giggles.

I'd had enough.

'Take your fucking hands off me!' I snapped, bursting into tears and tipping my jug of coffee into the nearest man's lap. His howls must have been audible from the kitchen as Marty was there in a matter of seconds, still brandishing his spatula.

'What the hell do you think you're doing, you dumb broad?' he yelled. 'Don't you know better than to assault my goddamn customers?'

'But he put his hand . . .'

Marty pulled me to one side and lowered his voice to a hiss. 'I couldn't give a toss where my customers put their hands as long as they end up putting them in their fucking wallets before they leave! Something these two won't be doing, since you couldn't even get your act together to take their goddamn orders! Now get out of my sight before I fire you – you dumb bitch!'

Shaken, I fled to the back room, where Trish found me a few minutes later. 'Jesus, Cin,' she said in a shocked tone. 'What were you playing at out there? You'll get us both thrown out of here.'

But when I explained what had happened she was sympathetic. 'Last time a guy tried it on with me,' she said, 'I took his scrambled eggs round the back and got everyone to spit in it.' She grinned. 'Including Marty's dog.'

'I don't know what to do,' I confessed. 'With the orders and everything – it must be the accident that made me forget.'

'Don't worry, buddy,' said Trish with a reassuring smile. 'I'll help you out. As long as . . .'

'More gas money?' I enquired acidly.

'Aw, come on Cin – I'm not that greedy. No, I was going to say, as long as you can take my Saturday night shift. It'll be good practice for you. I've got a date with this guy who says he can get me a part in *Baywatch*.'

CHAPTER 7

My first day at Marty's was an unmitigated disaster, but after a crash course in waitressing techniques from Trish I gradually managed to claw back some self-respect. I soon learned how to decipher the customers' orders – which often bore little relationship to what was printed on the menu – and how to silence the troublemakers among them with a suitably crushing retort. After a few weeks I was reciting the list of daily specials as if I had been doing it all my life, and asking, *'Soup or salad?'* with the weary familiarity of the true professional.

Marty and the rest of the male staff kept their hands to themselves after the story of the coffee incident spread, but I felt that I was tolerated rather than treated like the others. Despite my best efforts, I made no further friends. After I overheard two of the other waitresses bitching in the locker room, I realised it was all to do with the way I looked. The women were jealous and the men were simply desperate to get into my knickers. Even though Hollywood probably had the world's highest concentration of beautiful people,

Cindy's looks were still considered to be outstanding. If only I could find a way to use them to my advantage, I thought, I might be able to get out of this poverty trap. I hadn't sold my soul to Mephisto so that I could spend the rest of my life being a waitress.

Because Marty's Diner was in Hollywood, everyone who worked there was going to be a star. I overheard dozens of hard-luck stories from waitresses who were really up-and-coming starlets, and cooks who claimed to be talented actors on the verge of being discovered. They were all either 'resting', or 'temporarily down on their luck'. We were regularly short staffed due to half the shift being either in attendance at an audition or sulking in a darkened room after being rejected for some coveted part.

Many of the staff would practise their acting as they worked, usually restricting themselves to a lively recitation of the daily specials, but occasionally staging a crisis to attract more attention if they suspected a customer might have some connection with the movie business. Trish and the other waitresses spent their coffee breaks frantically scanning the pictures in *Variety* to be sure of recognising any movie moguls who might accidentally wander in. When in doubt, they preferred to be safe rather than sorry, so it sometimes happened that a bemused truck driver was treated to free entertainment while he ate, and received handfuls of business cards and agents' telephone numbers at the end of his meal.

Every night, Trish went out with a different man who had promised her an introduction to some close friend of Michael Douglas or Sylvester Stallone. She didn't seem to connect the process of being discovered with any actual need to be able to act, or to perform in any way. Trish believed in 'Star Quality', which was, apparently, all you needed.

'You either got it or you don't, Cin,' she said to me on numerous occasions. 'It ain't nothing to do with who you are or where you come from. Anyone can be famous if you try hard enough – so long as you got Star Quality. The important thing is, just never give up.'

I tried to point out that people were usually famous for actually *doing* something, but Trish wasn't so sure. She saw acting solely as a means to an end, and concentrated her efforts on trying to meet famous people. Deprived of her rightful place in Beverly Hills society by a cruel accident of birth, she was convinced that if only she could make contact with Hollywood's elite, they would immediately recognise her as one of their own.

Every night, while Trish was out seeking fame and fortune, I stayed at home in the apartment, too exhausted to move. My feet hurt from standing up all day, my limbs were weary and my brain ached from culture shock. I had never worked so hard or for such long hours in my life. One evening in the second week, I had just settled on the sofa to watch the early evening news when Trish appeared in the doorway, hands on hips.

'Come on, Cin – get your act together. We always work out on Wednesday night.'

'Work out?' I echoed weakly.

'Don't pretend you forgot, Cind. I let you off last time 'cause you only just got out of the hospital, but you've had a whole week to get better since then.' She came towards me and peered at my waist with an envious expression. 'You won't hold on to that dreamboat figure by sitting around on your ass all day.'

I felt like telling her to piss off and worry about her own waistline – which looked in greater need of attention than mine – but something stopped me. What if she was right? What if Cindy's gloriously slender body was the result of a punishing diet and exercise regime? What if I, as the new owner of this hot property, blew all her hard work through laziness and turned it into a monstrosity like Harriet? I would end up with less self-respect than ever before.

'You don't want to miss the new step teacher that started last week, do you, Cin?' wheedled Trish. 'He's got the most incredible bulge in his shorts and the cutest little butt I ever laid eyes on.'

'All right then,' I said wearily, getting up. She was obviously determined that I should come and admire this latest conquest. 'I'll be ready in a moment.' Half-way to my room, I paused. 'Trish?' I asked, turning helplessly to face her. 'What on earth am I supposed to *wear*?'

I spent the entire journey worrying that I would be a laughing stock in the clothes Trish had told me to put on but, when we arrived at the gym, I was relieved to see that other women were dressed in a similar way. I wore black leggings and a bright red leotard cut so high around the leg that it looked as if my thighs reached up to my armpits. My feet were encased in huge trainers and my wrists and forehead were circled with a variety of garishly coloured towelling sweatbands. I carried an armoury of accessories, including hand weights, water bottles, towels, support bandages and muscle spray.

We entered a large studio with mirror-clad walls. A number of muscular-looking women were there already, strutting and posing in front of low rectangular platforms which were spaced evenly around the room.

'Quick – grab a step,' hissed Trish, dragging me towards a pair of unattended platforms. We sat down on them and waited for something to happen. Several of the women turned and gave me hostile stares.

When the instructor arrived, I recognised him at once from Trish's description. He gave me a long curious look that ended in a wink, then clapped his hands together and began to shake his feet rhythmically as if he had just stepped in something nasty.

'*Come on, girls,*' he boomed, his head microphone whining with feedback as his deep voice echoed around the room. Flicking a switch, he engulfed us in mind-blowingly loud music. '*Let's loosen up!*'

He began to march his feet up and down in time with the music and the rest of the class did the same. I followed haltingly, finding it easy enough at first. Soon, however, the beat became faster, and everyone started to step up and down on their little platforms with rapid and complicated movements which were all too quick for me to keep up with. I looked despairingly at Trish, but she seemed to be in a trance, thumping her feet up and down and punching the air with a glazed expression.

The instructor's hands and feet moved faster and faster, until they were almost a blur, and the lycra-clad bulge in his shorts bobbed up and down to the beat of the music. Suddenly I felt his eyes on me.

'*Come on, baby,*' he coaxed, throwing me a smile of encouragement. '*Just let yourself go.*'

Something clicked in my head somewhere, and I found that if I stopped trying so hard, my body – Cindy's body – tapped into the rhythm.

'*Left, right, left, right, double sidestep, hands together, over the top and round the world . . .*' I was doing it! Cindy must have practised this routine dozens of times, and her body was performing it on autopilot.

I felt a surge of adrenalin. This was fun. Aware of the instructor's eye constantly upon me, I synchronised my frenzied motions with the rest of the class. Gradually, the pace of the workout quickened even more.

'*. . . and up and over and round and round and . . . oh baby, that's good . . . that's real good . . .*' The music reached a jangling climax and he made a series of strange jerking movements with his pelvis. '*You can do it, baby. Squeeze those glutes just one more time . . .*' A roomful of eyes were fixed on the legendary bulge, which seemed on the verge of springing out from his lycra waistband.

My heart was thumping wildly and my breath came in short gasps. My body was tingling all over with energy and a sensation of well-being. I had never felt like this when I was Harriet.

'*Oh baby . . .*' He looked directly at me for a moment, then turned a full circle on his step and changed his stance. He began to move to a slower beat, stepping rhythmically from one foot to the other. '*I'm gonna take you down now, real slow . . .*' The music became gradually slower and everyone reached for their water bottles.

'Jesus Christ,' panted Trish beside me. 'Did you go all the way, Cin?'

When the workout was over the instructor appeared at my side, sweat gleaming on his forehead. '*I didn't see you here last week, baby,*' he boomed. Everyone turned to stare at us, and he shook his head with annoyance. '*Always forget to switch this damn thing off,*' he muttered, removing his microphone headset. 'I'm Chuck Woodcock,' he added in a surprisingly ordinary voice. 'Call me Chuck.'

I felt his eyes travelling up and down my body as I introduced myself, shaking his outstretched hand.

'Hi, Chuck,' gushed Trish, leaning across eagerly. 'We met last week, remember?'

'You did real well tonight, Cindy,' he continued, ignoring her. 'Maybe you'd like to hear about some of my other classes? We could talk about them over a drink, if you're not in a hurry.'

'That's a great idea, Chuck,' said Trish loudly. 'I was thinking about taking some extra classes too.'

Chuck glared at her, then turned to me. 'I could give you a lift home later,' he offered hopefully. 'If your friend here needs to get away.'

'That's all right,' said Trish. 'I don't mind waiting around. After all, that's what's friends are for.'

As we showered and changed, I noticed that the other women in the changing room couldn't take their eyes off me. There was a hushed silence as I peeled off my sweaty leotard, and I was aware of surreptitious comparisons of waistlines and thighs taking place all round the room. I was surprised to see that the women who had looked so intimidatingly perfect when we first arrived were actually quite flabby when they removed the layers of elasticated fabric that held them in. Cindy's body was clearly something special – even by the standards of a Hollywood gym. I felt a tingle of smugness as I realised that I was the envy of every woman in the room.

Chuck Woodcock was waiting for us outside, and we went to a nearby bar.

'What do you want to drink, baby?' he asked me, swivelling on his bar stool so that his back was turned firmly towards Trish.

'Double scotch on the rocks, please,' I said decisively. I hadn't had a decent drink since I woke up as Cindy.

'I'll have one of those too,' added Trish. He didn't seem to hear her, so she tapped him on the shoulder and repeated her request, this time as he was ordering a double orange juice for himself.

'Have you ever done high-impact work, Cindy?' he asked. I shook my head and sipped my drink with relish. It was good to know that whisky tasted the same whichever body you were in.

'I didn't ask for orange juice,' squawked Trish indignantly, leaning forward and glaring down the bar at me. 'I want what she's got!'

'Better get a couple of implants then, sweetheart,' said a man beside her, staring at my breasts.

'And who the fuck are you?' asked Trish, swinging round angrily.

Chuck shifted his stool sideways and blocked my view. 'You should try my Hi-Energy Power Step class some time, Cindy,' he said, leaning towards me and gazing into my eyes as if my reaction was of the utmost significance. I felt a thrill of pleasure at being the focus of a man's attention – something which had rarely happened to Harriet.

'Maybe I will,' I said, smiling happily as the whisky glowed inside me. Chuck began to prattle on about adrenalin highs and pain thresholds, but I wasn't really listening. I was enjoying the touch of his hand on my arm and experiencing tingling pangs of sexual attraction.

'Endurance training's pretty good,' he said eventually, placing a hand on my knee, 'but it all comes down to mind over matter at the end of the day. Aren't I right?'

My mind was telling me not to touch a dork like Chuck Woodcock with a bargepole, while my body kept insisting that it didn't matter.

'Oh yes,' I said earnestly, struggling with my baser instincts. 'I know exactly what you mean.'

'Why don't we get out of here and go for a drive?' he asked, fixing me with a meaningful look.

'I, er . . . my friend . . .' I looked round for Trish, but she was deep in conversation with the man from earlier, who now had his hand up her skirt.

'Leave me alone,' she hissed. 'Can't you see I'm making progress? He says he's going to get me an introduction to a guy who knows Spielberg.'

'But I want to go home.'

'Well you should have thought of that before hoisting a flag with a pair of open legs on it in front of Chuck Woodcock,' she snapped. 'Don't be pathetic, Cin – he's not going to eat you.'

Chuck drove in tense silence when we left the bar. I had given him approximate directions to the apartment, but after a few turns it became clear that he was ignoring them.

'Thought we'd go up Mulholland,' he grunted, swinging the car around a sharp bend. The road began to twist and turn, climbing steadily all the time. 'Ever been up here before, Cindy?'

'No,' I admitted, unsure what this signified.

'Really?' He raised an eyebrow in surprise and began to chuckle. 'Well, there's always a first time.'

We pulled off the road and parked under a tree. Below and in front of us, Los Angeles was spread out in a glittering grid of lights – just like the scenes in the movies where the guy and his girl get it together. Warning bells began to go off in my head.

'Come here, baby,' he muttered, lunging across the car and pushing me back into my seat. I felt the pressure of his mouth against mine, and was unable to stop myself responding – I hadn't been kissed for over thirty years and the blood was surging in my veins.

'No, no,' I protested, struggling feebly, but secretly

enjoying it. I allowed his tongue to explore my mouth and was surprised to find how pleasant it felt.

'Hey, you're hot, baby.' he breathed, fumbling with a lever. With a sudden crash, my seat reclined into a horizontal position and he leapt on top of me. I felt the famous bulge pressing into my thigh as his hand thrust itself rudely under my skirt and began to tug at my underwear.

'Hey, stop it!' I squealed, reaching to pull his hand away. I hadn't intended to let things go this far.

'Give it to me, you horny bitch,' he grunted. There was a ripping sound and I saw my knickers disappear through the car window. Holding me down with one hand, he began to undo his zipper.

'Help!' I screamed, twisting in his firm grip and trying to reach the door handle. 'Get off me!'

'Don't you tell me what to do,' he snarled, slapping my face with a stinging blow. 'You cockteasing little cunt!'

Tears of anger and humiliation welled in my eyes as he straddled my body and pinned my hands above my head. I hadn't wanted my first sexual experience as Cindy to be like this.

His zipper popped open and the perpetrator of the bulge sprang into view.

'This big enough for you?' he groaned, thrusting it under my nose. 'This what you want?'

It was bigger than I had thought possible. I stared at it open-mouthed. Was this the giant redwood of the penis world? Relaxing his grip on me, he leaned back and began to stroke it lovingly, like a pet dog.

I knew nothing about self-defence, but I guessed that this was my best chance of catching him off guard. Taking a deep breath, I brought my knees sharply upwards.

'Arrgghh! You fucking bitch!' He keeled over, clutching his groin, and I scrambled to get out from beneath him and open the door. I began to search for my knickers, but quickly abandoned the task when I heard him moving inside the car.

Adjusting Cindy's short skirt to a semblance of decency, I took off my shoes and began to run. I needed to make myself scarce before my aptly named assailant recovered from the damage to his timber resources.

After running along winding roads for about twenty minutes, I slowed down and began to take note of my surroundings. I didn't have the faintest idea where I was, or even which direction I was facing. There were no road signs. Dense bushes and security fences lined the roadside, punctuated by the occasional unmarked gate. As I approached one of these gates in the darkness, a light flicked on and a camera swivelled to point at me with a series of sharp clicking noises.

It seemed logical to head downhill, but I kept coming to junctions where both roads led downwards in different directions. As I cut across an area of grass on a corner, I passed a sign which was dimly visible in the glow of a distant streetlight. *Danger – Private Security Force – Armed Response – Trained Guard Dogs.*

A siren began to wail and a flashing blue light appeared in the distance. The sound of a car engine approached. I started running again, but soon found myself in a dead end – trapped by another high steel gate which wouldn't open. The car crunched slowly towards me across the gravel road surface. When it stopped, a burly figure got out and thrust a searchlight in my face.

'Hey, Wayne,' drawled a man's voice. 'Come and see what I got here. Makes Sharon Stone look a real double bagger.'

First they wanted to take me to the police. When I finally convinced them that I wasn't Catwoman, and that I wasn't about to break into the homes of their clients, they wanted me to go with them to their security cabin. After much wheedling and for the price of one French kiss each, strictly timed to last no longer than one minute and not to be delivered until they had fulfilled their side of the bargain, I persuaded them to give me a lift home.

Trish was still out when I returned to the apartment. Noticing that she hadn't locked her bedroom door I had a quick snoop in her wardrobe, where I found a half empty bottle of whisky.

Just what I needed, I thought, taking it back to my room. I sat on the bed and took a deep swig, which made me feel better. The tight-fisted bitch had probably marked the level on the bottle, but I wasn't in the mood to worry about the finer points of ownership. I could always top it up with cold tea.

My new life wasn't turning out at all the way I had expected. I had always blamed the failures of my previous life on my lack of beauty. Now, with Cindy's looks, I had assumed that everything would be easy. But where were the benefits I had so fondly imagined? Where were the friends, the career, the dream lifestyle? Where were the opportunities for love and romance?

The pink teddy bear gave me a glassy-eyed look of reproach from the floor as I took another swig of whisky. 'Who do you think you're staring at, sawdust head?' I snarled, snatching it up by the throat and squeezing hard. It winked at me.

'Right, that's it,' I snapped, marching into the kitchen. 'I've had enough!' The waste disposal unit in the sink made short work of Cindy's beloved toy, liquidising it in a matter of seconds and dispatching it to a swift oblivion in the Los Angeles sewage system.

My future looked bleak. I had no money and I was trapped in a relationship of debt with Trish. Working at Marty's made even the job of librarian seem enviable. Every man I met treated me as a sex object, and tonight I had narrowly missed being raped.

Had I sold my soul for this?

'You bastard, Mephisto,' I muttered, wiping shreds of pink fur from around the stainless steel plughole. 'You've really screwed things up for me!'

'Who said it would be easy?' Mephisto's disembodied voice spoke suddenly inside my head. *'You've got what you wanted, haven't you?'*

'Where are you?' I demanded angrily. There was a ghostly, cackling laugh, straight out of a low-budget horror movie, and a shape began to materialise on the draining board in front of me. I watched, open-mouthed, as it solidified into Mephisto's familiar figure. He was wearing the same scruffy clothes as when I last saw him, and his boots were still covered in mud.

'How's it going, babe?' he said, glancing at his surroundings as he lowered his feet to the floor. He leaned against the sink unit and grinned, folding his arms. 'Nice place you've got here.'

I gave him a hostile glare. 'You did this on purpose, you bastard! Why couldn't you have left me in Guildford instead of bringing me to this hell-hole? Why didn't you tell me I was going to be trapped in somebody else's life?'

'You never asked, did you?' he replied smugly. 'You should always read the small print when you bargain with the Devil.'

'Can't you get me out of here?' I pleaded. 'All I want is a chance to be happy – a chance to have a decent life.'

'That's all most people want, isn't it? But they have to get it for themselves. Why should you be any different?'

'I . . . I don't know,' I said helplessly. 'But why did you choose me in the first place, if you weren't going to give me what you promised?'

'I've given you youth and beauty, haven't I? You're supposed to be the one with the brains – it's up to you what happens next.' He gave me a reproachful look. 'I hope you're not going to disappoint me, Harriet, after all the effort I've put into this. Do you have any idea how privileged you are to have been offered a Faustian pact?'

'What do you mean, privileged?'

He sighed. 'I thought you'd done your homework on this subject, but obviously not. Didn't you realise that Faustian pacts were phased out, let me see,' he counted on his fingers, 'over a hundred and fifty years ago?'

He gave me a look of exasperation. 'Standards are slipping in Hell,' he muttered, reaching for the whisky bottle. 'What we need is to get some of the old traditions reintroduced and brought up to date. There's a huge potential for evil in the Faustian pact, if only these hide-bound followers of the rule books would wake up and see it.'

'Why were they phased out, then,' I asked, 'if they were such a good idea?'

'Too much work involved in following them up, wasn't there?' His voice became bitter. 'Never mind job satisfaction – everything's measured against short-term efficiency these days. They decided it was a waste of resources.'

'Why do you have to follow anything up? What more can you expect to get, once someone's sold you their soul?'

'Plenty more,' he said, taking a long swig of whisky. 'We need to make sure that you're still on our side – working as a force for evil. Help you to fritter away the extra years in true Faustian style.' He placed the bottle on the draining board and I watched the liquid swirl back up to its original level, just as it had on previous occasions. It looked as if our dwindling supply of teabags might be spared this time.

'You've already passed the first stage with flying

colours,' he continued, giving me a conspiratorial look. 'It didn't take long to persuade you to accept my offer. But how do I know that you won't go running off to the opposition – sacrificing yourself to do good works, or some such feeble-minded nonsense? I have to keep an eye on you. Make sure you stay properly corrupted.'

'I'm not corrupted,' I protested. 'Besides, there wasn't anything in the pact about this. The bargain's finished as far as I'm concerned. I just want to get on with my life and be happy.'

Mephisto chuckled and glanced around at the sleazy kitchen. 'Is this what you call happiness? Not doing too well so far, are you?'

'That's not the point . . .' I faltered, seeing that his gaze was now fixed on a point just below my waist. Cindy's short skirt had once again ridden up too far. Remembering with a shock that I had left my knickers somewhere in the Hollywood Hills, I wriggled into a more modest position.

Mephisto let out a low sigh. 'You haven't realised quite how attractive you are, have you?' He moved towards me, leaning closer until I could feel his breath on my skin. 'How can you blame that poor boy tonight? After getting his hormones all fired up the way you did?' He reached out and lightly touched my face, tracing the outline of my cheekbone with one finger. 'How could anyone resist such temptation?'

Cindy's body trembled with suppressed urges, but I pulled away sharply just as his lips were about to brush mine.

'Get off!' I hissed, slapping his hand away. 'That poor

boy, as you call him, tried to rape me. There's no excuse for that!'

'My, my, we seem to have developed fine principles all of a sudden,' he sneered, taking a step backwards. 'I remember a time,' he added nastily, 'when you wouldn't have been so quick to turn me down.'

'If you touch me again, you know what you'll get,' I snapped. How would a devil's anatomy compare, I wondered, with that of a mere mortal such as Chuck Woodcock? Would everything be in the same place?

Mephisto bristled. 'I don't need to force anyone to find me attractive,' he said, folding his arms. 'You'll be the one who's begging for it by the time I've finished with you.'

'Never,' I said vehemently. 'Nothing could make me that desperate.'

Cindy's body continued to give out contradictory signals, but I ignored them. She had got me into more than enough trouble already tonight.

'I can wait,' said Mephisto in a knowing tone. 'Everyone gives in to temptation sooner or later.' He picked up the whisky bottle and took another long swig, eyeing me thoughtfully. 'Besides,' he added. 'There are plenty of other ways for me to win my bet.'

'What bet?'

'Ah, we always have a bet,' he replied with a smile. 'It's not much fun if you have to wait twenty-five years before you get any results.'

'Twenty-nine,' I murmured. 'You got your sums wrong, didn't you?'

'Forget the details,' he said impatiently, waving the

whisky bottle in a sweeping gesture. 'I'm going to shake up these old-fashioned rules and regulations in Hell. I've placed a big wager on this project. Full proof of corruption before the first annual review – that'll show them what I'm made of!'

He faced me with a look of pride. 'They might not think I've got it in me to handle a Faustian pact any more, but I'll show them! I'm no ordinary Devil, I'm Mephisto . . .'

'Arch regent and commander of all spirits.' I finished his sentence with him, unable to resist a smile.

'It's all a matter of selecting the right subject, really,' he continued, ignoring my taunt. 'It's never been done with a woman before, as far as I know. Much more fun, don't you think?' He grinned. 'Equal opportunities and all that – I'm sure you must approve.'

He took another noisy glug of whisky. 'Why do you think I chose you, Harriet? Why do you think I've brought you all the way to LA? Much more potential to utilise your new assets than boring old Guildford, wouldn't you agree? Much more of a chance to catch up on all the things you've missed?'

He spread his hands in an expansive gesture. 'You want to be successful, don't you? Money, fame, social position – all the good things in life are here for the taking. They can all be yours if you go about it in the right way.' He let out a giggle, accompanied by a small hiccup. 'Or rather, in the *wrong* way. Don't they have a saying out here – that beauty is only *sin* deep?'

'I'm sorry to be such a disappointment,' I said bitterly.

I had been too busy coping with mere survival to waste time on such idle fantasies.

'Never underestimate the power of beauty to corrupt.' I felt a shiver of discomfort as he paused to emphasise these words. 'You might think you're above all this, but you'll forget your fancy principles soon enough, once you've had a taste of the good life. You'll be out for what you can get – fighting for your slice of the cake with the rest of them – you just wait and see.'

'What taste of the good life?' I asked indignantly. 'I haven't seen much of that around here yet.'

'Ah, now that *would* be telling.' He began to laugh, the sound echoing unpleasantly in my head. I rubbed my eyes and stared at him. His image was blurred – dissolving into the air.

'What do you mean?'

'Wait and see,' he cackled, rapidly becoming transparent. 'Just remember that I'll be watching you.' The whisky bottle remained hovering in front of me.

'Come back,' I begged. 'Tell me what happens next.'

'*Sorry,*' he intoned in an irritating sing-song voice. '*No can do.*'

The bottle dropped unceremoniously into my lap and he was gone.

CHAPTER 8

A few days later, I was having my coffee break in the back room at Marty's when Trish rushed in.

'Quick Cin! Come and look!' she squealed. 'You'll never guess who just walked in – *Harley Brightman*!'

'Who?'

'Your accident, remember? The guy whose car you ran into?' She gave me a wide-eyed look. 'The owner of *Lapinique*! Do you think he's here for compensation?'

'Which one is he?' I asked, pressing my nose to the glass window of the kitchen door.

'Oh cut it out, Cin,' she said, rolling her eyes towards the ceiling. 'We watched him on that Larry King interview.' She let out a sigh of exasperation. 'He's not the short fat guy with the beard, is he? Or the jerk in the baseball cap?'

I followed her gaze to a table near the door, where a man in his thirties was consulting the menu. I barely had time to register his boyish good looks and fashionable clothes before a gaggle of waitresses broke into a song and dance routine in front of him, blocking my view.

'Trust those dumb bitches to get it wrong,' muttered Trish contemptuously. 'Tell me how a guy who owns a cosmetic company's going to get them a part in a movie.'

'What's going on out there?' Marty appeared beside us, a fried egg poised on his spatula. 'Holy shit,' he breathed. '*Harley Brightman* in *my* diner.' He pushed open the door. 'My wife'll never forgive me if I don't get his autograph,' he explained, handing me the spatula and scurrying towards the focus of activity.

A few moments later he returned with a puzzled expression. 'Cindy, honey,' he said. 'I don't know what you've done to deserve it, but he wants to talk to you.' He straightened my cap and pushed me through the door. 'Now get out there and be nice to the man. Make me proud of you.'

The other waitresses melted away in a flurry of giggles as I approached the table of the most eligible bachelor in Los Angeles.

'Cindy?' he asked in a gentle voice, holding out his hand. I was about to reach out and shake it when I realised I was still holding a spatula with a fried egg on it.

'Hi,' I said nervously, putting my hand quickly behind my back.

'You probably don't remember me,' he said, smiling. 'You were unconscious when I saw you last. I wanted to see you again – just to be sure that you were OK.'

I looked around anxiously for a place to get rid of the egg, but nowhere seemed appropriate.

'I don't usually drive the Rolls myself,' he added. 'It

was a bit of a shock – running into you like that. I felt somehow, well . . . responsible. It's a big relief to see that you're OK now.'

I looked at him closely. He had regular, clean-cut features with friendly eyes and light brown hair swept back from his forehead. Meeting my gaze, he raised his eyebrows and gave me a self-conscious grin.

'I was also, um, wondering,' he continued, pushing a hand through his hair and fiddling with the back of his collar, 'if you'd, um . . . if you'd like to have dinner with me tonight?'

Catching a movement in the corner of my eye, I looked through the window behind him and saw Trish standing in the car park, gesturing frantically to catch my attention. *Say yes*, she mouthed. Marty stood beside her, waving a menu and pointing to it with his other hand. *Ask him what he wants to eat,* he mimed.

'Thanks,' I said. 'Dinner would be great.' With a shrug, I held out the spatula with its congealed cargo. 'In the meantime,' I asked, 'would you like an egg?'

When I told her the details, Trish was white with envy. 'You lucky bitch,' she grumbled wistfully. 'I wish I'd been in that accident too.' She paused and gave me a hopeful look. 'Are you *sure* he didn't ask you to bring a friend?'

Back at the apartment, she helped me search Cindy's wardrobe for something to wear. If she couldn't have dinner with Harley Brightman herself, Trish wanted to be as involved as possible in preparations for the event.

'Just think, Cin,' she sighed, holding a series of different dresses in front of me. 'One of the richest men in LA, and he's still single. He might fall in love with you.'

'I hardly think so,' I replied with a dismissive laugh, though I was secretly rather excited by the whole thing. Why had he sought me out like this? Did it have some connection with the 'taste of the good life' Mephisto had been talking about?

We settled for a tight-fitting black dress with a plunging neckline. 'No point in being well-stacked if you don't display some of the goods,' said Trish, tugging at the stretchy material to ensure that a large portion of cleavage was exposed.

She fussed over every detail of my appearance from the colour and texture of my stockings to the precise shade of lipstick I should wear. When I was ready, she stood beside me in front of the mirror, admiring her handiwork.

'If he doesn't invite you out again,' she concluded, 'it won't be because of the way you look.'

The doorbell rang at precisely eight o'clock, and I found myself trembling with nervous anticipation. I hadn't been out on a date for at least thirty years, and I didn't have a clue how I was supposed to behave.

'Now don't blow it,' warned Trish as she escorted me to the door. 'If you don't know what to say, just say yes.'

Despite the darkness in the narrow hallway, Harley Brightman was wearing sunglasses.

'Hi Cindy,' he drawled, pulling them forward with one hand and twinkling his eyes over the rims like the star of some television commercial. How long had he been practising that particular move, I wondered?

'I'm Trish,' said Trish, elbowing her way into view and extending her hand. 'I helped her to get ready.'

'You look fantastic, Cindy,' he murmured, taking my arm. 'Ready to go?' Thrusting a five-dollar bill into Trish's outstretched hand, he turned and led me hurriedly down the stairs. 'I'm a little worried that something might happen to my car out there.'

The car turned out to be a pale blue Ferrari with tinted windows. As we approached, a group of youths scattered into the darkness, interrupted in the task of removing the windshield wipers.

'The Rolls is still in the shop,' said Harley, opening the door for me. 'It's also my chauffeur's night off, so you're going to have to take your chances with my driving again.' He peered at the dashboard with a frown. 'Now where did that button for the lights go?' he muttered, flicking switches on and off. 'Ah, found it!' Removing his sunglasses, he turned and gave me another twinkling look. 'I'll try not to run into anything this time.'

The restaurant was called Wagner's and was, to judge by the famous faces sprinkled around the Valkyrie Room, a highly fashionable place to be seen. A burly man in a dinner jacket rushed forward to greet us.

'Mr Brightman, sir,' he said with a heavy German accent. 'What a wonderful surprise!' His eyes flickered over me doubtfully, then returned to Harley. 'Just the two of you tonight, sir? Your usual table?'

'Thanks Heinrich,' said Harley, pressing a bill into his

hand. 'I love coming here,' he whispered, as we watched a well-dressed middle-aged couple being thrown out of their seats to make room for us. 'It's so much more intimate than Morton's or Spago, and Heinrich is such a character, isn't he?'

It didn't look particularly intimate to me. People bustled from table to table, exchanging greetings and kissing their friends, and the hubbub of voices rendered the operatic background music barely audible.

'What's going to happen to them?' I asked, as a waiter led the middle-aged couple away.

'Oh, they'll be going to the Nibelung Cellar in the basement,' said Harley with a knowing smile. 'Heinrich reserves it for the troublemakers and the tourists. Nobody who's anybody sits down there.'

Heinrich returned and presented us with elaborate menus. 'Great idea to base all the dishes around the Ring Cycle, eh?' murmured Harley, ordering a Brunhilde's Delight.

'What are these numbers written next to the names?' I asked in a whisper, hoping they weren't the prices.

Harley laughed. 'Oh, those are the calorie counts.' He patted his stomach. 'Helps keep a check on the waistline.'

I had never bothered to count calories before, but I knew that two hundred wasn't very many for a main course. I scanned the list for something more substantial. After paying Trish the various sums I owed her, I wasn't left with much to spend on food, and I had existed for most of the previous week on leftovers from Marty's kitchen.

'Could I just have a steak?' I asked tentatively.

Heinrich's mouth dropped open and a sudden hush fell over our section of the room. Heads turned to stare. The music stopped. Someone dropped a glass, which shattered noisily amid the silence, and a man at a nearby table began to cough. *'Did you hear that?'* whispered a woman's voice. '*Red meat!*' Someone let out a low whistle, and the buzz of conversation gradually resumed.

'Might I recommend the Siegfried Special instead?' said Heinrich in a clipped tone which told me I had little choice in the matter. 'Very rich in protein, but without the high cholesterol content.'

'Why don't you try it?' suggested Harley quickly. 'I've heard it's delicious.'

I nodded, embarrassed. Without consulting me further, he ordered mineral water to drink, so I guessed that alcohol was out for the evening as well.

'What star sign are you, Cindy?' he asked, handing the menu back to Heinrich. What was it with all these difficult questions, I wondered, struggling to remember Cindy's date of birth from her driver's licence. What sign was June, for Christ's sake?

'I bet you're a Gemini,' said Harley.

'How did you know?' I asked, trying to sound impressed and hoping that he was right.

'Oh, just a little knack I have,' he replied, looking pleased. 'I'm a Sagittarius myself,' he added, and proceeded to give me a detailed rundown of the current configuration of his star chart. Glancing around the room as I listened, I noticed that Clint Eastwood was sitting at the next table, and Richard Gere had just turned up at the bar. This looked like a highly favourable configuration of stars to me.

When the food arrived, I discovered that Brunhilde got her kicks from wholewheat pasta with wild mushrooms, while Siegfried's favourite dinner was apparently grilled salmon. Both were served with a slice of fresh orange on the side of the plate.

'Do you want a bite?' asked Harley, thrusting a fork full of linguine under my nose and spearing a piece of my fish at the same time. He grinned. 'My bioenergetics man tells me it's one of the most psychologically beneficial things you can do with another person – sharing food. It's like a primitive form of bonding.'

As I sucked the linguine into my mouth, a series of tingling sensations told me that Cindy's body was interested in doing some primitive bonding too. Could this be my big chance, I wondered?

Glancing at Harley's handsome features, I felt a shiver of anticipation and desire. I looked away, blushing. What should I do? I had waited over thirty years to find out what sex with a real man was like and I didn't want to blow it now. How was I to give out the right signals, without making him think I was too easy? I didn't want to repeat the mistakes I had made with Chuck Woodcock.

Play it cool, I told myself firmly. I reminded myself that although I might be a nobody by Heinrich's standards, I had a powerful weapon – Cindy's body – at my disposal. With Harriet's brains to go with it, I had to be in with a chance. I began to relax a little, talking about myself for the first time since I woke up as Cindy. It was a complicated amalgam of truth and fiction, but it didn't really matter. Harley didn't know me from before, either as Cindy or as Harriet. This, I told myself, was the real start to my new life. I could be whatever I wanted.

As my confidence grew, I found myself talking about books.

'You've read *Dickens?*' he responded in an admiring tone, as if I had done something really clever. 'I've got a set of those at home somewhere – I'll show you some time.'

I was so used to being ignored or talked down to in the past, that it was a new experience to be able to impress someone so easily. When I told him I had read most of Shakespeare, anyone would have thought I had discovered a new way of splitting the atom.

'That's amazing,' he said, gazing into my eyes. 'You're so young and beautiful, so unspoiled, but . . .' he spread his hands in a gesture of bewilderment, '. . . what knowledge of the world.'

For dessert we had Götterdämmerung cake, which turned out to be a minuscule slice of calorie-reduced chocolate mousse. Valhalla was obviously not the place to head for if you wanted a nourishing feed. I was wondering whether to make a joke about the twilight of the gods being precipitated by starvation, when I felt Harley's hand brush against mine.

'Cindy,' he murmured, facing me with a soulful expression. 'I'm really glad I've found you.'

'Me too,' I agreed, moving my chair closer and giving him what I hoped was a seductive smile.

'I shouldn't really tell you this,' he continued, pushing his fingers through his hair so that it stuck out in odd directions. 'But it's been on my mind ever since I first saw you.'

He paused, looking embarrassed. 'When I saw you there, Cindy, after the crash – lying there in the wreck – I . . .' He gulped. 'I fell in love with you.'

In love? I felt a shiver of excitement deep inside me to hear the magic words I had dreamed of for so many years. But how could it be true? People didn't fall in love like that – not in the real world. Or did they? I could hardly claim to be an expert on the subject, after all.

'But how . . . I mean, you hardly know me.'

'I don't need to know you, Cindy,' he said firmly. 'All I have to do is look into your eyes.' Reaching across the table he took my hand in his and began to rhapsodise about the eyes being the windows of the soul.

If they were, he obviously wasn't looking very hard. What would he think if he tweaked aside the net curtains and caught a glimpse of my raddled fifty-year-old soul, mortgaged to the hilt in a bargain with the Devil. Meanwhile, Cindy's hormone bomb of a body was responding to him in a big way, sending electric tingles to all my nerve endings.

'It's getting late,' observed Harley, checking his watch. 'Why don't I take you home?'

Home? That wasn't what Cindy's body had in mind. I was all wound up and ready to go, and he was sending me back to face the third degree from Trish. What had I done wrong?

'Don't worry,' said Harley. 'I wasn't planning to take advantage of you.'

'But . . .' I floundered for a moment, then gave up. There was no way of putting it elegantly.

One thing struck me forcibly as we left the restaurant. I had thought that being young and beautiful would make life easy, but I had been wrong. It made everything about ten times more complicated, and it was, in many respects, just as frustrating as my previous condition. How long did I have to wait, for Christ's sake, until Cindy managed to get herself laid?

I let myself quietly into the apartment, hoping to creep into bed without disturbing Trish, but she was waiting at the door of her room, eager to grill me about the events of the evening.

'Did you score?' she asked excitedly. 'What's it like in the back of a Ferrari?' She refilled her glass from her private whisky bottle and, after a moment's hesitation, poured one for me as well. 'Are you going to see him again?'

Feeling somewhat deflated, I described Harley's chaste goodnight kiss. After all his talk about falling in love, he had left me on the doorstep without any discussion about the future – not even the suggestion of another date.

Trish looked disappointed, but soon perked up when I told her about the restaurant.

'Wagner's?' she echoed in an awestruck voice. 'Wow, Cin, that's where all the famous people go. Who was there?'

I thought Clint Eastwood and Richard Gere might be enough for her, but she kept me up half the night demanding detailed descriptions of the occupants of every single table in the place.

'Are you sure he didn't invite you out again?' she asked eventually, tipping the last drops of whisky into her glass. 'Maybe you're just not his type, Cin. She paused thoughtfully and gave me a wistful look. 'So if things don't work out for you, maybe he'll date me instead?'

In the morning, as we were getting ready to leave for Marty's, the telephone rang.

'It's him!' squawked Trish, holding her hand over the mouthpiece. 'Quick! Make yourself decent!' She took her hand away and held the receiver to her ear. 'Hi, Harley,' she breathed in a husky voice. 'It's Trish here . . .'

When I finally prised the telephone from her grasp, Harley sounded puzzled.

'You really should sort out your answering service, Cindy. I've just had the weirdest lady on the phone. Listen, I'll pick you up in about half an hour, and we'll go for a swim before breakfast. Then I'll show you around the house and we can . . .'

'I'm sorry, Harley,' I interrupted. 'It's Wednesday. I have to go to work.'

'Can't you take a day off?' he asked in a surprised tone.

'I, er . . .'

'Of course she can,' said Trish, snatching the receiver

from me. 'Don't worry, Harl – I'll make sure she's there.'

'What do you think you're doing?' I demanded angrily as she hung up.

'You can't go to *work*, Cin,' she said in an exasperated voice. 'Not at a time like this! Hey, stop worrying – I'll fix it for you. I'll tell Marty that you've got an audition for the new Mel Gibson movie or something.'

'But . . .'

'Get yourself ready and stop arguing. What time did he say he was picking you up?'

To my relief, Trish had set off for Marty's by the time Harley arrived. I felt a twinge of embarrassment as I hurried him down the stairs, realising for the first time just how sleazy the place must seem to him. It looked even worse by daylight than it had the night before.

'You really should get some security cameras put in around here,' he observed, wrinkling his nose as he stepped over a steaming pool of urine on one of the landings. 'They're very effective at cutting down on crime and vandalism. An armed patrol unit can be a good idea too – at least, that's what we found in my neighbourhood.'

Who did he think was going to pay for that, I wondered? As we left the building, a group of surly young men pushed past us, each carrying a shiny new hubcap under his arm. A pale blue Bentley stood outside, its wheel nuts exposed to the elements.

'I meant to come in the Porsche today,' said Harley, absentmindedly handing a crumpled bill to a youth who was retrieving a jack from beneath the chassis. 'Trouble is,' he added, opening the door, 'you can never trust the staff to get the right car out of the garage. José's been learning English for six months now, and he still can't tell the difference between a Bentley and a Porsche.'

As we drove into Beverly Hills, I recognised Wayne getting out of a patrol car by the security booth and shrank out of view in case he should stop us to demand another French kiss. The whole place looked a lot more friendly in daylight and I gazed at the big houses, wondering why they all had such huge front doors. We passed one which looked like a giant version of Hansel and Gretel's gingerbread cottage. Another might well have been the home of the Addams family.

We stopped at the end of a cul-de-sac which bore a strong resemblance to the place where Wayne and his friend had caught me a few nights earlier.

'Damn,' muttered Harley, swinging the wheel to turn the car around. 'I must have taken the wrong turning.'

We passed the Hansel and Gretel house twice more before Harley finally recognised the entrance to the road where he lived.

'I'm not used to coming from this direction,' he murmured apologetically, pulling up in front of a huge pair of gateposts with lions on the tops. 'Besides, José usually does the driving.'

After a brief struggle with the coded keypad on the entry phone, the gates slid open on silent runners, and we approached a slightly scaled-down version of the palace at Versailles. An American flag flying above the doorway was the only indication that we hadn't been miraculously transported to the outskirts of Paris.

The entrance hall was about six times larger than my entire Guildford flat.

'Good morning, sir,' said a prim voice. 'I've made the pool house ready as you requested.' I looked round, startled by the familiar tones, and saw a portly middle-aged man in a dark suit carrying a silver tray.

'Hi, George,' said Harley. He paused, then turned to me. 'I guess his accent sounds kind of strange to you, eh, Cindy? Let me introduce you to George, my *English* butler.'

'Er, hi, George,' I murmured, unsure of the correct etiquette.

'Any messages?' asked Harley.

George took a notebook from his pocket and consulted it. 'Mr Armani rang about your new suit, sir,' he said. 'I've arranged a fitting for next week, as you'll see from your diary. You'll notice that I've also made an appointment with your dentist for the twelfth, as you're due for your monthly polishing.' He turned a page of the notebook and frowned. 'Some journalist fellow called wanting an interview, but I thought the publication sounded rather tacky so I told him you were out of the country. And there was a dinner invitation from the Stallones for next Friday. I said you were likely to go.' He gave a discreet cough and glanced at me. 'Though I'll have to let them know, sir,' he added, 'whether you'll be taking a partner.'

'I'll, um, catch up with you on that one later, George,' said Harley in a casual voice. 'Is that it?'

'I'll be in the pantry if you need me, sir. Just ring the bell.'

Harley watched his retreating figure with an indulgent smile. 'I don't know what I'd do without George,' he said thoughtfully. 'He runs this place like clockwork. I sometimes feel like I'm just getting in the way.'

He pushed his fingers slowly through his hair, then shook his head and turned to face me with a look of boyish enthusiasm. 'Let's go swimming, Cindy.'

He led me through a series of grandiose corridors to an indoor swimming pool that was decorated like a Roman bathhouse. Eat your heart out, Sally, I thought, remembering a similar project my friend had carried out for a local health club, albeit on a much smaller scale.

What was Sally doing now, I wondered? With a pang, I realised that I would never be able to tell her about my experiences in Los Angeles – never be able to confide in her again.

Harley showed me into a changing room which was kitted out with a row of bikinis in different sizes hanging from a rail. There was a silk bathrobe hanging beside them, and a set of *Lapinique* toiletries on the vanity unit. A heap of soft, pale-blue towels lay at one end of an elegant chaise-longue, each embroidered with the *Lapinique* logo.

I changed into a bikini and emerged on the poolside, nervously aware that ninety-eight percent of my body was on display. Harley was powering up and down in the water, completing several lengths to the minute.

Smiling, I entered the water in a graceful dive. In my younger days as Harriet, I could do a mean front crawl. I'd show Harley what I was made of.

It wasn't until I surfaced – and unexpectedly sank underwater again – that a horrible thought struck me. What if Cindy couldn't swim?

The next thing I knew, I was lying on the poolside spitting out water as Harley pumped my chest with his hands and prepared himself to administer the kiss of life. So much for my bargain with Mephisto, I thought. In one moment of carelessness, I had nearly blown all those extra years. I opened my eyes.

'Are you all right, Cindy?' asked Harley anxiously. 'I should have realised you weren't ready for it – right after your accident and everything. I'm so sorry . . .' He held out his hands in a gesture of helplessness. 'You must think I'm trying to kill you,' he added with a note of melodrama in his voice. 'First the accident, and now, this.'

I sat up, coughing. 'I think I'll survive,' I said in a choked voice. 'Any chance of a brandy to clear my throat?'

When Harley was satisfied that I had fully recovered, we changed back into our clothes and he began to show me around the house. The place was vast, and the number of rooms appeared to be matched only by the number of different styles and historical periods reflected in the decor. From the Roman baths we moved into a room done out in full-blown Regency elegance, which then led through to another whose textured white walls were festooned with African rugs and carvings.

'I've had a Feng Shui consultant in to check the whole place,' he said, as we passed through a room with a distinctly Japanese flavour. 'That's why I've got those lions on the gates out front – they're supposed to neutralise the negative energy flowing from the west.'

In an oak-panelled room which he referred to as the library, he led me to one of several matching glass-fronted cabinets. It contained rows of leather-bound books which looked as if they had never been opened, and I wondered if they had been purchased by the yard.

'Here's that Dickens I was telling you about,' he said proudly, unlocking the door and carefully removing a volume. 'These are worth a lot of money – feel the quality of that binding.'

I dutifully inspected a copy of *Bleak House.* Some of the pages were still uncut. I was about to make a scathing remark about people who collected books but never read them, when I caught a glimpse of Harley's face. For a moment, he had a vulnerable, boyish look about him – like a spoiled child anxious to show off his possessions. As I watched, he pushed his fingers through his hair, unconsciously ruffling it out of its neatly groomed style. I felt a twinge of affection towards him. He had treated me with more kindness than any other man I had met in LA, and he hadn't even tried to go further than a goodnight kiss.

Softening, I handed the book back with an appreciative murmur. Why should it matter so much if he hadn't read Dickens?

We admired the garden from the terrace, which looked like a paving manufacturer's showroom. A wide sweeping lawn was bordered by tall hedges, some parts of which were clipped into elaborate designs. There were peacocks, spirals, castellations, and several amorphous sausage-like shapes.

'José's learning topiary at night school,' said Harley, indicating a small, dark figure perched at the top of a ladder. 'I think the blobby ones are his.'

A fully equipped gym overlooked the garden. 'These workstations are specially designed for isolating triceps, biceps and quadriceps,' he said, taking me past a row of gleaming pieces of equipment. 'The one at the end is my favourite – it's a swimming machine.' Rolling up his sleeves, he clambered right into the workings of the fearsome-looking contraption. 'Come here, I'll show you,' he said, strapping himself in.

Why did he need a machine for swimming, I wondered, when he had an indoor pool? It began to make rhythmic clanking noises as Harley laboured to reproduce the movements of the breast stroke.

'I've set it for a couple of lengths,' he gasped. 'Then you'll see the computer print-out of my performance.'

Gazing out of the window while I waited, I saw George sauntering across the lawn with a silver tray in his hand. As he passed beneath José's topiary sausage, he paused and glanced around to see if he was being watched, then deliberately kicked the foot of the ladder.

A distant shriek of indignation rang through the air as José plummeted into the foliage. The bush began to shake wildly and the ladder fell to the ground with a clatter.

George continued towards the house with an impassive smile on his face. 'English asshole!' wailed the bush, just audible over the clatter of gym equipment. 'I get you for this!'

'What was that?' asked Harley from the depths of his machine. 'Did you say something, Cindy?'

The bush leaned over towards the ground, stretching the elasticity of its stem to the limit, then catapulted upright as a small figure dropped on to the lawn and scampered out of sight. The door opened quietly and George materialised at the side of Harley's machine.

'Lunch will be served in the conservatory in five minutes, sir.'

Catching my eye, he gave me a look which clearly warned me not to mention what I had seen. 'These Hispanics,' he murmured, moving to the window and nodding towards the swaying bush. 'They have no sense of responsibility – no grasp of safety procedures. I'm surprised he hasn't killed himself by now.'

A surly Mexican woman brought in our lunch – a meagre looking salad with soup and wholewheat rolls.

'Thanks, Maria,' said Harley, checking the items against a pocket calorie chart. 'You didn't forget the liquid seaweed supplement, did you?'

Maria shook her head slowly, her expression clearly indicating that she thought he was mad.

'She's the third housekeeper I've had in six months,' sighed Harley as she left the room. 'You wouldn't believe how difficult it is to make these people understand about balancing nutrients.'

As we ate, he chatted on about the house, but I wasn't really listening. Something was beginning to bother me. He might be showing me all his possessions, from his swimming pool right down to his personalised cuff-links embossed with the *Lapinique* logo, but he wasn't really telling me anything about himself. What kind of person was he? What was he like inside?

When I asked him questions about himself he seemed to be at a loss for words.

'You must have read all the magazine articles,' he said, fidgeting uncomfortably like a schoolboy caught stealing apples. 'And the Larry King interview – you must have seen that?'

I shook my head.

'It's just . . . they seem to describe me much better than I can,' he said sheepishly. 'I'm pretty ordinary, really. I don't have any great interests or hobbies or anything – I just happen to be kind of rich.'

The little he told me about his family background made it clear that he had been brought up in surroundings of privilege and luxury. His fortune was derived from the *Lapinique* cosmetic company, founded by his late mother, and was large enough to ensure that he would never have to worry about earning a living like other mortals.

Lapinique – for the woman who wants a little more. Their slogan had been a constant source of irritation in my previous life, underlining my failure to achieve any of the things that most women took for granted.

'It's not as easy as you'd think. Being rich, I mean.' Harley's voice interrupted my thoughts. 'There's lots of hard work involved in running a place this size. You know, there are accountants and lawyers to keep in touch with, investment decisions to make, cheques to sign, charity functions to attend – and there are only so many hours in a day . . .'

'What about *Lapinique*?' I asked. 'I'd have thought that would take up most of your time.'

'*Lapinique*?' He brightened. 'Yeah, *Lapinique*.' He stood up. 'Come on, I'll show you my office,' he said, taking my hand and leading me towards the door. 'I've got a surprise for you.'

He led me to a room which was decorated entirely in the now familiar *Lapinique* blue. Rows of framed advertisements for the various products hung on the walls – images which were familiar from the glossy sections of the Sunday newspapers back home. They all featured blonde-haired models with the same delicate, doll-like features and expressions of wide-eyed innocence. Inspecting them more closely, I felt a shock of recognition. It was the same expression that now confronted me whenever I looked in a mirror – each time disturbing me with its contrast to my previous appearance and taunting me with its failure to communicate anything about the way I felt inside.

'Welcome to the hub of the *Lapinique* empire,' said Harley with a grin. He stood behind a large desk at one end of the room, flanked by an array of smaller desks laden with telephones, computers, and other business paraphernalia. I felt like a prospective employee about to be interviewed.

A machine on one of the desks whirred into life, disgorging sheets of printed paper. 'We're linked directly to the head office here in LA,' he said proudly, patting the machine. 'And that's linked to all the *Lapinique* offices around the world. London, Paris, Rome . . .' He picked up one of the sheets and examined it. 'This one has just come straight from New York.'

'What is it?' I asked.

He scratched his head. 'Sales figures, by the look of it. Not my department really – David takes care of all that.' He tossed it into a large wire basket filled with similar sheets of paper. 'It pays to keep in touch, though. Keep tabs on all the latest developments.'

'Who's David?'

'My brother.' He smiled. 'He deals with the business side of things. You'll meet him soon enough.'

Taking a key from the desk drawer, he opened a cupboard and removed a large rectangular object wrapped in velvet cloth. 'Now for that surprise,' he announced, indicating that I should sit at the desk. He placed the object in front of me, handling it with reverence.

'This is for you, Cindy. A special present.'

I cautiously removed the covering to reveal a shiny pale blue box embossed with the *Lapinique* logo.

'Go on, open it,' he said eagerly. I undid a pair of miniature brass clasps and lifted the lid. Inside were a series of trays lined with pale blue velvet, which lifted out like the layers in a box of chocolates. Each tray was divided into sections and filled with rows of tiny pots, bottles and tubes.

'It's a complete set of the *Lapinique* range,' he explained, arranging the trays on the desktop so that I could see them all. 'We had them made up in a limited edition for a special promotion, and this is the last one. I've been saving it for a long time – waiting for a woman who deserves it.'

He gave me a shy smile. 'Let me show you,' he said, pointing to the trays one by one. 'Cleanser, moisturiser, and toner in this one – that's the Total Skin Control range. Then there's foundation, powder and blusher in here. Lipstick in that one – you can see we do a lot of colours. Eyeshadow and mascara in there . . .' He continued with a seemingly endless list, fondly stroking each product with his fingertips. Then he leaned across the desk and lightly touched my chin, angling my face towards the light.

'I want to show you what *Lapinique* can do for you, Cindy.' Opening a drawer, he took out a box containing brushes, sponges and pads of cotton wool. 'May I?' he asked, selecting a bottle from one of the trays. I nodded.

He produced a mirror from another drawer and set it up on the desk in front of me. Gently, he removed the remaining traces of the make-up I had hastily applied that morning, and set to work with the contents of the trays. As he became absorbed in the task, his face lost its usual self-conscious expression and acquired a look of childish concentration – like a small boy experimenting with a new paintbox. His touch was delicate, and I found myself taking pleasure in each gentle contact with my skin.

'There,' he said eventually, standing back to admire his work. 'The natural look.'

'Why do I need make-up to look natural?' I asked.

'Natural beauty takes work,' he replied with an air of authority. 'You need to make the most of a beautiful face – show it off. Without make-up, a face is unfinished – like a painting without a frame. Look in the mirror and you'll see the difference.'

I inspected my reflection. The make-up was barely visible, but my face had a glow about it – a sheen of sophistication. It was an effect I could never have achieved with the garishly coloured contents of Cindy's make-up tray. I smiled, feeling a new sense of confidence.

'You're the most beautiful woman I've ever met, Cindy,' he said. 'I should know. I'm an expert on beauty – it goes with the job. People say that beauty is only skin deep, but there's something special about you – something different – and it tells me that your beauty comes from the inside.'

I turned to face him, moistening my lips in anticipation. Surely this was it – the moment when he would take me in his arms and kiss me?

He held out his hand to help me to my feet but, instead of kissing me, he led me towards a doorway at the other end of his office. A bedroom, perhaps? A shiver ran through me as my thoughts raced ahead to the unleashing of my long-suppressed desires.

He opened the door. 'What do you think?' he asked,

showing me a room kitted out like a photographer's studio, with backdrops, light reflectors and an expensive-looking camera with a huge lens set up on a tripod. 'I had a friend of David Bailey's design it for me.'

Trying not to show my disappointment, I made suitable noises of admiration.

'I'd love to take some pictures of you, Cindy,' he said shyly. 'May I?'

I hesitated, remembering the folklore of some African tribes who thought that a camera could steal your soul. My soul was supposedly safe in the hands of Mephisto, but what if the developed photographs were to show who I really was – not Cindy, but the fifty-year-old Harriet?

Taking my silence for assent, he led me into the centre of the room and left me there. Lights flicked on all around me and I stepped back, shading my eyes from the glare. Stumbling, I threw out a hand to steady myself.

I was dazzled by a flashbulb. 'That's great, Cindy,' exclaimed Harley, triggering his motor drive. 'Just lean back a little further – do you mind if I take another one?'

As the camera whirred and flashed several more times, I found my body responding to his instructions as if it knew exactly what would please him. Had Cindy been trained as a model at some time in her short life?

'That's amazing,' gasped Harley, his eye glued to the viewer. 'Don't stop, whatever you do.'

Stretching and twisting in sinuous movements, I willed him to abandon his equipment and join me in the intoxicating warmth of the lights. I felt young, beautiful and sexy. I wanted Harley – wanted to feel the delicate touch of his hands on my skin again. I wanted him to peel off my clothes and make love to me right there on the studio floor – just as I had seen it happen in films.

'Harley,' I breathed, parting my lips and gazing into the camera lens with half-closed eyes. He responded with a rapid barrage of flashes which ended with a loud bang.

'Damn,' he muttered, watching a wisp of smoke rise from the camera. 'Motor drive's gone.'

I was left standing foolishly in the middle of the room while Harley struggled to rescue his film. Eventually, with the help of a large screwdriver, he prised it from the back of the camera. 'Better run you home now,' he said, glancing at his watch and opening the door to his office. 'I want to get these pictures down to the lab before it closes.'

Reluctantly, I straightened my clothing. 'OK,' I mumbled, feeling downcast. Why did people always become so mysteriously elusive and unattainable the minute you started to find them attractive?

'Oh, did I tell you?' he added casually. 'There's a party tomorrow night. I'll pick you up in the afternoon to go shopping first.' He eyed my clothing with a look of vague disapproval. 'I thought you might need something new to wear.'

He drove me home in the Ferrari. Much of the journey passed in silence. Harley seemed preoccupied, and my thoughts were focussed on a subject I didn't dare to broach. What was I doing wrong, I asked myself? Why hadn't he made a pass at me yet? It was possible that he simply didn't fancy me but, if so, why was he making such a fuss about my beauty and going to so much trouble to entertain me? What had happened to all that talk about love from the previous night?

Stealing a glance at him as he drove, I reminded myself that Harley Brightman was, according to the gossip columnists, California's most eligible bachelor. Could it be that I was setting my sights just a little too high? But I had scarcely done anything to bring about our acquaintance – it was he who had taken the initiative and made all the moves.

The Harley I had met bore little resemblance to the playboy described in the newspapers. He seemed so much more kind, considerate and sensitive than the thick-skinned profligate I had been led to expect. I pictured him, earlier that day, sucking a make-up brush as he frowned over the choice of shadow colour for my eyes. His expression had been that of an artist intent on his work – of a man with few worldly cares. Had I been given a glimpse of the real Harley Brightman – of the side of him no one else knew? Could it be, I wondered excitedly, that he was responding to *my* real self – to the personality of the woman inside Cindy's beautiful body? Might Harley be a knight on a pale blue charger – the man I had dreamed of during all those lonely years as Harriet?

My reflections were brought to an abrupt halt by our arrival at Trish's apartment.

'See you tomorrow, honey,' he murmured, pecking

me on the cheek as he leaned over to press a button on the dashboard which opened my door. I lingered for a moment, but he made no further move.

'See you, then,' I replied in a neutral tone. Sadly, I turned my back on him and approached the grim entrance to the building. My imagination had been running away with itself again. A man like Harley Brightman could have any woman he chose. What had possessed me to think that he could possibly fall in love with me?

CHAPTER 9

The next day, Trish told Marty I had been called back for another screen test and Harley collected me at lunchtime in a pale-blue Mercedes. This time José was acting as chauffeur. The local thugs watched with interest from a nearby street light as we approached the vehicle.

'George usually drives me when I go shopping,' said Harley, joining me on the back seat. 'But he's feeling a little under the weather today. Some little mishap in the wine cellar last night which I don't really understand – I can't figure out how he managed to lock himself in.'

A quiet snigger from the front of the car suggested that José might have been able to enlighten him. As we pulled away, there was a cheer from around the street light and I glanced behind to see a grime-encrusted youth pick himself up from the ground and make an exaggerated bow to his audience. In one hand he held a screwdriver, while in the other he brandished a car numberplate embossed with the letters HARL 3.

José dropped us on Rodeo Drive and we strolled past a series of lavishly decorated shop windows. Many of the names were familiar – Gucci, Armani, Chanel – names I had always despised as symbols of a lifestyle I could never have. Sleek young sales assistants lurked intimidatingly in the doorways while armed security guards mingled conspicuously with the pot plants on the sidewalk, their trigger fingers twitching in readiness. I didn't fancy the chances of anyone foolish enough to try checking the colour of a garment by daylight.

'Let's have a look in here,' murmured Harley, guiding me into a large and sparsely furnished shop. Inside, there were no racks of clothes to browse through, no bargain bins. A few discreetly positioned mannequins gave the only hint of the nature of the business being carried out.

I faltered in the doorway, aware that my stiletto heels were biting into the polished wooden floor. A sales assistant dismissed me with a withering glare and turned to Harley.

'Can I help you, sir?'

Harley looked at me expectantly. 'Why don't you try some things on?' he suggested. 'Don't be shy. See if there's anything you like.'

'I'll show you the Spring Collection, ma'am,' said the assistant, steering me firmly towards the back of the shop.

I had dressed carefully that morning, aware that Harley might find Cindy's clothes a little wanting in elegance. It wasn't until we passed a large mirror, and I saw my reflection in these restrained surroundings, that I realised with a shiver of embarrassment just how cheap and tacky I looked. It was time, I decided, for Cindy to smarten up.

I was expecting to see clothes that matched my impression of what rich women wore – elegant, well-cut, and with a hint of glamour – but the Spring Collection was something of a disappointment. I was presented with a series of oddly styled garments in dingy pastel colours, with the occasional highlight of muddy brown or grey.

'Haven't you got anything brighter?' I asked, climbing into a dress that looked as if it had been made from a potato sack.

'These are this season's colours, ma'am,' said the assistant in a condescending tone.

I held up a jacket which appeared to have four arms. 'Or anything a little more, er, conventional?'

'This, ma'am,' she replied haughtily, 'is a designer boutique.' Glancing around, she lowered her voice to an icy whisper. 'If you don't like the clothes, baby, get off my case and stick to shopping at Sears like everyone else.'

I didn't know about Sears, but I felt a sudden yearning for the cosy familiarity of Marks and Spencer. Why did fashion have to be such hard work?

Eventually, I presented myself to Harley in a gold-coloured suit that looked like a cast-off from the *Star Trek* wardrobe.

'Hey, that's very stylish,' he enthused, leaping to his feet as I approached. 'Pretty smart of you to pick something so different.'

Glimpsing the price tag, I became anxious to leave.

Surely even Harley would baulk at spending so much money? He insisted, however, on my modelling several different outfits, each more ghastly than the one before. I had a problem with Cindy's body. No matter what I put on, I still looked good. If I had slipped into a bin liner, the assistant would probably have flogged it to Harley for some extortionate price.

'We'll take them all,' he said eventually, handing his over his credit card. 'I knew this was the best place to bring you,' he added, turning to face me with a happy smile. 'Clothes say a lot about your personality, don't they? It's so important to get it right.'

We went to several more shops, where I was kitted out with shoes, handbags and other accessories. I kept protesting that he shouldn't be so extravagant, but Harley wouldn't listen. 'What good is all this money,' he asked, 'if I can't spend it how I want?'

Our last stop was at a shop so exclusive that we needed an appointment to get in. 'I hope you don't mind that I set this up,' Harley whispered, 'but there's a dress in here that's just perfect – the colours are right and everything. I liked it so much when I first saw it, that I asked them to put it aside. All I've been waiting for is the right woman to wear it for me.'

A flimsy creation in pale-blue silk appeared. When I put it on, his eyes became misty. 'Will you wear it for me tonight, Cindy?' he asked. 'To the party? I want you to meet my friends.'

I nodded, admiring myself in the mirror. The style of the dress was simple and feminine, quite different to anything Cindy might have chosen. I looked a picture of innocent beauty. Who would ever guess that I had sold my soul to the Devil?

When we returned to Harley's house, we spent the rest of the afternoon by the pool. I refused to go in the water again, but he was anxious not to fall behind in his daily exercise programme and insisted on swimming several dozen lengths. Relaxing on a comfortable chair, I sipped fresh orange juice and enjoyed a pleasant sensation of laziness. I could get used to a lifestyle like this, I thought, if only I could get my hands on a real drink.

Later, when Harley had finished entering the details of his swim on his computerised exercise chart, he took me to a guest room where I could get changed for the evening. The blue dress that had cost the equivalent of several months rent on my old flat in Guildford was being laid out on the bed by Maria. As soon as she had left the room I undressed and slipped it on, folding Cindy's cheap garments into a neat pile and leaving them on a chair.

When I had fixed my hair and applied my makeup, I looked just the way I had always imagined someone who had everything should look – glamorous, sophisticated and with a relaxed sparkle that came from not having to slave in a menial job every day. If only, I thought, gazing at my reflection in the mirror with a little shiver of excitement. Marty's Diner was beginning to seem a long way away.

'I hope you can see me now, Mephisto,' I murmured. 'Things are looking up.'

A faint, ghostly cackle echoed in my ears. *'Never underestimate the power of beauty to corrupt . . .'*

'Mephisto?' There was no reply. Had I imagined it?

'I'm not being corrupted,' I muttered indignantly to myself, remembering his words from our last encounter. 'Why shouldn't I get to enjoy myself for a change?'

'Cindy?' I jumped at the voice, then turned to see Harley at the door, resplendent in a dinner jacket and bow tie.

'Sorry,' he said, glancing round the room. 'I heard voices – I thought you were calling me.' He gave me a big smile. 'You look great.'

'Thanks,' I said, blushing as I sensed an emotion welling up inside me which was all too familiar from my time as Harriet. It was a pang of unrequited love – the very same feeling that used to cloud my judgement and undermine my self-confidence whenever I was with Andrew.

'Ready to go?' Harley held out his hand.

I joined him, thrilling at the touch of his fingers as he laced them through mine. This time, I told myself firmly, things were going to be different. Hadn't he talked about love at our very first meeting? Why else would he be treating me with such kindness?

I love you, Harley. I tried out the phrase in my mind. Maybe tonight, I might find the right moment to use it – find the courage to declare my feelings with the words I had never dared to say to Andrew.

Meanwhile, I decided, I wasn't going to fall into the old trap of having my every pleasure soured by thoughts of the further gratifications denied to me. I was going to live for the moment and make the best of what I could get. Hadn't Mephisto promised me a taste of the good life? I was more than ready for it. Surely I deserved a few lucky breaks?

George, looking somewhat bleary eyed and hungover, was waiting outside the front entrance with a pale blue stretch limousine. The interior of the car was vast – there was enough space inside to hold a small dinner party, complete with tables and chairs.

'How many cars *have* you got?' I asked Harley, as we pulled out of the driveway. 'You seem to have a different one every time I see you.'

'Oh, um, just the five,' he replied, scratching his head. 'If you count the Rolls. Or is it six?' He leaned forward. 'George, did we get rid of the Porsche? I haven't seen it for a while.'

'Neither have I, sir,' said George in a dry voice. 'Not since you left it on North Rodeo Drive with the keys inside, if you recall?'

We turned into another driveway and, after negotiating a huge set of security gates, pulled up at the end of a queue of cars that were waiting to disgorge their occupants at the entrance to a big white house. To judge by the distance we had travelled, the house belonged to Harley's next-door neighbour. By the time we reached the front of the queue and stepped out on to a red carpet which extended from the door, it had taken us over half an hour to get there.

The house was very different to Harley's. It was as if the architect had been so overwhelmed by the variety of competing styles on offer next door, that he had elected to design the entire building as an exercise in restraint. Surfaces were predominantly white and spaces seemed to flow one into another so that you could never quite pin down exactly which room you were in.

In what seemed to be the main living area, full-height glass panels opened on to a timber deck surrounding a swimming pool that was illuminated by floating white candles shaped like water lily flowers. At one end of the room, a small man who looked remarkably like Dudley Moore tinkled the keys of a white grand piano, his hands moving lazily back and forth as he conjured up the atmosphere of parties I had seen in Hollywood films.

Groups of elegantly dressed people stood around the poolside, creating a gentle burble of conversation as they cast flickering shadows in the twilight. I clung to Harley's arm, suddenly shy. Everyone looked so confident, so absolutely sure of themselves. What would these people think of me?

'Harley darling!' A tall woman with angular features detached herself from a group and swooped towards us with puckered lips. 'So glad you could make it!'

I stared at her open-mouthed, realising that our hostess was the actress Crystal Kelly. In her heyday, back in the late sixties, she had been one of Harriet's favourite film stars.

Harley grinned, seeing the surprise on my face.

'You could have warned me,' I hissed under my breath.

'Sorry,' he murmured. 'I thought you would be too young to recognise . . . mmmfurgh!' He was cut off as Crystal Kelly kissed him, first on the mouth and then several times on each cheek. She looked a lot older than I remembered from the films I had seen, and was wearing a flimsy dress which revealed more of her drooping cleavage than seemed respectable.

'I know it's not fashionable to exchange body fluids these days, my dear,' she said, turning to me and kissing the air on each side of my face, 'but Harleykins and I go back a long way.' She wagged a knowing finger at him. 'His mother and I were great friends,' she added, and began to laugh uncontrollably, as if she had just said the wittiest thing in the world.

'I don't think you've met Cindy,' said Harley. 'Let me introduce you.'

'Well, *hello*, my dear,' she said, placing a hand on my arm and facing me with a conspiratorial look. 'Where has Harleykins been hiding *you*? We *must* have a good long talk – just the *girls* – and you can tell me all about yourself. *Do* tell me how you met.'

'I, er . . . it's a long story,' I began, glancing at Harley for guidance. 'We kind of bumped into each other.' Harley nodded encouragement, but when I looked back at Crystal, she was staring over my shoulder with glazed eyes.

'I just love parties, don't you?' she said in a dreamy voice. Then her eyes flickered with recognition and she swung back into action.

'Look, there's Larry!' she exclaimed, pushing me gently to one side as she advanced towards a newcomer with outstretched arms. 'Larrykins, darling!'

'Crystal's a sweetheart, isn't she?' said Harley in an indulgent voice. 'She's so natural, you'd never guess she was an actress.'

As more guests arrived, I began to see a logic to the restrained whites and beiges of the house. They must have been carefully chosen – just like a backdrop to a film – to ensure that they didn't compete with the real stars of the occasion, the Hollywood people.

The men looked the way men always do – transformed by the universally flattering uniform of the well-cut dinner jacket into groups of identically good-looking penguins. It was the women who stole the scene, strutting like peacocks in vibrantly coloured creations, blusher striped like war paint on their cheekbones. I watched in fascination as a series of glittering apparitions strode into the room, their calf muscles bulging with the strain of walking in five-inch heels. They were all thin to the point of emaciation, and positively dripped with jewellery. One woman was wearing so much gold that she could have been Tutankhamen in drag.

I had thought myself sophisticated when I left Harley's guest room earlier this evening, but in comparison to these creatures, I felt that I looked like a vestal virgin. With a feeling of unease, I wondered if this had been Harley's intention in choosing my dress.

'Harley, how are you buddy?' A middle-aged man with a face like an old leather purse bore down on us, his jewel-encrusted wife in tow. 'So who's the little lady?' he asked, flashing me a smile that exposed rows of gleaming white teeth too perfect to be the real thing.

When he immediately turned his back on me and began to talk business with Harley, I concluded that it had been a rhetorical question. The man obviously considered himself far too important to waste his time talking to me.

His wife stood by, looking me up and down with a faintly hostile expression.

'I guess you're one of Harley's models,' she said eventually, with a note of distaste in her voice. 'Have you known him for long?'

'Er, no actually,' I replied. 'To both questions.' I ventured a smile.

'Oh really?' She raised her eyebrows. 'What *do* you do?'

'I'm a waitress,' I said, looking her straight in the eye. 'What do *you* do?'

A flicker of annoyance crossed her face. 'I don't need to *do* anything, my dear. Don't you know who my husband is?'

I shook my head. 'I'm afraid nobody's bothered to introduce us.'

She gave me a look which could have withered the contents of a flower shop. 'I think there are a few things you need to know, my dear,' she hissed, 'if you've just arrived by Greyhound from Hicksville. One, that my husband Aaron is one of the wealthiest and most influential men in Hollywood, and two, that my daughter Jessica is virtually engaged to Harley.' She nodded towards a younger replica of herself standing nearby. 'I wouldn't want you to waste your time.'

Pointedly, she turned her back on me and walked away to greet some new arrivals. Looking around for Harley, I saw him being dragged off to meet someone. A group of people pushed their way past, blocking me from following him, and I was left surrounded by strangers.

Several different conversations were taking place around me. One group of people were gossiping about Crystal Kelly's plastic surgery, while another discussed the latest techniques of colonic irrigation. A third group were deep into some kind of New Age philosophy, comparing notes on strategies for getting in touch with their Inner Child.

I needed a drink. Snatching a glass from a passing tray, I took a large gulp of what turned out to be sparkling mineral water. *Mineral water?* This was going too far, I thought miserably. Was everyone so busy nursing their Inner Child that they'd forgotten to lay on any drinks for the grown-ups?

'Hey gorgeous, come here,' said a man with a little pointed beard, snatching my hand and dragging me into his group. 'We're doing Chinese horoscopes. What year were you born?'

'Nineteen for – fif . . . ' I stuttered, doing rapid mental calculations. 'I mean, *seventy*-seven. I mean six. Nineteen seventy-six.'

'Well, make your mind up, darling,' said another man with a snigger. 'Anyone would think you had something to *hide*.'

'That makes her a Dragon,' said the bearded man with a twinkle in his eye. He turned to his friend, glancing down at a chart in his hand. 'Now, let's pretend you were born in – let's see – nineteen-fifty? That would make you a Pig, which it says here is highly compatible. Is romance blossoming here or what?'

'I wasn't born in nineteen bloody fifty,' hissed the other man, glancing round to see if anyone else had heard.

'Not if you're a Pig, you weren't,' I said. This was the one Chinese sign I knew, because it was Harriet's. 'It would have to be forty-seven.'

He glared at me. 'How the fuck would you know?'

'She's right,' said the bearded man, consulting his chart with a raised eyebrow. 'I was reading the wrong column.' He looked closely at his friend. 'I never would have guessed you were *that* ancient, Johnny.'

A third man beamed at me with a lecherous smile. 'What a wise head on such pretty young shoulders, eh?' He sidled towards me. 'What do you do, my dear? Teach math?'

'Actually,' I said frostily, 'I used to be a librarian.'

'Ha, ha, that's a good one,' he chortled, patting my bottom. 'You can stamp my library books for me any time, darling!'

I turned to retaliate, but there was a sudden commotion nearby and several people pushed into me. A knot of people surged along the poolside with a man struggling in their midst.

'Get that filthy man out of here!' barked a woman, bustling self-importantly in their wake.

'What happened?' asked someone beside me.

'Completely disgusting!' spat the woman. 'You wouldn't believe the things some people can do!'

'Did you hear?' whispered another woman excitedly. 'Someone tried to *light a cigarette!*'

The man was thrown unceremoniously over the

railing of the timber deck, and could be heard crashing through the undergrowth some distance below.

'Serves him right,' said a wide-eyed girl with a face like porcelain. 'Who was he?'

'Nobody important,' said her friend, who I recognised as Jessica. 'Just somebody's husband – not even on the B list.'

Jessica clutched a plate of smoked salmon in her hand, together with what appeared to be a proper drink – unless someone had peed in her mineral water when she wasn't looking. Her other hand was occupied busily transferring pieces of salmon to her mouth.

'So what did you think of Teddy?' she asked her friend. 'I thought he was great in the sack considering he's only a college kid. Mom got really heavy about me seeing him, though, so I've had to cut him down to two nights a week.'

'Actually, I preferred Chester,' giggled the other girl. 'Not many prospects, but a hell of a big schlong.' Blushing, she snatched the last piece of smoked salmon from Jessica's plate. 'What about you and Harley, though?' she asked. 'Have you scored yet?'

Jessica's eyes zeroed in on her empty plate. 'Shit,' she muttered. 'We'd better get some more of this before it runs out.'

I followed them closely as they made their way around the pool. Not only did I want to hear the dirt about Jessica and Harley, but I also wanted to find a real drink.

At the buffet table, I discovered that alcohol was dispensed on request by a dazzlingly handsome young waiter, and I began to down the white wine with a vengeance.

'Harley never talks to me these days,' continued Jessica with a sigh, taking up position at the edge of the pool and wading into a freshly loaded plate of smoked salmon. She leaned towards her friend and lowered her voice to an excited whisper. 'You'll never guess what – Mom tells me he's got some bimbo in tow tonight. Cheap little gold digger by the sound of it – apparently, she's a *waitress*.'

'I wouldn't lose sleep over it,' replied her friend. 'It saves him having to pay for it.' She began to giggle. 'Men have urges just like we do, Jessie.'

Jessica nodded vigorously. 'Yeah,' she mumbled, cramming another piece of salmon into her fat little mouth and chewing noisily. 'She's probably nothing but a two-bit hooker – let herself down as soon as she opens her mouth.'

I glanced around. No one was watching, so I stepped close to her and jabbed my elbow sharply into her back.

'Mmmrrgh!' She jerked forward with a muffled yelp, teetered on her stiletto heels, and pitched headlong into the pool.

'Oh my God!' screamed her mother. 'Jessie's drowning!' Everyone rushed towards the pool, eager for a ringside view.

Not wanting to share the fate of the friendless smoker, I slipped quickly out of sight into the crowd. Looking back from a safe distance, I saw a group of people heaving a dripping bundle from the pool, while others looked on in distaste at the scraps of half-eaten salmon and other miscellaneous contents of Jessica's stomach which floated among the ersatz water-lilies.

I still couldn't see Harley anywhere so, when the commotion had died down, I returned to the buffet table for some more wine. A pair of expensive-looking women were loading their plates with gourmet morsels.

'Gosh, Eleanor, these cream cheese and pastry thingies are unbelievable,' said one with a giggle. 'I can't seem to stop them jumping on to my plate.'

'I'm sticking to the caviar and water biscuits, darling,' said the other, brandishing a spoon with determination. 'If you're going to blow your calorie allowance, you may as well get a bit of flavour. How *is* the new diet going?'

'Well you know me, Eleanor,' said the first woman with a shrug. 'I have to be so careful. One calorie over the limit and I just *bloat*.' She glanced around. 'You do have to keep up appearances though. It would be so rude to waste all this scrumptious food.'

'There's always the emergency measures, eh, Sylvie?' said Eleanor, nudging her friend and discreetly pointing two fingers at her mouth. 'Binge and purge – have a good feed and deal with the technicalities later.'

Sylvie blushed. 'I don't . . .'

Eleanor touched her arm. 'I know you don't,' she said in a soothing voice. 'It's just that I can't understand how you look so slim.'

'Do I really?' asked Sylvie, preening. 'Maybe it's my new outfit – do you like it?' She was wearing a bright-purple dress with padded shoulders which made her look like a linebacker.

'It makes you look ten years younger,' said Eleanor without conviction.

Sylvie sighed. 'I bought it for Warren's birthday party and I had to lose nearly ten pounds to get into it. And he didn't even notice that I was wearing something new. I sometimes wonder why I bother.'

'I know darling.' Eleanor tweaked a single grape from a bunch on the table and popped it into her mouth. 'I felt like giving up when Arnie had his last affair. But you can't blame the men for fooling around if you don't make an effort. I went on a new diet, treated myself at the hairdresser's, and splashed out on a full course of *Lapinique* rejuvenation creams.' She stroked the skin of her scrawny neck with a pink taloned fingertip and gave her friend a knowing smile. 'I feel so much better now.'

I must have moved closer without realising, because she suddenly reached out and grabbed me by the wrist. 'If you're going to eavesdrop on our conversation,' she snapped, pulling me towards her, 'you better come and introduce yourself.' She regarded me with blatant curiosity. 'Who are you? And whose husband are you having an affair with?'

'I'm not having an affair with anyone,' I said indignantly. 'I'm a friend of Harley.'

'Harley Brightman?' She raised her eyebrows. 'He sure has been keeping you a secret.'

'Is that your natural hair colour?' asked Sylvie, sidling towards me. 'It's real pretty.'

I nodded, trying not to stare at the halo of sculpted

candyfloss that clung to her own head, the fruit of a lifetime's dependence on chemical enhancement.

'You don't know how lucky you are,' she said with a sigh of envy. 'When I think of all the time and money I spend at that hairdressers . . .'

'It's worth every penny, darling,' said Eleanor reassuringly. 'Some people might get all the natural advantages for free, but everyone has to pay for style.' She turned to me. 'You'll find that out soon enough, my dear,' she said in a patronising tone. 'You might be able to get away with it now, but the "natural look" doesn't get you very far at our age.'

Looking over her shoulder, I spotted Harley on the other side of the room, deep in conversation with our hostess. He waved and I made a movement to go and join him, but Eleanor blocked my way.

'Now we've met, my dear, let's have a nice little gossip. You must tell us all the latest news about *Lapinique*. Is it true that Harley's going to launch a new range of skin creams? It's too bad of him really – I'm still on the first stage of the *Two Year Total Skin Control Course*, and I would hate to switch treatments half-way through.'

'I'm afraid I can't tell you,' I replied. 'I, er, haven't known Harley very long.'

'I see.' She gave me a pitying look. 'I guess you wouldn't know about that article in *LA Weekly* either?'

'It's shocking,' added Sylvie indignantly. 'I pay ninety-five dollars for a bottle of *Total Skin Control*, and this journalist bitch has the nerve to say it's the same as ordinary cold cream.'

'Why don't you use cold cream, then?' I suggested. 'Save yourself some money.'

She gave me a horrified look. 'How could you even *think* that I would risk smearing cheap garbage like that on my face?' she retorted indignantly. 'I only use the very best skin products, and I'll have you know that I can afford to pay for them!'

Staring at the network of fine wrinkles which was clearly visible under her make-up, I wondered how much she would pay for Mephisto's brand of rejuvenation treatment.

'Anyhow,' she added, more thoughtfully, 'you don't get alpha hydroxy acids in cold cream. What would you do about exfoliation?'

'Look, isn't that Warren over there?' interrupted Eleanor, nudging her friend. 'Don't waste your breath, darling,' she added in a low voice, glancing at me. '*She* doesn't need to know about exfoliation. She probably couldn't even spell it.'

The two women exchanged elaborate kisses with Warren, a plump little man whose dinner jacket strained to cover his bulging stomach.

'Hi there,' he said, homing in on me with a beady glint in his eye. 'Who's this pretty new face?'

'She's Harley's girlfriend,' said Sylvie, taking him firmly by the arm.

'Well, well,' he said, ignoring her attempts to steer him away. 'Nice to meet you, my dear.' He gave me a patronising smile. 'Are you one of Harley's models?'

'No,' I replied irritably. 'I'm a brain surgeon.'

A flicker of doubt crossed his features, then he began

to laugh. 'Ha, ha – that's a good one! Of course you are!' He turned to Eleanor. 'Harley got himself a little comedienne here, eh? I love a girl with spirit.'

Why would no one take me seriously? 'Actually, I was fibbing,' I said angrily. 'If you really want to know the truth . . .'

The three turned to face me with quizzical expressions.

'I'm a fifty-year-old librarian who sold my soul to the Devil in return for youth and beauty. It's much more effective than a pot of cream, and the price isn't a great deal higher, by the sound of it.'

Sylvie opened and shut her mouth several times, while the other two exchanged looks of surprise.

Harley appeared suddenly at my side. 'Cindy, there you are! I've been looking for you everywhere.' He glanced at the others. 'Have you met everyone?'

Warren broke into a loud guffaw. 'We've met all right,' he said, slapping Harley on the back. 'You've got yourself a good one here! Great sense of humour.'

'Come with me, Warren,' said Eleanor, shooting me a poisonous look. 'I want you to help me find Arnie.' Sylvie turned to follow them, then paused, glancing at me with a wistful expression.

'You *were* only joking, weren't you?' she asked in a confidential whisper. 'I mean, it's obvious that you're not that old, but I just wondered . . . I mean, I thought it might be some new treatment you'd heard about.' She looked at me eagerly, her face pathetic with hope. 'If you'd just tell me the name . . .'

'It's called a Faustian Pact,' I said, chuckling to myself as she whipped out a notebook from her handbag and began to write it down. 'Rub it well into your skin before you go to bed at night and, when you wake up in the morning, you'll find that you're a new person.'

It was late by the time we left the party. I had scarcely spoken to Harley all evening and the optimism I had felt earlier was beginning to wane.

'I'm really proud of you, Cindy,' he said, as George drove us away from the house. 'You carried yourself with such poise – no one would have guessed you were only a waitress.'

What's wrong with being a waitress, I thought indignantly.

'I've been listening to compliments about you all night,' he continued happily. 'Everyone loved you.'

Couldn't he see through their smug hypocrisy? I felt a surge of loathing for these privileged creatures, for their obsession with looks and money. At the same time, I was pleased to know I had made an impression. I'm just as good as them, I thought. If I had their advantages, I could do something with my life.

'Where are we going?' I asked, noticing that we had passed the lions at the end of Harley's drive.

'I thought we'd go for a ride,' he said softly. 'Have you ever been up Mulholland Drive?'

To my dismay, we pulled off the road at exactly the same spot where Chuck Woodcock had tried to rape me only a few days earlier. My knickers were probably still out there on the grass verge.

George glanced over his shoulder at Harley, who responded with a discreet nod. 'I'll just, er, take a short walk, sir,' he said, opening the door and disappearing abruptly into the night.

'Alone at last,' murmured Harley, leaning forward to open a small refrigerator. 'I hope you like champagne,' he added, taking out a half-bottle and a pair of elegant glasses. He gave me a boyish wink. 'I've been saving up my alcohol units all evening for this.'

Handing me a frothing glass, he reached for a set of controls on a panel beside him. There was a brief hissing sound followed by a series of clicks and a soft melody began to drift through the interior of the car. With a smile, I recognised a favourite from my past – *That Devil Called Love*, sung by Ted de Vincy. I gazed at the twinkling lights of Los Angeles. If a moment was ever ripe for romance, this had to be it.

'Just look at that view,' said Harley, squeezing my hand. He turned towards me and I held my breath, waiting for him to pounce.

'If you married me, Cindy,' he said in a quiet voice. 'You wouldn't have to be a waitress any more.'

I swallowed my mouthful of champagne with a gulp and stared at him in surprise. Things were moving faster than I had expected. I had relished the thought of becoming his lover, his steady girlfriend even, but I hadn't yet got as far as fantasising about being his wife. I'd only known him for three days, after all, and he hadn't even given me a proper kiss.

'Are you sure?' I asked cautiously, hoping I hadn't mistaken his meaning. 'I mean . . . shouldn't we take things a bit more gradually? See if we're really, um, compatible, and all that.'

'I'm an old-fashioned kind of guy, Cindy,' said Harley dramatically. 'I've been waiting a long time for the right woman to come along and I was sure that, when she did, I'd know deep down that it was right. For me, this is it. It's all or nothing.'

He gave me a shy smile. 'I saw this movie once – *Pretty Woman*, I think it was called. It was about a rich businessman who falls in love with a, um, with a prostitute. He finds out that she's got better qualities inside her than all the shallow people who pretend to be his friends, and in the end he marries her – takes her away from it all and makes her respectable.' He sighed. 'I've always dreamed of a romance like that – you know, meeting somebody I could reach out and help. Somebody who would really appreciate the things I have to give, because they'd never had them before.'

He leaned forward and kissed me gently on the cheek. 'You're so fresh and unspoiled, Cindy. So different from all those people tonight. Won't you be my pretty woman?'

A small part of me bristled at the comparison with a prostitute, but my dominant feeling was one of pleasure at being singled out from the sycophants at the party. They would soon treat me differently if I was Harley's wife. And how could I resist the charm of a story whose fairytale ending fitted so neatly with Harriet's dreams? Wasn't this exactly what she had waited for all those years?

Glancing across at his eager face, at his compelling brown eyes and the way his hair flopped so artlessly over his forehead, I felt a stirring of emotion. This was it – my chance of happiness. I didn't want life to pass me by for a second time while I waited on tables in Marty's Diner.

> *. . . the temptations I've missed*
> *It's so hard to resist*
> *That devil called love.*

The words of the song conjured up a fleeting thought of another devil. Harley had money, fame, and social position – the very things Mephisto had taunted me with. Was I falling into some kind of trap? Suddenly, I didn't care. I had already sold my soul, after all. What more could he possibly take from me?

Closing my eyes, I surrendered myself to the pleasure of the moment. 'Yes Harley,' I said in a clear voice. 'Yes, I'll marry you.'

He kissed me gently on the lips, and I felt a tingling sensation in my veins. Tonight, I thought excitedly – tonight I'll find out what it's really like. I returned his kiss, pressing myself close against him. It would be my first real sexual experience since that sordid business all those years ago in the back of Barry Thompson's van.

I was about to reach for the bulge which had risen prominently in Harley's lap, when he pulled away sharply and made a show of examining his watch.

'Good God, is that the time?' he said in a surprised voice. 'I better get you home – your friend will be starting to worry.' He pressed a button, opening the window with a smooth whirr and letting in a gust of cool night air. 'George? Are you out there?'

'Right here, sir,' answered George, looming suddenly out of the darkness. His face had acquired a rosy glow in marked contrast to his earlier appearance.

I threw Harley a beseeching look. 'But I don't . . .'

'Don't worry, my darling,' he replied, squeezing my hand. 'I'll get you home in no time.'

Surreptitiously recorking a hip flask and slipping it into his pocket, George climbed into the driving seat and started the engine.

'It's OK, darling,' whispered Harley as we pulled back on to Mulholland Drive. 'I wasn't planning to take advantage of you. I'm an old-fashioned guy, remember?' He grinned. 'I want to wait until our wedding night for *that*.'

CHAPTER 10

I had assumed Harley's offer of marriage to be a vague declaration of intent – something to be considered in the future, when we knew each other better.

Harley, however, viewed things differently.

'Let's do it right away,' he urged, telephoning me at six o'clock the following morning. 'I'm so excited, Cindy – I don't want to waste any more time.'

'Do you think so?' I asked hesitantly. 'I mean, shouldn't we be engaged for a while, or something?'

'We love each other, don't we? What is there to wait for?' His voice took on a mildly accusing tone. 'You haven't changed your mind already, have you?'

Of course I hadn't. I was eager to escape from Trish and Marty's Diner and get on with my new life. I could free myself from the past – from Mephisto and his double-edged promises. Who would believe that the wife of a man like Harley would make a pact with the Devil? Conjuring up the highlights of the previous night in my imagination, I was swept up once again by a heady feeling of pleasure and excitement. Eat your heart out, Mr Darcy, I warned my soon-to-be-forgotten fictional hero. There's no substitute for the real thing.

'Are you still there, Cindy?' Harley's voice betrayed a note of concern. 'Is everything OK?'

'Of course it is,' I assured him quickly. 'I'll marry you as soon as you want.'

'I'll pick you up at the regular time, then,' he said. 'We have lots of organising to do. Maybe you could think about who you'd like to invite to the wedding. Give me a preliminary list for my security people to check out.'

'What am I supposed to tell Marty today, then?' asked Trish, emerging from her bedroom with a casual air, as if she hadn't been listening at the keyhole.

'Tell him I'm getting married,' I murmured dreamily, wandering back towards my bed.

'Getting married?' squawked Trish, her eyes popping. 'Getting married? Not to . . . not to Harley Brightman?' She stared at me open-mouthed. 'You're kidding? Jeepers, Cin, you'll be rich! You'll never have to work at Marty's again! You'll . . .' Unexpectedly, she sank into a chair and burst into tears.

'What's wrong?' I asked.

'It's not fair!' she wailed. 'Why wasn't I in that accident instead of you? It's not like you're a better person than me, or more special, or anything. Now I have to go to work and you can just lie around peeling grapes all day if you want!'

I looked at her guiltily. Why shouldn't I feel special? I deserved it, didn't I?

'You'll probably get all stuck-up and high falutin' now,' she muttered sulkily. 'Rubbing shoulders with the rich and famous and hanging out at swanky cocktail parties. No time for your old friends like me.'

'That's not true,' I said unconvincingly, knowing that it was. I could sympathise with how she felt – I had spent my entire life as Harriet watching other people getting the lucky breaks.

'Hey, wait a minute,' she said, suddenly alert. 'What about the rent?' She glared at me suspiciously. 'You can't just leave, you know. You're supposed to give me notice. You'd have to pay me compensation if you want to move out.'

'Don't worry, Trish,' I assured her. 'I'll pay everything I owe you.'

'What about the inconvenience?' she muttered. 'I mean, it's all very well saying you'll pay what you owe, but there ought to be something extra. It's not going to be easy finding someone else to live in that room.'

Not at all easy, I thought. Unless she could find a wealthy dwarf with agoraphobia who liked hanging out in cupboards.

'And there's the money you owed me from before your accident,' she continued craftily. 'I thought I'd let it pass since you lost your memory and everything, but it changes things if you're getting married to a millionaire.'

'How much?' I asked.

'Five hundred?' she suggested hopefully.

'Done,' I said. It would be a small price to pay to get Trish off my back.

'Hey, really?' she asked, her voice brightening. She

paused thoughtfully. 'Has Harley got any nice friends? Maybe we could double-date or something?'

I smiled weakly, imagining the chaos she would cause among the Warrens and the Arnies of Harley's world. She would certainly give them a run for their money.

'Have you chosen your colour scheme yet?' she asked excitedly.

'What colour scheme?'

'For the wedding, of course. I'll need to know.' She gave me a dreamy look. 'I've always wanted to be a bridesmaid.'

'Bridesmaid?'

'But you promised me, Cin.' Her voice filled with reproach. 'That I'd be your bridesmaid when you got married. Don't tell me you forgot?'

I wasn't too keen on the way this was going. What other promises might Cindy have made to her friend?

'I need to know what colours I'll be wearing,' she continued. 'So that I can plan my make-up and lingerie and everything. Are you going to wear your hair up or down?'

'We haven't, er, made any definite plans yet,' I murmured. 'But I wouldn't be surprised if it was pale blue,' I added with a smile. 'Like a certain cosmetics company we know.'

'Blue for a boy, eh?' giggled Trish, nudging me. She gave me a sly look. 'Hey Cin, you're not knocked up, are you? Is that why you're in such a rush to get married?'

'Certainly not,' I said, realising with a shock that I

hadn't given a single thought to contraception. Thank Christ I had remembered before it was too late – I had a few things to sort out in my own life before I made myself responsible for anyone else's.

'Oh shit!' howled Trish, staring at her watch. 'Look at the time – Marty's gonna kill me if I turn up late again! What'll I do, Cin? It's all your fault.'

'Why don't you call in sick?' I suggested.

'I can't!' she wailed. 'I've already arranged to be sick tomorrow so that I can go shopping with Sharleen.' She gazed at me in helpless desperation. 'Do you think I could get away with saying that my mother was dead again?'

'But I thought you saw her at Christmas?'

'I know,' she muttered miserably. 'I don't know what I'm going to do when she really does kick the bucket. I've already used up all my parents and grandparents with Marty. I'm down to funerals of aunts and second cousins now.'

'Why don't you tell him the truth?' I suggested. 'You could blame it all on me.'

'Hey, I never thought of that,' she said, perking up. 'I could say that you were dead. That would be good for a day off, wouldn't it?'

Things all began to happen faster than I had anticipated. By closing my eyes and saying that one word, *yes*, it seemed I had set in motion a vast piece of machinery which couldn't be stopped. Not until I had said the other two words which sealed my promise – *I do.*

The gossip columns went into a frenzy of speculation

after we were seen together at Crystal Kelly's party, and it seemed that the entire population of California was waiting with bated breath to find out what Harley would do next. By the time he announced our engagement, two days later, everyone had heard of Cindy Brown, the girl from nowhere who had captured the heart of their favourite bachelor.

Lapinique Heir in Fairytale Romance, said one newspaper. *Harley Brightman to Wed:* said another. *Prince Charming finds his Cinderella.*

Relatives I didn't know I had began to ask me for money. Babs sent me a bill for her last plane ticket. Three different men wrote claiming to be my long-lost father who, according to Babs, had left home when I was still a baby. A squad of journalists and photographers set up camp in the stairwell of the apartment building, causing a minor upturn in the local economy by purchasing food, alcohol, drugs and secondhand car parts from the more enterprising inhabitants. Harley decided, much to Trish's disappointment, that it was time for me to leave this particular neighbourhood.

I had expected to move straight into Harley's house, but he was determined to do everything correctly and booked me into a suite at the Beverly Hills Hotel.

'We don't want to be tempted before the wedding night, do we Cindy?' he said with a playful grin. 'We've waited so long now, it would be awful to ruin it at the last minute.'

He called this a long time? I'd been waiting for thirty years for someone to finish the job that Barry Thompson started, so I didn't think another few weeks were going to kill me. Glancing around at my luxurious surroundings, which included a well-stocked bar, I decided that I could just about bear the suffering.

Once the date of the wedding was set, I found myself sucked into a complex web of arrangements and social rituals which took up most of my time. Harley showered me with presents, one of which was a *Lapinique* gift box tightly packed with crisp fifty-dollar bills.

'Just a little something to cover your expenses until I've got your credit card arranged,' he said shyly. I accepted the money gratefully, relieved to know that I could finally pay Trish what I owed her and that I wouldn't have to return to Marty's again. I hadn't dared to go back there to explain my disappearance – especially after I heard that he was trying to cash in on the publicity by selling Cindy Brightman T-shirts and bumper stickers outside the diner.

Harley's parents were no longer alive, but there seemed to be endless numbers of relatives who were eager to inspect his intended bride. We visited a series of elderly aunts and distant cousins who treated me with exaggerated courtesy in front of Harley, but were hard pressed to conceal their hostility in moments when he was out of the room.

His friends were more attentive, but I soon realised that they saw me not as an individual, but as a kind of appendage to Harley. To them, I was just another route by which they could gain his attention. They were friendly enough but, as they talked to me, their conversation would transform by gradual stages into a sales pitch for some business venture which needed financial backing, or some good cause which required his support. If I would just mention it to him, they would hint, he would think I was so clever to have suggested such a good idea.

Eleanor, the woman I had met at the party, was particularly eager to befriend me and insisted that we go shopping and have lunch together. We passed a harrowing morning on Rodeo Drive. All my previously held notions about taste and style were laughingly swept aside as Eleanor bullied me into spending an obscene amount of money.

'You can't buy that – it's way too cheap!' she exclaimed, snatching a dress from my hands and examining the price tag. She thrust it back on the rail and turned to me with a pitying look. 'You can't choose something simply because you *like* it, Cindy dear! Think of your position. You're not a waitress any more – you have to keep up standards. People will want to know what labels you're wearing.'

Dragging me out of the shop, she reeled off a long list of designer's names I was to look out for, followed by an equally long list of names I was to avoid at all costs. For reasons which were not clear, these lists were subject to unpredictable fluctuations, and constant vigilance was required to avoid costly blunders.

'Did Harley ask you to tell me all this?' I asked, as we entered a restaurant and went through the ritual of obtaining a good table. 'Is he worried that I'm going to show him up by wearing the wrong clothes or eating with the wrong fork?'

'Let's face it my dear,' she said, sitting down. 'You are a little lacking in sophistication.' She glanced under the table at my feet. 'Like that outfit. Never wear those kind of shoes with narrow pants.'

'Why not?' I asked indignantly. 'They look perfectly all right to me.'

'It simply isn't done, my dear. Don't expect there to be any logic to it – that's the last thing you'll find here in Tinseltown. You have to learn the rules and play by them, otherwise you'll sink without trace. Are you going to listen to my advice or not?'

I nodded sulkily. I might be older and wiser than Cindy in many respects, but I had to admit that I was out of my depth here. Harriet's knowledge of fashion and society certainly wouldn't be harmed by a little polishing.

'As soon as you've learned to mix and match clothes correctly, you'll find that you can do much the same with people,' continued Eleanor, consulting the menu. 'It's all a matter of remembering who's on which list.'

She ordered mushroom salad for both of us, with Evian water to drink. White wine was being served at the table next to us, but there was no suggestion that we might have any. It was obviously not on the right list and neither, to judge by Eleanor's withering look, were the people drinking it.

'I'm sure you'll be having lots of parties,' she went on. 'You'll need to know exactly who to invite, and how to get rid of the rabble and the hangers-on. The best idea is for you to come to me for advice on these things because – to be quite honest – Harley doesn't have a clue. He has no idea of his social responsibilities – some kinds of people just shouldn't be mixed.'

'You mean he shouldn't be marrying me?' I asked, meeting her eyes.

She returned my gaze without flinching. 'You have to admit that you've put quite a few noses out of joint. Breezing in out of nowhere and scooping up the most eligible bachelor around. If people like Harley paid more attention to the rules, something like that just couldn't happen.'

She smiled. 'But you're here now, so we might as well make the best of it. Just take some advice from me and don't abuse your position. You might think you're invincible at the moment, but looks like yours don't last forever. When they're gone – that's when you'll find out who your real friends are. And they'll be fewer than you think.'

'Are you my friend?'

'Of course I am, Cindy,' she replied, giving my hand a pat of reassurance. 'I wouldn't be telling you all this if I wasn't.'

The waiter brought our lunch, laying the plates tentatively on the table while Eleanor watched over him like an invigilator at an exam.

'There's a splash of mayonnaise on this lettuce leaf,' she murmured quietly. 'And one of the mushrooms is off-grid, but I think we'll let it pass.' Dismissing the anxious waiter, she picked up her fork and turned to me with a smile. 'Now we can get down to the real business that we're here for.' She stabbed a mushroom and inspected it with a critical eye. 'Have you set your target weight yet? It's traditional to lose at least six pounds.'

It turned out that she was talking about the wedding, which she had every intention of organising for me.

'Why do I need to lose weight?' I asked in dismay. 'Surely I'm thin enough already?'

'You have to demonstrate your commitment,' she said firmly. 'Otherwise everyone will be expecting you to turn into a couch potato the minute you've got the ring on your finger.'

She made a rapid movement and the mushroom disappeared from her fork without the slightest hint that there was anything as crude as actual eating going on. 'I don't think you realise the seriousness of what you're doing here, Cindy,' she said. 'Marriage to a man in Harley's position is like taking on a full-time job.' She gave me a questioning look. 'You know this already of course.'

Another mushroom disappeared from her plate as if by magic. 'There are people out there – photographers mostly – who will be watching you all the time.' she said. 'They'll be waiting patiently to catch you with a mouthful of food on a bad hair day, or scratching your butt in public. You have to be switched on to them the whole time – there's no question of taking time off to schlep around in your old jeans.'

I tried to conceal my alarm at this news. Surely the rich and famous were allowed *some* privacy? Wasn't that why Harley paid for all the security gates and armed guards?

'Another thing,' said Eleanor, folding a lettuce leaf

into a tiny origami envelope with her knife and fork. 'How you reply to invitations is just as important as how you give them out. Remember that exclusivity is the key. Accept an invitation from some clueless piece of fodder like that woman at the next table and you'll be struck off the A-list faster than greased lightning.' She sealed the envelope with a dab of mayonnaise and popped it into her mouth. 'And if you don't get invited to something important, you must never, ever admit to it. Pretend you're out of town, that you've been rushed into hospital with skin cancer, or that your children have been kidnapped by a serial killer – anything rather than the truth.'

'You mean like that party Aaron whats-his name is giving next weekend?' I asked innocently.

'Who?' Her eyes narrowed. 'I wouldn't know anything about next weekend, I'm afraid. Arnie's taking me away to a luxury resort for a holiday. Too bad that I won't be around.'

She deposited her utensils on the empty plate with a click. 'Now listen carefully, my dear,' she said, changing the subject with practised ease. 'I'm going to tell you all about Arnie's new movie deal, and I want you to pass this on to Harley – he'd be furious if he missed the chance to come in on it.'

Eleanor seized control of the wedding arrangements like a general taking over a military campaign. I was expected to spend hours at her side while she created and revised an endless series of lists covering everything from the order of service to my depilation and personal hygiene schedule for the week before the big day.

The guest list and seating plan for the reception were major preoccupations.

'Who *are* these people?' she asked, pointing to a section of the list with an expression of disapproval. 'I don't know them.'

It was the section Trish had helped me fill in. 'They're my friends,' I replied, trying to sound suitably offended. I had never met most of them either, but Trish assured me I had known them all for years and couldn't possibly leave any of them out.

'I think we'd better put them in this corner by the door,' murmured Eleanor, reducing them to social outcasts with several brisk strokes of her pen. 'You can't afford to take any risks with people you don't know.' I nodded in silent agreement.

Trish, who was somehow under the impression that she was also helping to organise the wedding, visited me regularly with armfuls of bridal magazines. I struggled to keep her and Eleanor from meeting.

Trish was determined that every possible accessory should play its part in the success of the happy day.

'Look at these, Cin,' she whispered, pointing to an illustration. '*Express your individuality with custom-made table napkins in striking colours to contrast with your main theme*,' she read from the caption. '*Each napkin monogrammed in silver thread with the initials of the bride and groom*.'

I didn't care to think that my individuality could be summed up by the colour of a table napkin, but I let her have free rein in the hope that it would distract her from interfering with anything which actually mattered.

'You could have butterflies or white doves released as you say your vows,' she continued, turning a page excitedly. 'Or there's a thing here where they'll bury a time capsule for you: *Play your part in History. Capture your happiest moment with a selection of personalised mementoes for future generations to discover!*'

It seemed there were no limits to the tackiness she would embrace, but she reluctantly drew the line at *Tie the knot in free fall – special wedding packages for parachuting enthusiasts.*

'I suppose it is a bit too much,' she conceded sulkily. 'Especially if you've got vertigo.' She grinned. 'I bet it would look funny on the video, though. With your dress flying up over your head and everything. What would happen if you dropped your bouquet?'

Harley saved his closest relative until last. A few weeks before the wedding, he took me to the *Lapinique* offices downtown to meet his younger brother David.

José dropped us outside a skyscraper shaped like a giant lipstick tube with the *Lapinique* logo embossed all over its pale blue cladding. 'David has a brilliant idea,' said Harley as we travelled to the top floor in a high speed lift. 'Do you remember those pictures I took of you when we first met? Well, David's had some experts look them over and we think we could use you in the new campaign.'

I looked at him blankly. 'Use me? What do you mean?'

'As a model,' explained Harley excitedly. 'Apparently you have a face that captures the spirit of the modern age.' He hugged me with enthusiasm. 'I'm so proud of you, Cindy, sweetheart. You're going to have your picture everywhere – you're going to be famous!'

The elevator doors slid open to reveal a panoramic view over Los Angeles. A man stood by the window, fingering the lapel of his expensive-looking suit as he stared out at the city with a thoughtful expression.

'Ah, here you are,' he murmured, turning his head and moving swiftly to greet us. 'This must be Cindy. Even more beautiful than her picture.' I found myself face to face with a darker-haired and plumper version of Harley.

'David,' said Harley in a dramatic tone. 'Allow me to introduce the new Face of *Lapinique*.'

'It's a real pleasure to meet you at last,' he said, shaking my hand and retaining it in his own, which was warm and damp. Traces of perspiration were visible on his forehead. 'Welcome to the family.'

I pulled my hand away and dried it surreptitiously on the back of my skirt. There was something faintly repulsive about David, something sinister in his manner that reminded me for a moment of Mephisto.

He led us into a luxuriously furnished office and the two brothers began to discuss schedules for photographs and filming. On the wall was a mock-up for a billboard, with my face superimposed on it from the photographs Harley had taken. Behind me were a series of women wearing masks which hid their features. *Lapinique,* said the caption. *Be a face in the crowd. New with Formula B.*

'We can probably squeeze the whole thing into one session for the first phase,' said David, stretching back in his chair and linking his hands behind his head. 'The rest can be sorted out later.' He grinned at Harley. 'I know you guys are tied up ordering your outfits for the honeymoon and all that, so I won't take up too much of your time.'

Was there a sneering tone in his voice? I sat there without speaking for the whole meeting, angrily conscious that no one had consulted me about any of this. Harley had never asked me if I wanted to be a model – he had simply assumed that it must be the highest ambition a woman could possibly have. He was also making arrangements on my behalf as if I was incapable of doing it for myself, as if I were a child, or some kind of performing pet.

We left the office – the two men arm-in-arm with me tagging along behind – and went to a restaurant for lunch.

'Well Harley,' said David, ordering a bottle of champagne. 'The end of an era, eh? The Brightman bachelor boys bite the dust.'

'None for me, thanks,' said Harley, quickly placing his hand over his glass. 'I'm following a strict calorie monitoring programme this week.'

'All the more for us, eh Cindy?' said David with a laugh, filling my glass to the brim. 'Here's to my new sister.' Harley looked on with disapproval as we drank a toast.

'I'm looking forward to getting to know you better, Cindy,' murmured David. He leaned towards me and lowered his voice. 'Did Harley tell you about our special arrangement?'

I shook my head, puzzled.

'Well, it's like this, Sis,' he whispered, touching my knee under the table. 'Harley's a bit shy about the physical side of things, so he always gets me to try out his new girlfriends first.'

Shocked, I pushed his hand away and turned to check out Harley's reaction, but he was busy studying the calorie chart on the back of the menu and didn't seem to have heard anything.

There was an awkward silence for a moment, then David burst out laughing.

'I can see what you meant about 'fresh and unspoiled',' he said, turning to Harley and talking about me as if I wasn't there. 'You must have really scoured the boondocks for this one.'

He caught my indignant glare. 'Sorry,' he added. 'I was only joking, Sis.'

Swallowing my anger, I tried to remain calm. His behaviour was relatively inoffensive for the rest of the meal, and I made an effort to be friendly. I was too close to getting what I wanted to risk spoiling it all with some silly argument.

By the time I was due to be photographed for the new advertisement, I had forgotten my uneasiness about David. Harley dropped me at the *Lapinique* offices on the way to see his analyst, promising to collect me later.

'I'd love to stay and watch,' he said, 'but I don't dare cancel this appointment – my shrink's booked solid for the next six months.'

I expected the session to be rather like the previous one at Harley's house, but it turned out to be quite different. There were other models involved – tall, elegant creatures who drifted around in giggling clusters and borrowed each others lipstick and tampons. They didn't speak to me but, whenever I was nearby, their gossip ceased and they stared at me with hostile curiosity. Remembering the mock-up in David's office, I soon sensed their jealousy and resentment. Cindy Brown, the girl from nowhere, was now the face in the crowd, while they were just the crowd.

I was pushed and pulled around by wardrobe people, makeup artists, lighting technicians and, finally, by the photographer. Blinking in the glare of the fierce lights, I was bullied into one contorted pose after another.

'Make love to me, baby,' he urged, stroking my thigh before retreating behind his camera. 'Don't be shy.'

I felt vulnerable and exposed in the flimsy dress they had given me to wear. Everyone was staring at my body. Hot with embarrassment, I tried to follow his directions. Surely they wouldn't be treating me like this if Harley was here?

When it was finally over, David appeared out of the darkness at the back of the room. How long had he been watching, I wondered uncomfortably.

'Nice work, Cindy,' he murmured, catching me by the hand and leading me out of the room towards the elevator. He flashed me an oily smile. 'Come up to my office for a drink – Harley's just arrived and he's waiting for you up there.'

Why hadn't Harley come to fetch me himself? Half-way to the top of the building, David stabbed a button on the control panel and the elevator lurched to a halt between floors.

'OK,' he said abruptly, turning to face me. 'No one's going to interrupt us here. It's time we had a private talk.'

'What do you mean?' I asked, backing away in alarm. His veneer of charm had completely disappeared.

'You can quit playing the innocent with me now,' he said coldly. 'You might have taken in my dear brother, but I've got your number. I know exactly what you are.'

I shivered, reminded again of Mephisto. Surely David was bluffing? How could he possibly know the truth about me?

'A scheming little fortune hunter,' he continued. 'Thinking you can help yourself to the family money and then take Harley to the cleaners for a quick divorce.'

I felt a surge of indignation that was mingled with relief that he was nowhere near finding out about my real secret – my pact with the Devil. At the same time, I was confused by a faint pang of guilt. Would I be so interested in Harley if he wasn't rich?

'That's not true,' I said helplessly. 'Harley loves me . . .'

'He always was a fool for flattery.'

I took a deep breath, '. . . and I love him too,' I added,

experiencing a rush of romantic feeling as I said it. 'I want to make him happy.'

David gave me a contemptuous look. 'Well, you'd better start right now. I love my big brother as well, and I want to see him happy too. Happier than he ever thought possible. If I see him looking just the tiniest bit pussy-whipped, I'm going to know exactly who to blame.'

Tears welled in my eyes. Why should he doubt me?

'If I hear the slightest suggestion,' he continued, 'that you might be dipping too deeply into the purse or fooling with other men, then I'm going to put your ass in a sling so fast you'll wish you'd never laid your greedy little eyes on the *Lapinique* logo.'

He touched the button on the control panel and the elevator jerked back into motion.

'Don't mess with me, Cindy,' he added, savouring the melodrama of the moment. 'I can destroy you.' I began to feel like an extra in a low-budget thriller.

'I can destroy you like . . .'

The elevator doors slid open, interrupting the climax of his speech. Harley stood outside.

'There you are,' he said anxiously, pushing his hair out of his eyes. 'I was just coming to find you . . .' He stopped, seeing the expression on my face. 'What's wrong, Cindy?'

'Please take me home,' I whispered, stumbling out of the lift. 'I don't feel well.'

'What have you done to her?' Harley shot a suspicious look at David, then back at me. 'What have you two been up to?'

There was an uneasy silence in the car as José drove us back to the hotel. As we crossed the intersection with Sunset, I caught sight of a familiar figure shuffling along the sidewalk with a shopping cart. It was the woman with the 'Will Work for Food' sign – the one who had reminded me of Harriet. Her sign lay limply amongst her various grubby bundles as if she no longer had the energy to hold it on display.

I was afraid to tell Harley what David had said – he might begin to wonder if there was any truth in it. Why did I feel so guilty? Uneasily, I remembered Mephisto's words: *You'll forget your fancy principles soon enough, once you've had a taste of the good life. You'll be out for what you can get – fighting for your slice of the cake with the rest of them – you just wait and see.*

I began to be haunted by thoughts of Mephisto, by fear that he would unexpectedly return. When Harley and I went to visit the pastor to discuss the wedding arrangements, it occurred to me that a church service might not be the most appropriate option for someone in my position.

We perched on a low-slung wicker sofa festooned with scatter cushions and balanced cups of herbal tea on our knees while the Reverend Robert 'Call me Bob' Jackson paced back and forth in front of his desk, his thumbs hooked in the belt loops of his freshly ironed denims.

'Of course, we usually expect couples to attend services for at least six weeks prior to the happy day,' he murmured, glancing at Harley. 'In your special circumstances, however, and in view of the most generous donation to our Community Outreach Programme, I think we can dispense with most of these formalities.'

He launched into what sounded like his standard pre-nuptial sermon, while I stared at the poster over his desk which advertised a 'Habitat for Humanity Quilt-making Weekend' and tried to ignore the fact that I was on enemy territory as far as Mephisto was concerned.

In my youth – in my previous life – I had always dreamed of a white wedding. Religion never came into it – I just assumed it would follow in the natural course of events, like it did for everyone else. I never quite came to terms with the harsh realisation that it had passed me by. Now it was actually happening – the dream had finally come true. But to bring it about, I had made a pact with the Devil. How could a church wedding have any meaning now?

Feeling gradually more uncomfortable, I tried not to listen to what the Reverend Bob was saying and concentrated my attention on keeping my legs arranged so that he couldn't see up my skirt. But words kept filtering through: *a sacred bond . . . a union in the eyes of God . . . the blessing of the Church . . .* He matched the rhythm of his pacing to his words, and I felt his eyes turning towards me at each pause. Then he stopped and faced me with a smile, as if he had finally found a satisfactory viewpoint.

'Do you understand, Cindy, the serious nature of the commitment you are about to make?'

I nodded, shifting uneasily on the sofa and spilling

my tea. Harley flashed me a look of concern – he had been fussing about my welfare since my apparent sickness the previous day.

'Marriage is more than a bond between two people, Cindy,' continued Bob, his eyes fixed on my cleavage. 'The institution of marriage comes to us through God and his divine law – a covenant representing God's eternal fidelity to all who are faithful to him and follow his laws.'

Just because he spent his time organising quilt-making weekends to save the rainforest, I didn't see that he needed to use such a patronising tone. I had never believed in all this religious claptrap anyway. There were some moral precepts I had tried to follow in my old life – Polonius's advice to Laertes in *Hamlet*, for example: *To thine own self be true*. But which self? Was I really still the same person, or had I been changed by this new body? People treated me differently now – especially men – and I found I was getting used to it. Had I drifted into becoming more like Cindy than I knew?

I began to feel afraid – to wake up for the first time to the enormity of what I had done. What if God did exist after all? Would I be struck down by a thunderbolt at the altar? Or if I was spared this indignity, how long would I have wait in fear for divine retribution?

The Reverend Bob started pacing again. He seemed to have switched sermons while I wasn't listening, and he was now talking about forgiveness. Stuff about us all being like sheep and the blood of the Lamb washing our sins away.

His metaphors seemed a bit muddled, but was there something in it? I might not believe in God, but what if Mephisto did? He was with the Devil, after all, and how could the Devil exist if there wasn't a good guy on the opposing side? Could a marriage consecrated in a church drive Mephisto away?

Marriage was normal, solid, real – it was what ordinary people had, like the happy family on the back of the cornflake packet. Why shouldn't I have it too? It would give me some kind of status as a regular person, and I would be able to get on with my life without any gods or devils messing things up for me. Not only would I have Harley's love, but I would also be able to enjoy the simple pleasures which had in the past been soured by loneliness. I would be able to have ambitions, a career, a family, a future – to succeed where I had previously failed. I was only twenty-one, after all – there was plenty of time.

I wasn't going to back out now. Everything had been arranged – Eleanor had seen to that.

'I'll look forward to seeing you guys at the rehearsal, then,' said Bob, bringing the interview to a close. He handed us both leaflets for his next quilt-making weekend.

'You're a lucky fellow,' he added, patting Harley on the shoulder with a wistful smile. He turned to me. 'Think carefully, Cindy, about all that I've said. Marriage is a great adventure – a leap into the unknown. You can't be too well prepared.' His handshake was lingering and I thought I felt him tickle my palm with some mysterious secret sign. 'Remember it won't always be easy. The Devil is always watching for opportunities to lead us weak mortals astray.'

CHAPTER 11

I had expected the days to drag, to stretch out and smile at fate with the offer of endless potential for things to go wrong. But time passed quickly, and I found myself standing beside Harley in the church with the feeling that I wasn't quite ready – that such a significant moment deserved more of a build-up. *Wait,* I felt like shouting. *Slow down – it's all happening too fast!*

I could hear Trish breathing heavily behind me, tightly buttoned into a high-necked dress chosen by Eleanor. Little bridesmaids bobbed around my feet like a brood of ducklings, buffeted by the flounces of my voluminous wedding gown – white with a hint of pale blue. I blinked through my veil and watched the movements of the Reverend Bob's lips. He had exchanged his jeans for a surplice and his face had taken on an expression of solemn beatitude. He must be feeling pleased with himself, I thought. There were bound to be plenty of lucrative spin-offs from officiating at the society wedding of the year – the quilt-making circle was probably swamped with applications to join.

I heard myself repeating the vows, my voice a distorted whisper in a rustling, creaking silence. More words were mumbled. The ring slid on to my finger. Then the veil was lifted and Harley faced me with an ecstatic smile. It was done. There had been no sign of Mephisto, no thunderbolt from heaven. My new life had begun.

We left the church in a solemn procession with bridesmaids scattering rose petals before us while Bob's Sunshine Singers sang their hearts out in the hope of getting a mention in the media coverage.

Outside, ropes had been set up to restrain the enthusiastic crowd. It seemed as if the whole of Los Angeles had turned out to say goodbye to their most eligible bachelor. A hot-dog van was doing a brisk trade in the church car park and I glimpsed makeshift stalls on the sidewalk selling *Harley&Cindy* T-shirts. We were seized upon by a horde of photographers who buzzed around us like moths at a lightbulb as we struggled to make our way towards the car.

'Look,' said Harley, pausing on the gravel path and pointing upwards. A pale blue hot air balloon drifted overhead, our names entwined around the *Lapinique* logo on its side. Pale blue rose petals fluttered through the air, eliciting cheers from the crowd, who took this as a cue to throw confetti, rice and birdseed at us with enthusiasm.

'Isn't this great,' whispered Harley in a happy voice. 'I never knew we had so many friends.'

I yelped with pain as a handful of sunflower seeds stung me on the side of the face, bringing tears to my eyes.

'What was that, darling?' He turned to look at me. 'Oh, sweetheart – don't cry,' he begged, his voice trembling with emotion. He gave a loud sniff. 'You'll make me cry, too.'

When we arrived at the reception, which was held in a hotel so exclusive that it didn't appear to have a name, we were forced to go through endless rituals of greeting guests and posing for photographs before we were allowed to sit down for the meal. I was familiar with these things from other people's weddings, but it was strange to find myself at the centre of it all. I felt suddenly shy. I wasn't used to all this attention.

The catering was being personally supervised by Heinrich of Wagner's, which was apparently a coup of the highest order. To be on Heinrich's client list was akin to having a bronze star on the sidewalk of Hollywood Boulevard or, at the very least, a permanently reserved place in heaven. Hundreds of pairs of eyes followed me as I took a seat at the top table, which Heinrich had decorated with pale blue ribbons. In front of me was a glistening ice sculpture, shaped like a giant bottle of *Lapinique* perfume. Were guests going to be handed free samples and money-off vouchers when they left?

I looked round the room. Apart from a handful of people I recognised, they were all strangers. Why were they staring? They were supposed to wish me well, but I could feel hostility in their eyes. Were they jealous of my luck in marrying Harley? Were they all secretly hoping something would go wrong?

There was an uncomfortable silence in the room as the first course was handed out. Why weren't they talking, laughing, enjoying themselves? It didn't fit in with my faded dream of how *my* wedding should be. Then Heinrich's uniformed waiters began to circulate with bottles of wine. It was only an anaemic looking Chardonnay but it seemed to be a signal for everyone to relax. Snatching my drink from the table before the waiter could turn it into a spritzer, I downed it in one gulp and held out my glass for a refill. Eleanor shot me a disapproving glare from her seat nearby, but I didn't care. No one was going to make me worry about calories or alcohol units today.

Glancing towards the Siberia at the back of the room which Eleanor had reserved for Cindy's friends, I noticed that Babs hadn't been so reluctant to make the plane trip this time round. The doughy-faced man and row of little dumplings beside her were presumably Dale and the kids from Sioux Falls.

There was a sudden disturbance in the middle of the room as a woman claiming to be one of Harley's elderly aunts was unmasked as a reporter from a popular magazine of dubious integrity. A buzz of gossip travelled around the room as she was escorted out in disgrace – first it was said that she had a notebook in her handbag, then a tape recorder strapped to her leg. This became somehow translated into a miniature camera concealed in her hat and by the time she reached the door she stood accused of having an implant in her brain which was beaming live pictures via satellite to the entire country.

As she was ejected, a cheer went up from the table nearest the door, which contained a contingent from Marty's Diner as well as a handful of Trish's friends. It was the rowdiest table in the room and appeared, from the condition of its occupants, to have access to its own private supply of alcohol. As I watched, one of Heinrich's waiters slipped through the door with a bottle of vodka. Banknotes discreetly changed hands and he began to work his way around the table, dispensing shots.

Looking more closely, I noticed that one the revellers bore a suspicious resemblance to Chuck Woodcock. What on earth was he doing here?

Trish caught my eye from the end of the table. 'I knew you wouldn't mind, Cin, if I put him on the list. Now that you're hitched and out of the running, I thought I might be in with a chance of scoring myself.'

I tried to shut out the memory of my encounter on Mulholland Drive as the object of her desires leaned back in his chair and absent-mindedly began to scratch his balls.

'Do you think it's true that the thickness of a man's fingers is related to the size of his dick?' she asked, gazing longingly at his crotch.

Rapidly downing another glass of wine, I glanced sideways and caught Harley furtively checking out his hands. 'In the case of our friend over there,' I murmured, nodding towards the would-be rapist who thought it was cool to attend his victim's wedding. 'I'd guess it was directly related to the thickness between his ears.'

Halfway through the dessert, a peculiar confection of bilberries and pale blue meringue, I reached for my glass of wine and found that it had mysteriously changed colour from white to red. There wasn't a waiter nearby, so who had refilled it? Uneasily, I swallowed a large mouthful and replaced the glass on the table, watching it carefully out of the corner of my eye. The dark red liquid swirled in the glass and the level began to rise. Mephisto! Seized with panic, I stood up and stared round the room. Where was he hiding? What did he want with me now?

A few people looked at me oddly. 'Excuse me,' I muttered, heading towards the door. I didn't want Mephisto materialising in here. What if he suddenly turned me back into Harriet? How would all these people react if Harley's beautiful young bride crumbled before their eyes into a withered old woman?

In the hotel foyer, I collided with a waiter carrying a bottle of whisky on a tray.

'Put it on my bill,' I gasped, snatching the bottle. I badly needed a real drink.

Plunging through the door into the ladies toilet, I locked myself into a cubicle and struggled with the acres of frothy material which made up my dress, anxiously searching my body for signs of premature ageing. So far, it seemed to be intact. But I was afraid. With trembling hands I unscrewed the lid of the bottle. I hadn't tasted whisky since . . .

'How thoughtful of you to bring me a drink, Harriet.' I looked up with a guilty start to see Mephisto perched on the top of the cubicle partition.

'Go away,' I hissed. 'Leave me alone!'

'Did you doubt me, Harriet? Did you think I'd forgotten about you?' He reached for the bottle, brushing his hand against my bare shoulder. 'I expect you're looking forward to using that lovely body for its proper purpose tonight. Harley's a lucky man.'

Flinching at his touch, I tugged my dress back into position. 'What do you want?' I asked angrily.

'Just checking up on your progress. You're doing very nicely, Harriet – though you had me worried for a moment with all that business in the church. The holy estate of matrimony indeed!' With a shudder of distaste, he tipped the bottle to his lips and drank deeply. 'I'm afraid I wasn't there to witness whatever tacky deal you were making with the opposition – you could hardly expect me to follow you into *that* place.'

He wiped the neck of the bottle and handed it back to me. I gulped at it thirstily.

'But, on the whole, I'm rather proud of you,' he continued. 'You've adapted to the Hollywood ethos as if you were born to it. I didn't expect to get results quite so quickly.'

'What do you mean?' I asked, watching the level of the whisky rise back to the top of the bottle.

'Well, you haven't exactly wasted any time grabbing your share of the pile, have you?' He tilted his head to one side and fixed me with a questioning look. 'Trading off your newly acquired physical assets in exchange for money, power, influence and social standing?'

'But I . . .'

'I knew you wouldn't be able to resist it,' he added

smugly. 'You're turning out to be just as corrupt as the rest of them. It won't be long before I have all the evidence I need.'

'But it's not like that,' I protested. 'I'm not interested in Harley's money.'

'Oh, really?' He raised an eyebrow. 'So you'd still have married him if he was poor?'

'Of course I would,' I said defensively. 'I'm in love with him.'

'*In love?*' He laughed so hard that he lost his balance and disappeared into the next cubicle. 'Love?' he repeated in an incredulous tone, reappearing through the gap at the foot of the partition. 'I'm disappointed in you, Harriet. I didn't think you'd fall for that one.'

'What's wrong with love? Everyone else seems pleased enough with it – why shouldn't I get a chance?'

'Love, my dear Harriet, is an illusion created by mankind to compensate for their insecurity. Everyone wants to feel important – it's a cheap way to achieve power over someone else. You'll find out soon enough. What's happened to all your ambition, Harriet? I can't believe that you're going to throw away the chance of real power – the chance to get your own back on a world you claim to hate so much – for a pathetic substitute like that.'

'Well that's what I want to do, so why don't you piss off and leave me alone?' I said angrily. 'All I want is to be happy.' I took another swig of whisky. Why shouldn't I get a chance to experience things – to find out what they were like for myself? Why was I always being told what to do by other people?

'So you think you've got what you wanted, do you?' He hoisted himself back into position above me. 'Well, we'll see what happens. I hope you're not going to be disappointed.'

'You'll get your side of the bargain paid off when I die,' I muttered. 'Why can't you just go away until then?'

He reached down with a sinuous movement and stroked the back of my neck. 'You look so beautiful when you're angry,' he murmured. 'Are you sure you can wait until tonight?'

'Stop it,' I said mechanically, struggling to ignore the fact that my frustrated body was responding to his caress. I lifted my hand to push him away, but there was nothing there. He was becoming transparent – dissolving.

'Just remember that I'll be watching you. You'll realise soon enough what a mistake you've made. You'll be begging me to come back and rescue you, just wait and see . . .' His voice faded gradually away.

I looked down at the brimming whisky bottle in my hand. I took a few large mouthfuls and waited a moment, but this time there was no sign of replenishment. Mephisto had gone, taking his magical powers with him.

I was about to leave the cubicle when the main door creaked open to admit sounds of distant merriment. High heels clattered across the tiled floor.

'Jesus, I look like the Queen of friggin' Sheba in this lot!' It was Trish, her nasal drawl echoing through the thin walls of the partition. Here, help me undo some buttons, Sharleen. I'll need to show some tit if I want to get anywhere with Chuck Woodcock.'

I shrank back into my cubicle and perched on the toilet seat. I wasn't in the mood for a meeting with Trish right now.

'It ain't right, the way I'm being treated,' she continued, a whining tone creeping into her voice. 'Her best friend for three years and I wasn't even allowed to choose my own dress.'

'It sure as hell don't seem right to me,' agreed Sharleen. 'But she always was a stuck-up little bitch.'

'Did you see her out there?' demanded Trish indignantly. 'Kissing ass with all those high falutin' new friends of hers. I bet she thinks she's way too good for us now.'

'Just imagine how much money she must have,' said Sharleen thoughtfully. 'Now she's got his ring on her finger. This bash must have set them back a bundle.'

'With the kind of cash he has,' muttered Trish, 'you'd think they could afford to be less friggin' stingy with the liquor. Have you tasted that piss water they're trying to pass off as white wine?'

'You mean the *waite waine?*' giggled Sharleen in imitation of Eleanor. 'I don't know what it's like on your table,' she added, 'but we've had to bribe the waiter to get our hands on the hard stuff.'

'Better grab what we can while the going's good,' said Trish. 'The tight-fisted bitch never even gave me a Christmas present – I don't think she'll be waiting around to give us any free handouts.'

'What I don't understand,' said Sharleen in a low

voice, 'is what a guy like him sees in her. I mean, she might as well have had liposuction to the brain for all she's got between her ears. I wonder what she had to do to snag him?'

'It's what's between her legs that interests him, if you ask me,' giggled Trish drunkenly. 'She used to put on this virgin act all the time, but I wouldn't be surprised if she'd had half the schlongs in the neighbourhood up there. She's probably got some kind of trick pussy that does stunts like a performing seal.'

The partition shook and there was a rattle of bolts. 'Jeepers, I'm busting for a pee,' continued her voice from the cubicle next to mine. There was a rustling noise followed by a sigh and the hiss of water against porcelain.

I stood up angrily, determined to make my escape before they came out. If that was what they thought of me, I would have no compunctions in turning my back on them to start a new life. Harley's friends wouldn't treat me like this. I gathered up the folds of my dress and emerged cautiously into the room.

'Well, it's too late now, isn't it? I tried to warn him what a mistake he was making, but he wouldn't listen . . .' It was Eleanor's voice. I shot back into the cubicle as the main door swung open again.

'I can't believe the blind stupidity of the man,' she exclaimed, her heels clicking across the floor towards the washbasins. I heard the snap of a powder compact opening. 'Were you listening to those vows in the church, Sylvie? *For richer, for poorer* – I can guess which one *she* had her mind fixed on. She's going to bleed him dry, and he'll have no one but himself to blame.'

'*Forsaking all others . . .*' murmured Sylvie, 'Warren's never let that one cramp his style.'

'We're going to have to keep a close eye on her,' said Eleanor firmly. 'She's bound to slip up sooner or later – let everyone see what kind of cheap little bimbo she really is. Let's just hope he's been sensible enough to make her sign some kind of prenuptial, or the little bitch will clean him out when it comes to the divorce.'

'Did you see the way she was acting out there?' asked Sylvie in a shocked whisper. 'Putting on airs and talking to people from our set as if she was some kind of equal – a little nobody like her!'

'Did you see that dreadful sister of hers?' said Eleanor with a giggle. 'And as for that *unspeakable* bridesmaid . . .'

There was an indignant rustling in the next cubicle.

'. . . I mean, she might as well paint the word "whore" across her forehead . . .'

'Who the fuck are you calling a whore?' The partition shuddered as Trish threw open the door and steamed into battle. 'You stuck-up old bat!' There were sounds of undignified scuffling.

'Take your hands off me this instant!' shrieked Eleanor. 'Sylvie, help me!'

'You're just jealous because you've got a face like a douche bag,' hissed Trish.

'Give the old bitch what she deserves,' growled Sharleen.

'Oh my God,' bleated Sylvie.

'Let me go!' whimpered Eleanor.

The door creaked open again and there was a sudden embarrassed silence.

'They're looking for Cindy to cut the cake.' Babs' querulous voice echoed through the room. 'Has anyone seen her?' There was a another silence.

'Who the fuck are you?' demanded Sharleen.

'Just her only living blood-relative, I'll have you know,' retorted Babs in a shocked tone. 'Which gives me more right to be here than any of you.' Her voice quavered, then dissolved into an unexpected wail of anguish. 'My little sister! After all I did for her – she doesn't want to know me now that she's moved up in the world!'

Everyone began speaking at once, fumbling for niceties. *. . . such a beautiful service . . . not so much losing a sister as gaining a whole new family. . . . always a difficult time.*

'It was them vows that did it,' snuffled Babs. '*Forsaking all others* . . . I knew I'd lost her then.'

'In sickness and in health . . .' murmured Sylvie irrelevantly.

'For richer for poorer . . .' added Sharleen, in a sing-song voice.

'Until death do us part,' said Eleanor grimly.

'Ashes to ashes, dust to dust,' chanted Trish. 'Oops, sorry,' she added with a squeal of laughter. 'Wrong service!'

I huddled miserably in my cubicle, willing them to go away. A tear trickled down my cheek. Much as I had despised them, these people were my only friends. I hadn't ever realised quite how much they hated me. I began to think guiltily of my past life – of Sally and Andrew, who had been kind to me when I had nothing to offer in return. There was little I could do to thank them now.

All I had left now was Harley.

'Hey, look under there!' My reflections were interrupted by an excited screech from Trish. 'It's her dress! She's been hiding in there all this time! She must have been . . .' Trish's voice tailed away as she grappled with the logical conclusion of this train of thought. Her voice became a horrified whisper. 'Do you think she heard us, Sharleen?'

'Serve her right for eavesdropping if she did,' interjected Sylvie in an indignant tone.

'Cin? Are you in there?' called Trish.

I closed my eyes and prayed for some kindly god or devil to wipe them all out with a thunderbolt.

'Hang on a minute,' she squawked. 'I'll climb up and look over the top!'

I had to move fast. Finding that I still had the bottle of whisky in my hand, I lifted the lid of the cistern and jammed it inside. Then I arranged myself in what seemed an appropriate position for someone who had fainted. Peeping through half-closed eyes, I saw Trish's face loom eagerly over the top of the partition.

'Ooh, jeepers, look at this, Sharl! She's stone cold passed out!' There was a pause. 'Do you think she's dead?'

After another pause, containing much scuffling and grunting, another face stared down at me. 'Nah,' said Sharleen eventually. 'I can see her breathing.'

'I know what!' squealed Trish. 'I'll climb over and get her out!'

I continued to feign unconsciousness as they manhandled me out of the cubicle and carried me towards the reception room. At the door, I underwent a sudden recovery, leaping from their clutches and rushing across the room towards Harley. It seemed that he was the only person left who cared for me.

'Cindy, sweetheart! Where have you been? Are you all right?' There was tenderness in his voice.

'Look after me, Harley,' I whispered.

'Of course I'll look after you, darling,' he murmured in a possessive tone. 'You're all mine now.'

Everyone was more friendly towards me after this incident, as if motivated by some collective awareness that the mark had been overstepped. I played out my part in the charade with a feeling of numb detachment, sheltering beneath a protective layer of alcohol.

'Your friends are certainly boisterous,' said Harley, as we watched Marty leading a drunken conga procession through the foyer. He was wearing a red velvet waistcoat stolen from one of Heinrich's waiters and waved a frying spatula in each hand. Trish lurched unsteadily behind. She had been busy with the buttons on her dress and her improvised décolletage stopped just a few millimetres short of indecent exposure. Chuck Woodcock followed, his hips thrusting rhythmically back and forth.

I shuddered, once again remembering the incident on Mulholland Drive. Tonight would be different to that, I told myself. Tonight I would at last find out what love was really about. It would be the turning point in my new life – my release from all those years of celibacy and loneliness.

I had waited impatiently for this moment since the day I agreed to marry Harley, but as the door of the bridal suite closed behind us and we faced each other shyly across a wide expanse of pale blue bed linen, I felt a surge of panic. I couldn't think of anything to say, and I didn't know what to do next. I felt self-conscious, vulnerable, unprepared.

Harley cleared his throat. 'Would you, um, like to use the bathroom first?'

Nodding gratefully, I fled from his presence. Locking the door behind me, I struggled out of my clothes and inspected myself in the mirror, anxious for reassurance that Cindy's body was still there. When I was satisfied that no extra wrinkles had appeared, I wrapped myself modestly in a bathrobe, cleaned my teeth twice, and crept nervously back to the bedroom. I wasn't sure what to expect.

Harley was standing by the window, still fully dressed. He approached me with a smile, but as I prepared myself to fall into his arms he stepped to one side and disappeared through the door, muttering something about the bathroom.

I realised with dismay that he was nervous as well. This wasn't happening the way I had imagined it. In my dreams everything took place in a romantic whirl, without awkward pauses for changing the scenery.

The corner of the bedcover was turned down to reveal an embroidered *Lapinique* logo. Was the man so obsessed with his status that he had brought his own sheets with him? Feeling mildly irritated, I shed the bathrobe and climbed into bed, rumpling the covers so that the logo was hidden. Distant gargling sounds came from the bathroom.

Eventually Harley returned, clad in nothing but a pair of pale blue underpants. It was a shock to see him undressed like this – he looked smaller, less substantial than the Harley who had left the room a few moments before. Conscious of my own nakedness, I turned my head away and hugged the bedclothes to my body.

When I found the courage to look up again, he was standing beside me. I stared in fascination at the bulge in his underpants, realising that what I had taken for another *Lapinique* logo was in fact a patch of dampness. With an air of studied casualness, he hooked his thumbs into the elastic waist and pushed gently downwards.

A large pink penis bobbed into view, inches from the end of my nose. I closed my eyes in a hot rush of embarrassment, then quickly opened them again to get a better look. Too late – with a swift movement he was between the sheets, his hands roaming eagerly over my body.

'Cindy darling . . .' he moaned in a strangled voice. 'At last . . . you're all mine . . .'

This was it. I wrapped my arms around his neck and braced myself for entry, wondering if it was going to hurt. He appeared to be quite well endowed, and I had no idea whether or not there was any truth in Trish's speculations about the capabilities of my private parts.

'Does this feel nice, darling?' There was a tickly feeling between my legs.

'Mmm . . .' I replied, impatient for him to get on with it. Cindy's body – my body – felt hornier than a herd of antelopes, and the rest of my being was crying out for emotional satisfaction. The tickling carried on for some time, and I grew increasingly frustrated. When was he going to cut to the chase?

I racked my brains to remember details of the sex scenes in novels I had read. How was I supposed to tell him I was ready? Should I cry out? *Take me, Harley!* It seemed rather melodramatic. Or should I be more down-to-earth? *Fuck me, Harley, for Christ's sake!* I didn't want to risk offending him.

Eventually I just grabbed hold of him and pulled him towards me. Everything seemed to fall into place of its own accord and I forgot all about Harley as I wallowed in the emotional triumph of becoming a real woman at last – a sexually active human being. Here I was, after all those lonely years, *actually doing it.*

After some time I glanced up at Harley and realised that he had forgotten all about me as well. He was busily grinding away with his teeth clenched and his eyes tightly shut. Little beads of sweat had appeared on his forehead. It was a pleasant enough sensation – in, out, in, out – but after a while I began to feel bored.

I began to count the beads on the chandelier, which were jiggling gently in time with the motion of the bed. Mephisto swam into my thoughts, his face a contemptuous sneer.

So you think you've got what you wanted . . . I hope you're not going to be disappointed . . .

Was that voice really in my imagination? An echoing laugh rang in my ears, getting louder and louder. The chandelier began to rattle more violently. *Leave me alone,* I begged silently. *Go away!*

'I'm coming!' gasped Harley.

He made a final thrust and let out a long moan, then collapsed in a trembling heap beside me.

I waited to see what came next, but nothing happened. After a few moments I sat up and stared at him. He was asleep.

CHAPTER 12

In the weeks leading up to the wedding I had often found myself thinking of Guildford. When would I get the chance to go back there and find out what had really happened in Harriet's flat that night? Whenever Harley had mentioned the subject of a honeymoon, I dropped hints that I'd always wanted to visit Europe, particularly the south of England.

A few days before the wedding, however, Harley had announced that we were going to Barbados.

'Trust me – you'll enjoy this much better,' he said. 'The climate in England's always lousy at this time of year.'

It was hardly gracious to complain about being taken on a Caribbean holiday, so I made an effort not to show my disappointment. There was bound to be another opportunity before long. I looked forward to what I imagined would be a relaxing time spent basking on sun-soaked beaches, swimming in warm seas, and discovering the local culture.

These innocent expectations, however, were swiftly demolished by Harley on the first day.

'Good heavens, I hope you're not planning to go out in *that*!' he exclaimed, viewing my newly purchased bikini with an expression of horror.

'I, er, thought it would be the best thing for suntanning,' I faltered, wondering if I had unknowingly transgressed some fashion code.

'*Suntanning?*' He stared at me with disbelief. 'Have you any idea what damage the sun can do to your skin?'

'Or swimming?' I suggested hopefully.

'I wouldn't risk it if I were you, Cindy,' he said, shaking his head slowly. 'The ocean is out of the question of course – you've no idea what might be in it. As for the hotel pool, well, maybe I could have a word with the manager. Find out what chemicals they use. With a double application of *Total Skin Control Factor 12* you might be able to get away with a short dip.' He pushed his fingers through his hair and frowned. 'I don't know about the bikini, though.'

'What's wrong with it?'

He sighed. 'I hate the idea of other men looking at your beautiful body. Haven't you got something that covers you up a bit more?'

Feeling slightly dazed, I put on a dress. 'Let's go for a walk, then,' I suggested, wondering what hidden dangers he might find in this activity. 'We can stay in the shade.'

'That's a good idea,' said Harley, brightening. 'We can explore the hotel grounds.'

I didn't see much of Barbados beyond the hotel and its grounds for the whole fortnight. What was the point in coming so far, I wondered, to stay in a hotel all the time? We could have been anywhere. Harley seemed happy to lounge in a shady spot near the swimming pool, sipping wheatgrass juice and checking the glossy women's magazines for *Lapinique* advertisements. He managed to find some objection to every outing I suggested.

'I don't know why you want to expose yourself to such risks,' he said, waving the hotel guide at me. 'You have everything you need right here. That's what we're paying for. We've got a security fence all round us to keep out the undesirables and they spray the grounds at night to protect us from insects and disease. You get all the advantages of being abroad without any of the dangers.'

'What about, er, seeing a bit of the place?' I asked tentatively. 'Trying the local food and all that?'

'I can't see that you're going to enjoy it any more with a dose of food poisoning,' he said with a note of impatience in his voice. 'There's food from a dozen different countries in the restaurant here and they even have a special "Bajan Evening" when they bring in the natives to dance for you. What more could you want?'

I wanted a stiff drink. I had hoped that the health regime might relax a little for the honeymoon, but it seemed that alcohol consumption was still high on the list of dangerous activities.

'You can't be too careful about your health when you're away from home,' said Harley. 'This trip has messed up my colonic irrigation schedule, so I'm monitoring my toxin intake very carefully. I think you better do the same.'

I resorted to purchasing miniature bottles of vodka from the hotel shop and fortifying my orange juice from my handbag when he wasn't looking. Once we get to know each other better, I told myself, I'll be able to stand up to him. He doesn't really mean any harm – he's only thinking of my own good.

How dare he tell me what to do? said an angry voice inside me, but I pretended not to hear.

The only activity which didn't feature on the danger list was sex. Armed with a mental list of positions, erotic pressure points and foreplay techniques to rival the Kama Sutra, he dragged me up to the hotel room two or three times a day. In the evenings he was ready to retire as soon as dinner was over, viewing my requests to join in the hotel nightlife with suspicion.

'There's lots of time for that sort of thing when we get home,' he would say. 'Surely you're not bored with me already?'

I couldn't complain. It was pleasant enough to be catching up on a lifetime of enforced sexual abstinence. But it wasn't quite how I had imagined it would be: I felt like an audience to a grand performance each time – an adjudicator to a display of physical prowess. He went at it with the determination of an athlete in training, oblivious to any response from myself that might disturb his concentration.

'Was I all right?' he would ask afterwards. 'You did like it, didn't you? Was it better than last time?'

Was he keeping a scorecard? I was beginning to feel like a piece of overused gym equipment.

We ventured outside the hotel only once during

our stay. Determined to see something of Barbados, I dragged Harley on a chauffeur-driven tour of the island and persuaded him to eat in a local fish restaurant recommended by the hotel. The next morning he came out in a rash. He took to his bed complaining of dizziness and stayed there for three days, repeatedly bemoaning the folly of having ignored his own better judgement. I was forced to sit and listen. He wouldn't hear of me going out alone – not even to sit by the pool.

I told myself that some people weren't at their best on holiday. Things would be easier once we got home. I would have plenty of time to myself then, with Harley busy at his work. I should make the most of this chance for us to be together – make an effort to talk to him and get to know him better.

Each time I tried to make conversation, however, the subject would somehow stray back to health and beauty issues. After running through his diet and exercise programme with me for the third time, he seemed to run out of things to talk about.

I decided it was time to take the initiative. 'What kind of books do you like reading, Harley?' I asked. 'I know you like Dickens, but what do you think of Austen and Trollope? Or do you prefer to stick with the Americans? What do you think of *Huckleberry Finn*?'

I quickly discovered that the leather-bound volumes in his 'library' were there purely for show. His ignorance of literature astounded me. How could anyone get through life without having read any Shakespeare, or without ever realising that George Eliot wasn't a man?

How could I go to bed with someone who had never even heard of *The Catcher in the Rye*?

Never mind, I thought. I'll educate him.

I launched into a short history of English and American literature, briefly describing the plots of some of the classic texts and promising to get him copies to read. He listened patiently for a few minutes before interrupting.

'Really, Cindy,' he said, 'you don't need to do this.'

'What do you mean?' I asked indignantly, forgetting my resolve not to argue on our honeymoon. 'There are some basic things which everyone should know about, and I'm going to tell you whether you like it or not! There's no excuse for ignorance!'

'But Cindy, I never suggested that you were ignorant.'

What on earth was he on about?

'I know the kind of background you have – it's not your fault if you never had a good education. But you don't need to impress me with all this pretend intellectual nonsense. I love you just the way you are, Cindy.'

'But I'm not like that!' I shrieked despairingly. 'You haven't been listening to me! I'm an educated woman! I'm telling you about things that matter – things I care about!'

'There, there, no need to get upset.' He gave me a patronising smile. 'It's sweet of you to make an effort, darling, but you haven't been listening to me either. I'm telling you that it doesn't make any difference. Why would a pretty little thing like you want to trouble her head with all that nonsense anyway? Why don't you just come over here and give me a kiss?'

I stared at him with disbelief. How could I have any hope for the future if he disregarded my words like that?

'Piss off,' I muttered.

'What was that?' He gave me a reproachful look. 'You don't need to sulk, you know. I'm not mad at you.'

How dare he treat me like this? The inner voice became more persistent.

'Besides,' he added, 'I can't see what you're getting all upset about. We were only talking about books, weren't we? Made-up stories. What's the point in arguing about them?'

Had he no imagination at all?

Later that evening, when I begrudgingly forgave him so that we wouldn't miss out on that day's heats in the Sexual Olympics, I discovered that he *did* have an imagination. It seemed, however, to be confined exclusively to one subject area: my relationships with other men.

'Tell me,' he said, after grunting his way to a climax. 'Tell me about the others.'

'What others?' I prevaricated, thinking of Tess of the D'Urbervilles and her ill-advised confession to Angel Clare.

'You know perfectly well what I mean,' he said sternly. 'The men before me.'

What could I tell him? Should I invent a list of Cindy's conquests, or should I tell him about the back of Barry Thompson's van? I would have been happy to tell the truth if I knew what it was.

'But I love you, Harley,' I said feebly. 'Why should anyone in the past matter?'

'Is that what you said to Chuck Woodcock?'

'Who?' My heart skipped a beat. How did he know about him? 'But he's just the aerobics instructor at the gym.'

'Oh yeah?' said Harley, his voice taking on an ugly tone. 'Do you think I'm stupid or something? Do you think I don't know what goes on at those places?'

'He's nothing to do with me,' I said unhappily. 'He's one of Trish's friends.' What had the stupid bitch been saying?

'That's not what I heard. Someone told me at the reception that he was an old flame of yours!' Harley faced me with bulging eyes, his voice becoming shrill. 'I'd like to know what he was doing there – at *our* wedding! And as for you disappearing in the middle of the reception like that – it's all beginning to make sense now – I suppose you were with *him*! Making me look a complete jerk while you sneaked off for a quickie for old times sake!'

'It's not true.' Tears welled into my eyes at the unfairness of these accusations. 'Why don't you believe me?'

He shook me by the shoulders. 'Look, Cindy, I wasn't born yesterday. A girl as attractive as you – there must have been others. I need to know. Tell me the truth. How many were there?'

'I, er . . .'

'My God! Don't tell me there were too many to count!'

'No, it wasn't . . .'

'Stop! Don't say anything!' He threw the sheets to one side and sprang from the bed. 'I can't stand it! The thought of all those other men!'

'But . . .'

'Don't tell me – I don't want to hear!' He stalked across the room to the window. 'How can you torment me like this?' he added in a low voice.

I buried my face in the bedclothes and fought back angry tears. Why had everything gone so horribly wrong?

Harley said nothing. A moment later there was a rattling noise and a rush of cool air. The door of the balcony slammed shut.

I sat up in bed. 'Harley?'

There was no reply. Climbing out of bed, I tiptoed across to the window. Harley stood on the balcony, clad only in his pale blue dressing gown. He gripped the rail with trembling hands and stared out into the tropical darkness.

I opened the door. 'Harley?' He turned towards me with a stricken expression.

'Don't be an idiot,' I said softly. 'You're imagining things that never happened. Come to bed.'

'An idiot?' he repeated, backing away from my outstretched hand. His voice was cold. 'You put me through all this, and then you call me an idiot?' He pushed his hand through his hair and shook his head. 'I don't know what to think, Cindy. I really don't.'

'Oh come on,' I said, losing my patience. 'There's no need to sulk.'

'I never sulk,' he replied, folding his arms and turning away.

I went back into the room and waited, but the shadowy figure remained motionless on the balcony. Anger and resentment began to build up inside me. How dare he accuse me of sleeping with a monster like Chuck Woodcock? He was treating me like a whore. So much for his stupid daydreams about *Pretty Woman*. How would he have coped if I had really been a prostitute, like the character in the film? And how might that story have continued in real life? I pictured an ageing Julia Roberts squabbling with Richard Gere as she put the children to bed. He would turn round, halfway through cleaning his teeth, and fling it all back in her face – *How can you criticise me after all that you've done? If it wasn't for me, you'd still be on the streets . . .*

I counted slowly to a hundred, then locked the balcony door and switched out the light.

'Well, fuck you too,' I said to the empty room. An urgent tapping noise began at the window.

'Let me in,' said a muffled voice. 'Cindy, stop fooling around.'

I got back into bed and buried my head under the pillow so that I couldn't hear. Exhausted after a week of satisfying Harley's sexual urges, I quickly fell into a deep sleep.

The following morning he was penitent. 'I don't know what came over me,' he said, emerging stiffly from the damp wicker chair in which he had spent the night. 'I'm sorry, Cindy. I feel like such an asshole.'

His teeth were chattering, and his arms and legs were

covered with little red bumps. 'I think I've been bitten,' he said anxiously, rummaging through the multitude of *Lapinique* bottles and jars on the dressing table. 'Have we got any antiseptic cream?'

Later that day I came into the hotel room to find him sobbing on the couch with a pillow clutched to his stomach.

'Harley?' I asked anxiously. 'What's wrong?' It looked as if he was either seriously ill or going off the rails.

He let out an anguished howl, then sat up and gave me a smile.

'What? Did you say something?'

I stared at him speechlessly, fearing for his sanity.

'Oh sorry, these are just my bioenergetics exercises,' he explained sheepishly. 'I'm tapping into my childhood emotions to release the residual rage in my body. If you don't express it, or let it out somehow, it gets stored as tension.'

His eyes twinkled. 'It's not the only way to release tension, of course,' he added, glancing meaningfully towards the bed. 'Want to?'

In the circumstances, I felt obliged to perform, but something had changed. Sex was no longer an uncomplicated physical activity; it now carried moral overtones of punishment and possession. With every thrust, I heard his litany of accusations repeating themselves in my head. He couldn't bear to think that other men had enjoyed my favours, but how was he any different? I had offered him my body and he had seized it as a trophy – the proof of his manhood – making no attempt to see beyond Cindy's beauty to the person inside. I felt betrayed, defiled by his attentions. I hadn't expected love to be like this.

The next day I had an unexpected reprieve in the middle of our early-morning session.

'Oh my God, there's blood on the sheets!' exclaimed Harley, leaping from the bed as if he had been bitten. He looked down at his reddened genitals and fled to the bathroom with an expression of horror.

Sounds of running water and furious scrubbing came through the door. 'Don't worry, it's only my period,' I called after him. Eventually he reappeared with a towel round his waist.

'You must be so disappointed, darling,' he said, perching on the edge of the bed and offering me a box of tissues. 'I certainly am.'

'I think I can live with it,' I replied with a smile, trying to hide my relief at the thought of having my body to myself for a whole week.

'Never mind,' he continued. 'Maybe we'll have better luck next month.'

What did he mean, better luck?

'And there's one consolation,' he added, giving me an odd little smile. 'At least this way we'll be sure. I'll know it's mine.' He patted my stomach. 'I hope the first one is a boy, don't you?'

I sat up in bed and stared at him. 'But Harley,' I whispered. 'We haven't even discussed . . . I mean . . . aren't we going to wait a while before we . . . before we start a family?'

'What is there to wait for?'

I had a sudden vision of a series of miniature Harleys

dressed identically in pale blue, the heirs to the *Lapinique* empire. I wasn't ready for the responsibility of a family – I had my own life to sort out first.

'I . . .'

'Don't worry,' he said with a grin. 'You'll make a great mom.'

I decided not to mention the contraceptive pills I had obtained before the wedding. He was bound to get suspicious before long, but I would deal with that problem when it arose. Meanwhile, I would have to be especially careful to remember to take one every day. I didn't want there to be any accidents.

By the time the honeymoon ended, I was exhausted. I had never realised what a strain the constant company of another human being could be. Harley rarely let me out of his sight, jealously watching my every move – particularly if there were other men around. I felt like a prisoner.

I told myself that things would improve. It was still early days. Once we had got used to living together – once I had established myself in Harley's world – he would come to understand me better and respect me as an individual. I had to make an effort.

José collected us from the airport and drove us by an unfamiliar route towards Beverly Hills. I didn't recognise where we were until we turned on to Sunset Boulevard.

'Look,' whispered Harley, nudging me and pointing upwards.

I was startled to see my own face towering above

us on a huge billboard. The photographer had caught me with my lips slightly parted and a faraway look in my eyes. *Lapinique,* said the caption. *Be a face in the crowd.*

'You look so beautiful,' murmured Harley. 'I'm proud of you, Cindy.'

What had I been thinking of when the picture was taken, I wondered? Was I remembering the other woman I once was – remembering the hopes and dreams of poor, dowdy Harriet? I had come a long way, I told myself with a feeling of satisfaction. What would the people in Guildford think if they could see me now?

The poster wasn't just on Sunset, but on billboards all over the city. Smaller versions appeared on the prime advertising pages of the fashionable women's magazines and the image was prominently displayed at the *Lapinique* counters of all the big stores.

Harley took me to a special promotion at Neiman Marcus, where I was surprised to find myself surrounded by well-dressed, middle-aged women who wanted me to autograph their bottles of *Lapinique.*

'Don't worry,' said Harley, handing me a marker pen. 'It's standard practice. Just scribble off a few to keep them happy and I'll call security. Make sure they're on standby for when we want to leave.'

It gave me a thrill to be at the centre of attention like this – something Harriet had never experienced. I began to look forward to meeting all those people from Crystal Kelly's party again – the ones who had been rude to me, or treated me as if I was stupid. I would show them how wrong they had been.

I would give parties of my own – select gatherings of the best people – and watch them scrabbling for invites. Now that I was someone who counted, I would seek out the more interesting people – the ones *I* wanted to get to know. There had to be intelligent life somewhere in this town.

After a few social outings, however, it began to dawn on me that this was not necessarily the case. Everyone was friendly enough to me now that I was both Mrs Harley Brightman and the Face of *Lapinique*, but no one seemed to want to have a proper conversation. They weren't being rude – they were simply incapable of addressing themselves to anything that wasn't directly connected with their own self-advancement. I was shocked by the triviality of their talk and their obsession with petty gossip. It seemed that Mephisto had found me the one place on the planet whose inhabitants didn't have a fully functioning brain cell to share between them.

Despite Eleanor's frequent briefings, I didn't understand the value system which operated in this society. Why was it that people with such apparent power were ruled by the whims of gossip columnists? Why were men judged only by their achievements, while women were condemned for their age, their physical shape and the clothes they wore? Why was everyone so obsessed with labels – not only for clothes but also for people? Why, when men were expected to call you a person rather than labelling you by gender, was it still OK for them to put their hand up your skirt?

I was plagued by the attentions of these men – the

Warrens and the Arnies – whose talk was peppered with a form of crude innuendo which seemed to pass in these circles for sparkling wit. It seemed that I was considered fair game – perhaps even more so now that I was married to Harley. Before, I had been a nobody. Now, I was a challenge. I was pestered with repeated propositions to meet them for lunch, for dinner, or sometimes even in the parking lot outside.

Harley didn't seem to notice these blatant assaults on my integrity – he was far too busy imagining infidelities which didn't exist. If I was unwise enough to talk for more than a few moments with one of the more harmless men at a social gathering, he immediately grew restless and demanded to take me home.

'I didn't like the way you were paying so much attention to that guy,' he would say afterwards, facing me with a stern expression.

'But I was only being friendly. He was asking me if we enjoyed Barbados.'

'It isn't right to tell people all the details of our personal lives. You've got a lot to learn yet, Cindy. A careless word could seriously damage your reputation.'

He began to make excuses to stay at home. 'These parties can be such a bore,' he would say. 'Now that we've got each other, Cindy, why do we need to go out all the time?'

On the increasingly rare occasions when we did go somewhere, he would yawn and start checking his watch at nine o'clock in the evening.

'We don't want to overstay our welcome,' he would say, dragging me from a conversation in mid-sentence and leading me to the car. 'Besides, you need your beauty sleep. You can't go out living it up every night and expect to stay in condition.'

Harley's idea of living it up was to quaff a glass of dry white wine and sprinkle a little lime juice on his grilled chicken breast. He seemed to spend half his life worrying about what he put into his body, and the other half trying to get it out again.

'You really should try colonic irrigation, Cindy,' he would urge me. 'It's the most painless and efficient way to keep your body pure and free of toxins.'

My problem was not being able to get my hands on enough toxins. I wasn't just suffering from alcohol deprivation – I was also hungry all the time. I dreamed of the days when I could binge on a Marty's special – the one where you got a second portion free if you could finish the first – without any guilt. The last thing I needed was to further dilute the low-cal, low-fat, low-everything diet that Harley imposed on me by sticking a hosepipe up my butt and flushing it all away.

Lonely and bored, I spent long hours roaming through the over-decorated and lifeless rooms of the mansion while Harley was out having his biorhythms massaged or his nostrils waxed. I had to be very careful if I wandered outside as the security system was so sensitive the alarms could go off if a dog coughed in the neighbour's garden.

Gazing from the window of the conservatory where we had breakfast each day, I watched José's progress with his topiary work. After a week or two, the tops of the tall, sausage shaped bushes began to take on unusual contours – but I didn't get the joke until he wheeled a pair of sphere-shaped bay trees out of the greenhouse and positioned them symmetrically at the base of one of the taller bushes.

'Are you all right, Cindy?' asked Harley anxiously as I choked with silent laughter over my bran flakes and chopped prunes. 'Do you want me to perform the Heimlich manoeuvre?'

Eventually, I plucked up the courage to tell him how bored I was.

He stared at me with an expression of bewilderment. 'Bored?' he echoed, scratching his head. 'But how could you . . .' Then he broke into a smile. 'I know what the problem is, my sweetheart – your biological clock is ticking away . . .'

Biological clock? What did he think I was – a fucking time bomb?

'We'll just have to wait for a little while until we've got the TV commercial out of the way, but, once that's over, you can start picking out things for the nursery.'

'Harley, what are you talking about?' I asked. 'What TV commercial?'

He sighed. 'I wish I hadn't agreed to it now, but it was such a good idea of David's. After you did so well at the photo shoot. He's thinking of filming it in Italy, you know – he found a wonderful location.'

Agreed to it? Was I to get no choice in any of this?

I bit my lip. I didn't want to start an argument yet – not when we had only been married such a short time. My patience was wearing thin, however. Sooner or later, one of us was going to have to admit that something was wrong.

On the surface, everything was perfect. I had all the material things a woman could want, together with a husband who was handsome, loving, and always eager for sex. Was I ungrateful in wanting something more? What *was* it that I wanted?

He kept telling me he loved me, but what did this mean?

'You don't understand me, Harley,' I said tearfully one night.

'Of course I understand you, darling,' he replied softly. 'Now stop crying – it's bad for your eyes. Do you have any idea what kind of damage it can do to your complexion?'

'But you hardly know me.'

'I know how beautiful you are. What more could I possibly need to know? I love you, Cindy.'

The word meant different things to each of us. To him it meant possession. To me, love was all about respect, intimacy and trust. Had I got it all wrong? Was that kind of love only possible in fiction? Had I been taken in by all the romantic stories and spent my life yearning for something which didn't exist?

My dream marriage was rapidly turning into a nightmare. I had thrown away my freedom and condemned myself to a lifetime of physical exploitation and boredom. I had made a terrible mistake, and this time I couldn't blame Mephisto. It was all my own fault. I would have to get out of this one all on my own.

CHAPTER 13

I came to the conclusion that I needed to assert my independence. Waiting until Harley went out for his weekly aromatherapy session, I put on a large floppy hat and a pair of dark glasses, then called a taxi and took a ride to Venice. It was the perfect day for a walk on the beach.

I wandered along the boardwalk, browsing at the stalls and mingling with body-builders, roller-bladers, New Age prophets and the other assorted freaks and weirdos who come out of the woodwork in any town whenever the sun shines. Feeling rather daring, I bought a packet of scented candles and a pair of earrings shaped like surf boards. I watched a chainsaw juggler, a fire-eater and a limbo dancer, then sat outside a beach café drinking a cold beer. It was a relief to be able to feel like an ordinary person again – to mingle anonymously in the crowd without being stared at all the time.

What did the future hold for me, I wondered? Would we travel to Italy to make this new *Lapinique* commercial, as Harley had hinted? Italy wasn't all that far from England. Would I get a chance to go there – to return to

Guildford and answer some of the questions that had haunted me since I woke up as Cindy?

Watching a young couple go past hand-in-hand, I felt a pang of loneliness. I envied them their uncomplicated enjoyment of each other and of their surroundings. Harley would never come with me to a place like this – he would find it beneath his dignity. If I wanted to savour the ordinary pleasures of life, it looked as if I would have to indulge in them on my own.

I felt a tug at my jacket and looked down to see a small child with smears of ice cream around his mouth.

'My mom says you're Cindy Brightman,' he said in a small, but confident voice. 'If you don't want us to tell everyone, you'd better give us your autograph.'

He held out a pen. Looking around the nearby tables I saw two women, one of them presumably his mother, grinning and waving at me.

Scribbling my name on a napkin, I handed it to him with a smile and placed a finger to my lips. 'Shhh,' I said, winking. 'We don't want everyone to know our secret, do we?'

He stood there, staring at the napkin with an open mouth.

'Bugger off,' I hissed in a low voice. 'Leave me alone now, for Christ's sake!'

'Gee, Mom!' he shouted suddenly. 'You were right! Look – it says Cindy Brightman on here!'

Everyone turned to stare at me.

'Hey,' drawled a woman at the next table, who had previously been flicking cigarette ash on my shoes. 'Would you sign my menu? I'd really appreciate it.'

An elderly man in Bermuda shorts approached me shyly. 'If you wouldn't mind,' he asked, spreading a pile of napkins across my table and thrusting a plastic pen into my hand. 'It would be such a lovely surprise for my grandchildren.'

'Hey, Wilbur, go get the camera from the car,' shouted someone. A crowd began to gather.

'If you wouldn't mind doing them separately,' said the man with the napkins, 'I'll tell you their names.'

'Here, let me have a lock of your hair,' gurgled a fat woman in a pink tracksuit, lunging at me with a pair of nail scissors.

'I'm sorry,' I muttered, standing up. 'I have to go.' I looked around in panic for a telephone.

'You can't go now,' screeched a woman behind me. 'I was next!'

'No you weren't,' said another. 'I saw her first!'

'Stuck-up bitch,' shouted a girl on roller blades. 'What makes you think you're so special, anyway?'

Someone tugged at my clothes and I heard a ripping sound. I turned and began to run.

'Hey, I've got some of her slip!' said an excited voice behind me.

'I want some too!' said another.

I paused and slipped off my shoes, then began to run across the sand as fast as I could, heading for the main street. As my pursuers began to catch up with me, I turned and hurled my footwear at them. I glanced back when I reached the road and saw the crowd fighting over them like a pack of hungry wolves.

'I saw them first!'

'Let go, this one's mine!'

'Are you all right, ma'am?' I looked up to find a policeman standing beside me. 'Hey,' he added, his eyes flickering with recognition, 'aren't you, um . . . you know, whatsername?'

'Cindy Brightman,' I told him wearily. I gave him a hopeful smile. 'I'll let you have my autograph if you get me a ride out of here.'

He took me to the precinct, where I had to pose for photographs with what seemed like half the Los Angeles Police Department and sign a baseball bat for raffling at their next charity benefit before they would let me go.

Harley took a dim view of the whole business. 'Why on earth did you want to go *there*?' he asked with an expression of distaste. 'I can't think of a worse place to be.'

'No one was asking *you* to go with me,' I muttered sulkily.

'And why didn't you tell me where you were going? It's not very responsible, Cindy – anything could have happened to you.'

'I didn't realise I needed written permission,' I said. 'What's wrong with taking a walk on the beach, anyway?'

The next morning there were photographs in the *LA Times*. 'What are you trying to do to my reputation?' asked Harley, throwing the newspaper on the breakfast table in disgust. 'Are you completely stupid?'

'It wasn't my fault,' I said quietly. 'Why are you treating me as if I've done something terrible?'

'You don't seem to realise, Cindy,' he said in a tight voice, 'just how famous you are. You have responsibilities now. Everything you do reflects the name of *Lapinique.*'

I hadn't realised at all. It seemed that the latest batch of advertisements had captured the public imagination in a big way. Now everyone knew the story of the girl from nowhere who became the Face of *Lapinique.* David was currently negotiating with a well-known fashion designer to put my name on a major range of sportswear and there was even talk of bringing out a Cindy Brightman salad dressing.

'It'll be low calorie, of course,' said Harley. 'And one hundred percent organic.'

I could no longer do the things I wanted – the things I had dreamed of when I was Harriet. I couldn't go for a walk on the street, buy a dress in a boutique, or even make friends in the usual ways. Because I had such a beautiful body, I was no longer allowed the freedoms permitted to the ordinary and the ugly. The simple pleasures of life were forever out of reach.

Everywhere I went, people would point and stare. I was even pursued into the ladies room at Wagner's by two women who had climbed in through the fire escape. When I hid in a cubicle, they thrust a pen and a pair of autograph books under the door and threatened to set off their rape alarms if I didn't sign.

One evening, I was watching TV in the Regency drawing room when Eleanor appeared unannounced in the doorway.

'Harley's in the gym,' I muttered, avoiding her eye. I had scarcely spoken to her since I overheard her remarks about me at the wedding reception.

'I know,' she said, taking a seat beside me on the chaise longue. 'I just saw him. He thought it would be a good idea for me to have a little talk to you.'

'What about?' I asked suspiciously, edging away from her. 'Are you going to say sorry for calling me a cheap little bimbo?'

'Whatever makes you think I said that, my dear?'

'I heard you,' I said. 'At my wedding. Don't pretend you don't know what I'm talking about.'

Her gaze flickered around the room. 'Oh, the *wedding*,' she said in an unruffled tone, picking up the remote control from where it lay beside me and switching off the TV. 'You shouldn't pay attention to anything I say at a *wedding*.' She placed the remote control on the table, aligning it fussily with a box of tissues and a folded magazine. 'I always get too emotional at these things. My analyst tells me it stems from some deep childhood trauma. Apparently I'm always trying to sublimate my feelings by saying the opposite of what I really feel. Sounds ridiculous, I know, but it's the truth.' She glanced towards me, gauging my reaction, and let out a little tinkling laugh. 'I had to pay two hundred dollars an hour to learn that, so I'm not very likely to disagree.'

Grudgingly, I admired her sheer nerve. The woman could probably talk her way out of a locked safe if she put her mind to it.

'Let's speak honestly, Cindy,' she continued, quickly

changing the subject while the going was good. 'Harley's worried that there might be something wrong – something you might be too embarrassed to discuss with a man. Have you been to see your gynaecologist lately?'

I looked at her blankly. 'Why should I need one of those?'

'Oh dear.' She rolled her eyes and let out a sigh. 'I figured as much. Don't tell me that you haven't had your optimum reproductive flow chart plotted? Or your cycle monitored for lifestyle rebalancing?'

'I don't know what you're talking about.'

Reaching into her handbag, she clicked open her purse and handed me a card. 'My gynaecologist. I recommend you make an appointment as soon as possible. Take your calendar with you when you go – you'll need to have your periods monitored to fit in with filming schedules and everything.' She smiled. 'You can virtually design your own monthly cycle with the drugs they have now. You don't have to worry about water retention messing up your wardrobe planning any more, or whether you're going to get PMS at a really important dinner party.'

She frowned, glancing at the door. 'As for the rest, my dear, I know Harley's eager to start, but don't let him rush you. These things need to be planned. You can't just leave it to chance. You could end up with undesirable genes in the ascendent, the wrong eye colour, or even the wrong sex.'

'The wrong sex?'

'Well, I presume you want a boy and a girl – that's usual these days. There's a special diet you can follow to make sure you get them in the right order. In my opinion, it's better if the boy comes first. You can afford to make a few mistakes with boys – they're far more resilient, and it's good practice for getting things right when that beautiful little girl comes along.' Her eyes took on a dreamy look. 'Then you need to plan their schooling – decide what value system you want them to have. And you need to think about who's going to look after them every day. You can't just leave them with the Mexican maid, you know.'

'But I don't want children.'

'Of course you do,' she snapped. 'Everybody has them these days. People will think there's something wrong with you if you don't. They'll be the perfect asset for you if you get the timing right. By the time you're forty, the boy could be out of the way, earning his own living, and your little girl could be small enough – especially with the right clothes – that people would still see you as a young mother. When she gets older, you'll have someone to talk to when Harley starts to have affairs.'

'Harley have affairs!' I spluttered. For some reason I found the idea amusing.

'He will, you know,' said Eleanor with a worldly sigh. 'Believe me, they always do.'

'Do you have children then?' I asked.

'Only one,' she said sadly. 'A boy. Arnie's my second husband, you see, and by the time we got together, it was too late for another one. I wanted a little girl.'

I was damned if I was going to be a surrogate for her. 'What's he like?' I asked. 'Your son, I mean.'

Eleanor produced a compact from her handbag and

began to inspect her face. 'I don't really see him these days,' she murmured. 'He's got a life of his own and everything.' She paused, then lifted her eyes from the mirror to face me with a look of self-pity. 'He's going bald, for Christ's sake!' There was anger in her voice. 'How old are people going to think *I* am when they see me next to him? And he's so inconsiderate – he won't even wear a hat when he's with me!'

She twisted open a shiny tube and reapplied her lipstick with trembling hands. It seemed that the admission had rattled her. I smiled to myself, relieved to know that Eleanor had a weakness – that there was something less than perfect about her well-ordered life.

'What's this I hear about you going out on your own to some filthy public beach?' she asked, abruptly changing the subject the way she always did when it suited her. 'Didn't you listen to any of the things I told you?'

'Why shouldn't I go out on my own?' I retorted indignantly. 'Why can't I be like an ordinary human being?'

'Because, my dear girl – as I've told you before – you're not an ordinary human being. You, my dear, are the Face of *Lapinique*, not to mention being Mrs Cindy Brightman at the same time. You have responsibilities – a duty to your public.'

'What duty?'

'You don't really understand how this place works at all, do you?' she said with a sigh. 'Do you really think people would pay all that money for *Lapinique* products if they were endorsed by some nobody they might bump into when they were standing in line for a bus? Someone the same as them?'

'What does it matter who *endorses* them?' I laughed. 'The product doesn't change, does it? Surely that's what they're paying for?'

'That, my dear,' she said decisively, 'is where you're totally, completely wrong. They couldn't care less what the product is – it's *your image* they're buying. Every single time they buy some perfume or a jar of cream, they're buying a tiny little piece of you to put on their dressing tables and feed their dreams. If they choose *Lapinique*, they tell themselves, they might just get lucky like you did. They might wake up one day to find themselves in the fairytale where they turn out to be a beautiful princess and get to be rich and famous and marry the prince.'

She took a deep breath. 'If you go schlepping around on the beach and let them see you looking like an ordinary person, you're going to destroy that dream! You'll cheapen it – can't you see that?' She seemed to be overexcited and angry – as if I had somehow threatened her. Was she jealous of me, I wondered? Did she envy my youth and beauty – wish she could have had it herself?

'And another thing,' she continued heatedly, 'if you keep on acting like this, you'll wreck things for the rest of us. As soon as people start thinking that we're not better than anyone else – as soon as they start thinking that anyone can be rich and live in Beverly Hills – we'll lose our special status. The entire social fabric will crumble!'

She stood up unsteadily, getting ready to leave. 'There's only a limited amount of wealth to go round,' she said with a note of hysteria in her voice. 'You wouldn't want to have to share it out equally, would you?'

'No one's trying to take anything away from you,' I reassured her, following her to the door.

'I wouldn't be so sure,' she said grimly. 'Things are deteriorating already. Only the other day, there was a tramp rifling around in our garbage bins. I had to get Arnie to set the dogs on him.'

Trish began to plague me with calls, reminding me of the promises I had made to stay in touch, and telling me how she had known from the start that I would never keep them. Reluctant to let her be proved right so quickly, I invited her to visit.

She came one day when Harley was out having acupuncture to combat his obsession with health fads.

'Holy shit, Cin,' she whispered in an awed tone as I showed her around the house. 'You've landed on your feet here!'

I took her into the conservatory, closing the door behind us. 'Actually, Trish,' I said quietly, 'It's not as great as it looks. It's different from what I expected.'

'Well, excuse me for living,' she muttered, unable to suppress her envy for long enough to listen to what I was actually saying.

'My relationship with Harley,' I persisted. 'I'm not happy. It's not . . . it's not turning out as I hoped.'

Trish gave me a wide-eyed stare. 'But you're famous, aren't you? How can you be unhappy?' She fingered the material of the period reproduction sofa with an appreciative look. 'He must be rolling in it, for Christ's sake, Cin,' she added in a low voice. 'What do you have to complain about?'

'Money isn't everything, Trish,' I said. 'Or fame.'

She gave me a look of scornful incomprehension which told me that she thought they were. 'What is it, then?' she asked eventually. 'Is he not performing in the sack, or something?'

I shook my head slowly. 'It's not that, Trish . . .'

'You can't expect to have your cake and icing too, Cin,' she continued, not hearing me. 'A guy of Harley's age is hardly going to set the bed alight like Chuck Woodcock, is he?' She let out a long sigh. 'Not that I would know anything about that,' she added miserably. 'He went off with that bitch Sharleen straight after the wedding. Just when I thought I had a chance.'

'You don't understand, Trish. It's nothing to do with sex. That's the least of my worries – he won't leave me alone.'

'Won't leave you alone?' She shot me a look of envious disbelief. 'How often?'

'He's wearing me out,' I confessed. 'Two or three times a night. I can't get any sleep. But that's not the problem. It's that . . .'

'Sweet Jesus,' murmured Trish, leaning back on the couch and scratching her inner thigh. 'I could do with a bit of that myself.'

'. . . it's that I don't love him, Trish.'

'Love?' she snorted. 'Who said you could have everything?' She gave me a curious look. 'You're living in cloud cuckoo land, Cin. You've had some pretty weird ideas about the way the world works ever since that accident of yours. You need to get real.'

'How?' I asked in a mood of desperation. 'What can I do?'

'What you need, Cin,' she said in a reassuring tone, 'is to get yourself pregnant. How long has it been?' She paused to make some mental calculations. 'It'll make all the difference, you know – the patter of tiny feet.'

'But I don't want children.'

'Of course you do, you silly bitch.' She leaned towards me and lowered her voice. 'Once you have children, you have security. You can do what you like then – find yourself a lover, or whatever turns you on. Then, when it comes to the divorce, you can take him to the cleaners.' She shrugged. 'You can understand why he's probably being a bit careful about it – not rushing into things. Just try sticking pins in his condoms. That usually does the trick.'

'But . . .'

'It's perfectly legitimate really, seeing as you're his wife. What have you got to lose? Best get in quick before someone else takes his fancy.'

'Shhh,' I hissed, hearing voices in the hallway. It was Harley talking to George.

'Oooh, it's him!' squealed Trish.

The door opened and Harley came in. 'What's this I hear from George about that awful friend of yours . . .' He stopped, seeing Trish.

'Oh,' he said, blushing. 'You're still here.'

'Hi, Harley,' simpered Trish. 'We've been talking about you.'

'No, we haven't,' I whispered, kicking her. 'Shut up!'

'You know what your problem is, Harley?' she continued. 'Your little Cindy's getting desperate for kids. I've just been telling her about my sister-in-law's lovely little babies, and she's getting all down in the dumps wondering if she'll ever have one of her own.'

'What business is it of yours . . .' Harley stopped and stared at her. 'What did you say?'

'You heard me,' said Trish with a knowing snigger.

'Are you really, darling?' he asked, rushing eagerly to my side.

'I know you might think I'm out of line,' continued Trish loudly. 'But I can't help speaking my mind when there's something that needs saying. After all, she'd make such a great mother.'

'That's just what I've been telling her,' said Harley.

'Don't say I never do anything to help you,' Trish whispered in my ear. She turned to Harley with a dazzling smile. 'Now that we've been introduced at last,' she said, 'you have to tell me all about *Lapinique*. It's my favourite brand.'

'Is it really?' he asked, looking pleased. 'What skin type are you?'

They were soon deep in conversation about cosmetics. 'This is great stuff,' exclaimed Harley nearly an hour later. 'First-rate consumer feedback!'

I began to wonder if she would ever leave, but eventually she stood up.

'Well, I suppose I'd better be running along,' she said with a wink. 'Leave you two lovebirds alone.'

As I showed her to the door she pulled a sheaf of

papers out of her handbag. They were xerox copies of a photograph of Cindy and Trish posing outside Marty's diner.

'If you wouldn't mind just signing these for me,' she asked hopefully. 'I can get ten bucks each for them at Marty's stall.'

'Er, leave them with me,' I muttered, thrusting them quickly out of sight into a drawer. 'I'll see what I can do.'

'You know something, Cindy?' asked Harley that evening. 'I think I was wrong about that friend of yours. She seems quite nice when you get to know her. Sensible type. Maybe you should invite her here more often.'

'David's coming over to stay for a while,' announced Harley at lunchtime the following day.

'What for?' I asked, surprised. 'I mean, I thought he lived near here.'

'Why should he need a reason?' he asked, inserting a large brown envelope into his electric letter-opener. 'He likes a change of scenery just like everybody else and, besides, we have some business to discuss.' He looked up at me reproachfully. 'I know you don't like him much, Cindy, but he *is* my brother. Try to be nice to him.'

The gadget on the table let out a whirring noise and began to shred the envelope into thin strips. 'Damn!' he exclaimed, struggling to retrieve the document inside. 'Somebody put this thing on the wrong setting.'

'Is anything the matter?' I asked, watching a frown

appear on his forehead as he pulled out the tattered remains of a report and began to read it.

'Oh, it's these *Lapinette* people,' he said in an abstracted voice. 'The ones who do look-alike versions of our products and sell them on market stalls for a tenth of the price. I've had an analysis done of their face cream and it turns out to have exactly the same ingredients as the real thing.' He tugged at a stray lock of hair and twirled it thoughtfully between his fingers. 'I'd like to know where they got hold of the formula.'

I became attentive. This was the first time Harley had ever discussed the workings of *Lapinique* with me. Was he taking me seriously at last – showing me some respect as an equal?

'What's special about the formula?' I asked. 'What does the cream actually do?'

'Eh?' He shook the hair out of his eyes and turned to the opening of his next letter. 'Oh, it's too complicated to explain,' he said in a dismissive voice. 'You wouldn't understand.'

An alarm sounded on his watch. 'Time for your morning workout, sweetheart,' he said, checking the display. 'You better run along to the gym now.'

Condescending bastard. In a supreme effort to retain my self control, I stood up and left the room in an icy rage.

'Oh, Cindy,' he added, just as I was about to slam the door. 'We aren't going to have any cheating on the tricep dips this time, are we?' He gave me a knowing look. 'It really isn't worth it, sweetheart – you only end up cheating yourself in the long run.'

* * *

I spent an hour sulking upstairs, then decided that I might as well go to the gym as anywhere else. If I didn't feel like doing any exercise, I could always fix the mileage counter on the walking machine to keep Harley quiet.

Passing an open window, I heard voices on the terrace. David had already arrived. Looking out, I saw him lounging in a deckchair by the open door of the pool house. Harley lay in a special reclining chair in the shade of a nearby awning, wired up to a machine for measuring his cholesterol level.

I was about to continue on my way when I heard my name spoken.

'I don't know if Cindy's going to be doing much more of this, David,' said Harley in a disapproving tone. 'You said at first that it was just going to be one photo session. Then I agreed to the filming in Italy, and now you come back and tell me you want to do *another* commercial. Then there'll be another one after that . . . when's it going to stop?'

'You haven't been following the sales figures?' asked David in a voice of incredulity. 'Don't tell me you forgot how to read a balance sheet?'

Harley muttered something I couldn't hear.

'The figures for the perfume alone have broken all our previous records for a new marketing drive,' added David. 'And the survey findings are unbelievable – nearly eighty percent of the sample said they made their purchase as a direct result of seeing the ad.' He thrust a handful of papers under Harley's nose. 'Look, see for yourself! That girl could make us a fortune if we use her the right way.'

'She's my wife, goddammit!' spluttered Harley, tearing the wires from his wrists and struggling with the chair in an effort to sit up. 'I won't have all these other guys staring at her body! I won't allow it!'

'Before you make a final decision, big brother,' murmured David, 'hadn't you better remember where the money to pay for all this comes from?' He made a gesture to indicate their surroundings. 'Don't you think a little extra might be useful when the bills for that wedding of yours come in?'

Harley opened his mouth to protest but was distracted by his battle with the folding chair, which seemed to be trying to fold itself away.

Closing the window, I stalked angrily downstairs. They were talking about me as if I was some commodity – some piece of property they both wanted a stake in. What about my feelings? No one had thought to ask *me* how *I* felt about doing another commercial.

Rage bubbled inside me as I approached the door to the terrace. It was pure exploitation. I wasn't Harley's slave, for Christ's sake – I had a right to be consulted. If I was going to make anyone a fortune, it would have to be on *my* terms.

I reached the terrace just in time to see Harley's chair collapse, depositing him ungracefully in a heap on the floor.

'How dare you talk about me like that?' I exploded. 'I'll be the one to decide if I appear in a commercial or not. Just who do you think you are?'

'I'm your husband,' said Harley indignantly, picking himself up.

'Love you too, Sis,' said David with a sarcastic grin.

'And if I am going to be in any more of your lousy adverts,' I added, addressing myself to David, 'if I am going to 'make a fortune for you', as you so delicately put it – don't you think you ought to treat me the same as the others and actually *pay* me? Haven't you ever heard of the fucking minimum wage?'

'I'll deal with this, David,' said Harley with a frown. 'I think you'd better leave us to work this out.'

David uncoiled himself lazily from his deckchair. 'Well, I do have a few errands to run,' he murmured, gathering his papers together. 'What's the matter, Sis?' he added nastily, catching my eye. 'Harley's money not enough for you, so you want to keep up the day job as well? Or is it just that you don't like the idea of anyone else playing you at your own game?'

'Exploitative bastard,' I hissed at his departing back.

'Now, what's all this about, Cindy?' asked Harley, red-faced. 'Why can't you be civil to David, for God's sake? Is that too much to ask?'

'Did you hear what he was saying about me?' I spluttered. 'Did you hear what you were saying yourself, for that matter? I'm not some piece of property you can lend out to your friends and relatives when it suits you!'

'I don't know what you're talking about,' he said slowly. 'You weren't listening properly. I was telling David that I *didn't* want you doing any more commercials. I'm on your side, sweetheart!'

'But that's exactly . . .' I glared at him in frustration. He simply couldn't see what I meant – would never see. 'Maybe I should get an agent,' I said eventually. 'Somebody who could guide me in my career. They would know whether it was right for me to accept a job or not.'

'Agent? Career?' Harley clutched his forehead and stared at me wildly. 'What's come over you, Cindy? Aren't you happy to follow *my* advice any more?'

'What if I was offered a job by someone else?' I asked innocently. 'Someone who wasn't *Lapinique*, I mean. Wouldn't there be a conflict of interest?'

'I can't believe I heard that,' he said quietly. 'Work for someone else? How on earth can you think I would ever allow it?'

'It's not a matter of what you'll allow, Harley,' I said defiantly. 'I'm a human being with just the same rights as you, and if I want to work as a model then I damn well will! Whether you like it or not!'

His face went purple. 'I won't allow it!' he began. 'I won't . . .'

'Piss off, Harley,' I interrupted. 'I'll decide what I do, thank you very much.'

'How dare you talk to me like that, you . . . you little bitch!' Picking up the nearest object, which happened to be his mobile telephone, he hurled it into the pool. It sank like a stone.

I turned and stalked back into the house, too angry to speak.

'Cindy! Where are you going?' He was at the door, trying to block my path.

'Leave me alone,' I muttered, pushing past him and heading for the gym.

When I got there I took out the screwdriver I had hidden behind a pot plant and, with a few swift adjustments, logged up fifteen miles on the treadmill. Then I turned to the console of Harley's computerised exercise monitor and wiped out a whole month's accumulation of jogging miles.

Warning! said the screen. *Health Alert! Compiling emergency fitness plan . . .*

Leaving the machine bleeping with astonishment at Harley's irresponsibility, I locked myself in one of the guest bathrooms – the only place I had found where I could get some privacy. I had a bottle of vodka and several volumes of Dickens stowed away in the towel cupboard for emergencies.

I stayed there for the rest of the day, getting halfway through *Hard Times* before the vodka caught up with me. When I emerged, slightly unsteady on my feet, I tripped over a recumbent figure on the landing outside.

'Cindy, is that you?' Harley sat up blinking and rubbing his eyes. 'You've come back to me at last.' He held out his arms. 'I forgive you, darling. I know you were just upset – I know you didn't mean what you were saying.'

Forgive? I had meant every word of it. I was the one who would be doing the forgiving – in my own time. 'I'm going to bed,' I muttered.

'But Cindy . . .' He caught up with me in the bedroom. 'Didn't you hear me?' He gave me an indulgent smile. 'All forgiven and forgotten. We can be friends again now.'

'I'm tired,' I said, getting into bed.

'Not too tired for what I've got in mind, I hope?' he said, approaching the bed with a gleam in his eye.

I was sick of having my body abused like this – of being treated like a plaything, a life-sized doll for an overgrown child like Harley to comfort himself with. He was far too absorbed in his own vanity to look beyond the pretty packaging and make contact with the human being inside.

'Fuck off, Harley,' I said. 'I'm not in the mood.'

A look of deep anguish spread over his features. 'What do you mean by that?' he said in an affronted voice. 'Are you saying that I don't satisfy you any more?'

I turned over and pretended to be asleep, but he shook me roughly by the arm. 'Is there something you haven't told me, Cindy?' he demanded in a suspicious tone. 'Is there somebody else?'

I didn't get much sleep that night. Harley ranted and raved until the small hours, angrily demanding an explanation for this sudden withdrawal of his conjugal rights.

'There's something deeply wrong with our relationship,' he pronounced eventually, and stormed off to sulk in his study, slamming the door. It was the first sensible remark he had made all evening. Was the penny beginning to drop at last?

* * *

Harley moped around the house for much of the following day, jealously watching my every move and becoming increasingly suspicious of my extended trips to the bathroom.

'What are you doing in there?' he demanded, rattling the door handle.

'Telephoning my lover – what do you think?' I replied irritably, returning the vodka bottle to its hiding place under the pale blue towels.

How much longer could I put up with Harley? I needed to do something – to find a way of sorting out the mess I was in. Mephisto's mocking laughter echoed in my thoughts.

You'll realise soon enough what a mistake you've made. You'll be begging me to come back and rescue you, just wait and see . . .

'Oh no I won't,' I muttered angrily to myself. 'I won't give you the satisfaction.'

'Cindy?' Harley thumped insistently at the door. 'I can hear voices! Who have you got in there?'

In an effort to keep out of his way I stalked around the house, trailing through endless corridors like the ghost of Mrs Rochester. Was this how I was going to end up – imprisoned by Harley like a madwoman in the attic? I began to wish that he had a job like other men, so that I could at least have a bit of peace and quiet away from him during the day.

That evening, we had been invited to a party given by Nancy van Aspern – a figure of such importance in Hollywood society that Harley couldn't possibly afford to snub her. We were going to have to appear as a loving couple – or so he had instructed me in a stern voice through the bathroom door.

If the invitation had been from anyone else I would have told him to piss off, but Nancy van Aspern was an icon from my past. I had watched all her films when I was young, back in the days when I was Harriet. She played opposite Hollywood's most gorgeous men and she was the most beautiful woman I had ever seen. In my childhood dreams I used to imagine how different my life could have been if I had looked like her. She must be in her seventies by now, I realised. Would she still look like the same person I had worshipped on the screen?

George drove us to the party. Harley seemed to be practising his impersonation of a happily married man and twittered on cosily about domestic matters all the way to Topanga Canyon.

'What's Nancy van Aspern like?' I asked eventually, changing the subject. 'I'm really looking forward to meeting her.'

'Don't hold your breath, sweetheart,' advised Harley. 'She's a real recluse these days – it's even rare for her to turn up at her own parties.'

'Why does she give them, then?' I asked, puzzled and disappointed.

'Oh, it's habit, I expect,' he replied. 'Rumour has it that she keeps out of sight because she's embarrassed about losing her looks.' He laughed. 'You can't really blame her. She used to be a great beauty, you see, but now she's got about three chins and a face like an old prune.'

I stared at him coldly. 'And I suppose you'll be swanning around like a Playgirl pin-up when you're seventy, will you? Without so much as a wrinkle or an ounce of surplus fat on your perfect body?'

'I didn't say that,' he replied, flustered. 'What I meant was . . .'

'That women over a certain age should hide themselves away so as not to spoil the scenery? That it's a crime to get old or, heaven forbid, to actually look your age?' I heard my voice growing louder, but I didn't care. 'You might have a perfect body now, Harley, but it's a shame that you haven't got a brain to match it. Otherwise you'd realise that it's going to happen to you too one day!'

'Be quiet, Cindy!' he hissed. 'What will George think?' He pushed his hands through his hair and faced me with an angry look. 'I wasn't saying any of those things. It's just that I can't help wondering why some women let themselves go like that. When there are so many ways to keep yourself looking young and beautiful – lifestyle, diet, exercise, cosmetics, and even plastic surgery. It seems wrong to me not to make an effort.'

'And I think it's wrong to criticise people for the way they look. Not everyone was born beautiful, you know, Harley. Some people can't help it.' I was so angry, I was on the verge of telling him the truth. Would he include pacts with the Devil on his list of modern beauty aids? I sighed. What was the point? He would never believe me.

When we arrived at the party I headed straight for the bar in search of hard liquor. I was expecting to have to negotiate a private supply but, to my surprise, there was a row of serious-looking bottles on a shelf at one side.

'A large one of those, please,' I asked eagerly, pointing to a bourbon.

The barman hesitated. 'This one?' he asked, raising an eyebrow. 'You know what it is?'

'Of course I know what it is, young man,' I snapped. 'If I didn't, I'd be asking for fizzy piss-water like everyone else!'

There was a sudden silence around me, then everyone began to chatter loudly. *Young man?* What had I been thinking of? He looked older than me.

'Sorry,' he replied, hastening to pour me a large measure. 'It's just that you have to be careful around here.' He lowered his voice to a whisper. 'I got into big trouble once when the wife of a hot-shot producer asked me for a pint of margarita, thinking it was some kind of soft drink.' He grinned. 'You should have seen her face when she started knocking it back like cola.'

Taking my drink, I slipped through a door on to the terrace and looked for a quiet spot where I could get drunk. I didn't really care if Harley saw me – not after the row we had just had – but I wasn't in the mood to listen to his nagging.

A few moments later, Eleanor appeared and sat down beside me.

'Don't think I didn't see you creeping away like that. What's all this about you and Harley having problems?'

'Nothing,' I muttered, hiding my drink in a trough of flowers before she spotted it. 'What's he been telling you?'

'Oh, he didn't need to say anything,' said Eleanor. 'I can read between the lines. I only had to take one look at his face and I knew that something was wrong.'

I gave her a calculating look, wondering if I could trust her.

'I'm not happy,' I confided cautiously. 'He doesn't understand me, Eleanor.'

'Happy?' she asked in voice of disbelief. 'You've got everything a girl could want, Cindy – looks, money, fame, a good husband – surely that's enough to satisfy you? Surely you don't expect to be happy as well? Who *is* these days?'

'But I never asked for all this,' I complained.

'Didn't you?' Eleanor's eyebrows fixed themselves in an accusing slant. 'I didn't see you begging to be allowed to go back to that awful waitressing job and those tacky friends of yours. I didn't see you kicking and screaming at the goddamn altar refusing to go through with it.'

A smile flickered across her lips. '*For richer, for poorer?* I've no doubt you saw that as a one-way bargain. Let's see, maybe it's *forsaking all others* that's giving you such a problem.'

'I don't know what you mean,' I spluttered.

'You've got a lot to learn, my girl,' she said quietly. 'Maybe you don't realise that most Hollywood marriages are no more than convenient business arrangements – deals based on money, skills, position and looks. Love – if that's the missing ingredient you were thinking of – doesn't come into it.'

She folded her arms and gave me a knowing stare. 'So who is he?'

'What do you mean?'

'Your lover. It's the only explanation I can think of for your behaviour.'

I gave her a look of speechless indignation.

She sighed. 'All right, I didn't really expect you to tell me. Keep your little secret if you have to – but first listen to a word of advice from an older woman. In this town, it's not what you do that's counted as a crime, it's being found out. In your position, my dear, you can't afford to take any risks. Look what happened to April de Vincy.'

'You mean Ted de Vincy's wife?' I had already glimpsed the ageing rock star lurking around the bar with a scantily clad young woman.

Eleanor nodded with a grim expression. 'Caught in the gardener's room with the pool cleaner,' she whispered. 'Surely you remember? They even had pictures in the *LA Enquirer*. All because she was foolish enough to tell all to her manicurist.' She shook her head slowly, making little tutting noises of disapproval.

'Though it was rather unlucky,' she added, glancing around to check that no one was listening, 'that the nail girl happened to be the pool boy's fiancée. *And* having an affair with a freelance photographer.' She gave me a stern look. 'Now April's been struck off all the lists right down to the school-run at Beverly High and she's paying her lawyers a fortune to try to scrape some alimony out of the mess. Meanwhile Ted's shopping around for a new model – even though everybody knows he was playing hide the salami with the Mexican maid at the time.'

She shook her head sadly. 'It's an unfair system, but if you can't control your appetite and you're determined to snack between meals, you have to be careful what you nibble on, my dear.'

'But I'm not . . .'

'Choose your lover very carefully,' she continued, ignoring me. 'There are lots of cowboys out there who will want to hit on you, hoping they might press the right buttons and win the jackpot. They're all opportunists who've read too much Jackie Collins and figure they could try their luck at blackmail.'

'But I'm not going to have an affair,' I insisted.

'You might say that now, my dear,' murmured Eleanor in a world weary tone, 'but you'll come to it in the end. I can see it in your eyes. My advice will be just as good in twenty years, so you should take it on board. These are the rules: Be very, very discreet. Don't trust or confide in anyone, especially not your closest friend. Keep an eye on the servants. Don't even think about keeping a diary, or writing letters. And whatever you do, don't ever, ever fuck anyone who has less to lose by being found out than you do.'

She stood up, handing me my drink from the planting trough. 'This must be yours, my dear. I'll run along now and leave you to think over what I've said.'

I sat miserably sipping my drink. I was hidden from sight in my shadowy corner, but I had a clear view of the comings and goings on the main part of the terrace, where coloured lights had now been switched on and people were beginning to gather. I watched Harley strut self-importantly through the french windows, deep in conversation with Crystal Kelly. Ted de Vincy steered his nymphet across to join them – the latest model being taken out for a test drive, presumably. She looked young enough to be his granddaughter. I recognised Sylvie and Warren, Eleanor and Arnie, Jessica and her awful parents. Everyone was there.

The women had an air of brittle vulnerability as they stood there in their party dresses, clutching their glasses of Evian and clicking their heels against the flagstones. They wore the best clothes that money could buy – Chanel, Armani, Versace – but they were too thin. Their eyes had a hollowness about them and it didn't take much imagination to visualise the grinning skulls beneath their made-up faces. Why was the look of the famine victim so much admired?

As I watched, music started playing and Crystal Kelly began to dance with Arnie. They must both be in their fifties – maybe even their sixties – and I watched them closely, remembering what Harley had said. Crystal Kelly certainly hadn't 'let herself go' – she was strapped into a tight little sleeveless dress that left no doubt about the slenderness of her figure. But there was something about the crude exaggeration of her made-up features and the quality of her skin – the scrawny texture of her neck and upper arms – which made the whole outfit seem suddenly obscene. Why did she have to dress as if she was forty years younger than she actually was? Staring at her feet, at the muscles which strained with the effort of balancing on stiletto heels, I was unexpectedly reminded of my grandmother. At the same age, her feet were stuffed into comfortable felt slippers with slits cut in them to relieve the pressure on her bunions.

Both images were cruel stereotypes. Which was worse – to be a shuffling old woman with bunions, or to be derided as 'mutton dressed as lamb'? Was there no middle path a woman could take with dignity?

'Sad, isn't it?' said a voice beside me, making me jump several inches into the air. 'Sorry, I didn't mean to startle you.'

I turned to see an elderly woman dressed in a black tracksuit and trainers sitting beside me.

'Where did you . . . I didn't hear . . .' I stared at her. The likeness was unmistakable. 'Are you . . .'

'Nancy van Aspern,' she said, extending her hand. 'You must be Cindy Brightman.' She raised her eyebrows slightly. 'The Face of *Lapinique*?'

'Well, er, yes,' I mumbled, tongue-tied at meeting my childhood idol. I stared at her face with interest. She did have quite a lot of wrinkles – as Harley had suggested – but it was a kind face, a face with character. Her voice was like gravel coated in honey.

'I must admit,' she continued, 'that you sounded just like the rest of the empty-headed bimbos who flock to this town. Until you revealed your liking for good bourbon to my barman, that is. I thought I'd better meet you for myself when I heard about that. You've got taste, my girl.'

'Er thanks,' I muttered.

'I've brought you a refill,' she added, thrusting a well-charged glass into my hand. 'We can enjoy it together, eh? And stuff all those prissy creatures with their calorie counters and thought police.'

'I'll drink to that,' I said, perking up. The music changed, increasing in volume and tempo, and Crystal Kelly launched into a fresh series of gyrations.

'As I was in the process of observing,' said Nancy, 'it's sad the way they don't accept the passing of the years. Look, she's acting as if she was sixteen again. You wouldn't believe we were the same age.'

My mind raced to reconcile the widely differing estimates I had made.

'I don't have anything against people having a good time,' she added, lighting a cigar. 'It's just the pretence I can't stand. What's wrong with being sixty-five, for Christ's sake?'

'I don't know,' I murmured. 'It happens to most people in the end – so why not accept it?'

'Look at her,' repeated Nancy. 'She doesn't believe in her own beauty any more than we do, so why does she think she's fooling anybody else? Even young women like you feel insecure about your looks these days, don't you?'

'If I was ugly,' I said thoughtfully, 'I would probably sell my soul to look the way I do now. But if you have the looks, you spend half your time worrying about losing them. It makes you wonder whether the game's worth the candle.' I gave her a half-questioning smile. If only she knew the truth of what I was saying.

'I think it goes like this,' said Nancy. 'You create an ideal of beauty that no one can ever possibly achieve, and then brainwash everyone to believe that if they tried hard enough – did an extra set of pelvic thrusts, or whatever they do for exercise now, before breakfast each day – then they'd have a chance of getting there. Then you stand back and have a good laugh as you watch the poor saps trying.'

She drew deeply on her cigar and blew a perfect smoke ring. 'The whole damn thing's a conspiracy by men to make women feel inadequate, and we both know it, don't we?'

'Inadequate, insecure and, consequently, powerless,' I murmured. She had given me the words to express what I had been thinking since my disagreement with Harley.

'Just where the fuckers want us,' she growled. 'It doesn't matter whether you're a model or a Red Cross worker, whatever achievements you've made in your life will all fall by the wayside when it comes to the ultimate test of worth – whether or not your body conforms to some ridiculous shape chosen quite arbitrarily by men.'

'If only we could make them jump through the same hoops,' I said, glancing around with a smile. 'I'd like to see some of this lot get written off by society and turned down for jobs because they're looking a bit past it or because their dicks don't hang at the right angle.'

Nancy giggled. 'I'd like to see some of those fat little movie executives trying to fuck their way into a picture like they still expect us to. They wouldn't get very far if I was doing the casting.'

She paused, and a note of sadness crept into her voice. 'It's not until you're *really* old and ugly like me that you can finally summon up the courage to defy them,' she sighed. 'To say it doesn't matter. By then, of course, it's too late.'

'I think you're still beautiful,' I said shyly. 'And a brilliant actress – I used to love your films.'

'I'm pretty sure they were before your time, my dear,' she said gruffly, trying not to show that the compliment had pleased her.

'Do you mind if I ask – why do people say that you never go to your own parties? And if you don't like parties, why do you give them?'

She laughed. 'I don't mind telling you that. It's to remind myself how lucky I am. Sometimes I get a bit complacent and forget what a nightmare other people can be. Tell myself I ought to be more sociable and all that crap.'

She smiled. 'When this feeling comes upon me, I know it's time to have my annual party. It gets it out of my system. I usually don't feel the urge to socialise for about another year after that. It only takes about five minutes for the effect to sink in, so I tend to skulk around in the background for the rest of the time, like this.' She patted my hand. 'You get to meet the more interesting people this way.'

A shrill voice interrupted our conversation. 'Hey Duane, come quickly! There's somebody *smoking* over here!' A pert blonde in a skimpy dress appeared out of the darkness. 'Put that out at once!' she hissed in a commanding voice. 'Don't you know that nobody smokes any more?'

She took a step closer. 'Eeurghh!' she screeched. 'It's a *cigar!*'

'Get lost, you little asshole,' said Nancy dryly.

'How dare you talk to me like that!' shrieked the blonde. 'Who do you think you are?'

'Nancy van Aspern,' she said quietly. 'Your hostess. Pleased to meet you.'

'Ha, ha, very funny,' said the blonde. 'Everybody knows that the old bag never turns up at her own parties.' She peered through the darkness, inspecting us more closely. 'Holy shit!' she breathed. 'Quick, Duane! Come and look at this! I found Cindy Brightman!'

Nancy stood up slowly. 'I think it's time for me to be going,' she said. 'And I think I might hold out for two years after this.'

'Duane, hurry up! What are you playing at?'

'Meeting you has made tonight worthwhile, my dear,' added Nancy. 'If I wasn't such a misanthropic old bitch I'd say you were a kindred spirit. You do have a remarkably mature outlook for your years.' She coughed. 'I have to go now, though. I'm starting to get alarm signals that I might do something uncharacteristic like ask you out for lunch.'

She disappeared into the darkness and I heard the click of a door closing behind her. I could hear footsteps approaching, presumably belonging to Duane, and decided it was time to do something. Two could play at that game.

'Harley!' I screeched at the top of my voice. 'Come here at once! These people are being rude to me!'

'Cindy!' cried a small voice out of the darkness. 'Where are you? I've been looking for you all night!'

CHAPTER 14

The day after the party, I woke late with a hangover and spent a long time in the bathroom looking for something to take for my headache. Where some people have a walk-in closet for their clothes, Harley had a walk-in medicine cabinet. It was well stocked with vitamin and fibre supplements and contained enough homeopathic remedies to look after an entire New Age community, but there was no aspirin. Why not, I wondered? Were they fattening, or bad for you in some way? Was Harley so bloody healthy that he didn't need them? Or had he downed such a skinful the previous night that he had been there before me and used them all up? I couldn't remember the details of the latter part of the evening, but I suspected that he might have needed a drink or two to cope with my behaviour after Nancy left. I winced. Had I really danced on the table with that barman who gave me the bourbon?

I was on my way to ask George if he had any aspirin, when I heard a familiar voice through the door of one of the guest rooms.

'What do you mean you don't know when it's coming?

I sent you notification of the shipment two days ago. It'll be coming tomorrow, for Chrissakes!'

It was David, doing his macho business routine on the telephone. I could picture him strutting up and down in his Armani suit while he reduced some hapless employee to tears. I was about to continue downstairs when a name caught my attention.

'Don't ask me what happened to it,' said David aggressively. 'I sent it to the email address you gave me at *Lapinette*.'

Lapinette? The people Harley had been complaining about the other day. Why would David be speaking to them? I stopped outside the door and listened carefully.

'I've got the details here if you want me to read them over . . . hang on . . .' There was a sound of shuffling paper. 'What do you mean you need a frigging hard copy? Don't you trust me or something? How am I supposed to get it to you from here – I'm staying at my brother's place for Chrissakes!'

There was a sound of fingers drumming impatiently on a tabletop. 'Yes . . . yes . . .' He gave a theatrical sigh. 'OK . . . all right. If it keeps you happy. I think there's a computer around here somewhere – I'll put it on the email.'

There was a long pause before he spoke again.

'I told you I can't get any more,' he snapped. 'Not at that price, anyway. They're getting suspicious around here and I think we better give it a rest for a month or two.'

There was another pause.

'OK,' he said eventually. 'I'll have it through to you in an hour or so. Just don't fuck up on the transfer details this time. It's my Caymen account, not the US one, OK? I don't want the IRS after me again.'

There was a click of a telephone receiver being replaced and footsteps briskly approached the door. I leapt away in alarm, throwing myself through the door of an adjacent room which turned out to be a broom cupboard. Trembling in the darkness, I held my breath as the door to the next room opened and I heard his footsteps pass my hiding place and fade slowly away down the corridor.

It sounded as if David had a hand in the leaking of the *Lapinique* formula – as if he was actually selling the stuff to the opposition. I couldn't quite work out the logic of it all, but it certainly seemed that he was acting against his brother's interests.

Untangling myself from an assortment of mops and brooms, I emerged cautiously into the corridor and went downstairs to continue my search for aspirin. The only computer I knew of in the house was in Harley's study. As soon as David had sent his message, I was going to give myself a quick refresher course in electronic file management.

It would never occur to either Harley or David that I might know how to operate a computer. But then neither would it occur to them to consult me if they had an obscure query regarding the Dewey Decimal Classification System. How could anyone be expected to know that the Face of *Lapinique* belonged to a fully qualified librarian?

I had always resented not being given the opportunity to use my skills properly in Guildford. When Annette smartarse Baker went off on a three-day computer course and came back trilling about the benefits of technology, they bought her a PC and gave her a virtually unlimited budget to develop the in-house information system. They conveniently overlooked the fact that I had been attending evening classes and quietly campaigning to update the facilities for years.

Just because she had legs up to her armpits and tits to challenge Jean-Paul Gaultier, Annette Baker was hailed as the IT guru of the library. I was told to stop complaining and to remember that a younger mind was better equipped to cope with new technology. Like hell it was. I looked over her shoulder one day and saw that her so-called prowess was a complete bluff. She was still struggling with the first chapter of the manual.

When I entered Harley's study a little later, the seat at the keyboard of the computer was still warm. I hadn't been into the pale blue room since my first visit to the house, but it was just as I remembered it. How naïve I had been then – imagining that marriage to Harley would secure my freedom. I was more of a prisoner now than I had ever been.

Switching on the computer, I soon had the email programme fired up, but there was no trace of a recent communication. The fax programme was equally unhelpful. As I suspected, David had deleted his message immediately after sending it.

That wasn't the end of the story, however. In the recycle bin, I traced a file which had been created less than half an hour earlier. It was a matter of moments to get it fully restored and displayed on the screen.

Reading it, I saw that David was indeed selling *Lapinique* products to what should have been a business rival. A consignment of *Total Skin Control with Formula B* was about to be delivered to an address in the outskirts of LA in return for a substantial deposit into David's personal account at the Caymen National Bank.

I reached to turn the printer on, but was startled by a quiet cough at the door. With a pounding heart, I scrabbled to shut down the computer while praying that it wasn't David.

'I managed to find some aspirin in the Bentley's first aid kit, ma'am,' said an unctuous voice behind me. It was George, rattling a bottle of pills in his hand. 'You can always rely on a British manufacturer to think of all those unforseen eventualities.'

'Er, thanks, George,' I muttered, flicking my handkerchief at the keyboard to make it look as if I had been dusting or something.

'The printing on the label's a little worn, ma'am,' he continued, 'so I can't actually see if they're past their sell-by date. But the wax seal is still intact.'

Wax seal? Surely he was winding me up? I shot him a sidelong look, trying to catch him out, but his face was impassive. I dropped my handkerchief, realising how foolish I must look. *Dusting?* That was George's job.

I paced up and down on the terrace for some time, trying to decide what to do. How long was I going to store up this information about David? I was no longer the sort of person who enjoyed dithering around waiting for results. I needed to do something straight away. With this in mind, I went to look for Harley. We would see what he thought of his precious brother now.

'Really, Cindy,' exclaimed Harley, adjusting the straps on his swimming machine. 'Is this important enough to interrupt my simulated crossing of the Hellespont?'

'You must come and see for yourself,' I insisted, tugging at his arm. 'You probably won't believe me otherwise. I can tell you how those *Lapinette* people got hold of your formula.'

Eventually he shut down his oxygen supply and clambered out of the contraption.

'Well?' he asked. 'Where is it?'

I dragged him to the study and switched on the computer. 'Brace yourself, Harley,' I warned him. 'You might not like this.'

'What do you think you're doing?' he squawked. 'Leave it alone! You'll press the wrong button!'

'Hold your horses, Harley,' I murmured, scrolling through the list of files. 'I'm just going to bring up this message and then you can decide for yourself.' I shook my head and checked the list again. It wasn't there.

'Someone's wiped it out,' I said in a voice of disbelief. 'I was only looking at it an hour ago.'

'Wiped what out? What are you talking about, Cindy?'

George. It had to be him. I moved the cursor to the recycle bin, but Harley seized my wrist.

'That's enough of your silly tricks,' he spluttered. 'Didn't I tell you never to touch this machine?'

'But . . .'

'Computers are complex pieces of equipment,' he said, pushing me out of the chair and taking it himself. 'You could do all kinds of damage if you mess around with them.' He fiddled with the mouse, trying to hit one of the buttons, 'Oops! There we are!'

The computer turned unexpectedly multimedia on us, emitting a noise like the tinkling accompaniment to a Disney ride. A pack of playing cards appeared on the screen.

'What's that?' I asked, puzzled.

'It's Solitaire,' he said, taking my hand in his and guiding the mouse. 'Let me show you. You hold it like *this*, and when the little arrow is over the card you want, you simply press the button like *this,* and move the card – just like you were playing it in real life.'

I shifted a few cards around the screen to keep him happy. What kind of dork did he think I was?

'Look, Harley,' I said eventually. 'Someone's deleted the file I was going to show you, so I'll just have to tell you instead. It's David. I overheard him on the telephone and . . .'

'What's this?' he interrupted. 'Eavesdropping? Listening at doors? That's no way to treat my brother when he's a guest in my house.'

'But I wasn't . . .' With a sigh of frustration, I decided to come straight to the point. 'The thing is, Harley – it's David who's given your formula to *Lapinette*. He's actually selling consignments of cream to them.'

Harley stared at me open mouthed. 'But that's outrageous . . .' he said slowly.

'I know,' I replied. 'It's not very nice, is it? Cheating on his brother like that.'

His eyes bulged. 'I meant that it's outrageous for you to make an accusation like that,' he exploded. 'Really, Cindy! My own brother! How could you even think of such a thing?'

He stood up and paced across his office, shaking his head. 'I don't know what's got into you lately, Cindy. I think maybe you need to see a doctor. Or maybe I can get you an appointment with my analyst.' He picked up the telephone.

'No!' I shouted, surprising even myself with the loudness of my reaction. 'I'm not going to see an analyst!' I seized the telephone receiver from his hand and slammed it back in its cradle, then turned and fled from the room. What secrets would an analyst find in my head, I wondered fearfully? How would they make sense of the strange cocktail of two different people I had become? I didn't want to spend the rest of my time as Cindy locked in a mental institution.

I rushed through the door to the terrace and collided with David.

He caught me by the arm. 'Where are you going in such a hurry, little sister?' he asked in a patronising tone. 'I hope you haven't been upsetting my darling brother again.'

'You're a fine one to talk,' I said angrily, struggling in his grip. 'Don't you think he'd be upset if he knew you were stealing from him? Selling the *Lapinique* formula to his competitors?'

'How the devil . . .' He glared at me furiously. 'How

on earth . . .' He checked himself. 'Did I hear you say *formula*?'

'You heard me.'

He began to laugh. 'Oh dear, do you really think it has a formula? Do you think there's anything more to it than ordinary cold cream and a few fragrances? Plus maybe a couple of harmless vegetable extracts to keep the macrobiotic brigade happy?'

'That's not the point,' I retorted. 'You shouldn't be selling it to a rival company behind Harley's back.'

He frowned. 'I really thought you were brighter than that, Cindy. *Lapinette* are hardly our rivals. They're just a bunch of small-time cowboys at the bottom end of the market.'

'But Harley said . . .' I faltered. Could I really have got it all wrong?

'Never mind what Harley said,' snapped David. 'You've got a lot to learn if you're going to start interfering in the family business. You clearly don't know the first thing about modern commercial practices. It's standard procedure to sell off the surplus product when you get your wastage rate down.'

'It sounds like stealing to me,' I muttered sulkily.

'That only shows how little you understand,' he said with an exasperated sigh. 'Look, I don't see why I should have to account for this to you but, if you must know, I'm actually saving you a lot of money. Have you any idea how much the IRS could screw out of us each year if they got the chance? This so-called conspiracy you've dreamed up is nothing more than a routine reallocation of funds to avoid paying too much tax. It's perfectly legal – people do it all the time.'

I watched his expression become more complacent as he convinced himself that I believed the hogwash he was giving me. He obviously thought I didn't know about the personal bank account in the Caymen Islands. I might not understand the precise details of where the money was coming from, but I knew exactly where it was going.

'Next time you feel like accusing me of embezzlement,' he continued, 'why don't you stop and think about who pays for the extravagant lifestyle you've adopted so easily. Remember who pays for the clothes, the holidays, and the little luxuries you can't do without, before you bite the hand that feeds you. You're a Brightman now too, Cindy.'

I nodded dumbly.

'I hope you haven't been making a fool of yourself in front of Harley with all this,' he added with a hint of menace. 'I'm sure you don't want him finding out just how stupid you really are.'

I shook my head, trying to look suitably chastised. He really thought I'd swallowed it. So much the better, I told myself. Life would be a whole lot easier if he no longer saw me as a threat.

Fortifying myself with a hair of the dog from the towel cupboard of the guest bathroom, I tried to get my thoughts in order. All this business with David was distracting me from my real problem, which was sorting out my relationship with Harley.

He treated me as if I were a child, never listening to what I said or allowing me any control over my own life. If I didn't do something about it soon – didn't force him to give me some independence and respect – I would be no better than the other members of this society whose values I loathed. I had no intention of joining the ranks of the self-serving sycophants who pandered to him all the time.

I needed a proper confrontation with Harley – one in which I didn't back down at the first sign of resistance. We needed to have a long, frank talk.

I would stand up to him this time, I told myself, taking another swig from the vodka bottle. I would explain to him exactly why I was unhappy, and tell him what he had to do to put things right. I would lay down an agenda for our future relationship based on mutual co-operation and trust, and I would make it clear that we were both expected to make an effort.

Wasn't that what marriage was all about? Weren't people always saying that you had to work at it? My courage bolstered with vodka, I left the bathroom and marched downstairs in search of Harley. I was ready to take control of my destiny.

I didn't have to look far. I had just reached the hallway at the bottom of the stairs when he appeared at the door of the conservatory.

'Can you come in here a moment, Cindy,' he said. 'I want to talk to you.'

'Good – I'd like to have a talk to you too,' I replied, following him through the door. Had he anticipated my ultimatum, I wondered hopefully? Was he about to apologise for his thoughtless behaviour and tell me that he wanted to get our relationship back on the rails?

'We've been thinking,' he continued, 'and we've decided that things are getting out of hand.'

'I know,' I responded eagerly. 'I've been thinking exactly the . . .' I stopped. 'Did you say "we"?'

'David and I,' he elaborated – rather unnecessarily, as I had just seen David lounging in an armchair at the other side of the room. I threw him an unfriendly look. *We've* decided? How dare they discuss me as if I were their common property?

'We've decided that you've been under a lot of pressure lately,' continued Harley. 'We think you need a vacation.'

A vacation? That was the last thing I needed. What was the point of going away when we had all these problems to sort out right here at home?

'We're going to Italy, Cindy,' he went on excitedly. 'Remember the new commercial we're making? Well, the shooting starts next week – I forgot to tell you, with everything that's been happening here. David rented a house, and I thought we could go out there a bit early for a break.' He sighed and gave me a wistful look. 'You'll love it there, Cindy. Portofino's a really romantic place.'

'Hold on a minute,' I said quietly. 'Are you saying that you expected me to appear in a commercial in Italy *next week* and you *didn't think it was important to tell me?* What if I'd already arranged to do something else?'

'Oh, don't be silly,' said Harley with an indulgent laugh. 'What else would you be doing?'

I trembled with anger. How dare he speak to me like

that? I opened my mouth to tell him, once and for all, exactly what was wrong with his shitty chauvinistic behaviour.

'Oh, and I thought we might stop off in London on the way,' he added casually. 'You've always wanted to visit England, haven't you, Cindy?'

I closed my mouth again. London. My mind raced over the possibilities. Close enough to Guildford that I could sneak off for a day trip. I had unfinished business there which needed to be resolved before I could settle down to a new life, and this might be my one chance of getting there.

Gratefully seizing the opportunity to avoid the confrontation I had planned, I told myself that my reappraisal of our relationship would have to wait for a few days. I couldn't risk having an argument with Harley right now. He might change his mind if I upset him.

'That would be nice,' I said, managing a smile. 'I'd love to visit London.'

Harley beamed at David. 'What did I tell you,' he said in a triumphant voice. 'I knew she'd agree if I asked her the right way.'

That night, Harley pursued me into bed with enthusiasm.

'Cindy darling, I want you,' he murmured, his voice hoarse with passion. I tried to feign sleep, but he persisted.

Eventually he wore down my resistance and I begrudgingly let him have his way.

It was a mistake. Something had changed and I couldn't pretend any more.

I felt violated, invaded. It wasn't just Cindy's body which was being invaded, but something deeper inside – a part of my real self. I had convinced myself that I cared for Harley – but it wasn't true. I had mistaken the fleeting thrills of sexual intimacy for love. Now I knew that he would always be a stranger to me. I didn't just not love him – I despised him. I despised him for what he was – an empty-headed playboy manipulated by his ruthless brother – as well as for being vacuous enough to love someone like Cindy.

'My darling Cindy,' he gasped, thrusting into me. 'You're all mine again!'

Oh no, I'm not, I thought, bracing myself for the climax. I'm not anybody's Cindy. I'm not Cindy at all. I needed to make this journey to England so that I could get back in touch with my real self again and find out who I really was.

When we set off at lunchtime the next day, I was surprised to find that both David and George were travelling with us. José drove us to the airport, clearly relishing the idea of getting rid of George for a few weeks, but outraged that he should be riding in the back of the limousine with us.

'What a good idea that David suggested you come too, George,' said Harley in a jovial voice after we had all been staring at each other in gloomy silence for about twenty minutes. 'You'll be able to visit all your old haunts.'

'I must admit that I'm rather looking forward to the trip, sir,' said George stiffly. 'It'll be nice to pop down to Kempton Park and Windsor again. See how the lads are getting on.'

'Always good to catch up with old friends, eh, George?' said Harley in a patronising tone. 'Are those places where you used to live before you came to the States?'

'Oh, you could say something like that, sir,' replied George with a wistful smile. 'I used to travel around a bit. Bath, Newbury, Ascot, Sandown. You name the place and I've been there.'

'Lingfield?' I murmured. 'Goodwood? Fontwell?'

George's mouth dropped open. 'I say, Miss Cindy. You certainly know your way around the . . .'

'South of England?' I suggested quickly, winking at him. 'I was looking at the map last night,' I explained, turning to Harley.

We turned on to Sunset and, as we passed the *Lapinique* billboard, I found myself staring at the figures on the sidewalk. I scarcely knew what I was looking for until I saw her – the woman with the placard. She had lost her shopping cart since I saw her last, and she seemed to be walking with an even more dispirited stoop.

As we drew level with her, she lurched off the sidewalk into the road and began to weave her way unsteadily through the slowly moving queues of traffic. Horns began to sound.

'Christ,' muttered David in an exasperated tone. 'When are they going to clean up the streets around here? Get rid of some of these deadbeats?'

'When they find people like her somewhere to live,'

I said, fixing David with an angry stare. 'It's not her fault she's been squeezed out of the system by greedy bastards like you.'

José slammed on the brakes as the woman bounced off the side of a Cadillac which wouldn't give way and crashed against the front of our vehicle with a thud.

'Wait!' I shouted, fumbling with the doorhandle. 'Let me out – I have to see if she's all right.'

'Drive over the bitch,' hissed David. 'She asked for it.'

'Cindy, stay where you are!' exclaimed Harley. 'She might have a gun! You could be murdered out there!'

George raised his eyebrows, while José lifted his hands in a gesture of helplessness. I opened the door and stepped outside. The woman lay on the tarmac, her head inches away from one of the wheels.

'I didn't mean no harm, ma'am,' she gabbled hoarsely, her eyes wide with terror. 'I was only crossin' the road. Please don't call the cops – I ain't done nothin' wrong.'

'I know you haven't,' I whispered soothingly. 'Can you stand up?'

She cowered and flinched as I reached out my hand to help her. 'Come on, try,' I urged, taking her hand in mine. I stared at her face, fascinated by the faint resemblance she bore to Harriet. What was it that happened to old women, I wondered, that made them all end up looking the same?

More horns began to sound. 'Someone get those bitches out of the goddamn way!' shouted a voice from a distant car.

Whatever it was, I thought, it somehow made the rest of humanity conspire together to despise them. There was something about age in a woman which always seemed to frighten people – especially men.

Regaining her feet, the woman gazed at me with suspicion. She was clearly not used to kindness.

I opened my handbag and unzipped the inner pocket. It contained a rolled bundle of hundred dollar bills that Harley insisted I carried with me for emergencies. 'Hold on,' I whispered, arranging myself so that he couldn't see what I was doing. Peeling off one of the bills, I pressed it into her hand. 'Take this.'

She backed away, her eyes popping. 'You settin' me up?' she asked in a voice thick with distrust. 'Makin' it look like I stole it?'

'It's yours,' I urged. 'Please take it. Get yourself some food – or whatever you need.'

'Get back in the car, Cindy!' yelled Harley, winding down the window. 'What do you think you're doing? I won't have my wife walking around on the street with vagrants!'

I swung round and glared at his soft, pampered features. Did he have no feelings? No compassion for people who were less fortunate than himself?

'Wait!' I hissed, catching hold of the woman's arm. I took the rest of the bundle, which must have contained nearly two thousand dollars, and stuffed it into her pocket. 'Take that as well. Treat yourself.'

She felt her pocket and gazed at me with an expression of disbelief. 'You better not be foolin' with me,' she said eventually. ''Cause the minute you and me part company here, you won't be layin' eyes on these greenbacks again.'

With a little whoop of excitement, she darted away through the traffic and disappeared from view.

What the hell, I thought to myself, getting back into the car and outfacing the other occupants with a cool stare. Harley had plenty of money. Perhaps it was time I dispensed a little charity to those who needed it more than he did.

I pretended to be asleep for most of the flight to England so that I wouldn't have to talk to Harley. He passed the time by reading a large bundle of women's magazines he had bought at the airport, lingering over the *Lapinique* advertisements. Looking through half-closed eyelids, I caught him throwing furtive glances in my direction, comparing me with the image on the page in front of him. Was he wondering what had happened to the Face of *Lapinique*? Was he curious to know why the wide-eyed and innocent twenty-one-year-old he had married seemed to have grown up so fast?

When we landed at Heathrow, I experienced an incredible feeling of relief to be back in England. The area around the airport might not be one of the most attractive places in the world, but it wasn't until I saw this familiar landscape that I realised quite how much I hated America. I was home at last – back in the place where I belonged.

The taxi driver who took us into London sounded as if he had just walked straight off the set of *Eastenders*.

'That sure is quaint,' whispered Harley in my ear. 'They say you have to be born listening to the sound of Bow Bells to get an accent like that.'

I stared at him. *Bow Bells?* What kind of half-baked tourist guidebooks had he been reading? Did he imagine a London filled with Beefeaters, Pearly Kings and red telephone boxes? He'd be telling me next that the streets were paved with gold.

Gazing out of the window of our suite at the Dorchester I remembered all the times I had visited London in the past, when I was Harriet. On one occasion I had trudged halfway up Park Lane with heavy bags of shopping before I realised that I had taken the wrong turning, and had stopped outside this hotel, to check my *A to Z* and get my bearings. I remembered being fascinated by the expensive-looking people coming in and out of the foyer and wondering what it was that set the rich apart – making them almost a different species to ordinary people like myself.

I might appear to be one of them now I had married Harley, but deep down I knew that I didn't really belong. You had to be born into the breed to share their arrogant view of the world as a repository of riches to be plundered – as a storehouse whose sole purpose was to supply their needs. I hadn't been born rich, either as Harriet or as Cindy. Was this, I wondered, one of the reasons why Harley and I could never really understand each other?

I spent some time trying to work out how I was going to escape to Guildford. Should I pretend to have relatives I wanted to trace? It wasn't that far from the truth. Or should I simply say that I wanted to spend a day exploring London alone?

Something told me that Harley would never allow it,

and I eventually decided that the best course of action was simply to take off and leave the explanations until afterwards. I couldn't bear to be stopped now that I was so close to home.

The following morning, I waited until Harley was busy flossing his teeth in the bathroom and crept out. I left a note on the pillow. *Gone out on my own for the day. Don't worry, I'll be back later. Love Cindy.*

Love was hard to write, but I gritted my teeth. I didn't want him getting suspicious yet.

Taking a taxi to Waterloo station, I found the fast train to Guildford waiting on the usual platform. As it pulled out of the station and I looked out of the window at the familiar sights – the Houses of Parliament, Big Ben, the new MI6 building – I began to realise that my spiritual quest could also serve a practical purpose. I had no idea what I was going to do next, but I had a strong feeling that I wouldn't be returning to the States in a hurry. How would I live if I found myself alone in England, without Harley? I was no longer a British citizen. There were immigration laws and so on – things I had never learned about because I hadn't thought that they might ever apply to me. If Harriet's disappearance had not yet been discovered, a second identity, created with the help of her papers, might prove an invaluable asset. There were a few problems I wasn't sure how to handle, like the differences in age and appearance, but there was bound to be a way around them if I thought about it hard enough.

Forty minutes later, the train was approaching Guildford and I felt a pang of melancholy. How many times had I arrived here in my previous life – returning from a lonely shopping trip or theatre visit – a sad old spinster going home to her empty flat? Now, I was a young married woman – but did my life hold any greater hope?

Emerging from the station, I trudged up the hill, following the familiar route home through the crowds of shoppers on the High Street. The *Lapinique* advertisement hadn't arrived in the UK yet – I had checked this with Harley. I was safe from recognition for the time being. Scanning the faces as they went by, I wondered if I might see someone from my past. How would it feel to come face to face with Sally, or even Andrew, without their having the slightest idea who I was?

The spare key was where I had left it, wedged inside a convenient recess in the stone garden wall. Letting myself into the communal hallway, I crept quietly up the stairs, hoping the old lady on the ground floor wouldn't hear me. With trembling hands, I unlocked the door of my flat.

I stepped over a pile of junk mail and went into the living room. It was over three months since I had last been here, but it seemed as if it were only yesterday. Memories came flooding back as I gazed at the familiar objects – the books on the table, the dirty coffee cups, the empty whisky bottle – memories of my life as Harriet. Catching a glimpse of my reflection in the mirror over the fireplace, I felt a shiver of disorientation. How many times had I looked in that mirror and confronted an entirely different face?

My heartbeat quickened as I opened the bedroom

door. What would I find? I half expected to see Harriet's mouldering body, but the room was empty. I examined the unmade bed, pulling aside the crumpled sheets in search of some clue as to what had happened, but there was nothing there. In the interests of thoroughness, I went through the rest of the flat – checking the broom cupboard, the wardrobe, even looking under the bed – but I could find no trace of the bodily presence of the woman I had once been.

When I was certain that I wasn't sharing the flat with a corpse, I set to work collecting the things I needed – Harriet's credit card, chequebook, passport, and other documents I thought might be useful. I checked the calendar on the wall. I had paid my rent in advance, and there were a few weeks left before the next installment was due. By then, I would be in a position to decide about my future. Meanwhile, as long as I could avoid the woman downstairs, I had a bolthole – somewhere to hide out for a few days if I needed it.

Before leaving the flat, I glanced through the heap of circulars and bills on the doormat. The bills could wait – they always had in the past – but one of the brown envelopes was franked with a familiar slogan: *Dip into a good book – make the most of your library service.*

I opened it and found a cheque made out in Harriet's name. The redundancy money from the library – I had forgotten completely about it. It wasn't a fortune, but it was enough to live on for a few months.

Locking the door carefully behind me, I left the flat

and walked back down the hill to the High Street. I paid the cheque into Harriet's bank account, then turned down the narrow passage by the coffee shop which led to North Street. It was time for a visit to the library.

The foyer was crowded. Pushing my way through to the main hall, I felt a shock of recognition as I saw the familiar faces behind the desk. Cynthia Hoskins, one of the few staff members who had ever been friendly towards me, caught me looking at her and responded with a hostile glare. Simon Dawson, the assistant manager, flashed me a lecherous smile.

'Can I help you?'

I felt his eyes travelling up and down my body. He had never looked at me like that when he was berating me for late arrival in the mornings.

I smiled sweetly. 'Could you possibly direct me,' I asked, 'to the *Living and Learning* section?'

'Straight down at the back of the main hall – let me show you.' He stepped eagerly from behind the desk.

'Don't get lost on the way,' muttered Cynthia, stapling a sheaf of papers together with a fierce movement. 'Whatever would I tell your wife when she came to meet you for lunch?'

The *Living and Learning* section occupied a large open area which used to be filled with shelves. Padded chairs with tubular steel frames were arranged in tasteful groupings, interspersed with low tables and pot plants. The books were confined to display racks along two sides of the space and to a handful of revolving stands containing paperbacks. A row of computer terminals lined the third wall, and on the fourth, flanked by racks of newspapers, magazines and videos, Annette Baker presided over the enquiry desk.

It looked more like an airport departure lounge than a library, and I fought back an impulse to ask when the next flight was boarding. One thing pleased me immensely – despite the crowds in the foyer, this part of the library was almost deserted. It looked as if the *Living and Learning* project was not the runaway success everyone had expected.

I sat down at one of the public access terminals. Selecting the 'search catalogue' option, I scrolled through the subject headings and soon found a title which would suit my purpose.

Annette Baker eyed me suspiciously as I approached the desk.

'Have you got a copy of *The Tribal Myth – A Study of Social Groupings in West African Villages*?' I asked.

'I'll have to look it up,' she said irritably, turning to her computer screen. She looked tired – older and less glamorous than I remembered. Her 'smart little suit' – the same one she had been wearing the last time I saw her – looked shabby next to my expensively tailored outfit.

'I'm afraid it's in the reserve collection,' she said finally, as if that was the end of the matter. I could have told her that – it was the reason I had chosen that particular book.

'May I see it, please?'

She gave me a look of exasperation. 'I'll have to go all the way down to the basement for it, you know?'

'That's all right,' I replied with a smile. 'I don't mind waiting.'

As soon as she was gone, I slipped into the seat behind the desk and began to tap rapidly away at the keyboard. My password was out of date, but it was a simple matter to assign myself a new one. Glancing around to make sure I wasn't being observed, I gained access to the main programme and typed in a series of commands.

Warning! said a message on the screen. *Are you sure you wish to delete all files in the Living and Learning directory? Y/N*

With a feeling of pleasure, I pressed the letter *Y* and hit the return key several times to be on the safe side. Then I emptied the recycle bin. Moments later, I was mingling with the shoppers on North Street, attracting curious glances from everyone who saw the broad smile of satisfaction which spread irrepressibly across my face.

I didn't want to leave Guildford without making some kind of contact with Sally and Andrew – even if just to see them from a distance, to reassure myself that they were still there. I didn't quite know how to achieve this, and I walked the streets for some time, racking my brains for an idea. Eventually I plucked up my courage and rang Sally's number from a telephone box.

'My name's Mrs, er, Brightwater,' I said when she replied. 'I've had your name recommended to me as an interior designer – I have a large house in LA which needs a complete overhaul.'

'LA?' asked Sally, sounding surprised. 'Well, I haven't worked in the States before, but I've just set up on my own, so there's no reason why I shouldn't diversify. Perhaps you could give me a few details?'

'The point is,' I said, 'I'm passing through Guildford at the moment, and I wondered if it might be convenient to drop by – have a look at your portfolio, that sort of thing?'

'Of course,' said Sally. 'What time would suit you?'

'No time like the present,' I said gaily. 'Are you busy right now?'

I waited for half an hour in a pub before walking the short distance to Sally's house, not wishing to arouse her suspicions by seeming too keen. I had only remembered at the last moment to go through the motions of asking for directions.

'Do you mind my asking,' she enquired as I followed her into the house, 'where you heard of my name? I mean, I don't advertise or anything – I still do a lot of my work for a consultancy.'

'A mutual friend, I believe,' I said, taking a seat at the familiar pine table in the kitchen. 'A lady I met in Barbados recommended you most warmly.'

'What was her name?' asked Sally with a puzzled frown.

'Ah, now there's a question,' I murmured, removing my coat. Sally rushed to take it from me and laid it carefully over the back of a chair.

'Coffee?' she asked anxiously. 'Or do you prefer tea?'

I felt guilty deceiving my friend like this. But what else could I do? She would never believe me if I told the truth.

'I think,' I said slowly, 'the lady was called Harriet.'

'Harriet!' exclaimed Sally with wide eyes. 'Whatever was she doing in Barbados?'

'I seem to remember something about a world cruise . . .'

'Gosh,' said Sally, almost to herself. 'So she did it after all. Good old Harriet.' She gave me a searching look. 'How was she? Was she all right? I mean, was she enjoying herself and all that?'

'Oh yes,' I said quietly. *Sally*, cried my inner voice. *Sally, it's me – Harriet! Don't you recognise me?* This meeting was more painful than I had expected.

Eager to get the deception over with, I rattled out a load of nonsense about the work I needed doing – about my ideas for the redesign of Harley's mansion in LA.

'It's terribly fashionable at the moment to have a British designer,' I assured her. 'You really ought to make a few contacts out there – they'll love you to bits.'

If I ever went back to the States, I thought, I would give her the job. Harley needed to get that eclectic mish-mash of styles sorted out before his house gained a reputation as a museum of international bad taste.

'I'm interviewing a number of top designers,' I added, hoping to soften her disappointment if nothing came of it. 'I don't expect to make my final choice for a week or two.'

Sally nodded, a sudden look of tiredness on her face.

'Are you all right?' I asked anxiously. 'The lady I met – Harriet – seemed concerned about you. She was very keen that I should look you up.'

'Really?' asked Sally. She sighed. Things *have* been a bit difficult lately, what with Duncan leaving and everything . . .'

'Duncan leaving!' I exclaimed. 'Er, who's Duncan?' I added quickly.

'My husband. Ex-husband to be. I threw him out last week.'

'What happened?'

She looked at me with interest. 'Do you really want to know? I mean, this isn't very professional, is it? Why would a successful woman like you want to hear about my problems? Especially if you're thinking of employing me to do a job?'

'Don't worry about the job,' I said with abandon. 'It's yours already. And I'm not successful – my husband's the one with the money.' There was no reason why I couldn't persuade Harley to commission her anyway, whether I returned to the States with him or not.

'Well,' said Sally slowly. 'It all started when he came home with a new BMW . . .'

Gradually, with encouragement, she opened up and poured out her story. Two hours and a bottle of wine later, I knew the truth about Sally's 'dream marriage'. I heard how Duncan had pushed her into a career she didn't enjoy, how he worked long hours at his job, leaving her to look after the children she had never really wanted, how he cared about nothing but money – money and prestige. How she was worn out trying to keep up with the lifestyle he imposed on her, throwing parties and spending money in the belief that it would impress people. How she longed for nothing better than to have some peace and quiet on her own to do what *she* wanted and to get to know herself properly for the first time.

'Harriet was right,' she said sadly. 'The woman in Barbados, remember? She was so independent – she never needed a man to prop up her self-esteem.'

'Harriet told me,' I said softly, 'that if I did look you up, I was to send you her love.'

I left Sally's house with tears in my eyes. How blindly I had judged her – how wrong I had been. If I had been a better friend to her, I might have known all this before – might have been able to help her.

There was one more thing I had to do before I went back to London to have things out with Harley. I had to see Andrew again.

CHAPTER 15

I had remembered, half way through my talk with Sally, that this was the day Andrew taught his creative writing classes at the university. I looked at my watch. There was plenty of time to get there before the evening session began.

I spent some time wandering the campus before I found the building where evening classes were held. An enthusiastic woman at the front desk tried to sign me up for pottery-making and raffia work, then directed me to the wrong classroom, where I blundered into a lecture on quantum physics.

Returning to make further enquiries, I turned a corner and walked straight into Andrew, spilling his armful of papers all over the floor.

'Oh, I'm sorry,' I gasped, bending to help pick them up. 'Let me . . .'

'That's all right,' he muttered, scrabbling around at my feet. 'My fault. Should have been looking where I was going.'

'I'm a bit lost, actually.' I said. 'Do you know where the writing class is?'

'I certainly do,' he replied, snatching a stray paper from behind a radiator. 'I'm going there myself.' He stood up, brushing dust from his trousers, and looked at me for the first time. 'The thing is . . .' He paused, frowning. 'You're new here, aren't you?'

I gazed at his familiar face – the face I knew so well. Had he recognised something about me? Was it my voice?

'Well, I guess you could say that,' I replied, improvising an exaggerated American drawl. 'I'm just over on a visit, really. I was kinda wonderin' if I could sit in on one of these writing lessons – see how you do them over here?'

'Well, well.' He looked confused. 'The class is oversubscribed, really . . .'

'You mean *you're* the tutor?' I asked, feigning surprise. 'Now that's what I call a coincidence!' I gave him a playful smile. '*You* could get me in, then, couldn't you?'

Andrew was clearly pleased at this allusion to his authority. 'I . . . er . . . suppose we could make an exception just this once,' he said, looking as if he had just sanctioned a major breach of the university rules. 'I don't see that it would do any harm.' He glanced at his watch. 'We'd better hurry up, though, or I'll have a mutiny on my hands – I'm ten minutes late.'

The class was composed mainly of middle-aged women, whose chatter ceased abruptly at Andrew's entrance. They turned attentively towards him, adoration written in their eyes, as he took his place at the front.

'We have a new student with us this evening, ladies,'

he said, throwing me a conspiratorial smile. Several pairs of eyes shifted in my direction and registered looks of annoyance.

'This is . . .' he hesitated. 'What *did* you say your name was?'

'Cindy,' I simpered, fluttering my eyelashes.

'I thought this class was full,' said a plump woman with horn-rimmed glasses and a blue tint to her hair. She glared at me. 'My friend Janice has been waiting ages for a place.'

'Cindy's just visiting,' said Andrew, shuffling his papers. He looked up and grinned. 'I don't think we should turn her away from our seat of learning, seeing as she's come all the way from . . . *where* exactly was it?'

'LA,' I purred, growing in confidence. 'Beverly Hills, to be precise.' I surveyed the rows of smug, well-dressed matrons. These were exactly the kind of women who used to intimidate me so much when I was Harriet. 'We have quite a few writers in our neighbourhood, actually,' I added, with a tone of condescension borrowed directly from Eleanor. 'I often run into them at our little parties.'

'Do you know Jackie Collins?' asked one of the women excitedly.

'What about Quentin Tarantino?' enquired another with a giggle.

'Now, now,' said Andrew, looking flustered. 'We don't want to embarrass our guest, do we? Let's get started on some readings. Who wants to go first?'

Regaining control, he began to bask in the glow of

their attention. I sat in silence through a dozen or so offerings, which varied from bodice-ripping yarns to impenetrable meanderings about the meaning of life. Andrew made comments from time to time, setting off flurries of debate as the women vied to impress him with their critical skills.

'I'm not entirely convinced,' said one woman airily, 'by the way Rosie's heroine reacts to finding her husband in bed with another woman.'

'That's the way it happened,' muttered Rosie sulkily.

'Would it be an idea,' said another, 'to do it as a flashback – or even a dream sequence?'

'I feel it's more of a conversation piece,' said Janice's friend.

'Why not tell it from the husband's viewpoint?' suggested another, cattily.

'I think you have to be careful,' said Andrew in a diplomatic tone, 'when you're dealing with material of an autobiographical nature. There's a temptation to tell the story too literally – to lose sight of the author's role in arranging the structure of the plot. These sixteen pages of invective about the woman's character – while they might express the true feelings of the, er, fictional heroine – tend to distract us from the, er, the essential drama of the situation.'

'But aren't we trying to reproduce real life on paper?' asked Janice's friend. 'Shouldn't we be trying to show things as they really are?'

'Up to a point,' said Andrew. 'But it would make rather dull reading if you simply wrote down everything that happened. Most of us lead very boring lives.'

He caught my eye and smiled. 'What do you think, Cindy?'

A dozen pairs of hostile eyes turned to stare at me. 'I don't know that you're entirely right there,' I said boldly. 'Don't people say that truth is stranger than fiction? If you wrote down what really happened, then sometimes no one would believe you.'

'Cindy here,' said Andrew with a grin, 'obviously leads a much more exciting life over there in America than we do in boring old Guildford.' The class broke into titters of amusement.

'Have *you* brought anything to read out tonight?' asked Rosie bitchily. 'To show us how it should be done?'

'I . . . er . . .'

'Ah!' exclaimed Andrew, checking his watch. 'Nine o'clock!' He glanced impishly in my direction. 'Saved by the bell!'

Chairs scraped back and notebooks were packed into shopping bags. 'Anyone for the pub?' he added casually, precipitating a flurry of last-minute rescheduling.

'Derek's picking me up, but I could always ring and ask him to wait.'

'I have to get back in time to record that wildlife programme for Brian, but I could probably stop by for a few minutes.'

'I shouldn't really – I'm driving the new BMW tonight – but I could always have a soft drink.'

'Why don't you join us, Cindy?' suggested Andrew. 'You can tell us all about literary life in LA.'

Andrew, myself, and a handful of the women made

our way to a nearby pub. Andrew bought me a double whisky, while the women clustered round the bar and squabbled about whose turn it was to buy a drink for him.

'I hope you enjoyed our little session tonight, Cindy,' said Andrew, guiding me to a seat. 'Tell me, have you done much writing yourself?'

'I, er . . . haven't really started anything yet,' I said evasively. 'I'm kinda still thinking things through.'

Andrew launched into one of his standard spiels about the therapeutic value of creative writing and I listened with glazed eyes, remembering the times I had heard it before. Would he have expressed himself with quite so much enthusiasm, I wondered, if he knew who I really was?

The women returned from the bar with trays of drinks. It seemed the dispute had not been resolved – several separate half pints of beer were placed in front of him.

'Oh dear,' he said with a laugh. 'It looks as if I'll have to drink them all! Wouldn't do to show favouritism, would it?'

'I've bought you some crisps,' said the woman called Rosie, laying a packet on the table and patting it fondly. 'Salt and vinegar – they're your favourite, aren't they?'

I glanced up at her. She was about Harriet's age, smartly dressed, and had an air of primness – as if she considered this trip to the pub to be rather daring. But she had an attractive face with a kindly smile. Had she ever been my rival for Andrew's affections, I wondered? I looked back at Andrew, experiencing a surge of the old jealousy. Why had he never recognised how much I felt for him? And why did I still feel so much, even now?

Conversation continued much as if we were still in the class, with Andrew preening and showing off with obscure quotations from Shakespeare.

Unfortunately for him, I knew his routine. He had practised it on me in the past, over tea and crumpets. When I successfully identified six quotations in a row and countered them with others I knew he was saving for later, he stared at me with admiring disbelief.

'You certainly know your Shakespeare, Cindy. Have you studied literature at all?'

'Only in the library,' I replied with a laugh.

One by one, the women departed to catch buses and trains, pointedly ignoring me as they lingered over their goodbyes to Andrew. Rosie was the last to leave, a wistful look in her eye.

There wasn't much time before the last train left for London – how would Harley react if I didn't return that night? Suddenly, I didn't care. I had unfinished business with Andrew that I wanted to conclude. I wanted to teach him a lesson – to show him what it felt like to be the seduced instead of the seducer, to be the one without power.

Last orders were called at the bar. Andrew drained his fifth half-pint and added the glass to the row of empties in front of him.

'Another?' I suggested coyly. 'One for the road?'

'I'll get them,' said Andrew eagerly, standing up and reaching in his pocket. 'Same again?'

I nodded, offering my empty glass with a flirtatious

smile. When he returned from the bar, I moved my seat closer, leaning forward and extending my hand so that it almost touched his.

'I just love the way you English men are all so *masculine*,' I purred, meeting his eyes with a provocative gaze. 'I'm told you have real passionate natures behind all that famous British reserve.'

'Do we really?' he asked, looking surprised. 'I must say, you've been a breath of fresh air yourself this evening, Cindy. We do tend to get a bit set in our ways – in the class, I mean – without any, er . . . new blood.'

'You're quite some teacher, Andrew.' I traced a line on the back of his hand with my fingertip. 'Maybe you could teach me some more.'

'I'd like to very much,' he replied, looking pleased. 'I don't know how long you're staying over here, but I was hoping you might be able to come to the class again next week . . .'

'Why wait until next week?' I breathed huskily, reaching under the table and gently squeezing his crotch.

His eyes bulged with surprise. He continued to talk as if nothing had happened but, after a few moments, I felt a tentative hand on my knee. Clasping it firmly in mine, I deliberately guided it under the hem of my skirt.

'Would you like to come back for a coffee?' he whispered, unable to hide the excitement in his voice.

There it was. The invitation I had longed for all those years. You little tart, Andrew, I thought bitterly. You don't know anything about me, but you're prepared to leap into bed with me on the strength of a couple of lousy bits of Shakespeare and a quick feel. How many of your students have you done this with before?

Back at his flat, I waited on the sofa while he went through the motions of making coffee. The familiar surroundings triggered memories of my last visit as Harriet, diminishing my confidence and forcing me to remind myself that I was no longer the same person. When Andrew returned, however, he was clearly far more nervous than I was.

'Don't be shy,' I murmured, patting the cushion beside me as he hesitated between the sofa and the armchair. Leaning towards him as he sat down, I whispered a phrase borrowed from Mephisto into his ear:

'Sometimes indiscretions/Are our most valuable possessions.'

'That's from Faust, isn't it?' said Andrew, giving me a puzzled look. 'Now is it Marlowe or Goethe?' He scratched his head. 'Funny you should pick that one . . .'

'Why?'

He shook his head, blinking. 'Nothing. Just reminded me of something . . .'

Something or someone? It didn't occupy his thoughts for very long, however. Moving closer, I slid an arm around his neck and kissed him firmly on the lips, a kiss I had dreamed of for years when I was Harriet.

He responded, cautiously at first, then with increasing enthusiasm as he realised that I wasn't about to push him away. His breathing became faster as his hands explored my upper body, caressing my breasts through the flimsy material of my blouse.

'Mmmm,' I said, taking his hand. 'Where's the bedroom?'

I had intended to humiliate Andrew – to lead him on to the point of no return, then pull away, feigning disgust at our actions. I would apologise – blame it on the drinks he had plied me with – and tell him I didn't know what had come over me. I would point out that he was old enough to be my father and ask how he thought a young woman like myself could possibly find him attractive. Then I would depart, leaving him in a state of frustration and self-doubt.

In his bedroom, an inner sanctum I had never entered in my previous life, he kissed me for a long time before gently attempting to remove my clothes. I couldn't bring myself to stop him – not yet. I wanted to satisfy my curiosity first.

When I was Harriet, I had spent many lonely hours directing this scene in my head, rerunning it over and over with different settings and dialogue, trying to imagine what it would be like. I had wondered what Andrew would look like without his clothes – whether I would find his ageing body attractive or not. I had also worried what he might think of my body – whether it was possible for a man to love a woman with flabby thighs and drooping breasts.

Now it was really happening. It was happening to Cindy, not Harriet – but as he threw aside the last of his clothes and our naked bodies came together, something changed inside me and I was Harriet again. Abandoning my thoughts of revenge, I pulled him towards me and caressed him with the tenderness I had always longed to show.

His body was just as I had expected – slightly overweight in some places, showing signs of sagging and wrinkling in others – but I adored every inch of it. I was still in love with him – in love with the person inside.

I wanted to tell him, to whisper *I love you* in his ear, but I thought it might sound rather odd coming from someone he had met only a few hours before. Instead, I concentrated on the pleasure of the moment. Andrew's lovemaking was more passionate than I had expected, though somewhat uncoordinated.

'Sorry,' he said, as our noses bumped together.

'Ouch, sorry.' Our teeth clashed in the frenzy of a kiss.

'I've just thought of something,' he said suddenly, from somewhere near my navel. He surfaced with an expression of dismay. 'I haven't got any condoms.'

I had expected an old philanderer like him to have a rack of them by his bedside. 'Never mind,' I said, reaching for my handbag. 'I think I've got something here.' I took out the pack of three I had found in Cindy's bag on the first day in the hospital. I had kept them – just in case of emergencies. Andrew glanced at the packet doubtfully, then tore away the cellophane with his teeth and got down to business.

He came with a gentle moan of pleasure, quite unlike Harley's melodramatic cries. Then he shuddered and let out a strange whimpering sound.

'Andrew, what's the matter?'

'I'm sorry,' he muttered, reaching for his shirt. 'I should never have done this. I've taken advantage of you.'

'No, you haven't,' I said softly. 'You'll never know how much I enjoyed that.'

'The thing is,' he said slowly. 'The thing is . . .'

'It's all right,' I said, holding him close, not wanting this precious moment to end.

'I hardly know you,' he spluttered, pushing me to one side. He stood up and began to put his clothes on. 'I've never done anything like this before – I got carried away . . .'

He dressed rapidly and strode out of the room. I sat up in bed, miserably wondering where I had gone wrong.

Eventually I got dressed myself and went into the living room. He sat by the fireplace in his usual chair, moodily twirling the toasting fork in his hand.

'Do you want to talk?' I asked.

He sighed. 'You wouldn't understand – a young girl like you with your whole life ahead of you.'

'I might.'

'I'm sorry about the way I behaved,' he said. 'It's just that, well, I have a lot of young female students – none as attractive as you, mind – and a man of my age can't help having thoughts, fantasies, about what it might be like if . . . well, you know. When you touched me like that in the pub, I just couldn't resist . . . it seemed too good to be true. I didn't stop to think of the consequences.'

'What consequences? Why should there need to be any consequences?'

'Oh, I know there won't be any for you, my dear,' he said in a weary tone. 'Ships passing in the night and all that. But the problem for me is . . . well, the emotions play funny tricks on you at my time of life. The truth is, you remind me of someone I used to know. Your voice, mostly – though I can't imagine why because she wasn't American. Maybe it was just something you said. I'm afraid I've been sitting here thinking about her.'

'Did you love her?' I asked, trembling.

'Yes,' he said sadly. 'I never realised until it was too late. She went away – I'll probably never see her again.' He swung round and faced me. 'I'm sorry – I can't expect you to understand this – but I feel I've betrayed her.'

You stupid plonker, Andrew, I thought. Why didn't you think a bit harder? If only you had said something – given me the faintest encouragement – I could have seen to the rest. I wouldn't have listened to Mephisto then. None of this would ever have happened.

Now, it was too late.

'Listen, Andrew,' I said. 'I'm just as much to blame – I mean, I started it, didn't I?'

'What on earth do you see in me?'

I hesitated. 'You can't always explain these things,' I said eventually. 'Sometimes they just happen.'

'You've been terribly understanding,' he said. 'I don't deserve it really. Can I see you again? Make it up to you?'

'No,' I said firmly. 'It wouldn't work. Not now.'

What was I doing? Rejecting the man I loved? But I knew it wouldn't work – even ignoring the ridiculous age difference, he could never love me for the right reasons now.

'There are just two things you can do for me,' I added.

'What?'

'May I sleep on your sofa?' The last train had departed hours ago, and I didn't want to return to Harriet's empty flat.

'Of course,' he said, looking puzzled. 'If you want to. What's the other thing?'

'The woman you were talking about – the one you loved – what was her name?'

'Why on earth do you want to know that?'

I wanted to hear him say it. 'Please tell me.'

'Harriet,' he murmured softly, almost to himself. 'Maybe she'll come back one day.'

'Who can tell?' I said, wanting to comfort him. 'Maybe she will.'

If only he knew.

I slept on Andrew's sofa, fully clothed, in front of the fireplace where we used to toast crumpets together. The memory of those times seemed precious, even though I remembered only too clearly how unhappy I was then. Imagining what might have been, I was overtaken by a sense of sadness. By becoming Cindy, I had achieved the material things I had always wanted, but it was a hollow victory – the happiness I might have found with Andrew was now forever out of reach.

The following morning I left while he was still asleep and caught an early train back to London. What was Harley going to say about my absence? More importantly, what was I going to say to him? I stared out of the window at the drab suburban landscape. To me, it was rich in memories and associations. This was the place where my heart belonged – I would never feel truly at home in the designer fortresses of Beverly Hills. The train rattled over the points and Mephisto's words came unbidden into my head:

Never underestimate the power of beauty to corrupt.

He had been right, after all. I *had* been corrupted. I had been prepared to sacrifice the things which mattered – love, truth and friendship – for the material rewards that Harley had to offer. Not satisfied with getting a double measure of youth and beauty, I had wanted my cup to overflow with fame and fortune as well. In order to get these things, I had allowed myself to be seduced by the glamour of Harley's lifestyle and had confused the desire to be in love with him with the feeling itself.

Now I had been back to Guildford – now I had met once again with the man I really loved – I couldn't go back to America with Harley. What was I going to do? I remembered the remarks I had overheard at the wedding: *Cheap little bimbo . . . clean him out when it comes to the divorce* . . . I wasn't like that, I told myself angrily. I didn't want his money. I didn't want the notoriety of being the Face of *Lapinique* either – the novelty of that hadn't taken long to wear off.

All I wanted was to be happy. I didn't know what the

future held, but if I wanted to find love – the real kind of love which went deeper than surface appearances – I would have to leave Harley and find a new life of my own.

No one could recognise me in England. I had a ready-made alias in Harriet's identity which would serve my purposes for the time being. The redundancy money from the library would keep me going until I could work out the details – where to live, how to support myself and how to get around the immigration laws. By the time the new *Lapinique* advertisement came out, I could easily have changed my image enough to preserve my anonymity.

Would I ever find someone to love – someone to grow old with? My beauty, I realised, was a handicap which stood in the way of real relationships with other human beings. Men chased after me, women envied and hated me, but nobody took me seriously. Nobody tried to make contact with the lonely person trapped inside.

Arriving back at the Dorchester, I let myself quietly into the suite. I had hoped to delay the moment of confrontation, but Harley appeared straight away at the bedroom door.

'Cindy!' His face looked haggard, as if he hadn't slept for a week. 'Where the hell have you been? I've been worried sick.'

'I, er, missed the train,' I said lamely. 'I'm sorry – I should have telephoned.' I paused. This wasn't going to be easy. 'Listen, Harley,' I said. 'Things aren't working out too well, are they? We need to have a serious talk.'

'Where did you spend the night, then?' asked Harley suspiciously, ignoring my last remark. 'Or should I ask *who* you spent it with? Have you been with another guy?'

I shook my head, realising as I did so that I had in fact committed adultery the previous night. 'I stayed in a hotel,' I muttered. 'Listen, Harley. I need to spend some time on my own. I'm not happy, and I'm not making you happy either . . .'

'A hotel!' exploded Harley. 'Are you telling me I married some two-bit hooker who turns tricks in hotels?' He paced back and forth several times across the room, striking his hand against the wall on each turn, then whirled round to face me. 'Who is this guy?' he demanded in a melodramatic tone. Disgust flooded into his voice. 'Some stranger you picked up on the street?'

'There's no one else,' I said emphatically, meeting his gaze. 'I just need to go away for a while.'

He stared at me with a bewildered expression. It seemed to be sinking in at last. 'What do you mean, go away?' He followed me across the room to the sofa. 'What are you talking about?'

I sat down and took a deep breath. 'The thing is, Harley . . .'

'How can you say we're not happy?' he interrupted angrily. 'Haven't I looked after you? Given you everything you need?' He resumed his pacing, making circles round the coffee table. 'How can you be so unappreciative?' he added in a hurt voice.

'I'm not unappreciative, Harley,' I said quietly. 'I'm

really grateful for everything you've done. It's just that . . .'

'I won't allow you to do this!' He came to a halt in front of the sofa and looked down at me with a stern expression. 'I don't know who's been putting these crazy ideas into your head, but you better start forgetting them right now!' He folded his arms. 'You're my wife, Cindy, and you're staying right here with me where you belong.'

'How can you make me?'

He looked surprised. 'Didn't you hear what I said? I told you, I won't allow it.' He reached out and patted my shoulder. 'Now come on,' he said in a conciliatory tone. 'You're overtired. Why don't you have a rest, and we'll try to pretend that none of this ever happened.'

Why wouldn't he listen? Brushing his hand away, I stood up and faced him. 'It's not that simple, Harley,' I said, looking him in the eye. 'We don't love each other. What's the point in pretending?'

His eyes filled with a mixture of hurt and disbelief. 'Of course we love each other!' he burst out angrily. 'We proved that in bed every night.' He turned away and strode towards the window, then swung round abruptly. 'Are you telling me I'm not good enough? Are you saying that I can't satisfy you?' His face took on a tortured expression. 'Have you found somebody who can?'

'I told you, Harley, there's no one else.'

'I don't believe you!' He clutched his forehead and stared at me wildly. 'What other explanation can there be for this cranky behaviour of yours!'

'But, you don't understand . . .'

'Goddamnit – do you think I was born yesterday? I know the way you dumb broads operate.' He moved towards me with a threatening gesture. 'I thought you were different, Cindy. Now you betrayed me . . .'

'But . . .'

He seized me roughly by the shoulders and dragged me to my feet. 'Tell me the truth,' he snarled. 'I won't let you make a fool of me!'

I opened my mouth to protest.

'Stop!' he cried. 'Wait! Don't say anything!' He threw me violently back on the sofa.

'I can't stand it – the idea of you making out with some other guy – it's too much . . .' His face crumpled and he turned and fled towards the door. 'I never thought it would come to this,' he wailed, struggling with the door handle. There was a loud scuffling noise as the door flew open and George fell into the room.

'Treachery everywhere!' exclaimed Harley, pushing him roughly aside. 'I can't trust anybody any more!' He rushed through the door and disappeared down the corridor with an anguished cry.

George shot me a malevolent glance, then picked himself up and went after him.

'Wait, Mr Harley, sir!' His voice trailed away as he pursued him towards the lift. 'Come back!'

Left alone, I extricated myself from the sofa and went into the bedroom, rubbing my shoulder. Harley hadn't hurt me badly, but the violence of his reaction had shaken me. In a sense, I deserved it – I had married him under false pretences, convincing myself that there was love where none existed. Guiltily, I wondered whom I had deceived the most – Harley, or myself.

I sat on the bed and thought about this for a while before reaching a decision. Then I opened one of my suitcases and rapidly repacked most of the clothes I had brought with me. It would be best to leave immediately, while he was out of the way. No sense in making the parting any more painful.

I was at the door, suitcase in hand, when I heard voices in the corridor conversing in hushed tones. Harley and George were back already, damn them, and they had been joined by David.

'OK,' said Harley, sounding considerably calmer than when he left. 'If you're sure that's the best way to play it, I'll let you set it up.'

'These contacts of yours better be reliable, George,' said David. 'We can't afford any bad publicity with the UK launch coming up.'

George muttered something inaudible. I strained to hear more, but they must have gone into David's suite next door.

Then Harley's voice returned. 'I'll just check on her to see how she is.'

I jumped back and retreated into the bedroom, sliding the suitcase out of sight under the bed.

'Cindy, sweetheart.' Harley stood at the door looking abashed. 'I'm sorry – I didn't mean to be so rough. Forgive me?'

Why couldn't he have stayed away just a few minutes longer? Gritting my teeth, I gave him a weak smile. I couldn't face another argument – another scene. He was bound to come after me if I tried to leave – far better to slip away quietly, when no one was expecting it. I would have to put up with his recriminations until I found an opportunity to escape.

'I've been thinking,' he said. 'Maybe it is my fault that I'm not making you happy. My bioenergetics consultant did have a few problems with my body communication skills at my last session. Do you think we should go into joint body therapy? It's supposed to do wonders for a relationship if you can work together on the core issues – release the hurt and the deep rage from childhood.'

I stared at him, aghast. He was joking, of course. Surely he was joking?

He looked at his watch. 'It's a bit early to call LA yet, but I could get on to the clinic as soon as they open and have them fly a specialist over. I'm sure we can arrange for a soundproofed room to be made available.'

I gulped. There was no way I was getting involved in any of this New Age touchy feely stuff. Letting out my anger about not getting that new bicycle for my tenth birthday was hardly likely to make me change my mind about whether I loved Harley.

I smiled sweetly. 'If that's what you really want to do . . .'

No point in getting him suspicious. With a bit of luck I would be well out of the way before any of his witch doctors turned up.

'In the meantime, honey,' he continued, 'I'm going to take you out for dinner. Maybe I have been neglecting you lately – I've been kinda wrapped up with business and things.'

I hadn't noticed him deviating much from his usual leisured routine.

He gave me a patronising smile. 'Cindy, we can manage anything that comes our way. We both need to work at this marriage if we want to make it happen.'

Where on earth did he get hold of all this can-do bullshit?

He behaved perfectly towards me for the rest of the day, but I smelt a rat. Body therapy or not, I didn't believe that the rage he had exhibited earlier could really have disappeared so quickly. I didn't need to be an expert in male psychology to know that something was going on.

I woke early the following morning and felt under the bed for my suitcase. I wasn't going to wait around to find out what Harley, David and George had been plotting the day before. By the time they were awake, I would be well on my way to Guildford and out of their lives forever.

CHAPTER 16

The room was silent. Taking a final glance at Harley's sleeping figure, I tiptoed quietly out of the bedroom and opened the main door.

'Goodbye, Harley,' I whispered softly, stepping out into the corridor. After all my qualms and indecision, the actual departure was easier than I had expected. Outside the lobby I hailed a taxi which took me to Waterloo station. An hour or so later, I was standing in the concourse of Guildford station for the second time in three days, wondering what to do next. This was it – my new life. I needed to make some plans.

I didn't want to arouse suspicion by spending too much time at Harriet's flat, so I would have to find somewhere else to live as soon as I could. I would also have to find a job. Harriet's redundancy money wasn't going to last forever. Eager to start tackling these problems straight away, I deposited my suitcase at the left luggage office and crossed the bridge to the centre of the town. My first port of call was the Job Centre at the bottom of the High Street.

Scanning the boards, I realised that I needed to get

myself some qualifications if I wanted my new life to be any better than Cindy's old one. I didn't want to be a model any more, but I hadn't realised quite how far down-market I would have to go to find unskilled employment. *Part-time cleaner . . . kitchen porter . . . garage forecourt attendant* – the jobs on offer were hardly likely to form the basis of a brilliant new career. *Catering assistant required for American-style diner in local retail park* was an unwelcome reminder of Marty's, offering an hourly rate which would scarcely keep body and soul together. Glancing uneasily at the row of suited staff waiting to pounce if I approached the counter, I decided to wait a few days before testing out the credibility of my new identity. Leaving the Job Centre, I bought a local newspaper and went to a café on North Street.

I browsed through the paper, glancing occasionally from my comfortable window seat at the world outside. Sipping hot coffee, I began to savour a new feeling of independence. I was free at last – free to have a life of my own. I would make a completely fresh start – meet new friends, form new relationships. With luck, I might meet someone special – someone to drive away the pangs of loneliness and brighten my prospects for the future.

The jobs advertised in the paper weren't much better than those in the Job Centre, but I knew that I would have to start somewhere. Then I could find some evening classes – not in creative writing, but in something more useful which built on my existing skills. I knew how to work a computer – maybe I should try to develop my interest in that field. I drew circles around a couple of advertisements which sounded faintly promising, then turned to the property section.

Glancing again through the window, I noticed a man staring at me from the opposite pavement. He was a stocky, pugnacious-looking type, with a red face and a balding head. Despite the chill in the air, he wore only a short sleeved T-shirt, and seemed to be keeping himself warm by swinging his arms and rocking from one foot to the other with a self-conscious swagger. There was something strangely familiar about him – something I couldn't quite place. Watching discreetly over the edge of my newspaper, I saw him take a mobile telephone from the pocket of his jeans and dial a number. Then I remembered – I had seen him at Waterloo station that same morning, lurking by the ticket barrier with the telephone glued to his ear. We must have arrived in Guildford on the same train.

I turned back to the newspaper and read through the column of flats to let. When I looked up again, the man was still there. He seemed to have lost interest in the café, and was waving and gesticulating at someone further down the street. Idly curious, I glanced in that direction and saw a figure in a large overcoat scurrying up to meet him. They exchanged a few words, then both turned to stare at the café window. My heart skipped a beat – the second man was George.

Cowering behind my newspaper, I realised that he must already know I was there. The first man had undoubtedly followed me from Waterloo – or even from the house – keeping in touch with George by telephone. I remembered Harley's words to George the day before: *'I'll leave it to you to fix it up . . .'* Did he think I would lead them to the lover he imagined I had found? Or were they planning to take me back by force? Either way, it seemed that Harley wasn't going to let me go without putting up a fight.

My only comfort was that I hadn't gone straight to Harriet's flat. I still had a hiding place, if only I could get there without being followed. Leaving money on the table for my coffee, I stood up and mingled with a group of women who were leaving the café. If I could get outside quickly and unobtrusively – before George and his companion realised I had seen them – I could lose them in the maze of alleyways which connected the main streets.

The women clustered in the doorway, dithering with coats and shopping bags, then emerged in a gaggle on to the pavement. Keeping my head down, I attached myself to the group.

'Hello,' said one of the women, regarding me with a frown of uncertainty.

'Hi,' I said brightly. 'Lovely weather for the time of year.'

We crossed the road in tight formation, passing quite close to where George was standing, and swung eastwards up the hill.

'Do remind me, my dear,' said the woman in a chatty tone, 'I can't quite remember where we met before. Are you here for a holiday?' I was trying to think of a suitable reply when the group came to an abrupt halt outside the rear entrance to the Army and Navy. A swift cheek-pecking session ensued, and the women began to disperse in different directions.

'I've got a sister who lives in Florida,' continued my companion, detaining me with a gloved hand on my arm. 'Which part of the States do you come from? I'd so much like to go there one day.'

Looking behind, I saw George scanning the street with an angry expression. Before I had time to move, his head swivelled in my direction and our eyes met. 'Sorry. Must dash,' I muttered, diving towards the shop doors.

'There she goes!' George's voice followed in my wake. 'Stop her!'

I raced through the luggage section and pushed my way up the stairs which led to the front of the store. Speeding through the cosmetics department, I ran full tilt into a white-coated sales assistant wearing a pale blue sash.

'Sorry,' I gasped, pausing to steady myself.

'That's all right, madam,' she giggled, looking me up and down. 'I was going to stop you anyway – that's my job. Can I offer you a free makeover? It's a special promotion this week by . . .'

I stared at the familiar logo on her sash. *Lapinique*. Was there no escaping the bloody stuff?

'I'd rather burn in hell,' I said angrily, pushing her backwards into a pyramid of pale blue bottles. A series of tinkling crashes rang in my ears as I continued on my flight, but I didn't have time to look back and admire my handiwork.

I could hear George's footsteps behind me as I plunged

through the doors to the High Street. I turned downhill, running as fast as I could, then darted into an alleyway on the right. Two women with prams were approaching, blocking my path. Cursing, I looked around wildly for an escape route. A brightly painted door stood slightly ajar. Taking a deep breath, I pushed it open and went inside.

The hot, smoky atmosphere caught in my throat and stung my eyes. When I was able to focus on my surroundings, I saw a scruffy assortment of men regarding me with interest, their attention momentarily distracted from a row of television screens. It was a betting shop. A half smile crept across my face. They would never think of looking for me in here.

'Hello darling,' said one of the men with a leering smile.

'Hot tip for a nice little filly over there, Frank,' murmured another, winking at his companion.

I glared back at them. I had just as much right to be there as they did. With as much dignity as I could muster, I walked past them to an unoccupied corner and pretended to study the sheets of newspaper pinned to the wall. There were a few more inaudible comments, but they soon lost interest and turned back to their betting slips. I decided to wait for twenty minutes or so, then make a dash through one of the alleyways towards the castle. From there, I could find a way through the back streets to Harriet's flat.

The lists on the wall told me the names of the horses running that afternoon, together with a lot of cryptic information in small print which meant nothing to me.

One name caught my eye: *Devil's Dance*, running in the 3.30 at Newmarket. If I had the faintest idea how to do it, I would have made a bet. I felt I deserved a lucky break.

A man came into the shop carrying a mobile telephone, and the others turned to him with expectant faces.

'Nothing yet,' he muttered, stashing the telephone in his pocket. 'The boss says to wait for him to call again.'

'Bloody hell,' said one of the men in an aggressive tone. 'How long are we expected to hang around here, for Christ's sake? I'm supposed to be at Kempton Park this afternoon.'

'I told you I didn't like the sound of this job,' said another. 'It's not as if it's in our regular line of work. As for dragging us out to the sticks at the crack of dawn . . .'

'Stop whining,' snapped the man with the telephone. 'Is the car ready?'

'Pete's driving it round the one-way system like you told him,' said the man who had leered at me. 'Sounds like he'll run out of petrol before anything happens. Right bloody fiasco if you ask me.'

I stared at him for a moment, then looked away quickly as he caught my eye and fixed me with a lecherous stare. What had I stumbled upon? Were they waiting to rob a bank?

'I've never done an abduction before,' said one of the men quietly. 'What's the score?'

Abduction? A horrible suspicion began to form in my mind.

'Keep it down, you berk,' growled the man with the telephone. 'I told you it's all above board. It's not abduction as such, just taking her home to her husband where she belongs. Ask Wilkie if you don't believe me.'

'Who the hell's Wilkie?' asked the first man.

'Bloody hell – you don't know Wilkie?' The man with the telephone became misty-eyed. 'King of the each-way double, they used to call him – that was back in the Eighties, before he went to America. Rang me out of the blue last night, he did. This could be a nice little earner.' The man sighed. 'We had some fine old times together down at Newbury – old George Wilkins and me.'

My stomach churned as I realised who they were talking about. I needed to get out fast, before they recognised me. George had spared no expense on hiring the muscle, and I had blundered right into their hands.

Before I could move, the man's telephone rang.

'That'll be him,' he said, removing it from his pocket. He listened for a moment, then let out a grunt of annoyance. 'He's coming back here,' he said to the others. 'Sounds like they've lost her.' I began to sidle quietly along the counter, heading towards the back of the shop where I had seen another way out.

'Leaving us already, darling?' asked one of the men with a grin. I broke into a brisk walk. As I reached the door, it opened from the other side. George appeared, followed by his friend in the T-shirt. Their mouths dropped open when they saw me.

'What the hell . . .' breathed George. I turned and bolted through the shop towards the other exit. The men stood watching me with expressions of surprise.

'Stop her, you idiots,' shouted George. 'It's her – the one we're looking for!'

I had my hand on the door when they caught up with me. I struggled to escape, kicking wildly at my assailants, but I was outnumbered. Pinning my arms to my sides, they manoeuvred me into the alleyway and held me against the wall. I tried to scream, but a hand was clamped over my mouth.

'Can we rough her up a bit?' asked one of the men hopefully.

'Shut up,' said the man with the telephone. He spoke into it angrily. 'Pete? Where the fuck are you?'

After a few minutes, during which the men crowded around to hide me from the eyes of passers-by and various parts of my anatomy were surreptitiously tweaked and stroked, a man loped into the alleyway clutching a large MacDonald's carton.

'What's the problem, boss?'

'Get the car open, you stupid shit,' hissed the man with the telephone, knocking the carton from his hand and spilling chips all over the pavement.

'Pick that up, young man,' squawked a passing woman, stopping in her tracks. 'Don't you know that it's an offence to litter the streets?'

'Mmmrghh!' I tried to attract her attention, but to no avail. I was manhandled along the alleyway and into the waiting car. Looking back, I saw two of the men crawling around on the pavement, gathering up chips, while the woman stood over them with a vindictive smile.

'What are you waiting for?' snapped George, climbing into the front passenger seat. 'Those two can find their own way home.'

The car sped away from the kerb, then lurched almost immediately to a standstill as we joined the queue of cars in the one-way system.

'Bugger!' muttered the driver, scrabbling in his pocket for cigarettes. The car quickly filled with smoke. Sandwiched between two thugs on the back seat, I fought back pangs of nausea, gazing helplessly at the familiar sights as they crawled past. The thug on my right began to pick his nose, examining the results with interest before wiping them on the upholstery.

George busied himself with his mobile telephone, then turned and thrust it abruptly into my hand. 'Call for you, Miss Cindy,' he said in a smugly facetious voice. 'I think your *husband* would like a word.'

I held the telephone cautiously to my ear. 'Harley?'

'Cindy! Thank God you're safe.' His voice was a distant squawk, mingled with hisses of interference. 'What on earth did you think you were doing – running off like that?'

'I'd like to know what *you* think *you're* doing,' I said angrily. 'Did you send these thugs after me?'

'Thugs? Sorry – can't hear you properly. Listen Cindy . . .'

'I won't be treated like this,' I shouted. 'Tell them to let me go!'

The line crackled, then became clear again. 'Listen,

Cindy, this is for your own good,' he continued. 'You've not been well lately – I don't think you know what you're doing. What you need is a good rest. Now, I couldn't get hold of the clinic in LA, but I've found a doctor here and . . .'

'I'm not seeing a fucking doctor,' I said loudly.

'What's that? This line's not very good . . .'

I made a hissing noise through my teeth. 'Sorry, Harley. The signal's breaking up . . . I can't hear you . . .' Unable to control my anger and frustration, I flung the telephone at the windscreen. It bounced against the glass with a loud thud and flew back towards the driver. He ducked, swerving violently, and George swung round in his seat with a threatening gesture.

'You little bitch . . .'

'Shall we sort her out, guv?' asked the thug on my left, clenching his fist in readiness.

I glared at George. 'Don't forget that we'll still be living in the same house when we go back to the States,' I reminded him coldly. 'I'm a dab hand with a pair of scissors and I've also been known to sleepwalk so, if you don't want to wake up one morning with your testicles stuffed in your ears, you'd better tell these thugs to leave off.'

Uneasy laughter rippled around the car.

'Shut up, you lot,' growled George, turning back to inspect the windscreen for damage. The rest of the journey passed without incident.

When we arrived back at the hotel, Harley was waiting on the pavement outside the entrance. He faced me through the car window with a stern expression. 'You better come upstairs,' he said. 'I think you need to lie down for a while.'

Under George's direction, the thugs marched me forcibly through the lobby and into the lift.

'Help!' I shouted. 'I'm being abducted!' A few heads turned but no one lifted a finger to help me.

'I hope she's feeling better soon,' said the man from the reception, holding open the lift doors for us. 'I'll send the doctor straight up when he arrives.'

When we reached the suite, I was pushed unceremoniously through the bedroom door and a key turned in the lock behind me. I fell on the bed, sobbing.

Voices floated in from the main room as Harley concluded his business with George and his henchmen. Then I heard David's voice. I tried to listen at the door, but they were speaking in low tones and I couldn't quite catch what they were saying.

I rattled at the door. 'Harley,' I shouted. 'Let me out! I want to talk to you.'

Nothing happened. When I listened again, it sounded as if they had gone. Angrily, I began to pound my fists against the door. 'Let me out!' I bellowed. How dare they leave me here like this!

It was nearly an hour later when Harley returned. He opened the door and came in, locking it behind him and placing the key in his pocket.

'You bastard!' I shouted, flying at him in a rage. He caught my wrists and held me still, showing a strength I didn't know he possessed.

'Calm down, honey,' he said gently. 'The doctor will

be here soon – you'll be sorted out and better in no time.'

'I'm not seeing any doctor,' I protested. 'There's nothing wrong with me. Why won't you let me go?'

'There, there. Everything's going to be all right.' Still holding my wrists, he sat me on the bed and faced me with a look of anguish. It seemed that the poor fool had persuaded himself that I had a screw loose. How else could he come to terms with my behaviour?

'I've just been talking to David,' he said eventually. 'We decided that what you need is a change of scene. We're going to go straight to Italy. They won't need you for the first week – they'll just be setting up, doing background shots and stuff – so you can have a little vacation.' He gave me a hopeful smile. 'That'll be nice, won't it?'

A sense of weariness overcame me. What other choices did I have?

'All right,' I said eventually. 'As long as I don't have to see any stupid doctor.'

'That's great, honey,' said Harley excitedly. 'I knew you'd see it my way if we talked. I'll just go and tell David to sort out the tickets – he'll be so pleased that you're feeling better. We'll leave tomorrow if we can get a flight.'

He went away, locking the door behind him again. After about ten minutes, he returned with a cup of tea. 'Drink this,' he said. 'It'll make you feel better. Then we'll have another talk.'

The next thing I knew, Harley was shaking me awake. Bright morning sunlight filtered through the curtains. It seemed that I had somehow slept through the rest of the day and the whole of the night as well.

'Come on, honey,' whispered Harley. 'You need to pack some things – we're going to Italy, remember?'

'What happened?' I asked groggily. 'That tea you gave me . . .'

'Just a mild sleeping pill,' said Harley in a soothing voice. 'The doctor decided it was the best thing under the circumstances. We'll take you for a check-up when we get home.'

'But . . .'

'No buts,' he said, in a voice of cheery determination. 'Trust me – everything will work out OK.' He glanced at his watch. 'But you better hurry up now, sweetheart, we have to catch a plane.'

Packing was somewhat tricky as my essential belongings were still in the case I had left at Guildford station. I gathered together the few things that remained and put them into my second bag. It looked as if I was going to have to go through with this charade until I could convince Harley that it was safe to leave me on my own. Then I would find a way to escape.

When Harley was out of the way in the bathroom, I checked through the inner pockets of my handbag. I was worried that I might have lost something in yesterday's struggle, but Harriet's passport and chequebook were still there. Taking out my other passport – the one in Cindy's name, I opened them both and laid them on the dressing table. It was unnerving seeing the two photographs side by side. I stared at the two faces, seeing them objectively for the first time. Harriet didn't look quite as old and ugly as I remembered, while Cindy's superficial beauty gave her a bland, characterless appearance. I knew them both intimately, inside and out, but I realised with a sudden shock that neither of these women were really me.

Glancing in the mirror, I could see that I was now a different Cindy to the one in the photograph. I looked slightly older, more serious. My face was more thoughtful, bearing little trace of the expression of vacuous surprise which had been captured by the camera at the photographers. Inside, I no longer felt like Harriet. I had lost the sense of gloomy futility which had once restricted her actions and governed her moods. I might be unhappy still, but I now had something to strive for – a belief that I could change my life for the better.

I stared into the mirror, wishing I could penetrate the surface of my reflected features and see the true identity of the person inside. If I wasn't Harriet or Cindy, then who the hell was I? Had Mephisto unwittingly created a brand new person – a whole which was more than the sum of the parts?

My stomach churned uneasily. I was still suffering from the effects of whatever they had put in my tea. Thrusting the passports back into my handbag, I rushed into the bathroom. Harley sprang up from the toilet with a cry of alarm, his trousers round his ankles, and watched with dismay as I was violently sick all over the bath mat.

I sat queasily beside Harley on the flight to Genoa, vowing to be careful what I ate and drank in the future.

I wasn't going to let the bastards drug me into submission. I wasn't going to give up either. I would have to be more devious, now that they were watching my every move. Sooner or later, I would find another opportunity and, when I did, I would plan my escape carefully – checking it out from every angle. There weren't going to be any mistakes the next time.

The previous night must have taken its toll on Harley. He sat staring grimly ahead, with dark shadows under his eyes. A short time after take-off, he fell asleep.

A few minutes later, David appeared in the aisle beside me. 'Hi Sis,' he said, perching on the arm of my seat. 'Too bad we couldn't all sit together, eh?'

I gave him a sulky glare.

'We'll have a cosy little holiday,' he murmured, touching my arm in a gesture of familiarity. 'Just the three of us. I sure hope we're going to get along.'

'We'll get along just fine if you keep out of my way,' I snapped, brushing his hand away.

'I hoped we were going to be friends, Cindy,' he said in a low voice. 'I'm sure we have more in common than you think.' He paused thoughtfully, then leaned towards me, bending his lips close to my ear. 'But if that's how you feel,' he added with a snarl, 'you better watch your step. Remember what I told you – if you divorce Harley, I'll make sure that you don't get a penny.'

'Maybe I don't want his money,' I suggested quietly. David gave me a look of scornful disbelief.

'Why else would you marry him?' I opened my mouth to speak but he interrupted. 'Don't give me any of that crap about love,' he said with a dismissive wave of his hand. 'I can tell just by looking at your face that you hate his guts.'

I turned away in embarrassment. Was it that obvious? When I looked up again, David had gone – I could see his back retreating down the aisle. A new figure had taken his place.

'Remember me?' he asked. I shrank back in my seat, catching my breath with surprise. It was Mephisto.

'What do you want?' I faltered, staring at him. He wore a black tracksuit with oversized, fashionable trainers – the type that were all laces and floppy tongues. His chin sported bristles of dark designer stubble, and a pair of earphones hung loosely round his neck, emitting a tinny rhythmic sound.

'I was just wondering what the hell you think you're playing at,' he hissed angrily. 'Helping old ladies in the street with charity handouts? Running away from your wealthy husband when you could be taking him to the cleaners? What's come over you, Harriet?'

'Leave me alone,' I muttered, glancing around and wondering if the other passengers could see him. Harley was snoring gently beside me. 'Why should it matter to you? It's none of your business.'

'Oh, but you're wrong there, Harriet,' he said in a menacing tone. 'I'm afraid it is my business. I've got my reputation riding on this pact, you see. Not to mention a substantial wager. I've been counting on you to come up with the goods.'

There was a crackling noise and the lights in the cabin dimmed as a stewardess walked briskly down the aisle and appeared to pass straight through him. I shivered, thinking of the empty miles between us and the ground.

'How am I supposed to prove that you're corrupt if you're going to start playing the bloody Good Samaritan?' he asked in a vexed tone. 'All this moralistic behaviour of yours is starting to attract attention.'

'What do you mean, moralistic?' I replied sulkily. 'I've committed adultery, haven't I? Isn't that corrupt enough for you? I thought you'd be pleased.'

'Oh yes, thrilled to bits,' he said sarcastically. 'Especially when they told me that it didn't bloody count. That it wasn't proper evidence of corruption because you *loved* him.' His mouth twisted into an expression of distaste. 'Really, Harriet – how could you be so pathetic? He's old enough to be your . . .'

'It's not pathetic . . .' I began. Then I stopped, curious. '*Who* exactly told you that it didn't count?'

'My superiors,' he said bitterly. 'The half-assed apologies for devils who've managed to lie and cheat their way into the ranks above mine – even though they'd probably be too spineless to set off a firecracker at a prayer meeting. Thanks to your antics, they're all taking far too much interest in this Faustian pact of mine. They're treating it like some kind of soap opera – tuning in every day to find out what happens next. Standards are dropping, let me tell you.'

I tried to look suitably remorseful, but the idea of Mephisto having to kowtow to his superiors brought a smile to my lips.

'It's not funny,' he snapped. 'They're threatening to

cut back my powers if I don't come up with some real evidence pretty soon.' He stared at me in exasperation. 'Why can't you just quit fooling around and do something properly immoral, for Christ's sake! It wouldn't do you any harm, and it would make life a whole lot easier for me.'

'Who says it wouldn't do me any harm?'

He sighed. 'Look, I haven't got time to stand around arguing about details. If you won't co-operate, we'll just have to carry on with this charade until you come to your senses. You will in the end, you know – just you wait and see. You'll be only too pleased to do anything I ask.'

'Don't hold your breath,' I said.

'Don't worry, I won't,' he said. 'I'll just wait until you call me.'

He stood and began to walk up the aisle, then paused and looked back. 'If you're so sure of yourself,' he murmured with a sly smile, 'how is it that you didn't have the courage of your convictions yesterday? It wouldn't have done you any harm to have trusted me then.'

'What do you mean?'

'*Devil's Dance*, remember? The 3.30 at Newmarket?' He gave me a look of disappointment. 'Don't tell me you didn't realise I had it all fixed up for you. It came in at 33 to 1.'

He turned and continued down the aisle with a springing step – like astronauts I had seen on the television – and disappeared through the wall of the cabin. The lights dimmed briefly once again, then flickered into brightness.

'Damn!' muttered a stewardess, spilling coffee over the man in front of me. She inched her trolley forward and peered at me with an anxious expression. 'Are you all right madam? Can I get you anything to drink?'

I quickly composed my face into an expression of normality. 'Double scotch,' I muttered, taking a quick glance to make sure Harley was still asleep. 'No ice.'

A chauffeur-driven car was waiting for us at Genoa airport and it dawned on me for the first time that George was no longer with us.

'He's staying in London to visit some old friends in some place called Pentonville,' said Harley when I asked him. 'Then he's going back to LA to keep an eye on the house.' He grinned. 'Stop José getting into any mischief on his own.'

Leaving Genoa, we followed the coast, driving along winding cliff-top roads. Sitting between Harley and David in the back seat, I wondered why my life seemed to consist of journeys taken against my will. The sea sparkled beneath us, an intense deep blue, and the hillsides were adorned with olive groves. It was just like an illustration from an upmarket travel brochure – *Bask in the dreamlike beauty of Liguria.* I thought of films I had seen in my younger days – in my previous life. Sean Connery, Michael Caine, Cary Grant, they had all been here – or places very like it – driving through breathtaking scenery in fast and glamorous cars to mysterious assignations. How I had envied them, trapped as I was in the eternal English winter with no money and no romance in my life. Now I was here, but it was all wrong – I couldn't enjoy it.

'You're going to love the house,' said David, talking across me to Harley. 'So romantic – perched on top of the cliffs with magnificent views.' I felt the pressure of his knee against mine. 'So inaccessible too.'

After driving for about half an hour more, we pulled into a small layby at the side of the road.

'This is it,' said David, in an unexpectedly gleeful voice – like that of a child anticipating a surprise. 'What are you waiting for? Get out of the car.'

'But, where . . .' Harley stood at the roadside gazing around in puzzlement.

'Come with me,' said David, leading us to a gate in a wall which blended almost imperceptibly with the cliff face. 'Leave the baggage – Giorgio will bring it up later.'

He pressed a series of buttons on a panel set in the wall, and the gate slid open. Inside, the hillside loomed above us, clad in dense vegetation. A strange looking contraption, a kind of glass box on wheels, stood at the bottom of an inclined track which rose steeply through a cutting in the rock.

'It's a funicular elevator,' said David proudly, stepping into the glazed enclosure. 'Come in, it's perfectly safe. This is the front entrance to our house.'

When we were inside, David pressed a series of buttons on a control panel. There was a gentle hum of machinery, and the box began to move up the track at an impossibly steep angle. As we rose above the level of the wall, the sea came into view, stretching out towards the horizon, and we could see the miles of winding coastal road we had travelled on to get here.

'Fabulous, isn't it?' David smiled. 'Watch out, there's a change in the gradient here.'

I clung to Harley as the machinery slowed and we seemed about to tip back over the precipice. I closed my eyes. When I opened them again, we were still upright, and the view was spectacular.

'Automatic correction,' said David, laughing at our frightened faces. 'It's all pivoted at the base – the very latest technology.'

'This place is right out of one of those James Bond movies,' said Harley, peering anxiously upwards. 'How much farther do we have to go?'

Our destination came into view as he spoke, an unprepossessing looking building nestled into the hillside at the top of the track.

'Don't be fooled by appearances,' said David, turning to Harley. 'It's pretty impressive inside. Remember that Armenian financial guy I told you about – the one who wants a franchise on Formula B? It's his summer place – specially designed by a top architect. I visited him here last year. He doesn't usually rent it out, of course, but he's off on his yacht right now and he fixed this up as a special favour to me.'

Inside, the house was cool, spacious and strangely complicated in its layout. It seemed to follow the contours of the hillside in a series of staggered levels, so it was difficult to say whether you were upstairs or downstairs in any given place. My room – separated from Harley's by a connecting door – was in a section which cantilevered out over a steep slope. Checking the window, I saw at once that there was no possibility of escape in that direction.

The three of us had an early dinner, served by a wizened old Italian woman in a glass-walled dining room overlooking the sea. Succulent olives dressed in oil and garlic melted on my tongue, and aromatic Mediterranean sauces adorned the main course of baked fish. We drank tumblers of harsh local wine, poured from an earthenware jug. Everything was perfect – straight out of the articles in the Sunday supplements which glibly assumed that these delights were a commonplace event for anyone with a smattering of culture. I had dreamed for years of being able to afford a holiday in Italy. Now I was here – doing it in style – and I wished more than anything else in the world to be back in Harriet's flat in Guildford. Good food and fine views were a poor substitute for freedom.

After the meal, David smoked a cigar on the balcony, and we watched the glass box descend slowly through the olive groves to the roadside. It contained the old woman who had served our dinner, together with an assortment of surly looking young men.

'The housekeeper, the cook, the gardener, the handy-man . . .' David counted them off as they passed. 'All going home for the night.'

'What about Giorgio?' asked Harley.

'Oh, he stays here most of the time,' said David.

The spluttering of a car engine pierced the silence. 'Not tonight, though,' he added with a smile. 'I understand he has a date with a young lady in Santa Margherita.'

'Can you get a car up here?' asked Harley. 'I thought the elevator was the only way.'

David laughed. 'Giorgio's the only one crazy enough to attempt the back road. Have you seen how steep it is? I'm sure he'll bite the dust one of these days – tearing round a hairpin turn with too much alcohol inside him. It's a mystery why he doesn't park down in the lay-by like everybody else.'

At bedtime, Harley accompanied me to my room. 'I know you must be exhausted after the journey, darling,' he said, pecking me on the cheek. 'I'll leave you to get some rest.'

He disappeared through the connecting door, closing it softly behind him. After a few moments, I heard a key turning quietly in the lock. I crept across the room to try the main door, but it refused to yield. I was a prisoner.

I was too tired to worry about it that night. There would be ample time to make plans to escape when I had explored my territory more thoroughly. Revelling in the luxury of not having to share my bed with anyone else, I climbed between the sheets and quickly fell asleep.

CHAPTER 17

The following morning, after breakfast, Harley and David closeted themselves in the study to discuss the filming schedule.

'Can I go outside?' I asked hopefully, poking my head around the door. 'Get some fresh air?'

'Feel free,' said David with a benevolent smile. 'Don't worry,' he added in a low voice, glancing at Harley. 'She can't go very far – there's a security fence all around the place.'

Wandering around the house in the bright sunshine, I saw that the opportunities for escape were few indeed. A series of small terraces ran along the side of the house facing the sea, connecting between different levels with short flights of steps. Beneath these, the ground dropped away, steepening into an almost vertical cliff face before it reached the road. The only way out on this side was by the funicular elevator, and I knew without asking that the gate at the bottom would be locked.

Following a narrow path around the house, I came to a gravelled courtyard, enclosed on three sides. Herbs grew in terracotta pots and the smell of coffee drifted through an open doorway. Peering cautiously inside, I saw the old woman from the previous night hunched over a wooden chopping block. Wielding a large knife, she muttered unintelligibly in Italian as she performed a grisly filleting operation on a huge lump of meat.

I retreated quietly back into the courtyard. On the side that was open, a narrow track led through clumps of bushes and turned out of view. The rough surface bore imprints of tyres.

Glancing around to make sure that no one was watching me, I ventured along the track. At the turning, it began to descend, winding through a steep-sided cutting in the hillside. David had talked about the dangers of this road, but it looked ordinary enough compared to those we had travelled along the day before. Had he merely been trying to put me off? I continued through the cutting, my eyes gradually adjusting to the shadowy gloom. After about ten minutes, I emerged, blinking, into the sunlight again. Ahead, the sea filled the horizon, and the road swung sharply into a hairpin bend which jutted out over the cliff. There was no barrier at the side. Peering over the edge, I could just see the coastal road directly beneath, tucked tightly against the cliff face. Below it was another steep drop, at the foot of which waves crashed over dark, jagged rocks. Feeling a rush of vertigo, I moved quickly away from the edge. I didn't fancy trying to escape in that direction.

Continuing along the road for a short distance, I found a narrow pathway which ascended the hillside. I took this pathway and, after a short climb, found a vantage point where I could take stock of my surroundings.

I was on a ridge of higher ground between the house and the road. The house lay slightly below me on the right, and I could just see Harley and David on one of the terraces, deep in conversation. On the left, the road continued downwards to a large, industrial-looking gate. Looking carefully, I could just make out the line of a high mesh fence that led away from the gate and snaked around the base of the hillside. It was all as David had described – I might as well have been in a prison camp. I glanced around, half expecting to see machine gun turrets on the hillside. This Armenian, whoever he was, seemed a trifle paranoid about his security.

The sound of a car engine floated through the stillness. Looking down, I saw that the gate was now open. A battered-looking car lurched into view, accelerating up the winding road towards me at an alarming rate. The gate closed smoothly behind it, presumably operated by remote control. Retracing my steps towards the road, I reached it just as the car hurtled past, and caught a glimpse of a wild-eyed figure crouched behind the wheel. It looked as if Giorgio was late for work.

When I arrived back in the courtyard, the car was outside the kitchen door, parked at a rakish angle. A pair of wide, curving tracks now decorated the gravel surface, terminating at the rear wheels of the vehicle, and wisps of steam rose gently from the radiator. I approached cautiously. Looking through the grimy window, I could see the keys dangling in the ignition.

'Don't get any ideas,' said a voice in my ear. I jumped

guiltily away from the car and looked up to see David standing at the kitchen door.

'You wouldn't get very far,' he said with a gloating smile. 'That gate's made of solid steel – built to withstand a tank. You'd more likely end up in the sea.'

Later that morning, we went into Portofino to inspect the filming location. Giorgio, looking considerably spruced up since I last saw him, drove us there at a sedate pace in a hired car.

'You'll just love Portofino, Cindy,' said Harley with enthusiasm. 'It's a really cute little town – really pretty and unspoiled. I think I like it better than anywhere else in the whole world.'

Rounding a bend in the road, we met a queue of traffic and Giorgio slowed the car to a crawl. Flashing lights were visible ahead.

'What's happening?' I asked.

'It's all right,' replied Harley. 'It's just the traffic control system. Portofino's very popular with the tourists, you see, but the road's a dead end. If they didn't control the cars, they would just keep on pouring into the town and everything would jam up. Once it was full, this road would get clogged up and no one would be able to get out again.'

We passed a sign with flashing lights on it. *Welcome to Portofino*, it said in several languages. *Minutes to wait before entering the town: 10.* The number flashed on and off, then disappeared, to be replaced by a zero. The traffic moved forward. We entered the main square and were directed by a uniformed official towards a ramp which led into an underground car park.

Unspoiled? So far, the place fitted quite neatly with descriptions I had read of Disneyland. After a lot of messing around with parking tickets, we left Giorgio to his own devices and emerged into the town itself. A narrow street lined with souvenir shops led us down to the harbour, where tables spilled from restaurants on to the cobbled pavements and expensive-looking boats crowded the waterside. Groups of people milled around, jostling against each other as they posed for snapshots and gaped at the menu boards outside the restaurants.

I had to admit that the place was quite pretty, but once we had walked around the harbour, which took about five minutes, I could see its limitations. At least Disneyland offered the visitor something to do – here, there was next to nothing.

We lunched in a restaurant in the centre of the square, where the standard of food was roughly equivalent to an English transport café, except that the portions were much smaller. A smarmy-looking waiter quickly identified us as people with more money than sense, and pestered us throughout the meal with offers of 'house specialities' and overpriced tickets for boat rides. I ordered *pasta al pomodoro*, and got exactly that – a plateful of soggy, overcooked spaghetti with a spoonful of cold tinned tomatoes dolloped grudgingly on the top.

After lunch, we walked up to the church which perched photogenically on the hillside above us, following a string of walkers with backpacks and families with whining toddlers. We frequently had to step aside on the narrow path to allow people to pass in the opposite direction, and I realised that this too must be a dead end. How long before they installed traffic lights on the pathway as well?

Outside the church, I could hear nothing but the whirr of cameras.

'Look at the view,' said Harley. 'Isn't it perfect?'

I surveyed the scene in front of me with bad grace. The pretty pastel-stuccoed houses hugged the base of the hillside, forming a colourful backdrop for the bustle in the harbour. Yes, it was perfect – too perfect. It looked as if it had been put together by a crack team of set designers. Everything about it was false. The harbour, once a shelter for fishing boats, was now crammed with luxury yachts. The houses were no longer houses, but restaurants and hotels. Who could live in a place where the shops sold nothing but souvenirs and cheap trinkets and there was a permanent traffic jam to stop you from going anywhere else?

There weren't even any streets to speak of – the hillside rose steeply behind the buildings, which couldn't have had much of a view from their rear windows. The whole thing was like a cardboard cut-out – the beauty it offered was skin deep. Harley couldn't have picked a better location for the filming of a *Lapinique* advertisement.

We walked further up the narrow path, following signs which promised us a lighthouse. The crowds were thinner in this section, which was steeper than the first part of the climb. Clutching the flimsy hand-rail, I fantasised about pushing Harley and David over the edge, unexpectedly precipitating them to a watery grave. As if he could read my thoughts, David gripped me firmly by the arm. 'Nice walk,' he murmured. 'It'd be so much better if we were friends . . .'

Harley stopped abruptly, slapping his pockets. 'My indigestion pills – I left them in the car!' He turned, clutching his hand against his chest. 'I can feel heart-burn coming on. That lunch . . .'

After a short conference with David, he disappeared rapidly down the path.

'Just you and me now, baby,' said David, taking my hand. 'Let's go back and have a closer look at that church.'

Retracing our steps, we arrived at the church again. David pushed open a small gate in the wall and led me inside. It was the graveyard. No one else was in there.

Anxious to avoid conversation with David, I developed a sudden interest in Italian burial customs. Many of the headstones bore photographs of the deceased, and I found it rather eerie to be surrounded by rows of faded photographs of people who were dead. Some graves had two photographs – a husband and wife. Looking closely, I saw that the women were generally much older than the men – captured on film in their widowhood long after their husbands were dead and forgotten. With a shiver, I remembered my real age, and imagined Harriet's photograph coupled with Harley's. What would people think if they saw us together?

'Penny for your thoughts, Sis?' I started as David appeared at my side, slipping his arm around my waist.

'Leave me alone,' I said irritably, slapping his hand.

'Oh, come on,' he said smoothly. 'Quit fooling around. You know as well as I do that there's a chemistry between us.' His grip tightened and he pulled me close against him. 'I know you're not getting on too well with Harley right now, so how about trying it with another member of the family instead?'

'Let go, you pervert! I'll tell Harley . . .' I struggled to escape, but he pinned me up against a tombstone. I could feel a different kind of family member swelling against me as he slid his hand under the hem of my skirt.

'Come on, Sis,' he gasped. 'You know you want it. We have a lot in common, you and I – we'd make a great team. Think of all we could do together. Harley would never suspect a thing.'

I looked around for a weapon, but there was nothing in sight. His legs pressed closely against mine, forestalling any possibility of employing the Chuck Woodcock technique.

He began to move rhythmically against me, breathing heavily. 'Oh Cindy,' he moaned. 'You've got such a great body . . .'

'Cut it out, David,' I whispered in his ear. 'Or I'll tell the IRS about your deal with *Lapinette*. And your account in the Caymen Islands.'

He pulled away sharply with a look of alarm. 'What do you mean?' he hissed. 'I thought I made it clear that stuff was all above board?'

'Leave me alone, David,' I said. 'Otherwise I'll do it. And I'll tell Harley as well. See what he thinks of his darling little brother when he knows you've been siphoning off the company funds.'

'You little bitch,' he muttered, moving towards me with a threatening gesture. 'You can't prove anything. No one would believe you.'

'With the evidence I've got?'

He glared at me. 'What evidence?'

He couldn't know for certain that I didn't have any. If George hadn't disturbed me at the computer, I would have been able to get a print of that email. 'You'll see,' I said softly.

'You're full of shit!'

'What if I am?' I said. 'Are you going to take that risk? As long as you keep your hands off me, no one need ever find out.'

'I'll get you for this,' he growled between clenched teeth.

'Come on, brother-in-law,' I said in a friendly voice, taking his arm. 'Don't you think it's time we went to look for Harley?'

That evening, David went out straight after dinner. I stood by the door with Harley and watched him descend in the elevator.

'Where's he going?' I asked.

'I don't know,' replied Harley, rubbing his stomach with a pained expression. 'David's a dark horse sometimes.' He made a small belching noise and turned to me with a look of embarrassment. 'I've been feeling kind of weird since lunchtime,' he whispered apologetically. 'I think I'd better, um, just go find the bathroom.'

'Serves you right for guzzling all those oysters,' I muttered, as he vanished in the direction of the nearest lavatory. As soon as he was gone, I peered through the dusk to check the progress of the elevator. The glass box had disappeared from view, but the machinery was still whirring softly. It took about four minutes to get to the bottom, and I guessed that David would by now have reached the steepest part of the descent.

I examined the control panel, but was disappointed to find no button marked 'stop'. It would have been most satisfying to leave David stranded on a near-vertical cliff face for an hour or two. I pressed the up and down buttons in different combinations, but they didn't seem to affect the smooth progress of the machinery. A few moments later, a camera monitor flickered into life above the control panel to show the elevator arriving safely at the foot of the track. David's shadowy figure emerged and went over to the gate.

I watched the screen intently, hoping I might be able to see which numbers he punched into the keypad on the wall, but the picture was too indistinct. Halfway through, he glanced over his shoulder at the camera and shifted his position to block my view.

'You bastard,' I murmured softly. He must have known I would be watching him.

Strange gurgling noises were coming from the nearby lavatory.

'Harley?' I tapped on the door. 'Are you all right?'

'Is that you, Cindy?' His voice was an embarrassed whisper. 'You couldn't possibly, um, find me another roll of, um . . .'

'Toilet paper?' I asked loudly.

'Shhh!' he hissed. He seemed to have forgotten we were alone in the house. Giorgio had gone out earlier on some errand and hadn't yet returned. 'Yes please,' added Harley in a small voice. 'I knew I shouldn't have eaten those oysters – I think they were bad.'

'You wait there,' I said in a reassuring voice. 'I'll be right back.'

I headed towards the back of the house. There was a small lobby at the entrance to the kitchen, and I pushed open a door to find the room where supplies were kept. Shelves stacked with provisions lined the walls and slabs of Parma ham dangled from hooks in the ceiling. There was a sweet, musty smell.

I paused, glancing back into the lobby. There was another door facing the storeroom, which I had seen Giorgio using. It was standing slightly ajar. Realising that I might never get another chance like this to be alone in the house, I opened it and looked inside.

It was a small room containing a chair, a desk, and an impressive looking bank of buttons, switches and monitors, which I guessed to be the controls for the security equipment around the house. This was my chance to find out how to open the gate.

I went in, feeling like a character in a James Bond film. In these films, the character always knew exactly which sequence of buttons to press – usually conveniently labelled with brightly coloured warning signs – to blow the villain sky-high with his own technology. I didn't have a clue what any of the buttons did, so I started pressing them at random.

Nothing happened. After a while, I noticed a number keypad in the corner of the panel. A small digital display screen next to it bore the words 'enter user code'.

I stared at it angrily. Without the code, I couldn't even turn the bloody thing on, let alone operate it. Hoping that someone might have written the number down, I began to search through the drawers of the desk.

The top drawer contained the usual detritus that accumulates in the drawers of even the best-run households – pens with their caps missing, elastic bands, half-burnt candles, assorted batteries and a broken tape dispenser. There were a few scraps of paper bearing illegible scrawls in Italian, but nothing which remotely resembled a code number.

The next drawer was full of magazines – a sordid collection of pornography half-heartedly concealed beneath a single faded copy of a local newspaper. So this was how Giorgio entertained himself on his nights at home.

The bottom drawer was stiff, and didn't seem to have been opened for some time. Inside, I found a further selection of magazines, covered in dust. Underneath them was something soft, carefully wrapped in a plastic bag. Curious, I undid the fastenings and peered inside. It looked like a blonde wig, with a colouring very similar to my own hair. I picked it up to examine it more carefully, but then dropped it with a squeal of alarm. It was attached to something floppy – something with the texture and colour of skin.

After a moment's panic, during which I conjured up visions of butchered bodies scattered in bits around the house, I plucked up the courage to look at the thing again. I discovered that it was a life-sized inflatable doll – complete with realistic hair. Taking it from its bag, I laid it out on the floor. It was a sad caricature of a woman's body, its proportions reflecting the typical masculine view of how a woman should look. The hair wasn't the only thing that was realistic, but I didn't care to inspect the other parts too closely – I didn't know what they might have been used for last.

An idea began to form in my mind. Forgetting my original purpose of finding out how to open the gate, I stuffed the doll back in its bag and took it upstairs to my room. I wasn't yet sure of the details, but I had a feeling that this doll could play a useful part in my escape plans. Hiding it carefully at the back of my wardrobe, I sat down on the bed to think.

It was some time later that I heard a plaintive voice calling up the stairs, and remembered that Harley was still waiting for his toilet paper.

The next morning, Harley had made a full recovery. He announced that we were going back to Portofino with David to watch the first day of preparations for filming.

'I've got a terrible headache,' I said, lingering reluctantly at the door. 'Can't I stay behind and rest?'

'But you have to come,' said Harley, glancing at his watch and running his fingers through his hair. 'I've got something special arranged for today – a surprise.'

'What surprise?' I asked suspiciously. I wasn't in the mood for a surprise of any kind – unless it consisted of a plane ticket back to England and the freedom to use it.

'You'll see,' he said with a smile. 'Believe me, it'll really cheer you up – help get you on your feet again.'

David appeared from the side of the house, accompanied by Giorgio, and held open the door of the elevator. 'Get in, you stupid bitch,' he hissed in my ear.

I looked anxiously at Giorgio, who gave me an unfriendly scowl and muttered something to David in Italian. Had he missed his inflatable doll?

I tried to listen to David's reply, but Harley nudged me and bent close to my other ear.

'I bet I know what those two are up to,' he whispered with a giggle. 'I think Giorgio set up David with a date last night – you know, a girl. He's asking him how it went.'

David concluded his conversation with a loud chuckle and an obscene gesture.

'Looks like he scored,' I murmured, pitying the poor creature who had suffered the fate I so narrowly avoided in the churchyard.

Harley made a quiet clucking noise of disapproval. 'I wish David would settle down one of these days,' he whispered as we descended in the elevator. 'Find himself a wife and stop fooling around.'

I didn't reply. I was timing the descent on my wristwatch. It took exactly four minutes, which meant that at least eight minutes would pass before the elevator could return to the house. A lot could happen in eight minutes. All I needed now was the password for the control panel in Giorgio's room.

* * *

Portofino was a bustle of activity when we arrived. A large section of the area around the harbour had been cordoned off, and was clogged with vans and trailers from which quantities of equipment were being unloaded. Tourists swarmed around the barriers, eagerly taking photographs of a man with a megaphone who was pleading with them in several languages to keep back.

Once we had fought our way through the crowd, David and Harley were besieged by an assortment of people who tried to bear them off in several different directions at the same time. David began to strut self-importantly from one group of people to another, barking orders into a mobile telephone, while Harley hung back indecisively, holding my hand.

'Will you be OK on your own for a few minutes?' he asked anxiously. 'I need to talk to the producer.' He led me to a roped-off area containing tables and chairs, then scuttled away to join David.

It suited me just fine to be left alone, though a small part of me was feeling mildly offended that I hadn't been fussed over more. Wasn't I supposed to be the star of this commercial? Everyone seemed far more interested in David and Harley than in me. I toyed with thoughts of escape. Could I melt away in the crowd without being noticed? I didn't think I would get very far before they caught up with me, so I decided that it was better to lull their suspicions – let them think I had given up hope of escaping. I sat and watched the activity on the quay side, waiting for something to happen.

After a while, I realised that nothing much was happening at all. A lot of people were rushing around with clipboards, directing groups of bored looking technicians from one part of the set to another. Camera equipment was set up, then dismantled, then moved to a different location and set up again. Each operation involved one or two people doing the work, and half a dozen others standing around watching them. There was no sign whatsoever of any actual filming taking place.

A taxi drove into the square and nosed its way towards the barriers, causing a flurry of interest among the spectators. I looked up to see Harley rushing towards me with an excited smile.

'Remember what I told you about a surprise,' he said gleefully. 'This is it – come on!' Seizing me by the hand, he dragged me over towards the taxi. 'I figured you might get bored out here by yourself,' he explained breathlessly. 'With David and me being tied up with getting ready for the filming, I thought you needed some company.'

The door of the taxi opened. 'Surprise!' squawked a familiar voice, and Trish emerged on the quay side, clutching several carrier bags from the duty-free shop. She tottered forward to greet me, her high heels wobbling unsteadily on the cobbled surface.

'Jeepers Cin,' she squealed, holding out her arms like a long-lost lover. 'I bet you didn't expect to see me here!'

'Hi, Trish,' I said weakly, returning her embrace. Her breath smelled of gin.

'Wow,' she breathed, gazing at her surroundings with starry eyes. 'A film set! Is there anyone famous here? Apart from you, I mean.'

Taking her over to where I had been sitting, I explained that it was only a commercial, but she wasn't listening. Shading her eyes with her hand, she scanned the crowds. 'What about that guy over there with the telephone?' she asked, pointing. 'He looks a bit like Richard Gere.'

It was David. 'That's Harley's brother,' I said quietly. 'I'd keep out of his way if I were you – he's not very nice.'

'Aw, come on Cin,' she whined. 'Don't be so greedy. You can't have two gorgeous hunks like that all to yourself, it's not fair.'

'Don't say I didn't warn you, then,' I murmured.

'Why are you so fed up with them, anyway?' she asked petulantly. 'Always complaining – that's your problem, Cin. Well, I'll tell you something. I won't hear a word against your Harley – not after everything he's done for me.' Her eyes became dreamy.

'What do you mean?'

She sighed. 'It's just what the doctor ordered, Cin. An all-expenses-paid holiday with first-class travel and a personal spending allowance. It's just like winning one of those game shows on TV.'

'Er, Trish,' I asked. 'How long are you staying, exactly?'

'That's what I was trying to tell you, Cin,' she said happily. 'He's a real decent guy, your Harley. He said I can stay just as long as I want.'

Harley had turned out to be cleverer than I thought. Trish was a more effective gaoler than any number of thugs. She followed me everywhere with her continuous prattling, and I could hardly think straight – let alone formulate plans for escape. The day developed into a long, slow nightmare.

She dragged me round the gift shops of Portofino, spending copious amounts of her 'personal allowance' on shoddy trinkets. At regular intervals, we trailed back to the film set to check the new arrivals – Trish clung firmly to her conviction that Richard Gere was going to turn up, and nothing I said would make her believe otherwise.

When we ran out of gift shops, she started on the restaurants – guzzling food and drink with a vengeance. After we had both consumed a few drinks, I tried to talk to her.

'This isn't at all what it seems, Trish,' I said earnestly. 'I want to leave Harley, but he won't let me. He's keeping me a prisoner here.'

'A prisoner?' She paused with a dripping spoonful of tiramisu halfway to her mouth and stared at me with wide eyes.

'Won't you help me, Trish?' I pleaded. 'Help me escape?'

'Are you crazy?' she asked eventually in a voice of disbelief. 'Why would you want to escape from all this?' She waved her spoon to indicate her surroundings, splattering the people at the next table with droplets of cream. 'You've got everything you could ever want, and Harley's a fantastic guy . . .' She shook her head slowly. 'You don't know what's good for you, Cin – that's your problem.'

'But I'm not happy,' I said hopelessly.

'Now listen to me, Cin,' said Trish, with a note of determination in her voice. 'At times like this you need a friend there for you – a friend who knows what's best for you. I'm going to keep an eye on you from now on – make sure don't do anything dumb that you might regret later. You need somebody to protect you from yourself.'

'But . . .'

'I know,' she said, swallowing her spoonful with a noisy gulp. 'You probably think I'm being hard on you, but you'll thank me in the end. Now I don't want to hear any more of this nonsense. I'm on holiday, remember? I want to enjoy myself.'

That evening, Trish changed into a sequinned dress for dinner. She consumed an alarming quantity of wine and flirted outrageously with David, who eyed her throughout the meal with a look of distaste. As soon as dessert was finished, he excused himself and left, disappearing into the elevator.

'He'll be back,' whispered Trish loudly in my ear. 'I know his type – they pretend to be Mister Cool, but underneath they're desperate for it. I could tell by the way he was looking at me.'

'Be careful,' I muttered softly. 'You might get more than you bargained for.'

'So what shall we do now?' asked Harley in a jovial voice. 'I seem to have hit the jackpot tonight!' He grinned. 'Two gorgeous ladies all to myself!'

We ended up sitting in a row on the sofa, watching videos. There was an extensive collection to choose from, but Harley found a copy of *Pretty Woman*, and insisted on seeing it again.

'It's such a romantic story,' sighed Trish dreamily, as the film drew to a close. 'I wish something like that would happen to me.'

'Well, you never know,' said Harley, wiping a tear from his eye. 'Some day it just might.'

'If Richard Gere turned up on your film set . . .' she murmured thoughtfully, 'he'd be sure to notice me – especially if I was wearing my new pink dress . . .'

Harley glanced at his watch and frowned. 'It's getting late, darling,' he said in a meaningful voice. 'How about we go to bed?'

Trish was sorting busily through the video boxes. 'I can't find any more Richard Gere movies,' she said. 'But there's another Julia Roberts one here.' She took the cassette out of the box and stared at it on both sides, as if a close scrutiny would reveal the contents of the film.

'Cindy?' Harley stood up, gazing at me fondly, and I realised that he was still under the spell of *Pretty Woman*. I wasn't in the mood for a passionate reconciliation tonight – or any other night, for that matter.

'I'll, er, join you later,' I said innocently. 'Trish wants to watch another movie.'

His face clouded with disappointment. He turned to Trish. 'Can I just have a quick word with you,' he muttered, 'about the sleeping arrangements?'

They conducted a whispered conversation, then Trish

got up and followed him out of the room. She returned a few minutes later clutching a bottle of Strega.

'Look what I found in the kitchen,' she said triumphantly, uncorking the bottle and filling our empty wine glasses to the brim. She jammed a video into the machine and flopped back on the sofa. 'Just you and me, Cindy babe,' she said, 'Just like old times, eh?' She took a large gulp of the bright yellow liquid.

'What did Harley just say to you?' I asked.

'Eeurgh!' she spluttered, staring into her glass. 'This stuff tastes like a skunk's fart.'

'What did he say, Trish? When you were talking outside?'

She wiped her mouth with the back of her hand and took another cautious sip. 'Oh, nothing much,' she replied evasively. 'He was just telling me about locking up for the night.' She fumbled with the buttons on the remote control and the television screen flickered into life.

'What do you mean, locking up? Is he paying you to guard me, or something? Stop me from escaping?'

'Aw, Cin,' she moaned. 'Don't start going on about that again. I thought we were going to watch the movie.'

I snatched the controls from her hand and switched the television off.

'Are you going to lock me in my room tonight, then?' I asked bitterly. 'I thought you were my friend.'

She turned from the blank screen to face me, blinking uncertainly as she grappled with the logic of this remark. 'Of course I'm your friend, Cin,' she said eventually. 'It's for your own good. I'm here to help you get better.'

'What do you mean, get better? There's nothing wrong with me.'

'Aw, Cin, I wasn't supposed to say anything, but Harley explained everything to me. About you being sick, I mean. How it makes you keep acting all cranky and saying things you don't mean.' She shook her head sadly. 'If you ask me, Cin, it's that accident that did it. Before you met Harley, I mean.'

She poured herself another glass of Strega. 'You get to hear about these things, you know. People who come out of hospital after a knock on the head and walk around looking as fit as a fiddle and thinking they're better. Then one day – wham! They go berserk with an Uzi in McDonald's and take out thirty people. Or they might just drop down stone dead when they're walking along the street.'

I stared at her, unable to think of anything to say.

'Come on, cheer up, Cin,' she sighed. 'You look like somebody really rained on your parade. If you'd quit acting like this, we could be out there partying instead of being stuck here in this place.' She glanced at her watch. 'Do you think David's going to come back soon?'

Despairingly, I switched the video back on, fast forwarding through the trailers to the start of the film, which was called *Sleeping with the Enemy*. By a curious twist of irony, the plot turned out to be about a woman trying to escape from her husband.

'I don't see the point of this,' complained Trish after a few minutes. 'Why doesn't she just walk out on him?'

'Maybe he won't let her,' I suggested, intrigued by the parallel with my own situation.

'Ooh look,' she squawked a moment later 'He's beating her up!' She turned and gave me a curious look. 'Has Harley ever done that to you?'

I shook my head, wishing she would shut up.

'I don't know why she puts up with it,' she snorted. 'I'd have the cops on him right away if I was her. Look at the size of their house – she could get half of that in a divorce.'

The wife seemed to be plotting some complicated trick to get away from her husband, and I watched with bated breath to find out how she would do it.

'What's that silly bitch playing at now?' demanded Trish in an exasperated tone. 'This is about the dumbest movie I've ever seen.' She reached for the remote control and switched to an Italian pop video.

'Hey!' I squealed indignantly. 'I was watching that!'

Trish ignored me, splashing more Strega into her glass. 'This stuff doesn't taste too bad once you get used to it,' she said in a slurred voice, tapping her feet to the music. 'It's too bad we have to stay in – I'm in the mood to hit the town right now.'

'I don't think you'd get very far in the state you're in,' I muttered.

'Whadd'ya say?' Trish glared at me with unfocused eyes. 'I'm not drunk.'

I listened patiently as she chattered through half

an hour of mindless pop music, her remarks becoming increasingly unintelligible. After a while she fell uncharacteristically silent. Glancing across at her open mouth and slack features, I saw that she was asleep.

It took a few moments to prise the remote control from her sticky grasp, but I was then able to watch the rest of the film without interruption. When it was finished, I removed the video cassette from the machine and put it in my handbag. The film had given me an idea, and I didn't want anyone else in the house to see it.

As I was leaving the room, Trish began to stir. 'Hey, Cin,' she mumbled. 'Where ya going? The night's still young, ain't it? When are we gonna party?' She groped around for the Strega bottle and raised it to her lips.

'Good night, Trish,' I murmured softly.

She slumped back on the sofa and didn't reply. As I left, she began to snore heavily, a rivulet of bright yellow liquid trickling from the corner of her mouth.

CHAPTER 18

I stayed awake late into the small hours thinking about the idea the film had given me, then fell into a deep and contented sleep. The next morning I rose early and went down to the living room to see what had happened to Trish.

It wasn't a pretty sight. She lay more or less where I had left her, reeking of stale alcohol. Her make-up was smudged over her face and her clothing was in a state of disarray, as if she had tried to undress herself but given up half-way. She opened her eyes, gazing at me blearily, then sat up with a start.

'Where's David?' she asked, glancing down with a look of alarm and pulling her dress back over her thighs.

'David?' I asked, puzzled. 'Why do you want to know where he is?'

'Ooh Cin,' she whispered, clutching at my arm. 'You'll never guess what happened last night after you went to bed. David came back in the middle of the night and . . .'

I looked at her dishevelled state with dawning

comprehension. 'Oh no, Trish,' I said sadly. 'Don't tell me that you . . .'

'The trouble is, Cin,' she said in a worried voice, 'that I can't remember anything much. I don't know if . . . hey, wait a minute.' She began to rummage around on the sofa.

'What are you looking for?'

'It must be here somewhere,' she muttered, reaching under her dress and fiddling around. 'Hold on, there's something here . . . got it!'

I recoiled in disgust as she held up a small limp object. It was a used condom.

'Well, what do you know, Cin?' She faced me with a triumphant smile. 'It looks like I scored!' She paused, her expression becoming thoughtful. 'Hey, Cin,' she whispered excitedly. 'Do you think he might ask me to marry him? You know – like it happened with you and Harley?'

My answer must have been written on my face. 'All right,' she muttered sulkily. 'It was just an idea – you don't need to look at me like that.'

I went out on to the terrace for some fresh air, and walked straight into David.

'You pig,' I hissed in a low voice. 'How could you do something like that?'

He faced me with an insolent grin. 'Well, I did have to hold my breath so I didn't pass out from the fumes. Did you know she put away a whole bottle of Strega?'

'You bastard,' I muttered. 'Taking advantage of someone who was drunk.'

'The bitch asked for it,' he said nastily. 'She got what

she deserved. And you'll get the same if you don't watch out.'

'Over my dead body,' I snarled, advancing towards him with a look of hatred. 'You lay one finger on me and I'll . . .'

'What's going on out here?' Harley appeared on the terrace, blinking in the sunlight. 'It's a beautiful morning, isn't it?' He rubbed his hands together. 'Are you all ready to set off? We're going to start shooting backgrounds today.'

Trish was eager to get back to the film set, but her face turned a sickly shade of green when she hit the fresh air. 'Oh, my God,' she whispered, sinking into a chair on the terrace. 'I don't feel very well.' She gazed piteously towards David, who promptly turned his back and walked away.

'Never mind, Trish,' I said. 'I'll stay here with you. You'll feel better in no time, and then we could go shopping or something.' I gave Harley a questioning glance. 'That's all right, isn't it, darling? I need some new clothes, remember? You could send Giorgio back with the car and we could run into Santa Margherita for the afternoon.'

'Well, I don't know,' he said, eyeing me doubtfully. 'Will you be all right by yourselves?'

'Don't worry, darling,' I whispered sweetly. 'Let me show you that you can trust me. I promise I won't run away.'

Trish groaned quietly beside me while Harley paced up and down the terrace, pushing his fingers through his hair as he struggled to reach a decision.

'All right, Cindy,' he said eventually. 'I guess I have to trust you. You need a new dress for our party tomorrow night, anyway. I meant to tell you.'

'Party?' asked Trish, making a sudden recovery. 'Who's coming?'

'Oh, it's just a few people from the film set,' he said, throwing her an indulgent smile. 'Just a small dinner party, really – no big deal.' He gave me a fond look. 'I thought it might do you some good to socialise a bit, darling. Cheer you up a bit.'

'Hey, Cin,' said Trish, tugging at my sleeve as I watched Harley and David descend in the elevator. 'Do you think Richard Gere might turn up?'

I sent Trish indoors to sleep off her hangover and spent the rest of the morning prowling around the house and grounds, checking out the details of the plan which was forming in my mind.

All the ideas I had previously considered had one common weakness – which lay not in the escape itself, but in what I did afterwards. Harley was a rich and powerful man, who wouldn't think twice about spending vast sums of money to track me down. Sooner or later, he would be sure to catch up with me.

Now I had a solution. Harley wouldn't come looking for me any more if he thought I was dead.

In the film I had watched the night before, Julia Roberts had escaped from her sadistic husband by faking her own death. She had arranged it – rather clumsily, I thought – in a boating accident, where there was a risk of actually drowning if something went wrong. I didn't want to take any chances like that – Cindy couldn't even swim, after all, and there wasn't enough time to learn. I had a much better idea. There were still a few minor details to resolve, but on the whole, I didn't see how it could fail.

Giorgio arrived at lunchtime and drove us to Santa Margherita, which was only a few kilometres away. I deposited Trish in an expensive boutique with a promise of free rein on my credit card, and went off to do some serious shopping.

Most of the items on my list were easy enough to find: dark-coloured jeans and a sweater, a lightweight travelling bag with a shoulder strap, a sensible pair of shoes and a knitted hat that I could pull down over my ears. The last item, a length of rope, was harder to obtain as there wasn't anything appropriate in my phrasebook. Resorting to gesture and mime, I was offered balls of string, reels of cotton, spools of fishing line and even a lavatory chain by a series of puzzled shopkeepers. Eventually I found a yachting supply shop whose proprietor spoke some English and was able to purchase what I needed.

I returned to the boutique to find Trish clad in an outfit that made her look like Scarlett O'Hara.

'Do you think it's too dressy for daytime?' she asked, admiring herself in the mirror. 'I thought maybe if we were going down to the film set, I could leave it on and get them to wrap up my other clothes.'

'We're not going to the film set today,' I said firmly. 'I'd save it for tomorrow night, if I were you.'

'Aw, Cin . . .'

'Take it off,' I said, propelling her into a changing cubicle. 'Or I'll change my mind about the credit card.'

As soon as she was out of the way, I hastily tried on a few dresses myself. Selecting one, I approached the assistant, phrasebook in hand.

'Er, *due di questi, per favore.*'

'*Due*?' repeated the assistant, raising her eyebrows with surprise.

'*Due*,' I said decisively.

With a shrug, she went into a back room, returning a moment later with a second, identical dress. She began to wrap them slowly in tissue paper, glancing up at intervals with an expression which told me she thought I was mad. I drummed my fingers impatiently on the counter, willing her to hurry up and finish before Trish returned.

'What did you buy, Cin?' Trish appeared at my side as the assistant slid the packages into a bag. 'How come you got two things when I only got one?'

'The second one's a surprise,' I said, signing away a large chunk of Harley's money on the credit card slip. 'You'll just have to wait and see.'

Time dragged for the rest of the day. I had a few small tasks to carry out in preparation for the following night, but once these were completed, there was nothing to do but wait. When Harley returned, he was so pleased to find I hadn't run away that he decided to take us all out to a local restaurant.

'I knew a change of scene would make you feel better, darling,' he said happily, as the waiter filled three glasses with a cheap sparkling wine he had sold to Harley as low-calorie champagne. 'I think we're starting to work through our problems, aren't we?'

I nodded, forcing a smile. Trish glowered at me from the other side of the table, where she sat in regal solitude in her Scarlett O'Hara dress. She had been sulking ever since David made last-minute apologies outside the restaurant and drove off with Giorgio to some unknown destination.

'Here's looking at you,' said Harley, raising his glass. He winked at Trish. 'To the *two* special ladies in my life.'

Enjoy it while it lasts, I thought, swallowing a large mouthful of the acidic bubbly liquid. By the end of tomorrow, you'll find that you've only got one.

I was ready for him when he knocked on the connecting door later that night.

'Come in,' I said wearily, switching on the light.

He peered round the edge of the door, then stepped tentatively into the room, clad in his pale blue dressing gown.

'Cindy,' he whispered, approaching the bed. 'I thought . . . now that things are better between us . . .' He hesitated. 'Do you still love me, darling?'

I couldn't pretend to make love to him knowing what I was going to do the next day. Clutching my stomach, I let out a low moan. 'That food we ate tonight . . . I don't think it was quite fresh . . .' I rolled over in the bed. 'I don't feel very well.'

'Oh, darling.' He rushed to my side, reaching for my hand. 'Should I call a doctor?'

I shook my head. 'No, no, I'm sure it'll be out of my system by tomorrow.' I made a loud retching noise.

'Should I get a bowl?' he asked, jumping back in alarm.

'Don't bother,' I said. 'I'll use the bathroom if I need to.' I gave him a sly smile. 'You did always warn me about eating in fancy restaurants, didn't you?'

'I wasn't thinking,' muttered Harley, his face a picture of guilt. 'I should have known better . . .'

'Never mind, darling,' I said, smiling sweetly. 'I'll be fine by tomorrow night. After the party. Wait until then and I'll show you how much I love you.'

Eventually, I got rid of him, but it was a long time before I managed to sleep. Doubts began to creep into my mind. Was I doing the right thing? What would happen if something went wrong? And if I did manage to escape at last, could I really make a new life on my own?

There were people all around the world trapped in unhappy marriages. Was this the harsh reality – the way things were meant to be? People like Trish would give their right arm to be in my situation – so why didn't I just accept it, and make the most of Harley's social and financial advantages? Was I being arrogant in thinking I deserved something better?

All the happy endings in the romantic stories I used to read involved marriage. If I was honest with myself, I still clung to the idea that there was a man out there somewhere who was right for me. As Harriet, I had missed my chance with Andrew. Where could I find the man who would make Cindy's life complete?

What if he didn't exist? Could I be happy as a single person? There were plenty of ordinary people who had managed it, I told myself sternly. But then, I had to remind myself, I wasn't an ordinary person. I had sold my soul to the Devil. I had been so absorbed in my plans to escape from Harley that I had forgotten all about Mephisto, who was probably listening to my thoughts right now, rubbing his hands together with glee. If I really wanted to find happiness, it wasn't just a matter of getting away from Harley – I would somehow have to defeat Mephisto as well.

As the hour of the party approached, I grew increasingly nervous. I half expected Mephisto to materialise out of nowhere and thwart my plans.

I got myself ready in plenty of time, putting on one of the dresses I had bought the day before. When I had fixed my make-up, adjusting it several times, I ran out of things to occupy myself and went to help Trish.

'You're a bit antsy tonight, Cin,' she commented, as I helped her into the Scarlett outfit. 'Are you sure there isn't someone famous coming that you haven't told me about?'

The first guests to arrive were the English producer of the *Lapinique* commercial and his wife. Bill Bellman was a ferret-faced man with designer stubble and an accent like Michael Caine.

'Nice set-up you've got here, Harl,' he said, glancing around and rubbing his hands together as he stepped out of the elevator. He turned to me with an appreciative smile. 'So we get to meet the famous Cindy Brightman at last,' he said, shaking my hand with a lingering touch. 'The Face of *Lapinique*. You look every bit as lovely as your photograph, my dear.'

'Are we there yet, Bill?' His wife hovered uncertainly at the elevator door. 'This thing gives me the willies. Is it safe to get out?'

'Give over Beryl, you daft cow,' laughed Bill, reluctantly letting go of my hand and helping himself to a glass of champagne from a tray proffered by Giorgio. He winked at David. 'You should see her on the ski lifts at Gstaad.'

Harley rushed to her assistance while David began to talk to Bill, bragging about the people he knew in St Moritz.

'Blimey,' she gasped, patting her elaborate hairstyle into place as she tottered through the door on Harley's arm. 'I feel like I'm in one of them James Bond films.'

'Shaken but not stirred, eh?' said Bill with a loud guffaw. Trish giggled nervously.

'You know I don't like heights,' said Beryl, snapping open a powder compact with bejewelled fingers and peering anxiously at her reflection. She looked up, noticing Trish for the first time. 'Oh dear,' she said in a plaintive voice. 'I've got it all wrong again. Why didn't you tell us it was going to be fancy dress.'

A buzzing noise announced the arrival of more guests. David held a muttered conversation through the intercom and pressed the button to send the elevator down again.

'That must be Richard,' said Bill, handing Beryl a

drink and taking another for himself. 'I thought I passed him on the road.'

'Did you hear that?' whispered Trish, nudging me. 'You never know, that might be *him*.'

Richard turned out to be a small balding man wearing dark glasses and a leather jacket.

'Hi darlings,' he trilled, kissing everyone on both cheeks. 'What an entrance! I just love your fairground contraption out there. It made me feel just like . . .'

'James Bond,' said Harley, Bill and Trish in unison.

'Well, actually,' he giggled, approaching the drinks tray with a mincing step. 'I was going to say Pussy Galore.'

'Oh gawd,' sighed Bill, rolling his eyes. 'He's off again.' He nudged Giorgio in the ribs. 'Better keep your back to the wall tonight, Guiseppi,' he said with a knowing wink. 'Comprendez? He goes in for you dark-skinned types.'

'Richard's the artistic director,' whispered Harley in my ear. 'He's very talented – he'll do a great job on the commercial. You have to ignore his little eccentricities.'

One of these, presumably, was not bothering to introduce himself to the people he was going to work with. He glanced at me with an expression of mild boredom, then turned back to Giorgio and began to whisper in Italian.

The next guest to arrive was a corpulent businessman in his fifties, accompanied by a tall dizzy-looking blonde who couldn't have been much more than sixteen. He shook hands with Bill, David and Harley and disappeared into a corner with them, muttering about share issues and stock options. Beryl began a whispered conversation with Trish, ignoring the blonde, who stood gazing around with a helpless expression.

'Hello,' I said, feeling sorry for her. 'I'm Cindy.'

'Ooh, really?' she squealed excitedly. 'The Face of *Lapinque*! Wilbur said I'd get to meet you here!' She gave me a sympathetic smile. 'I hope you're not getting too bored – locked up here all the time.'

The room fell suddenly silent and everyone looked in our direction.

'Did I say something wrong?' she asked innocently, turning to Wilbur, who was looking embarrassed. 'You told me everyone knew about it, honey,' she whined loudly. 'How their marriage was on the rocks and she was going to run off with his money.'

'Let me offer you some refreshment,' I said, thrusting a glass of champagne into one of her hands and a plate of canapés into the other. 'These ones are particularly nice,' I added, picking up a handful and, with a swift movement, stuffing them into her open mouth. 'Don't you agree?'

'Mmmff,' she spluttered, spilling champagne on her white dress.

'Oh dear,' I said. 'You'll want to clean that up. Come with me.' I led her out of the room and pointed her in the direction of the most distant bathroom in the house. 'No need to hurry back,' I hissed in her ear. 'We'll struggle on somehow without your conversational skills.'

When the elevator doors opened to admit the last guests, I caught my breath with surprise.

'Cindy my dear!' Eleanor disengaged herself from

Arnie's arm and swooped towards me. 'You look divine! I told Harley a change of climate was just what you needed.'

'What are you doing here?' I asked weakly.

'We're on Arnie's yacht, of course,' she said, 'We stopped in Portofino this morning.'

I stared at her face. There was something odd about it. What had she done?

'I've just been to a special beauty clinic in France,' she said, observing my expression. 'They've given me this amazing new chemical exfoliation treatment – it peels off all the old wrinkly skin and you get this fresh new layer forming underneath.' She leaned towards me. 'I'm starting to notice the difference already. Can you see?'

I peered at her features. Seen close up, her skin was flaky and sore-looking. Large blotchy patches were visible beneath her make-up. She looked dreadful. Was there no limit to what she would suffer for her appearance?

'Er, yes,' I said hesitantly. 'It's certainly beginning to show.'

'There's a bit of excess peeling to start with, of course,' she said, touching her cheek thoughtfully. 'But the long-term effects are supposed to be amazing. Pretty soon I'll be looking ten years younger.'

Bill began to bray with laughter at something Harley had asked him. 'That's a good one, Harl,' he spluttered, reaching for another drink. 'I'm buggered if I know!'

Richard surfaced abruptly from his whisperings with

Giorgio. 'Did I hear someone use the B-word?' he squealed. 'Was that an invitation, Billy boy?'

A frown crossed Eleanor's features. 'Tell me, my dear,' she whispered, leaning back towards me. 'Who *are* all these dreadful people?'

'Hey, Cin,' said Trish, appearing at my elbow with disappointment written all over her face. 'Is that it? Isn't anybody else coming?'

Eleanor gave her a disdainful stare and swept away to greet Harley and David. Trish glared at her departing figure. 'What's that old bitch doing here?' she demanded in a belligerent tone. 'And why haven't you invited a date for me? I'm not going to sit next to that faggot.'

'Never mind, Trish,' I said in a consoling voice. 'Maybe we'll be able to get Richard Gere next time.'

Eventually the guests were rounded up and assembled in the dining room. Trish hung back from choosing a seat, presumably weighing her chances with each of the men.

Wilbur positioned himself next to David, still muttering about finance, and the big-mouthed blonde, who had only just found her way back from the bathroom, sat beside him. Arnie, with a twinkle in his eye, swooped into the next seat. Richard wandered down to the far end of the room where Giorgio was arranging the hors d'oeuvres, and Eleanor found herself flanked by Bill and Beryl on the other side of the table.

Trish was left with no choice but to take the remaining seat next to Richard. She was about to sit down when Giorgio jerked upright with a squawk of indignation and fled the room with an embarrassed face.

'He can't say I didn't warn him,' cackled Bill, nudging Eleanor in the ribs.

'Excuse me?' she asked frostily. He leaned over and whispered something in her ear.

'Arnie!' she commanded, standing up and moving round the table. 'Change places with me now, please! The light's in my eyes here.'

Arnie surrendered his seat to Eleanor while Trish, with a look of desperation, plumped herself into Eleanor's empty seat. Arnie was left stranded. Everyone jumped to their feet at once, offering seats and swapping places, and it was several minutes before the company was finally arranged.

'OK, let's start,' said Harley, beckoning a reluctant Giorgio back into the room.

'Sorry,' I said, standing up. 'I've just got to visit the bathroom.'

Everyone groaned. 'Oh, do start without me,' I pleaded. 'I'll only be a moment.'

Closing the door behind me, I went quietly across the hall to the front entrance and slipped out on to the landing, where the lift stood waiting with open doors. It was dark outside now and the lamps which lined the sides of the track had switched themselves on, glowing softly on the hillside beneath me. Checking to make sure that I couldn't be seen from the dining room windows, I descended a small flight of steps that led to the terrace and reached into the shrubbery. The things I had hidden earlier that day were still there, undisturbed.

I pulled out the travelling bag and crept round the

side of the house to the courtyard. A cloud of steam issued from the open kitchen door, accompanied by the clatter of pans and unintelligible screeching noises. Glancing inside as I passed, I saw the ancient housekeeper scuttling across the tiled floor, hopping from one foot to the other with the movements of some primitive tribal dance. She clutched a saucepan lid in one hand and waved a rolling pin in wide circles above her head with the other. Strange whistling noises came from a large pot that bubbled on the stove.

Giorgio's car was parked in the usual place, its door unlocked. I felt to make sure the keys were still in the ignition, then dropped my bag on the back seat and returned to the front of the house.

The second item I had left in the bushes wasn't very heavy, but it was large and awkward to handle. Lifting it from its hiding place, I manoeuvred it carefully up the steps and propped it inside the lift. After a few minor adjustments to get the position right, I stood back and admired my handiwork with a smile. It would be clearly visible through the glass as the elevator made its descent. Everything was ready. Taking a deep breath, I went back to the dining room.

Guffaws of laughter greeted me as I opened the door. I flushed, thinking they were directed at me, then realised that Bill was telling a joke.

'Anyway,' he continued, spluttering with mirth, 'then the Paki turned to the Irishman and said, "Now watch the monkey trying to put the cork back in!"'

'Ooeer!' squealed Richard. 'Sounds like my kind of monkey!'

'Looks like the shit hit the fan!' roared Wilbur.

'I knew a guy who fell into a septic tank once . . .' began Trish.

'Why would anyone want to put a cork up a pig's fanny?' asked the dizzy blonde.

'Same reason why they'd want to put one in your mouth,' said Eleanor icily. 'Keep the crap inside.'

I returned to my seat unnoticed, and kept quiet. When Giorgio went to fetch the main course, I held my breath, hoping he wouldn't look into the lift. As soon as he was safely back in the dining room I would be ready to make my move.

When he returned, I could see why the housekeeper had been having problems. The main course was lobster and, to judge by the size of the steaming heap on his platter, we were getting a whole one each. He moved around the table, depositing them on plates with a series of ungracious clunks.

'Watch out for the claws,' giggled Richard, as Giorgio skipped hastily past his chair. 'Miaow!'

'I prefer a bit of tail myself,' chortled Bill, leering across the table at the dizzy blonde.

'Put your eyes back in!' snapped Beryl, making a swift kicking movement under the table with her foot.

'Arrghh!' howled Trish, who was sitting between them, clutching her leg. 'You did that on purpose, you bitch!'

I had intended to cause a scene of some kind before running out of the room and setting my plan into motion, but I didn't see that I stood much of a chance of being noticed in the uproar that ensued.

'Leave me alone!' screamed Beryl as Trish advanced towards her brandishing a fork.

'Sit down, you silly bitch!' hissed Eleanor. 'Can't you see you're making a fool of yourself?'

'Now, now, girls,' said Harley, standing up at the head of the table. 'Calm down.'

'I'm not doing anything wrong, darling,' said Richard, patting Arnie playfully on the knee.

'Take your hands off me, you faggot!' shrieked Arnie, leaping to his feet.

'I'll sort him out for you,' said Wilbur in an aggressive voice, rolling up his sleeves.

'No, stop it!' wailed the dizzy blonde, clutching at his arm. 'Your heart condition . . .'

It was too late to turn back.

'Shut up, all of you!' I bellowed, rising from my seat. A hush fell suddenly over the room and they all turned to look at me. I trembled. This was it.

'I've had enough!' I screamed hysterically. 'I don't belong in this fucking nightmare! I'm leaving!'

'But, darling . . .' Harley stared at me with an expression of horror. 'You can't . . .'

'I fucking well can,' I said, picking up the lobster from my plate and hurling it across the room towards him. 'Goodbye, Harley!'

The lobster fell short of its target, landing with a dull crunch in the centre of the table. Heads swivelled to follow my progress to the door, their outraged features splattered with greasy droplets of sauce.

I left the room, slamming the door behind me, and ran across to the lift. Slapping my hand on the 'down' button, I kicked off my shoes and made for the kitchen. The machinery whirred into life behind me as the glass box began its journey down to the roadside.

Pausing briefly in the lobby, I heard a distant hubbub of voices as the door to the dining room opened and people began to spill out.

'She's going down in the elevator!' called a voice. 'I can see her in there!'

'Don't worry,' said another, which sounded like David's. 'She won't get far. I can bring it straight up again before she has time to get out.'

The old crone was slumped at the kitchen table, presumably overcome by her exertions with the lobsters, and didn't look up as I crept past on stockinged feet. Closing the door on her silent figure, I picked my way across the gravel to Giorgio's car. Inside, my hands shook as I fumbled with the unfamiliar controls, but the engine started on the second attempt. Gripping the wheel tightly, I drove out of the courtyard as quietly as I could and headed down the road into the cutting. I had exactly eight minutes before they came after me. Eight minutes before the elevator returned to the top of its track and the doors opened to reveal Giorgio's inflatable doll dressed in an identical outfit to mine.

CHAPTER 19

As I emerged from the end of the cutting, the darkness ceased and the road was bathed in bright moonlight. I slowed the car to a crawl and travelled the last hundred yards to the hairpin bend with my foot hovering above the brake. I didn't want to make any mistakes about what happened next.

It always looked so easy when they did it in films. You simply stopped the car on a suitable gradient, released the handbrake as you jumped out, and stood back to admire the result. It was the jumping out bit that bothered me most. Images crowded into my mind of doors slamming shut, clothing snagged on handles, seat belts twisted around ankles, and helpless bodies being dragged over cliffs. Natural justice dealing out its sentence to those who sought to profit from malicious plans.

I didn't believe in that kind of justice – you only had to look at people like David to see how ineffective it was. My plans weren't particularly malicious either, but I didn't want to take any chances. Dumping my bag at the edge of the road, I stood outside the car with my feet planted firmly on the ground and held my clothing carefully out of the way as I reached inside and released the handbrake.

Letting go, I leapt backwards, staggering against an outcrop of rock, and braced myself for the crash.

Nothing happened. The car stood motionless where I had left it, the engine gently humming. I went to the back of the car and pushed as hard as I could, but I couldn't get it to move. Looking down, I saw that there was no question about the gradient, so the only explanation seemed to be that the handbrake had stuck. I moved around to the open door and was just about to reach inside again, when a metallic creaking noise made me hesitate. With a gentle crunching of gravel beneath the tyres, the car began to move slowly forward.

I felt a brief pang of sympathy for Giorgio as it rolled towards the cliff edge, gathering momentum, and disappeared from view. He may have been an unwitting accessory in the conspiracy against me, but he had done nothing to deserve this arbitrary destruction of his property.

The loud series of crashes and explosions which followed drove these thoughts from my mind. I rushed forward to peer over the edge. Bright flames were visible far below, and I was glad to see that it had cleared the coast road and landed on the rocks beneath. The waves were already at work, extinguishing chunks of burning wreckage and sweeping them out to sea.

Hearing distant voices from the direction of the house, I ran back to collect my bag, then retraced my steps, following the road down towards the gate. Just before I reached it, I plunged into the bushes and clambered up the hillside towards a small hollow I had discovered the previous day. Once I was safely inside it, I knew I had a good vantage point where I couldn't be seen from the road.

I unzipped my bag and began to undress, removing my party frock and replacing it with the practical clothing I had bought in Santa Margherita. The rope I had taken so much trouble to obtain was no longer in the bag – I had taken it out that morning and positioned it in its intended place. Peering through the bushes I could just see it, dangling from the top of the security fence a short distance away from the gate.

The distant voices grew louder, and soon I heard running footsteps approaching the bend in the road.

Harley came into view first, closely followed by David. 'I don't understand,' wailed Harley. 'Where did that inflatable doll come from? Where's my Cindy gone?'

'She didn't get into the elevator, you fool,' hissed David. 'It was a trick to make us wait while she went off down the back road. Hurry up – she'll be down by the gate somewhere!'

Giorgio sprinted around the corner after them, babbling wildly. '*Al ladro! Mi hanno rubato*!'

As these three figures hurried down towards the gate, the rest of the party straggled slowly around the bend. The only ones missing were Wilbur and his dizzy blonde, and I experienced a brief moment of pique that they hadn't bothered to make the effort.

There couldn't be many dinner parties where the wife of the host launched herself into oblivion, and I wanted as many witnesses as I could get for my brief moment of glory.

'Hey, Cin!' Trish's voice cut harshly through the air. 'Quit goofing around – the dinner's getting cold!'

Eleanor scurried after her. 'Keep your voice down,' she hissed. 'People will hear you!'

'What people?' asked Trish loudly. 'I can't see anybody.'

'There are friends of ours moored in the bay. Really, I don't know what could have come over the girl to make her behave like that! How embarrassing!'

'Cooee! Georgie-poos! Where are you hiding?' Richard pranced unsteadily behind them, waving a bottle of wine above his head. 'This is such an adventure!'

'Stop whining, Beryl,' muttered Bill, leaning against a rock and shaking stones out of his shoes. 'Wait and see – it'll turn out to be one of those party games just like I told you.'

'But you know I can't take heights, Bill,' she wailed. 'Look over there. Have you seen how far down it is?'

Harley, David and Giorgio had reached the gate.

'Cindy!' bellowed Harley, clutching the bars. 'Where are you?'

'Well she can't have got out, can she?' snapped David. 'It's still shut.'

'Hold on a minute, what's that?' asked Harley in a weak voice, pointing.

'Looks like a rope,' muttered David, clambering up the bank. I shrank back into my hiding place.

'*Mia macchina*!' shrieked Giorgio, standing in the middle of the road and staring wildly around him.

'She could never have climbed this,' said David with a laugh, pulling the rope away from the fence. 'Look, it's not even tied properly.'

'What's he saying?' asked Harley, pointing at Giorgio.

'I always thought she was pretty dumb,' muttered David, picking his way back down the bank to the road, the rope in his hand.

'*Mia macchina*!' repeated Giorgio insistently.

'Hold on a minute,' said David. 'Where *is* Giorgio's car?'

'Christ almighty!' shrieked Bill, peering over the edge of the hairpin bend. 'Come and look at this!'

As Giorgio sprinted up the track to join him, a distant wail of sirens pierced the still night air. Glancing across the bay, I saw a flickering blue light moving towards us along the coast road. 'What is it?' called Harley, breaking into a run.

'*Mia macchina*!' howled Giorgio.

'Holy shit!' screamed Trish. 'It's Cindy! She's gone and killed herself!'

Harley rushed forward with a wail of anguish, and it looked for a moment as if he was going to hurl himself after the wreckage. 'Cindy!' he bellowed. 'Cindy! Come back to me!'

'Steady on, Harl,' muttered Bill, putting out a hand to restrain him as he teetered dangerously on the edge of the precipice.

'She might still be alive!' gasped Harley, struggling to free himself. 'I have to go to her!'

'I wouldn't get your hopes up, mate,' said Bill, glancing downwards. 'She'd have to be made of rubber to survive a drop like that.'

'What's going on?' barked David, appearing out of the shadows. 'Who called the cops?'

'She's dead!' sobbed Harley, collapsing in a heap on the roadside. 'My Cindy's dead!'

His words filled me with a heady sensation of relief. I had finally freed myself from Cindy's identity, and the woman who had met her fate in that other car accident, months earlier, could now be properly mourned. Harley would give her a good send-off, never knowing that the woman he thought he loved had been dead all the time. I could hardly feel sorry for him – it was his own fault, after all. If Harley hadn't driven into the back of her car on the Pasadena freeway, the original Cindy would still be alive today.

'I don't understand this,' said Bill, glancing up and down the road. 'If that gate's locked, like you say it is, why was she driving hell for leather down here? She wouldn't be able to get out.'

'She must have planned to leave the car and climb over,' said David, twirling the rope thoughtfully between his fingers. 'Stupid bitch. I don't know where she got hold of this, but it's not the right sort of rope for climbing. She can't have thought it through very clearly. Even if she made it to the other side, what would she have done then? We'd have caught up with her in no time.'

'Why on earth would she want to run off like that anyway?' asked Richard, brandishing a half-eaten lobster wrapped in a napkin. He giggled. 'You must have done something pretty dreadful to make her that desperate . . .'

'Mind your own business,' snapped David, turning away.

'Yeah, shut up, you old faggot,' said Trish. 'That's my friend you're talking about.' She paused thoughtfully. '*Was* my friend,' she added, a note of distress creeping into her voice.

Harley remained motionless on the roadside, clutching his head in an attitude of despair. 'I know how you feel, Harley,' whined Trish, tugging at his sleeve. 'She was just starting to get better as well, and now this had to go and happen.' She burst into tears. 'It's not fair! I was looking after her really well – just like I promised you – and now I'm going to be sent back home!'

'Arnie and I have been discussing the situation,' said Eleanor, emerging from the shadows at the other side of the road. 'This is a terrible tragedy, of course, but it's not going to help anyone if we all catch pneumonia standing on the road. I suggest that we go back to the house and wait for the police to arrive.'

'We really should be getting back to the yacht soon,' added Arnie anxiously. 'I'm expecting an urgent fax from the States tonight.'

'Oh, oh,' said Bill, nudging David. 'Looks like the fuzz are here already.' Everyone turned and looked down towards the gate, where a flashing blue light had appeared.

David strode across to Giorgio, who stood gazing mournfully at the wreckage, and held a muttered conversation in Italian. 'Come on,' he said, turning to the others. 'Giorgio's going down to explain. We'll have to go back up to the house anyway to open the gate. May as well wait for them up there.'

It took them some time to persuade Harley to abandon his vigil at the roadside, but eventually he stumbled to his feet, supported by Trish and Eleanor. David strode on ahead, closely followed by Arnie and Beryl, while Richard and Bill straggled at the rear, finishing off the wine Richard had brought with him.

'It makes you think, doesn't it?' twittered Richard. 'How little it takes for life's brief candle to be extinguished, and all that.'

'Speak for yourself, mate,' said Bill, reaching for the bottle. 'Christ!' he added, quickening his step. 'We'd better get back to the house and get that rubber doll out of the way before the police see it – they'll think we're a bunch of pervos.'

As they disappeared around the bend, I crept from my hiding place and made my way quietly towards the gate. Crouching in the shadows a few metres from the edge of the road, I listened to Giorgio negotiating with the policemen through the bars.

A short while later, there was a creaking of machinery and the gate slid open. The police car drove through, pausing to allow Giorgio to climb in, then headed slowly up the hill. The gate began to close. Waiting until the last possible moment, I ran down the road towards it and slipped through the diminishing gap. I was free at last.

A short distance from the junction with the coast road,

there was a scene of bustling activity. Flashing lights illuminated the darkness and an ambulance waited hopefully as policemen searched the road above the wreckage. No one noticed the silent figure that turned and crept along the edge of the road in the opposite direction, heading for Santa Margherita.

It was less than three kilometres to the town, and I had reckoned it would take me about an hour to walk there. Time passed slowly as I trudged along the road, retreating into the shadows at the foot of the cliffs each time a vehicle passed. Allowing my thoughts to roam, I ran through the events of the last few months in my mind, scarcely able to believe what had happened to me. After all I had suffered, I felt I deserved my freedom.

As I approached a bend in the road, a lorry swung suddenly into view, headlights blazing, and came towards me at an alarming speed. I leapt for safety, but lost my footing and stumbled, landing in a small ditch at the roadside. I cowered, rigid with fear, as the lorry thundered past inches from my nose, and it wasn't until I tried to get up that I felt a stabbing pain in my ankle.

I could just about stand on it, but walking was agonisingly painful. Limping slowly along the road, I forgot about everything except my immediate problem as I concentrated my mind on trying to blot out the pain. If I didn't get to Santa Margherita before the last train left for Milan, I would be stranded for the night.

The next few hours extended into a long torture. Several times I saw the lights of the town twinkling in the distance, only to round another bend in the road and find that I was scarcely any closer than when I set out. Each time I checked my watch, the hands had crept forward a little more than I expected. Twenty minutes before the train was due to leave, I still hadn't reached the outskirts of Santa Margherita, and I reluctantly admitted to myself that I wasn't going to make it.

When I finally arrived at the edge of the town, I realised that I was too exhausted to go any further. The railway timetable had been difficult to decipher when I visited the station the day before, and I wasn't at all sure whether there were any other trains that night. My throbbing ankle convinced me that a small hotel would be the best option. I had plenty of money stashed in my bag that I had drawn from the bank the previous day, so I could pay cash and register under a false name.

Entering an anonymous looking hotel at the end of the seafront, I found a girl in her late teens varnishing her fingernails behind the reception desk.

'*Dica?*' she muttered, glaring at me.

'Una camera singola?' I pronounced hesitantly. 'Per una notte?'

'Il passaporto, per favore,' she replied sulkily, blowing at her fingertips. She wore a short-sleeved dress and there was an angry-looking bruise on her upper arm.

'Passaporto?' I asked doubtfully. I had two passports in my bag – Cindy's and Harriet's – but I didn't want to reveal either unless I had to.

'Ah, domani,' she said irritably, fumbling in a drawer.

'Domani?'

'Tomorrow,' she snapped, pushing a registration form across the desk. 'La sua firma qua.' With an exasperated sigh she thrust a pen into my hand and pointed. 'Sign here.'

I hesitated for a moment, then wrote 'Annette Baker' in an untidy scrawl.

'Quant'è?' I asked, proffering a handful of notes. She counted them with a thoughtful smile, extracting a single note of a small denomination which she handed back to me.

'Terzo piano,' she muttered, tossing a key on the desk.

It took several attempts to persuade the elderly elevator to function, but once it was moving, it seemed eager to demonstrate its versatility. I visited the fourth floor, the basement, and even caught a further glimpse of the delights of the lobby before I finally coaxed it to admit me to the sanctuary of the third floor.

The room was basic, but contained everything I needed, including a bathroom. I soaked my aching body in hot water, massaging my swollen ankle with my fingers and hoping I hadn't caused any permanent damage. Later, wrapped in a warm towel, I switched off the lights and surveyed the view from the window, which faced the sea.

Along the coastline, I could see distant flashes of light as a helicopter circled over the scene of Cindy's departure from this world. I counted the chimes as the sound of a church bell rang through the air: nine, ten, eleven. With a shiver, I remembered a line of Marlowe's which Andrew had once quoted to me:

The stars move still, time runs, the clock will strike,
The devil will come, and Faustus must be damn'd.

Looking down at the promenade, I observed what I presumed to be a typical late-night scene in an Italian resort town. Courting couples strolled along the wide pavements, arm in arm, while groups of young people sat at tables outside the few bars which remained open. It all looked so safe, so normal. Surely Mephisto would never follow me here?

I was idly watching the activity around a nearby bar, when a car drew up outside the hotel. The passenger door opened and I stared in horror at the familiar figure that emerged. David. I stepped back from the window in alarm. What was he doing in Santa Margherita?

When I found the courage to look again, I saw that the girl from the reception desk had joined him on the pavement. Slipping her arm round his waist, she pressed herself against him for a kiss, then broke away with a peal of childish laughter and leaned through the open window of the car to talk to the driver.

I felt dizzy. Out of all the hotels in this god-forsaken place, what twist of fate had led me to choose the one containing David's mysterious girlfriend? And how, I asked myself angrily, could he behave like this – slipping away to visit his floozy on the same night that his sister-in-law had perished in a tragic accident?

The car pulled away, leaving David and the girl on the pavement outside. Linking arms, they began to walk slowly along the promenade. I watched their receding figures, wondering what I should do next. Would they come back here, or did they have somewhere else to spend the night? Would he tell her about the events of his evening, and if so, would she connect them with the arrival of a single woman at a suspiciously late hour?

I was hesitating over the best course of action when the two figures stopped, talking furiously, and turned back towards the hotel. The girl reached out her arm to slow David's progress, but he shook her off, breaking into a run.

I stepped back from the window in confusion. I had to do something – had to escape before he found me – but where was I to go? I needed to move fast.

There wasn't time to dress properly, so I slipped into my underwear and threw on a coat I had brought with me in my bag. Stuffing the rest of my possessions back in the bag, I left the room, closing the door behind me and limped down the corridor. Should I risk using the elevator? I hesitated with my finger over the button, then changed my mind and took the stairs.

At the bottom of the gloomy stairwell, I peered through a window in the door into the lobby. It seemed to be empty, but before I could venture out the front door opened and David strode in, followed by the girl.

'What room did you say she was in?' he snapped. '*Che camera*?'

Muttering in Italian, the girl reached behind the reception desk and produced a key. She went with him to the door of the elevator, which arrived with much creaking and grinding, but seemed reluctant to accompany him inside.

'Get in, you dumb broad,' muttered David, stepping

aside to let her go first. The elevator doors closed with a bang and the machinery began to whine.

This was my only chance. I headed for the front door with a scuttling limp and reached for the handle. It wouldn't move. There was some kind of security device attached to it – a series of complicated levers. As I bent to inspect them more closely, I heard a crashing sound behind me.

'What's wrong with this damned thing?' said David's angry voice. The elevator door slammed open. 'We'll have to . . .' His voice trailed away and I could feel his eyes boring into my back. I turned helplessly, immobilised by fear, as he stepped out of the elevator and walked slowly towards me.

'Well, well,' he said softly. 'If it isn't my little sister-in-law, back from the dead.'

'David,' I whispered. 'Let me go, please.'

'I knew there was something that didn't add up tonight,' he continued. 'That little charade you put on for us seemed just a little bit too neat to be true.'

'Please,' I repeated. 'I don't want anything from you. All I want is to be free.'

'Free?' he said with a bitter laugh. 'You should have thought about that before you rushed into those marriage vows. I suppose you were too busy dreaming about the big bucks you were going to get your filthy little hands on.'

'You know that's not true,' I said angrily, reaching behind to fumble with the levers on the door.

'I suppose all that talk about blackmail wasn't true either,' he said, moving closer. 'Do you really think I'm going to let you loose so that you can blab all my secrets to the world?'

'I'm not interested in your filthy secrets,' I muttered sulkily. A lever clicked into place, and I felt the door begin to move.

'Take your hands off that!' he snapped, reaching out and seizing me roughly by the arm. He dragged me away from the door, pulling it closed behind me. 'You're not going anywhere tonight!'

'Leave me alone, you bastard!' I screamed, struggling.

'Shut up!' His hand struck my face with a stinging slap and bright colours swam before my eyes. A dull throbbing commenced in my head, travelling through my body to merge with the pain in my ankle, and the little strength I had left seemed to drain away. Too weak to fight back, I sank to the floor with a whimper.

The girl screamed and David swung to face her, jabbering rapidly in Italian. I allowed my body to go limp, feigning unconsciousness to avoid a further confrontation. Inside, I was burning with rage and humiliation. How could I have been so stupid as to let myself be caught like this – so close to achieving my freedom? If I had been a character in a film, or a novel, I would have made plans to cover every eventuality. At this very moment, I would have been reaching into my pocket to grip the handle of the small revolver I carried everywhere with me.

'Nice try, David,' I would have said, as he turned and gazed with horror into the uplifted muzzle. 'But there's one small thing you've overlooked.' A gentle squeeze of the trigger, and he would be staggering backwards across the foyer in slow motion, clutching his chest. Hitting the opposite wall, he would slide to the floor, staring in disbelief at the blood which trickled through his fingers. My problems would all be solved.

Or would they? I didn't fancy being had up for murder – especially in a foreign country. Maybe it was just as well that I had nothing more offensive in my pocket than a half-eaten packet of mints and a snotty tissue.

Concluding a heated exchange in Italian which had been taking place over my slumped body, David and the girl began to drag me across the floor of the foyer. They manoeuvred me into the elevator, which, as if to compensate for its earlier blunders, rushed us to the third floor at breakneck speed and announced its arrival with a series of tinkling chimes.

Back in the room, David threw me roughly into a chair. He ripped a sheet from the bed and began to tear it into strips, causing the girl to protest loudly.

'Get lost, you dumb bitch,' he muttered, seizing her by the wrist and ejecting her from the room. Closing the door behind her he turned back to face me, twisting a length of torn sheet into a makeshift rope.

'Please, David,' I begged softly. 'Let me have another chance. Let me go, and I'll give you anything you want.' Undoing my coat, I slipped it from my shoulders to reveal that I wore nothing beneath it but my underwear.

'I'm sure we can come to an understanding,' I whispered huskily, attempting a seductive pose.

'Nice try, Cindy,' said David with a contemptuous

laugh. 'But I'm afraid there's one small thing you've overlooked.'

'What's that?' I asked.

'If I let you run away, everyone's going to think you're dead, you silly bitch.' He approached my chair and seized me by the wrist. 'You're hardly going to be much use to me then, are you? I couldn't even use you for the commercial. What do I have to gain?'

'But . . .' I tried to pull my hand away, but he held it in a vice-like grip and eyed me coldly.

'You didn't really think it was just that pathetic little body of yours that I wanted in the churchyard, did you? Bimbos like you are two a penny – I can get *that* any time I want. I had something much more profitable in mind – a business arrangement.' He shook his head. 'But it's too late now. I know you can't be trusted.'

I struggled feebly as he bound my wrists together. 'But I thought you said . . .'

'Oh yes,' he replied with a shrug. 'It would have been a nice bonus; the pleasure of knowing that my darling brother's wife – his precious little Cindy – was no better than a cheap hooker.' He paused, concentrating on tying my ankles to the chair legs. 'But that's nothing compared with the pleasure,' he continued, 'that I'm going to get from seeing the expression on his face when I bring him through that door.'

As I opened my mouth to protest, he thrust a strip of torn sheet between my teeth, reducing me to muffled moans of outrage.

'Something tells me,' he murmured, tying the gag behind my head, 'that my dear brother Harley might not be quite so lenient with you in the future. Not when he finds out how you tricked him.'

He paused at the door. 'I'll be back,' he said with a grin. 'Try not to run away this time.'

As soon as he was gone, I struggled to get out of the chair. If it wasn't for the gag, I might have been able to free my wrists by using my teeth, but he had tied it in such a way that any attempt to move my mouth was painful. I looked around for sharp edges on the furniture which might fray my bonds with repeated rubbing, but made little progress when I tried to shuffle the chair across the room. After nearly upending myself on the floor, I gave up this idea and began to realise how hopeless my situation was.

He might at least have let me put my coat back on, I thought miserably, shivering in my underwear. I started to cry, but even that brought no relief as I merely succeeded in blocking up my nose and making it difficult to breathe. Forcing myself to be calm, I tried to think clearly. There had to be some way of getting out of this – some means of escape I had overlooked.

Then the church bell chimed the half hour, and I found my thoughts turning reluctantly to my only remaining hope of rescue. Mephisto.

He had said that he would be waiting for me to call him, but I hadn't realised quite how impatiently. His name had barely shaped itself in my mind, when the air in front of me shimmered and he stepped into my presence, stamping his feet and rubbing his hands as if to restore the circulation after a period of inactivity.

'I was wondering how long you were going to take,' he snapped in a petulant tone. 'Do you find it amusing to leave me hanging around in limbo while you decide whether to remember my existence or not?'

I blinked and stared at him in surprise. He was wearing a weird kind of black leather suit festooned with metal studs, zips and chains, which made him look like a strange hybrid between a motorcycle courier and a fashion victim of the punk era.

'Mmmff!' I said. *Take this thing out of my mouth.*

He leaned across and slowly unknotted the gag, brushing my neck with his fingers. I spat the twisted cloth from my mouth, wincing at the ache in my jaw.

'Please untie me,' I croaked, holding out my bound wrists.

'Not so fast,' he said. 'Why should I help you? What have you ever done for me?'

'Please,' I begged. 'I'll do anything you . . .' my voice tailed away to nothing.

'Pardon? I didn't quite catch that.'

'. . . anything you ask,' I finished in a sullen tone, angry that I had allowed myself to be trapped into saying it.

'It's about bloody time, too,' he snarled. 'Have you any idea of the trouble you've caused me?'

I shook my head miserably, wondering how long I had before David came back with Harley and ruined my chances of escape forever. How could I possibly live with the consequences of what I had done?

'You thought you were being really clever, didn't you?' said Mephisto bitterly. 'All these smart-assed plans and so on. I don't suppose you stopped to think about me – about how you've screwed up my career and landed me in a right goddamn mess!'

He began to pace up and down in front of me. 'I thought I had you when you married that dumb jerk for his money,' he muttered. 'I thought you were all set up for the decadent lifestyle – ready to join in with the bribery and cheating, ready to fester in corruption like the rest of these pathetic mortals who suddenly find themselves ahead of the game. But, oh no, not you.'

He swung round, pointing at me with a gloved finger. 'You had to start questioning things – just like a typical goddamn woman. What makes you think that you've got a special exemption from the laws of human nature?'

'But I'm not . . .'

'Don't interrupt me,' he snapped. 'You had to go and spoil things, didn't you? You had to start doing good deeds and getting all sentimental about your old boyfriend. You had to get all self-righteous and idealistic about being *happy*.' An expression of disgust flickered across his features. 'I thought this little spell of imprisonment out here might sort you out – make you see sense – but it seems to have made you worse. Then you go and pull a stupid stunt like this and land me right in the shit!'

'But how does it affect you?'

'They were all watching, weren't they? My superiors. You're Hell's favourite soap opera, just in case you'd forgotten. They're all so hooked on your antics that nobody's been getting any work done down there for the last week – we've got a backlog of uncommitted sins that would make your average government department look efficient by comparison.'

He pulled a metallic hipflask from one of his zipped pockets and unscrewed the lid. 'I've had to sit there listening to them wittering on about fair play and what a jolly good show you've put up,' he said in a bitter voice, taking a swig from the flask. 'Crappy home-spun philosophy about acts of kindness transcending human fallibility. Then they start saying that I ought to admit that I've been beaten and let you go.' He gave a snort of contempt. 'That would never have happened in the old days – it would have been fire and brimstone and straight to Hell with no questions asked. These wishy-washy liberals make me want to throw up.'

'But doesn't that mean that you *could* let me go if you wanted to?' I asked hopefully.

'Shut up!' he snarled. 'You haven't heard half of my problems yet. You've been causing such a stir down there that some desk jockey in the personnel department woke up from a two-thousand year sleep and started waving red tape at me. Some nonsense about *ultra viries* – that I'd exceeded my powers in setting up this pact. They even dug out some ancient piece of legislation which says you can't make Faustian pacts with *women*.' He sniffed. 'Nobody told me about that, did they? Now they're talking about taking away my powers and putting me on ordinary duties.'

He faced me with an attitude of righteous indignation. 'I'm damned if I'm going to spend the rest of eternity helping old ladies under buses and getting cats stuck up trees! I'm Mephisto . . .'

'. . . arch regent and commander of all spirits,' I interjected, unable to resist a smile.

'Don't laugh, you stupid bitch,' he said, in a voice which was suddenly serious. 'Don't you realise what this means for both of us?' He took a long swig from his hipflask, then offered it to me. 'I think you might be needing this when I tell you.'

'You'll have to untie me first,' I said, holding out my bound wrists.

He placed the flask on the table and began to fumble with the knots. 'Shit,' he muttered, glancing at my watch. 'There's not much time.'

'Time for what?'

He sighed. 'You just don't get it, do you? If they take away my powers, all the magic will be undone. We'll both return to our natural ages.' He jerked the knot undone, freeing my wrists, and thrust the hipflask into my hand. 'Which means that you'll be an old woman again, Harriet.'

I caught my breath, took a deep draught of what turned out to be whisky, and stared at him. 'But . . .'

'I thought that might wake you up,' he said grimly.

'But . . .' Tears welled in my eyes. After all my efforts – after all I'd been through to try to escape from Harley, I would be right back where I started. It just didn't seem fair.

'Is there nothing you can do?' I asked eventually.

'There's only one way out,' he said, savouring his moment. 'But as we agreed earlier, this time it's *your* turn to do the work. I hardly think you're in a position to refuse.'

My mind was spinning with confusion. 'What do I have to do?'

'Can't you guess?' He glanced over my shoulder. 'They've given me until midnight to prove that this Faustian pact wasn't a waste of resources. I'll need to demonstrate conclusively that you really have been corrupted after all.'

I swung round and stared at the clock on the wall behind me, nearly falling from my chair in the process as my feet were still tied together. There were only a few minutes to go.

I heard the sound of a zip opening and turned back to see Mephisto reaching inside his trousers with trembling fingers. His face was flushed red and a vein pulsed in his neck.

'There isn't time to do it any other way,' he grunted, rearranging his underwear. A penis of statuesque proportions nosed into view, like a Zeppelin emerging from its hangar.

'No!' I screamed.

'You don't have any choice,' he said, advancing towards me with a menacing gesture. 'Harley will be here any minute. You won't stand a chance of getting away from him without me.'

'Wait!' I protested, twisting away from his grasp and holding out my hands to push him away. If I did what he wanted, how could I trust Mephisto to help me escape from Harley? Was the alternative as terrible as it seemed?

'For Christ's sake, Harriet,' he gasped, dropping to his knees in front of me. 'You can't let me down now. Please . . .'

The hands of the clock inched forwards.

Stand still, you ever-moving spheres of Heaven,
That time may cease, and midnight never come;

Faust had never really had a chance – he was doomed from the start. But I suddenly saw that I had been offered a way to escape from Harley once and for all – if I had the guts to choose it. Could I give up a double measure of youth and beauty in exchange for freedom? Could I face life as Harriet once more, now that I had tasted fame and fortune?

I didn't have any more time left to think. Trembling, I made my decision.

'I won't do it,' I said quietly.

'What?' He looked up at me with incredulity written all over his face. 'But you can't . . .'

'Oh yes I can!' I folded my arms and faced him with a look of defiance. 'You can't force me. Rape wouldn't count, would it?'

I could almost hear the seconds ticking away.

'You bitch!' He lunged towards me, but at that moment the church clock began to chime. There was a crackling in the air and sparks danced before my eyes as Mephisto floated into a kind of freeze frame. We stared at each other as the bell tolled, slowly counting out the final moments of that day . . . ten, eleven, twelve. Midnight.

He slumped to the floor with a strangled cry. A sulphurous smell invaded my nostrils, and I gazed in horrified disbelief at the scene taking place at my feet. His body was twitching, seized by mysterious convulsions. The flesh seemed to be moving on his bones – as if hundreds of buried insects were wriggling beneath the skin. His head rolled sideways and I let out an involuntary shriek as I found myself looking into the wizened face of an old man.

A dribble of saliva trickled from his toothless mouth.

'Oh shit,' he whimpered feebly. 'Look what you've gone and done now . . .'

Aware of a strange itching sensation in my own body, I looked down and realised the full extent of what had just happened. Mephisto had spoken the truth when he said that the magic would all be undone. He had returned to his natural age – whatever that was – and so had I.

Gazing at the familiar sagging contours of my old body, I let out a whimper of relief. The nightmare was over. I was Harriet again.

Before I had any time to accustom myself to this sudden change in my life, a key rattled in the door, which flew open. Harley and David burst unceremoniously into the room.

'There she is,' said David, pointing. 'Now will you believe me?' He turned to face me and his mouth dropped open in disbelief.

'My God!' squawked Harley, taking in the scene. 'It's a whorehouse!' He turned to David with an outraged expression. 'Is this your idea of a sick joke?'

'Sorry,' muttered David, retreating through the door. 'I must have the wrong room.'

I could hear them arguing in the corridor. After a moment, the door swung open again. 'Sorry,' said David. 'Sorry to disturb you.' He gazed slowly around the room, his eyes lingering on me with suspicion, then shook his head. 'I can't understand it,' he said. 'Somebody's been playing tricks on me.'

'Your imagination, I should think,' squealed Harley in a hysterical voice, slamming the door shut again. 'Have you any idea what kind of trauma I've been through tonight? My wife's lying dead at the bottom of the cliffs and all you can do to comfort me is come up with some cock and bull story about her still being alive! You need your head examined, you little shit-bag!'

'Don't call me that,' snapped David.

'I damn well will! I've let you get away with talking down to me for too long, and I've had enough! It's time there were some changes around here . . .' Their voices began to fade down the corridor.

I waited until they were gone, then set to work to untie my ankles. Shaking off the limp strips of cloth, I stood up and walked nervously towards the mirror.

I wasn't disappointed. 'Hello, Harriet,' I murmured, gazing fondly at the features I knew so well. 'Don't look so worried. I promise I'll treat you much better this time around.'

I dressed myself slowly, examining my body as I did so. I felt a sense of wonder at the way it had reassembled itself with such accuracy – every blemish, every wrinkle and scar in the exact same place where I remembered it. Why had I been so dismissive of this imperfect composition of flesh and bones that had faithfully contained my spirit for fifty years? It had never let me down. Why had I been so eager to trade it in for a newer model?

Crossing the room to collect my bag, I was pleased to note that my ankle no longer gave me any pain. I felt healthier than I had done for the last few months.

I paused at the door. Mephisto was still lying on the floor with his zip undone, the shrivelled remnants of his proud Zeppelin nestling limply in his groin. He groaned softly as I shook his arm to see if he was still alive.

'Come on, granddad,' I said, pulling him into a sitting position and handing him his hipflask. 'Make yourself decent. We need to get out of here before someone starts asking questions. It doesn't look as if you're going to be floating through walls any more, so would you like a hand getting to the lift?'

CHAPTER 20

I took Mephisto to a late night bar on the promenade and ordered two large grappas.

'Don't leave me here,' he croaked, clutching his glass with wizened fingers. He scarcely had the strength to lift it to his lips. 'I can't . . .' His voice trailed away to a hoarse whisper.

'Can't what?' Leaning forward to hear him better, I became aware of the foul stench of decay on his breath.

'. . . can't even speak Italian,' he gasped, anxiously touching the folds of withered skin which now hung from his scrawny neck. He seemed to be getting older by the minute – almost decomposing before my eyes.

'You should have thought of that before,' I said, raising my glass. 'Cheers,' I added, swallowing the fiery contents in one gulp.

'But Harriet . . .'

'I have to be going now.' I stood up, throwing a handful of coins on the table. 'That should cover the drinks. I'm afraid you'll have to fend for yourself from here.'

He waved his arms in a frenzied attempt to get up

and stop me, but the effort was too much for him. He sank back in his chair, gasping for breath.

'Wait . . .' he croaked, his bloodshot eyes sparkling with frustrated anger.

'So long, granddad,' I said with a grin. 'Don't get up to anything I wouldn't do.'

Walking along the promenade to the nearby taxi rank, I noted gratefully that men no longer stared at me. Nobody paid me any attention at all. I was just an ordinary middle aged woman, safely cloaked in anonymity.

Finding a taxi driver who spoke some English, I negotiated a fare to Genoa airport which left me with just enough of Harley's money to buy a plane ticket home. I couldn't have done this as Cindy – if I had used her passport, there would have been too much risk of David or Harley tracking me down. I had originally planned to travel through Europe by train – hoping that, by the time I reached the Channel, I could have dreamed up some way of getting across without a passport. But now I was Harriet again, I could travel home by any means I chose.

It wasn't going to be comfortable waiting overnight at the airport, but I didn't want to go back to that hotel room. I was impatient to be on my way and I intended to be on the very first flight to London in the morning.

As the taxi drove along the promenade, I caught a final glimpse of Mephisto's shrivelled figure, sitting outside the bar in exactly the same position as when I left him. I craned my neck for a closer look as I passed, but it was impossible to tell if he was alive or dead.

* * *

By lunchtime the following day, I was back in Guildford. Collecting my other bag – which contained clothes no longer suited to a person of my age and dimensions – from the left luggage office at the station, I made my way up the High Street. Sunlight reflected on the cobbles, casting its generous warmth over the familiar scene and lifting the spirits of weary shoppers with the promise of the approaching summer. Despite my tiredness, I felt a surge of optimism. No one was going to come after me now. My transformation had given me back my freedom – a freedom I could never have found while I was trapped in Cindy's body. My life was my own again. I had a second chance.

My flat was just as I had last left it, with the addition of a small heap of brown envelopes on the doormat – angry letters from the utility companies threatening the imminent withdrawal of their services, and the landlord, demanding his rent. Stuffing them out of sight behind a pile of books, I went straight to bed. They could wait until I had sorted out the more important things in my life. I hadn't escaped from the clutches of the Devil himself to be thrown into a panic by the likes of the gas board.

I slept for the whole of the afternoon and most of the night. The following morning, I had a long bath, washing my body thoroughly in a symbolic purging of the experiences of the last few months. I wandered naked around the flat, rediscovering the pleasure of being alone and answerable to no one but myself for my actions.

When I was ready to face the world again, I went to visit Sally.

'Harriet!' she exclaimed, throwing her arms around me. 'You're back! I thought you'd disappeared forever.'

'So did I,' I murmured, returning her embrace.

'But you look wonderful! Your holiday's done you a world of good – you look about ten years younger!'

This was an exaggeration, but I knew from my mirror that I looked better than before. There was a healthy glow to my complexion and my expression was somehow more alert – more alive.

'You'll find a few changes here since you left,' said Sally, leading me into the house. She explained about Duncan's enforced departure, telling me little that I didn't know already. It was a relief to be able to respond to her confession this time – to say the things I hadn't been able to say as Cindy.

'Don't be too sorry for me,' she interrupted with a laugh. 'It was pretty tough at first – I have to admit – but I'm over the worst of it now, and I'm starting to feel happier now than I've ever been before.'

'Why didn't you ever tell me?' I asked. 'I always thought you were so happy with Duncan – you seemed like the perfect couple.'

'Well, you know how it is,' she said evasively. 'No one likes to admit what a mess they've made of things.'

'You've no idea how jealous I was,' I said impulsively.

'But, Harriet,' said Sally, her eyes widening. 'I was the one who was jealous of you. There you were, all free and independent, while I was trapped in a rotten marriage – clinging to a little shit like Duncan because

I was too afraid of what would happen to me if I was on my own . . .' She paused, glancing at me for reassurance.

'Go on,' I said.

'Well, if it hadn't been for you, Harriet, I don't think I would have found the courage to do it. I wanted to be more like you – to be able to get on with my life without constantly having to rely on another person to solve my problems for me.' She sighed. 'Now it looks as if I got it all wrong. Are you really so unhappy?'

'Not any more,' I said with a smile. 'I've learned a few things while I was away.'

'Oh, I forgot to tell you,' she exclaimed. 'That American woman you met in Barbados – Mrs Brightwater or something – she came to see me, and more or less promised me a commission on the strength of your recommendation! Nothing's come of it as yet, but you never know. It was awfully sweet of you, Harriet. Whatever did you tell her about me to impress her so much?'

'Oh, nothing but the truth,' I said guiltily, wishing I had remembered to do something about it. 'I'm sure you'd do the same for me.'

'Does Andrew know you're back?' she asked suddenly, with a meaningful look in her eye. 'I'm sure he'd love to see you.'

'Not yet,' I said. 'But don't worry, I'm going to call on him very soon.' I returned her meaningful look with one of my own. 'I'm planning to surprise him.'

Before I went to see Andrew, I felt a need to visit the library again – to confront the memories it held for me.

The next morning, I walked down through the town and approached the familiar building on North Street. A cry of recognition came from the front desk as I stepped cautiously into the foyer.

'Harriet!' Cynthia Hoskins waved at me excitedly. Handing her date stamp to a junior, she lifted the flap in the counter and scurried over. 'Where have you been? We were all wondering what had happened to you!'

'I didn't realise the terms of redundancy included a duty to report on my activities,' I murmured dryly.

'Oh Harriet,' she said, flushing. 'That was all such a terrible mistake. We've all really missed you, you know. Everyone said that little Miss Antsy Pants was no good for that job – which, of course, turned out to be . . .'

'Miss Antsy Pants?'

Cynthia giggled. 'Annette Baker, remember? The way she used to wiggle her bottom when she walked – that's what we used to call her. Anyway, when the scandal came out in the papers . . .'

'Scandal?'

'You must have seen it – it was all over the front page of the *Advertiser*.' She let out a little gasp and put her hand to her mouth. 'You mean you don't *know*?'

'Know what?' I asked, trying to conceal my impatience. 'I've been away, remember. You don't tend to see the *Surrey Advertiser* on the news stands in LA.'

'LA?' she echoed, wide eyed. 'You've been to *Los Angeles*? Oh Harriet, you must tell me all about . . .'

'What happened?' I pleaded. The one thing which hadn't changed in my absence was Cynthia's inability to get to the point.

'The Living and Learning section's all been dismantled now,' she said, taking my arm and leading me up the stairs. 'Let me show you.' She paused. 'Of course, you wouldn't have seen it in the first place, so you probably won't notice any difference. Everything's been put back to how it was when you left.'

We went through the doors into the main hall and I saw that this was indeed the case. The bookshelves were back in their rightful places and the only remaining traces of Annette Baker's pet project were the tired pot plants which stood awkwardly at the ends of the rows, ready to be tripped over by unwary browsers.

'We didn't have the heart to throw them away,' said Cynthia apologetically. 'The new manager's fond of plants.'

New manager? Eventually I wormed out the details of the story. I had been right about Annette, after all – she and the manager had been caught *in flagrante* on a sofa in the Living and Learning department by the manager's wife, who had grown suspicious of his irregular working hours. The local paper had got hold of the story, instigating cries of outrage from the worthy citizens of Guildford who had demanded an immediate investigation into the way the library was being run. When they came to look at the computer records, it was discovered that the system was in complete disarray.

'It turned out she'd messed it up with her new project,' said Cynthia scornfully. 'Half the main catalogue had disappeared. They still haven't sorted it out yet – we've had to go back to the old manual system.' She sniffed. 'If you ask me, we'd have been better off sticking with that in the first place. I'd rather have a good honest card index any day, instead of all this new fangled stuff.'

I felt a pang of guilt. I hadn't realised that my deletions had been quite so extensive.

'So now we're all topsy turvey,' she continued. 'We're running short-staffed until they find a replacement for her, and the new manager's too busy trying to sort out the mess on the computer to get the rotas organised properly, and we don't know whether we're coming or going.'

'A replacement?' I asked. 'You mean she's gone?'

'Sacked on the spot,' said Cynthia with a smile of satisfaction. 'And I can't say she's going to be missed.'

'But I thought . . .' I was going to say that I thought everyone liked her, but I was beginning to realise that the old Harriet's perceptions of the world around her had been more than a little confused. If I hadn't been so wrapped up in bitterness and self-pity, I told myself, I might have had a few more friends.

'Oh, but Harriet,' exclaimed Cynthia. 'I've only just thought . . . the new job!' She let out a squeal of excitement. 'You were always so good with the computer, and you know how the system works and everything. It would be perfect for you!'

'What makes you think they would have me back,' I asked doubtfully. I certainly needed a job, but I hadn't envisaged anything like this.

'The new manager's really nice,' she said eagerly, taking my arm. 'Come on, let's go and find him. There's no harm in asking, after all.'

When I came out of Guildford library an hour later, it looked as if my days in the ranks of the unemployed were numbered. Subject to approval by the library committee, which the manager had assured me was a mere formality, I would soon be returning to my old place of employment. This time, however, I wouldn't just be an ordinary librarian. I would have the title of 'Information Systems Manager', a newly created position which commanded, I was pleased to learn, a salary substantially exceeding my previous one.

I telephoned Andrew to make sure he was in, but hung up as soon as he answered. I wasn't going to waste time fishing for an invitation like I used to in the old days.

'Good God, Harriet!' he exclaimed, opening his door after I had knocked several times. 'I thought you'd gone away for ever!'

He stared at me for a long moment and my confidence began to evaporate. Had I interrupted something? Was he alone?

'I can come back another time . . .' I began.

'Goodness, no,' he said hurriedly. 'Come in, come in at once.' He stood aside to let me through the door. 'I was just . . . well, surprised to see you. Where on earth have you been?'

'Oh, travelling around,' I murmured. 'Los Angeles, Barbados, places like that.'

'Barbados?' he echoed with a startled expression. 'Goodness me, that's rather adventurous.' He grinned. 'It must have been quite a change from boring old Guildford.'

'It was,' I assured him, smiling.

'It seems to have done you a world of good,' he added shyly. 'I hardly recognised you at first – you look ten years younger.'

I gazed around the familiar living room. I had last seen this room through Cindy's eyes, but now I was Harriet again. Andrew's platonic friend Harriet. Would we revert to our old relationship, measured out in toasted crumpets and talk of literature? Or was I a different person now? A person who could change things?

The grate of the fireplace was empty now that the warmer weather had come. The toasting fork lay idle on the hearth, one less instrument of social ritual for Andrew to distract me with, one less impediment to real communication.

'Would you like some tea and biscuits?' he asked, anxiously fingering his beard, which looked as if it needed a trim.

I glanced at a heap of papers spread over the table. 'Am I disturbing you?'

'Oh goodness, no,' he replied with a self-conscious laugh. 'They can wait.'

I watched him assemble the paraphernalia of the tea tray, a scruffy middle-aged man surrounded by his books and domestic clutter. It was hardly a setting to stir the emotions to a romantic frenzy, but I felt a pang of deep affection for this unworldly figure who wouldn't have recognised a designer label if it slapped him in the face. Andrew cared about the things that mattered – things of which Harley had known nothing.

The books on Andrew's shelves were tattered and dog-eared from constant use, and held a far greater value to their owner than the expensively bound volumes in Harley's cabinets.

I had spent most of the journey back from Italy thinking about Andrew, anticipating our meeting with hopes and fears born out of the new knowledge I had acquired as Cindy. I had rehearsed speeches in my mind, both mine and his, and had played out in my imagination several different versions of the happy ending I had dreamed of for so long. Now, faced with the reality of a concrete Andrew, hovering nervously in front of me with a teapot in his hand, I was tongue-tied. Was *he* going to say anything? What if I had misunderstood him? Or what if he had found someone else while I was away? What if I was too late?

I felt myself slipping back into the familiar pattern of doubts. The toasting fork caught my eye once again, taunting me with reminders of my failure to act in the past. If I said nothing, I was no better than the old Harriet. I would never change anything.

'Andrew,' I said softly. He looked up, caught in the task of unrolling a knitted tea cosy over the gently steaming pot.

I took his hand, which was warm and dry, and guided him away from the table. 'Never mind the tea,' I said. 'This is more important.'

Putting my arms gently around his waist, I pulled him towards me and kissed him on the lips.

For a moment, he faltered, and I thought that I had imagined it all – that I had precipitated a mess of explanations and apologies, and ruined our friendship forever. Then he returned my kiss, wrapping his arms around me and whispering my name in my ear.

There was a jangle of crockery as we backed into the table, and I put out my hand to catch a teacup as it fell from the tray.

'Sod the tea,' said Andrew, taking the cup from my hand and tossing it into the wastepaper basket. 'I've been making tea for you all these years, Harriet, instead of doing what I really wanted.'

We made love on the sofa in front of the empty fireplace with a surprising lack of embarrassment. I never even thought to worry about whether he had left his socks on.

'I love you, Harriet,' he whispered.

'I love you too,' I replied. This feeling was real – it had nothing to do with Mephisto and his tricks, nothing to do with the charade of my marriage to Harley. I was happy at last. I was being appreciated for the right reasons – by someone who knew what I was really like, who knew the person inside.

Afterwards, I allowed him to make some fresh tea. 'Will you marry me?' he asked, placing a cup and saucer in my hand.

'No,' I replied firmly.

'But . . .' He looked hurt.

'How about trying out a relationship first?' I asked, 'See how it goes, and all that? I didn't wait all this time just to wind up washing your dirty socks.'

I might have imagined it, but I thought I saw a look of relief cross his face.

'We both need space of our own,' I continued. 'I've learned a few things about that while I've been away.'

He smiled. 'Well, I suppose it might be a bit of a sudden change for both of us. How about dinner tonight instead?'

We had dined together before, but this time it was different. The physical intimacy seemed to have melted down the barriers of reserve which had always stood between us, and I found out more about Andrew that night than I had in all the previous years of our friendship. I realised that I had yearned after the romantic stereotype – the scruffily handsome professor with an answer for everything. I had somehow believed that intimacy with Andrew would grant me access to the imagined font of wisdom where he drank – that I would magically acquire the power to sail confidently through life without the need to depend on other people. As I discovered the real Andrew, the person who was lonely and afraid just like myself, I realised that we weren't that different from each other after all. Andrew wasn't going to give me a miracle cure for life's problems, but having him around might make them easier to bear.

Over the next few months, I had little time to worry about anything. The library committee approved my appointment and I was flung into the demanding routine of a new job. Faced with the huge task of sorting out the computer system, I began to enjoy my work properly for the first time. Once I had proved that I knew how to operate the thing, I was treated with a new respect which made all the difference between this and my previous job.

I was relieved to find that I wasn't the sole perpetrator of the problem – my deletions had been of a fairly minor nature compared with the mess Annette Baker had made of trying to cover them up. I had to work long hours, studying manuals in my spare time to catch up on the skills no one had ever bothered to teach me, but I found it much easier than everyone told me it would be.

'It's amazing how quickly you've picked it all up,' said the new manager, peering anxiously over my shoulder at a screen of programming commands. 'I've dabbled with it myself, but I have to admit that it's all a bit of a mystery to me.'

I looked up at him, a fresh-faced young man in his thirties whose passions in life were botany and archaeology. 'I don't know how you do it,' he continued. 'Our older staff are usually the most reluctant to embrace new technology. Or new methods of working – anything that's unfamiliar territory. They do say that you can't teach an old dog new tricks.'

'Speak for yourself,' I murmured. 'I wouldn't write people off so readily, if I were you. You'd be surprised how much they can change if they really want to. It's all a question of attitude.'

It was easy enough to say, but in a way, he had a point. It had taken an encounter with the Devil to shake me out of my negative ways of thinking. How many women of my age were plodding on in misery without the benefit of my experience? I wished I could find them – wished

I could be in a position to tell them that life was there for the taking if only they could see it. I wanted to reassure them that it didn't matter what you looked like on the outside – that true beauty could only come from within.

I had been lucky. I had been given a glimpse of life among the privileged few who conformed to the present day ideal of how a woman should look. I knew what others hoped, but didn't dare to believe – that it wasn't all it was made out to be. Youth and beauty didn't bring the automatic happiness everyone assumed they would.

Mephisto had brought me another piece of luck, which I didn't appreciate until my next visit to a doctor. Anxious that my double transformation might have caused some hidden damage to my body, I went for a check-up. I was relieved to be given a clean bill of health, accompanied by the usual warning to go easy on the drinking.

'You're in excellent condition for your age,' said the doctor, a woman in her fifties. 'I can't see anything that's likely to give you any problems.' She peered at her computer screen, scrolling thoughtfully through my medical records. 'You're luckier than most,' she added. 'No problems with the menopause. It looks like you've sailed through it in record time.'

'The menopause?' I stared at her. 'But I haven't . . .'

'I wish I could swap places with you,' she murmured, a wistful note in her voice. 'If you knew what it was like – the hot flushes, the headaches, the feeling of being a time bomb about to explode . . .' She shook her head and turned to face me with a smile. 'You don't need to worry about any of that – it's all safely behind you. You can get on with life now. Enjoy yourself.'

Sally telephoned me one day in a state of confused excitement.

'Remember that American women I told you about?' she asked. 'The one you met in Barbados who came to see me?'

I made a vague noise of assent, nervously wondering if some unforseen repercussion from my past was about to catch up with me.

'Well, I didn't make the connection at first, because I got the name wrong. It was Bright*man*, not Bright*water*. She was that famous model who got killed a few months ago. You know – the Face of *Lapinique*? You must have realised who she was, Harriet, but you never said anything.'

'I, er . . .' I floundered. 'It kind of slipped my mind.'

'Oh Harriet, you are hopeless,' said Sally with an affectionate laugh. 'Her husband was *Harley* Brightman. The owner of *Lapinique*. Didn't you ever read the story that was in all the papers about how he fell in love with her when she was just a waitress in a café? How he married her and made her into a famous model? A bit like the story of . . .'

'*Pretty Woman*?' I interrupted with a smile. I hadn't realised that Sally had been following my career so closely.

'How did you know I was going to say that?' she asked suspiciously. 'Are you sure you didn't read it yourself?' She gave a low chuckle. 'I know you like to make out how highbrow you are, but I bet you read the gossip columns just like everyone else when you think there's nobody looking.'

'Well, maybe something might have caught my eye,' I murmured. 'Why are you telling me all this?'

'He rang me up, didn't he?' she said excitedly. 'Harley Brightman! He's given me a commission – a complete refurbishment of his house in Beverly Hills! Apparently the latest thing out there is to hire an English designer, and he found my business card in his wife's things.'

I felt a vague pang of guilt at the thought of Harley living all alone in his palace. Had the decor become an unbearably sad reminder of his dead wife?

'He's flying me out there next week to have a look at it. I'm so excited, Harriet – after all the time I've spent trying to get started on my own, things seem to be suddenly taking off!'

'I'm so glad, Sally,' I said, meaning it.

'He hasn't let the grass grow under his feet,' she continued with a laugh. 'He's just got married again. Apparently his new wife's got some pretty strong ideas about how the place should look – all red velvet and gold leaf and so on.' She made a puking noise. 'I can't understand why these rich people always have such bad taste.'

Married again? To whom? After a moment's puzzled silence, I realised there was an obvious candidate.

'Er, Sally,' I asked. 'This new wife – do you happen to know what her name is?'

'Why do you want to know?' She sighed. 'Hang on, I'll see if I wrote it down.'

I heard her fumbling with pieces of paper. 'Patricia,' she said eventually. 'Mrs Patricia Brightman – sounds like one of these typical rich bitches born with a silver spoon in her mouth.'

Patricia? I began to laugh. Trish certainly hadn't wasted any time in snaring her man.

'What's so funny?' Sally's voice squawked tinnily from the receiver as I succumbed to a fit of helpless giggles. 'Harriet? Are you all right?'

The next morning at the library, I spent a rewarding hour exploring various international news archives through our newly installed Internet connection. Some superstition had prevented me from doing so before, but I now felt it was safe to read about the world's reaction to Cindy Brightman's death.

FACE OF LAPINIQUE IN DEATH PLUNGE, said one headline. *TRAGIC END TO FAIRYTALE MARRIAGE*, said another. *REAL LIFE PRETTY WOMAN IN FATAL CRASH.*

The descriptions of the incident were straightforward enough. Cindy had lost control of the car she was driving and skidded over the edge of a dangerous cliff top road. There was no suggestion of foul play, no mention of the scene at the dinner party with the inflatable doll, and nothing about a woman who looked like Cindy being seen in Santa Margherita the same night. Someone had done a pretty good whitewash job on the story.

Browsing through the main stories in the week of the accident, I found a series of follow-up articles:

SEARCH FOR BODY CONTINUES IN VAIN. BIRTH OF A LEGEND: THE TRAGIC STORY OF THE FACE OF LAPINIQUE. MOURNERS FLOCK TO SITE OF ITALIAN DEATH CRASH.

I skimmed through a badly researched piece that had Cindy growing up in a trailer home before being rescued from life on the streets of LA by her childhood friend Patricia. It was accompanied by a photograph showing groups of middle-aged women laying cellophane-wrapped bouquets at the security gate of the Italian hilltop house.

'She meant so much to us all,' said an interviewee. 'We could feel her inner beauty reaching out to touch ordinary people. Somehow, we felt a need to come out here – to connect with her spiritually.'

A further article described the growth of a new tourist industry catering to the needs of 'pilgrims' visiting the Santa Margherita area. Roadside stalls peddled Cindy Brightman dolls and pots of counterfeit *Lapinique* creams, while a number of hotels in the area had set up special 'beauty therapy' weekends. Rumours of 'miracles' were beginning to circulate, with a housewife from Bakersfield claiming to have experienced a spontaneous facelift after washing with seawater at the site of the crash.

Several weeks further on, the story cropped up again:

BRIGHTMAN WIDOWER TO WED A SECOND TIME. IS THIS THE NEW FACE OF LAPINIQUE?

A blurred photograph showed Trish looking as if she had just woken up from a heavy night on the Strega and several columns were devoted to reporting the cries of public outrage at such a hasty coupling. Trish, I learned, had been forced to settle for a quiet wedding and a honeymoon at home as a mark of respect to Harley's dead wife. I smiled, remembering her vast collection of bridal magazines and wedding planners. She couldn't have been very happy about that.

The final item listed under my search for the name Brightman had nothing to do with Trish or the wedding. It came from the business section of one of the Internet news services.

DAVID BRIGHTMAN FACES CHARGES OF EMBEZZLEMENT AND TAX EVASION.

Reading the article, I found that he was being investigated by the IRS for his dealings with *Lapinette*. The evidence of his misdeeds had been leaked to the press, it said, by a disgruntled former employee, George Wilkins, who was now living in retirement in Surrey, England.

So George had also turned the tables on the Brightmans – it looked as if he and I had more in common than anyone might think. How much had he been paid for his story, I wondered? Enough to set him up in his old way of life? I smiled. Who knows, I thought? Maybe I'll run into him at Kempton Park one day.

Sally didn't seem to have any idealistic scruples about accepting Harley's commission.

'I don't care if it sounds like I'm selling out,' she said. 'I know it's not going to put me at the forefront of international design, but I could do with the money.'

Visiting me after a 'teleconference' with Mrs Patricia

Brightman, she was less restrained in expressing her views. 'I'm going to deserve every penny I get,' she muttered. 'Have you any idea how awful that woman is?'

I made a noncommital noise.

'She's wanting gold trim on everything, by the sound of it, right down to the bloody toilet seat.' Sally pulled a face which she kept in reserve for the most serious errors of taste. '*Pink satin heart motifs* in the bedroom,' she whispered. 'Can you *believe* it?'

I handed her a cup of coffee with a smile. It looked as if the pale blue *Lapinique* logo had finally met its match.

'Still, I'm looking forward to going to LA,' she said with a sudden grin. 'Duncan's really jealous, or so the children tell me. Apparently he's been wanting to go there for years and he can't afford it now he's got the alimony payments to make.' She stirred her coffee thoughtfully. 'You went to LA, didn't you, Harriet? You must tell me the places to visit – I want to make the most of this trip.'

I hesitated. I had avoided talking about my 'world cruise' in any detail – I didn't want to get caught out by all the inconsistencies which were bound to creep into my story.

She gave me a curious look. 'Tell me, Harriet,' she asked. 'When you were in California, you didn't by any chance go to one of those rejuvenation clinics, did you? The ones you read about? It's just that you really do look about ten years younger.'

'Well, not exactly,' I murmured evasively. 'I think it was just that I needed a holiday.'

'If this trip does me half as much good as yours did you,' she said with a laugh, 'it would almost be worth selling my design principles to the Devil!'

'I wouldn't be so sure of that,' I said quickly, startled at the thought of Sally being as easily corruptible as myself. 'I'd be careful if I were you.' How many others would have done as I did, given half the chance?

She gave me a teasing look. 'I thought you'd be the last person to go all moralistic on me, Harriet. By the way, when *are* you and Andrew getting married?'

'I wouldn't hold your breath,' I advised her.

'Oh come on, Harriet. Why not? I always knew the two of you were right for each other.'

'I don't really think I'm cut out for marriage,' I said. 'Besides, the statistics aren't very encouraging, are they?'

'I wouldn't judge it by my experience,' she said with a shrug. 'I've got nothing against marriage, as long as it's not to a pig like Duncan. I just happened to pick the wrong man.'

'I don't think it does any harm to keep a bit of distance in a relationship,' I said slowly. 'How close can you really get to another person, after all? Did you tell Duncan all your innermost secrets?'

'I wish I hadn't,' she said ruefully. 'He never told me any of his. I'd have left him long ago if I'd known what he was really like.'

When Sally had gone, I sat down and breathed a sigh of relief. Each time I saw her, I felt a burning urge to pour out my secrets – to tell her the story of what had happened to me. Each time, so far, I had resisted the temptation.

Who could I tell? Not Andrew – he would never believe me anyway. Besides, he had secrets of his own – no amount of subtle prompting on my part had ever led him to mention the night he spent with Cindy.

Andrew had no idea that he had bedded a famous model – he had never even heard of *Lapinique*. I obtained a copy of a women's magazine which had run the original Face of *Lapinique* advertisement in this country, which I kept as a kind of souvenir. One day, I couldn't resist opening it in front of Andrew, ostentatiously folding it back so that he could see Cindy's picture while I pretended to read.

Watching him surreptitiously, I saw that his eyes kept wandering back to the page. 'What's the matter?' I asked. 'Did you want to read my magazine?'

'No, no,' he muttered, backing away. 'I just saw a picture that reminded me of someone.'

I turned the page and stared at Cindy's face with an expression of deliberation. 'One of your students?' I asked innocently. 'An old girlfriend, maybe?'

The following Christmas, Andrew bought me a bottle of *Lapinique* perfume. It was the best gift I had ever received.

I never did tell him – or anyone else, for that matter – the truth about what had happened. I felt it was wiser to remain silent. I hadn't broken my side of the bargain with Mephisto – it was he who had broken his – but I still had occasional nightmares about him returning to claim my soul.

In my old life I was too busy being miserable to worry about death, but now it was often in my thoughts. I came to the conclusion that it was because I was happy – because I now had something to lose.

Goethe's Faust had been snatched up to heaven at the very moment he admitted being happy, but that, I reminded myself, had been part of his original pact with Mephistopheles:

> *If ever, as Time flows by us, I should say:*
> *'This moment is so beautiful – let it stay!',*
> *that is the moment when you will have won.*

I was glad I hadn't made any rash promises like that. Now that I had finally learned to appreciate life, I wanted to stick around to enjoy the time I had left.

Had I really outwitted Mephisto, or did he still have some kind of claim on my soul? I would probably never find out what my true age was – whether I had gained extra years or lost them. What good would it do me, anyway? How could anyone know for certain what their lifespan was going to be?

There seemed little point in wasting my time worrying about dying when I could be getting on with enjoying the business of living. With this in mind, I decided to turn my back on the past. Pouring myself a double measure of whisky, I drank a toast to my new life.